To those who feel like the walls
may one day cave in.
I know your pain, and I see you.
I hear you.
There is hope.
You are loved.

AUTHOR'S NOTE

Dear Reader,

While this book will make you swoon, smile, laugh, and fall in love with the cowboys of Randall, Texas, it also contains mature themes. Here is a list of what you can expect throughout *Rope Me In:*

Spanking
Rope Bondage
Dirty Talk
Talk of Body Image
Insecurities/Mild Fatphobia
Negative Self Talk
Emotionally Manipulative Relationships
Addiction
Alcoholism
Anxiety
Depression
PTSD
Grief
Suicidal Thoughts

For a complete list of content warnings, please visit my website: www.kaylagrosse.com. If you or someone you know is struggling with depression or needs help, please contact the 988 Suicide & Crisis Lifeline by calling or texting 988, or visit the website: www.988lifeline.org for help.

As always, please take care of yourself, and know that you are never alone.

Xoxo,
Kayla

ROPE ME IN PLAYLIST

"War with My Mind" Flatland Cavalry
"Friends in Low Places" Garth Brooks
"Beer Never Broke My Heart" Luke Combs
"I Am a Man of Constant Sorrow" Alison Krauss &
Union Station
"Hurricane" Luke Combs
"Here for a Good Time" George Strait
"Stay a Little Longer" Brothers Osborne
"If You're Gonna Play in Texas" Alabama
"Something in the Orange" Zach Bryan
"The Devil Went Down to Georgia" The Charlie Daniels Band
"Biblical" Calum Scott
"The Kind of Love We Make" Luke Combs
"Pitchin' Fits" Drayton Farley
"Honky Tonkin's What I Do Best" Marty Stuart & Travis Tritt
"The Night" Morgan Wade
"Duet (Feat. Stephanie Briggs)" Penny and Sparrow
"It's a Great Day to Be Alive" Travis Tritt
"Invisible" Hunter Hayes
"If You Love Her" Forest Blakk
"Home" Phillip Phillips

CHAPTER 1

Kade

GRIEF. IT'S A FUNNY and horrible thing. Like your lungs, it expands and contracts. The more life you breathe into it, the larger it gets. But the longer you starve it, the more painful it becomes. Like when you walk into frigid winter air after a hard workout and the very sustenance you breathe becomes ice inside your chest. I rub my sternum like I can feel it right now.

"Kade?"

I'm broken from my thoughts by my cardiologist, Dr. Ellis. She looks at where I'm rubbing my chest and then into my eyes, her face etched with confusion.

"Sorry. You were saying?"

"Are you feeling okay?" she asks.

I look at my hand and force it down to my side. The pain I was feeling has nothing to do with my actual heart, but I'm not going to tell her that. "Yeah, sorry. Just an itch."

For a moment, I think she's going to press me further, but then she relaxes. "I was saying everything looks good."

I exhale a sigh of relief and give her a grateful nod. "I'm cleared to start work again?"

Dr. Ellis smiles warmly. "Don't go crazy. Keep stress at a minimum, but everything looks normal. I'm going to keep you on beta blockers, but it's just a precaution. I want to keep that heart muscle strong, especially considering the type of manual labor you do."

"Alright, then," I say, not happy about having to take medication. It makes me feel lethargic sometimes. And I read that it could be why I keep having strange dreams and nightmares. But it is what it is. I'm not going to complain about it if it keeps me alive. However, I *am* concerned about the cost, something I'll have to figure out later.

"And what are you planning to do for stress relief?" she asks.

I stare at my doctor, the one I've come to trust over the last three months. A hard thing to do when I grew up listening to a dad who told me to walk it off when I got hurt. And that all doctors were a bunch of money-hungry quacks.

"You want me to do goat yoga or some fancy shit you city people like to do?" I say, a teasing tone to my voice.

She chuckles. "If you like goats and yoga, then yes. I would say it could be a great stress reliever. Especially the yoga part."

I crack a half smile, unable to stop myself from being flirty. It's always been my way of dealing with people: to handle any tense situations and keep things nice and breezy.

"There are other great ways to relieve stress, you know." As soon as the words are out of my mouth, I regret them. Her back stiffens at what I inadvertently implied, and she stands from her rolling chair. *Way to fucking go, Kade. You creeped out your doctor. Your very married doctor.*

My eyes go to the giant diamond on her finger then to the floor. Sometimes I can't help what comes out of my mouth. It's second nature at this point. I've always been the town flirt and, eventually, the town playboy. I slept with a lot of women. It's not something I'm ashamed of; it's just a fact.

And while I haven't fucked anyone since I've been on the mend—and I've gotten better at watching what I say since I stopped drinking—it's been getting harder and harder recently to keep myself from reverting back to my old ways.

Dr. Ellis clears her throat, and I bring my eyes to meet hers. "I'm sorry, that was inappropriate."

She must hear the regret in my voice because her features soften, and she takes a step toward me. "You've been through a lot in the last few months, Kade. I'm not a psychologist, but I would consider seeing one if you haven't. After a major cardiac event, depression isn't uncommon. It also wasn't just your heart that was injured. You broke your arm and received a concussion from your fall. That's a lot for a body to take. If you'd like, I can have my physician's assistant get you some referrals."

I roll my shoulders back and grimace. The last thing I want to do is see a headshrinker. They'd probably lock me up in a padded cell for all the thoughts I've got swirling around in my head. Not to mention that my friends wouldn't let me hear the end of it. I'm only twenty-two, for god's sake. I refuse to believe I need to talk to someone. I've always dealt with my shit, even when I was a kid. And I'll keep dealing with it like I always have.

"I'll think about it," I tell her, trying to make it sound convincing.

"Okay, great. Then we're all done here. I'll have you come back in a year for a checkup."

"A year?"

"Yes. You can see your primary in between or use the online portal if you have questions. But your heart is healthy."

"Okay, thanks," I say, thinking about how I don't have a primary doctor. Or at least I haven't in a very long time.

She stands, cracking open the door to leave. "And Kade?"

"Yep?"

"You're going to be fine. This was a little hiccup. Keep your stress down, and enjoy life. Don't be so hard on yourself; you're too young to be back in my office anytime soon."

I attempt to smile at her. "I'll do my best."

Her eyes crinkle at the corners, the shine in her brown irises dimming as if my words have saddened her, like she truly cares for me. But after a few quick blinks, they're warm and friendly again. "Take care of yourself, Kade."

Once the door closes, I change out of my gown and make my way to the end of the hallway. I go through the motions, handing a credit card to the woman at the front desk then booking my checkup for a year from now before I walk back to my red truck in the attached parking garage. Once I'm inside, I check my silenced cell phone and turn the ringer back on. I have several missed text notifications, but I don't have to see the name to know who they're from.

Gavin, my overbearing older brother, wanted to come to this appointment with me. I insisted I would be fine, that I needed the space to think and had a few errands to run. Finally, after some bickering—which isn't abnormal for us—he let me come to the doctor myself. They were a little late seeing me, so I'm not surprised that he tried to reach me.

GAVIN: How did the appointment go? Momma and Gran are worried.

KADE: Is it Momma and Gran who are worried, or is it you?

GAVIN: Kade.

KADE: Gavin.

GAVIN: Just tell me—everything okay?

KADE: Yes, everything looks good.

GAVIN: Thank god.

I leave out the part where I have to take medication and that she told me to see a shrink. But I *am* physically okay—that part is true. Gavin would be even more of a helicopter brother if I told him the other stuff. He'd also be worried about the cost of the meds, just as I am. We have insurance, but it's not that great. On top of that, we've already had to get on a payment plan to pay off my visit to the emergency room, surgery, specialists...the list goes on.

His girlfriend, Blake, may have taken care of the debt our dear old dad had accumulated against the Montgomery Family Ranch with her barrel racing winnings, but that doesn't mean we aren't still tight on cash. And the last thing I'm going to do is ask Blake for more money, even if she's become like a sister to me after she saved my life the day I ruined her late brother's five-year remembrance at the cemetery. Guilt pools in my stomach when I think about it, about the pain I caused not only to Blake and her family but also to my own.

I remove my ball cap and run my fingers through my feathered dusty blond hair then down my face covered in scruff. I replay those twenty-four hours from my accident in my mind multiple times daily.

I let my temper get the best of me that day, the very same temper Dad had. But when I found out that Gavin was lying for nine months about the debt Dad left our family in then discovered the business plan Blake made for us to turn our land into a dude ranch, I was furious. More than furious.

I think anyone would be if they found out their brother had been lying to them about something so serious for that long. And in my defense, I thought Blake's business plan meant she wanted to purchase our land to turn it into a dude ranch for her family, not that she wanted to invest in us.

So I lost it, and I let my rage fuel my decisions from that point on. I hardly remember driving to the cemetery and sucker punching my brother to the ground in front of half the town. Or getting in a physical altercation at a city bar with the brother of a girl I'd slept with a few times. But I do clearly remember coming home to find my family sitting at the kitchen table with Blake. They looked so happy without me—laughing over barbecue and acting like life was so fucking sweet—that any remaining thread holding me together snapped.

I grabbed a full bottle of whiskey and got drunk before deciding to take one of our ATVs out for a ride to Devil's Rock, a canyon on our property that Dad used to take me and Gavin to all the time. I don't like to think about what happened next, what led me to stand on that edge, what brought on my cardiac arrest. But the next thing I knew, I was being brought back to life by Blake. Then I was in the hospital.

I rub my tired eyes. Every day, I wonder how I survived. *Why* I survived. Maybe it's God's way of punishing me. Killing me would have given me an easy way out.

My phone rings, this time with a call. When I see who it is, I can't help the grin that tugs at my lips. It's Jake, my friend and boss at our local bar, Night Hawk. Gavin and I have worked there since Dad died. First, it was for the extra money, but I actually really enjoy it. I've missed being able to get out and have fun with the folks who come through. It's always a good time. Especially when we get city girls in for their bachelorette parties.

"Hey, man," I say into the phone.

"I heard you've got the all clear. Congrats."

"Well, shit. My brother's turned into a town gossip. Soon, he'll be worse than Old Abbey Allen."

"I'll tell him you said that."

"Good. He's turning into a meddler."

Jake chuckles. "In all fairness, I happened to be standing next to him when he got your text. He was dropping in with some provisions he picked up for me. But I waited to call you until after he left." He says the last part with an almost playful tone, which piques my interest.

"Tell me more."

"Would you feel up to teaching line dancing tomorrow night?"

"Tomorrow?"

"Yeah, customers have been asking when you'd be back. If not, I can do it or beg Gavin to do two-stepping again. Though that always turns into Blake and Gavin showing off and kissing on the dance floor."

This time, I'm the one chuckling. It's no secret that Jake has always had a crush on Blake Tanner, but she's Gavin's girl now. He's supportive of it, even cheered for them to get together, but I imagine it still doesn't feel great to see them as a pair. Especially considering they're the type of couple that can't keep their eyes or hands off each other.

"I'm sorry you've had to take the brunt of that."

"Please. She's on your ranch enough I'm sure you've seen more than your fair share of PDA."

I grunt, thinking of the times I've walked in on them doing more than I care to see. "True."

"If you don't feel up to it, it's okay. I'll figure it out."

An itch of excitement builds in my stomach at the prospect of getting my body back in action. Sure, I've been doing physical therapy and little things around the ranch, but I've been dying to go full speed. I don't like sitting idle; it gives me too much time to think. And this will help me pay for my meds as well.

"Yeah, I'm in."

"Yeah?"

"I wouldn't miss it."

"Thanks, man, I appreciate it. It's been so crazy here. I've hired a new bartender who starts tomorrow, too, so with you on the floor, she can shadow Gavin on the bar most of the night. It'll be great to have another Montgomery boy riling up the ladies."

"Are you saying I'm good for business?"

"You know it."

I laugh. "Don't tell Gavin this plan. He'll be doing his mother-henning and probably try to lock me in my bedroom to keep me from coming if I tell him I'll be dancing, even though I feel good." *At least physically.*

"Wasn't planning on tattling."

I exhale a breath. "Thanks, Jake."

"I've got your back, man. See you tomorrow."

After I hang up, I see I've got another text from Gavin. Proving I'm right about his mothering, he's texting me to ask where I'm heading and when I'll be home.

I think over my options for a while. I could go back to the ranch and let my family see that I'm "okay." I could sit and smile and have them all believe I'm on the path to being the boy I was before Dad died. The one who played cards with Gran instead of going to bars. The one who smiled and laughed, keeping things happy and upbeat on the outside.

Then we'd sit at the dinner table, and the three of them would talk about anything and nothing, making sure they avoid discussing the elephant in the room: me. Because while we've talked about the events leading up to my accident, and apologies were said, the conversation has remained surface-level, like it often does. They're still too afraid to ask the hard questions. To ask me the details of my accident. To talk about why Gavin lied to us all for so long or the reasons Dad kept us in the dark before he died.

Though I'm no better. Because I know if they really ask, they won't like what I have to say. That's part of the reason we've all been tiptoeing around each other—nobody wants a repeat of three months ago. Nobody really wants to know how I'm doing, either. So they continue to ask if I'm okay. I continue to say I'm fine. And we move on.

Ping! I look down at my cell.

GAVIN: If I don't hear from you soon, I'm
calling you.

I start up my truck, the engine roaring to life. As the vibrations of the vehicle shake through my body, I let the images of that plausible family dinner tonight fade to the back of my mind. For the last three months, I've been good. I've done my PT exercises, gone to my doctors' appointments, and haven't touched a drop of alcohol or been to a bar to pick up a girl and get my frustrations out with a good hard fuck—preferably while she's tied up and begging for my cock.

Every muscle and tendon in my body tightens, and my hands itch to feel my favorite rope sliding over my skin, to worship the warm body of a woman writhing beneath me. I'm not going to lie; it feels good to finally let myself imagine it. I long to give into the side of myself that craves and loves control, the side that helps me keep my negative thoughts at bay. The side that lets me shove them down deep and keeps me numb yet allows me to feel everything all at the same time.

I flex my hands, swearing I can feel the textured rope in my palms right now. Fuck, I don't think I can hold back any longer. And maybe I shouldn't. It would be nice to escape myself for a while. To temporarily be free of my endless self-loathing. To pretend as if I'm just a twenty-two-year-old with no fucks to give.

Like Dr. Ellis reminded me, I'm young. I need to enjoy life. And isn't sex and drinking part of that? Why am I required to feel so fucking much? Why am I trying to please my brother and my family when they live their lives the way they see fit? Especially Gavin.

With that in mind, I pull out of the parking lot and head to a bar I know is twenty minutes from here. Some would call what

I'm about to do avoidance or maybe say I'm an idiot to throw three months of sobriety and abstinence down the drain, but fuck it. I'm sick of only thinking about money, work, lies, and my dad's death. I'm sick of feeling.

My cell rings, the sound grating on me. I somehow manage not to throw it out the window and put the call on speaker as I drive down the busy two-lane road.

"What is it?" I ask gruffly.

"You didn't answer my text," Gavin says, clearly panicked.

"I'm driving."

"You on your way home?"

"No."

Gavin pauses. A heavy silence passes between us. "Everything okay?"

"I'll see you in the morning. Don't wait up."

"Kade—"

I don't let him finish. Instead, I turn my phone off and continue to the bar, shutting away the part of me that wants to keep my brother happy. Shutting away every part of me that wants to keep anyone happy. Even myself.

It's time to feel good. Or better yet, numb.

CHAPTER 2

Presley

I STARE AT MYSELF in the bathroom mirror, smoothing out my platinum-blonde hair that blends into various shades of purple. A little over seven months ago, my hairdresser in the city talked me into the change, saying it would go perfect with my complexion and sleeve of black-and-gray floral tattoos that cover my left arm. She was right.

At the time, this hair made me feel more like a version of me that was brave, like a woman on the brink of something new. Like the girl I was in college who dared to dream big and be edgy. Like a woman who took risks.

Now...now, this hair just makes me stick out like a sore thumb. Paired with my tattoos, it says, *Look at me! I'm different!* Which isn't great when you chose to move to a small Texas town whose population of under six thousand people could fit into a small stadium.

I shake out the nerves in my body then look into my blue eyes staring back at me in the mirror. "You can do this, Presley. You've played shows all over the South! Stop being like this. This is just bartending, for crying out loud!"

I huff out a breath and try to smile, but it doesn't quite reach my eyes. This is the tenth pep talk I've given myself in the last ten minutes, and none of them have worked. It's silly that I feel so scared to go tend bar when only last month I was playing fiddle to a crowd of thousands. But playing fiddle and being around new people in a new town are two completely different things.

Not to mention, I live here now and want to make a good first impression.

Knock! Knock! Knock!

I jump, hand flying to my chest as I remember that I'm not in the comfort of the tiny little guest house I rented three days ago on the Delgados' ranch. I'm at my new bartending job for my first shift, the very one where I'm trying to make a good first impression.

"Everything okay in there?" a deep voice booms from outside. The voice sounds like Jake's, the man who hired me. I believe he owns Night Hawk, but I'm not quite sure. All I know is he's my hot boss and he's the one who hired me with only a phone interview. Who even does that these days? I thought he'd at least want to meet me once, but nope.

"Hello?" he asks again.

Crap. I look in the mirror one more time and decide I look okay, I guess. Not that I ever think I necessarily look good, especially in uniforms. Thankfully, this one is a black T-shirt with Night Hawk's logo on it and a black waist apron to match. I'm also wearing a pair of high-waisted dark-wash jeans that hug my very full heart-shaped butt and keep my generous stomach tucked tight, a must-have for me after the years of my ex-boyfriend and now ex-bandmate, Derek, pointing out the things he didn't like about my body.

With a final sweep of my favorite lip gloss over my downturned lips and a deep breath, I open the door to a very concerned-looking Jake.

"You okay?" he asks, his dark chestnut eyes boring into mine from beneath the brim of a red cowboy hat. I bite the inside of my cheek. He's *gorgeous*. Tall, broad, dark, and handsome. But more importantly, from my limited experience, he's super nice, something I'm not used to anymore.

Between Derek, my band, and the years I've spent trying to navigate the music industry, I've become jaded, often assuming the people I meet are only nice to get something from me or for show. But so far, Jake hasn't given me a reason to believe any of those things about him. He seems genuine, a trait I'd forgotten exists.

It also helps that he doesn't know me. He doesn't know where I'm from or that I play fiddle. He doesn't know that my mom and I haven't spoken in five years or that my fifteen-year-old half-sister doesn't even know that I'm a musician. He doesn't know that my boyfriend of five-and-a-half years cheated on me and then dumped me this past Valentine's Day because he felt like I "no longer cared" about myself. Derek told me he wanted his girlfriend to put effort not only into her own looks but also into him and his needs.

Moreover, Jake doesn't know that I gave up the opportunity of a lifetime four days ago, the kind of opportunity that I've been working toward since before I even graduated from Berklee College of Music when I was twenty-two. All those massive dreams of making it big as a fiddle player, and I'd said no.

He doesn't know any of that—and hopefully, he never will. Because I never plan to tell him. I'm going to come here, do my job, go to my little guest house during the day, and try to figure out what the hell I plan to do with my life and music career.

Jake clears his throat, one of his dark eyebrows lifting as he continues to stare at me. That's when I realize I still haven't said anything. *Great job, Presley. Way to make a good first impression.*

"Yeah, I'm fine. Sorry. I was having a slight wardrobe malfunction."

Jake doesn't stop his gaze from moving down my form before he looks into my eyes again. "Do you need a different uniform? I think I have more in the back."

I shake my head. The lie I made up was silly at best. "Nope, all good to go now. Sorry I took so long."

He stares at me for another beat before he nods then waves at me to follow him down the small bathroom hallway toward the main room. "I'll show you around before Gavin gets in. You'll shadow him at the bar tonight and help him with anything he needs. Eventually, if you feel comfortable, you can start helping customers on your own."

"Great."

"Oh!" He snaps his fingers, stopping once we reach the bar top. "Kade will be in tonight. It's his first night back teaching line dancing after a little hiatus, so it's going to be a packed house. Just a fair warning."

"Thanks." I smile.

"I know you said on the phone you have some experience bartending, but as I mentioned, the city folk can get a little handsy and demanding. Especially when we get busy and they have to wait to be served."

City folk. His verbiage makes me want to laugh. When I thought about where I would go after I made maybe the dumbest decision of my life earlier this week, I never would have dreamed I'd end up in Randall, Texas. But as I doom-scrolled through social media with a ninety-nine-cent meat stick in my hand from the mini-mart and tears streaking down my face, I came across a shirtless man on a mechanical bull. He was cute—and too young for me but old enough—so I stopped to take a closer look.

It was then I realized it was an ad for a job as a bartender, a smart way to get people's attention, if you ask me. When I looked it up, I saw it was only a couple of hours away. Far enough that I could pretend the city didn't exist but not far enough that I had to worry about moving to a different state or changing my driver's license. It too meant I didn't have to deal with the anxiety of figuring out how to pay for expensive big-city apartments or how to make my meager savings last for more than a couple of weeks.

"I can handle people from the city," I say.

Jake eyes me, his gaze discerning. "You from there?"

I swallow, my throat now dry. I was born in a suburb outside of Dallas then moved to another suburb called Lynn with my mom and her new husband, Greg, after my parents divorced when I was five. They still live in that same suburb, in the same house, and my dad lives in California with a girlfriend that is half his age whose name I don't know. But I don't want to tell Jake that.

"Yeah," I say instead. "I look like it, don't I?"

He chuckles, a warm sound that reminds me of a nice hug. "If you get yourself a pair of cowboy boots and a hat, maybe some worn jeans, you'll fit in better."

I answer with a smile instead of commenting on how cliché that would be. At least the people in this town are real cowboys and ranchers, unlike the people I came across playing gigs at bars and clubs in different cities who like to play pretend. I'll have to order a pair of cheap boots or see if the Delgados' daughter, Lyla, has an extra pair for my wide calves and size-nine feet. But I imagine getting quick shipping to a town like this isn't a thing. I should also be saving my money, not spending it on something to help me blend in.

I hold back a sigh. All these thoughts have me annoyed at myself for not packing better. I have boots and a hat among my belongings somewhere in Derek's storage unit, but my exodus and new life here in Randall wasn't exactly well-thought-out.

"Well, then, I guess I don't need to explain city folk to you," Jake says. "Most of the people are fine, but when we get bachelor parties, the men can get kind of rowdy. The bachelorette parties do, too, but most of our bartenders don't care if they get handsy—especially Kade." He smiles to himself like he just told a funny inside joke.

"I can handle myself," I affirm. And that's the truth. If I can handle Derek getting drunk after shows and acting like a fool at three am, then I'm not worried.

"If anyone gets to be too much, yell for me, Kade, Gavin, or Stu. We're the crew that works most weekends," Jake says.

"I can do that."

Jake gestures to the long bar top we're standing in front of. It's placed along the wall near the back so I can see the entire layout of Night Hawk, from the small stage and dance floor to the padded mechanical bull pen. The place isn't huge, but it's large enough to fit a couple hundred people and has the kind of kitschy country charm that makes me smile. There are even peanut shells on the floor that crunch beneath my feet when I walk.

"Typically, Gavin will work the right side of the bar and Stu will work the left. If I'm not in the back doing paperwork, I'll take the tables or sub for Gavin when the mechanical bull is running. When Kade is here, if he's not teaching line dancing, he goes where he's needed, floating between tables, the bar, and sometimes, the bull. Once you get the hang of the place, I'll float you as well. But as I mentioned earlier, tonight you'll shadow Gavin, and he'll direct you."

"Got it," I say, awkwardly giving a thumbs-up to the information. Jake looks at my thumb, the ghost of a smile teasing at the corner of his lips. I try not to blush with embarrassment at my weird reactions to things.

With my anxiety and the aftereffects of Derek's constant belittling, I'm not that great with people. I know how to turn on a certain set of social skills, especially when I'm onstage playing or when I get comfortable with someone, but one-on-one with new people or in new group settings? I get awkward. Especially with people I'm trying to impress. Thankfully, Jake brushes off my awkwardness and continues to show me around.

"That right there," he says, pointing to a brown-and-white spotted mechanical bull, "is our pride and joy, Tornado."

"Fitting name." I grin.

"Thanks. He makes us a lot of money—he's the whole reason we've even got all these wedding parties coming here. Well, that and the shirtless mechanical bull riding my friend, Blake, convinced us to add in once a month."

"Smart," I say, trying to make conversation and be a normal person.

"That she is. The bull already was bringing in a big crowd, but add in shirtless cowboys, and now we're at capacity almost every weekend."

"That's great."

"It's why we needed the extra help and why I'm grateful you applied so quickly. It's hard to find consistent workers in such a small town. Most of the folks here already have their hands full with their own ranches and family businesses."

"Thanks for hiring me with the limited experience I have."

He tips the brim of his cowboy hat. "It's easy work, though it can get overwhelming." He pauses after he says that, probably thinking about how awkwardly I've presented myself since I walked through the door. "Any questions, come find me."

When a concerned look returns to his face, I know he's definitely thinking about it. I mentally smack myself for being so weird; I know I can present myself better. I did on the phone interview, though I didn't have to look him in the eye for that. I was also running on pure adrenaline after deciding to leave the band. I was highly motivated to get a job and get out of the city quickly.

I plaster a smile on my face. "I will." Though I know I won't. I'll work through anything I feel on my own, like I always do. I'm determined not to make a fool of myself further and keep this job, at least until I figure out what to do next.

Jake opens his mouth to say something else but gets cut off by the sound of a door opening. I turn my head toward the entrance and see two cowboys walk in. Even in the dim light and the glow of neon signs, I recognize one of the men right away. He's the one I saw riding the mechanical bull shirtless—the whole reason I found this job and why I'm here right now.

"You need to take it easy, Kade," the taller one says in a strained voice.

The one apparently called Kade doesn't look back at the man as he says, "You're not my babysitter, big brother. I'm fine. For the last time, lay off."

"I'm not trying to babysit you, I'm—"

"Like hell," he spits, spinning to shove his finger into his purported brother's chest. They both stop, glaring at each other. I start to get uncomfortable. They must not realize they have an audience because they're too focused on whatever is going on between them.

"I'm just trying to talk with you," the man says to Kade. When he goes to say something else, Jake clears his throat loudly. The two men both turn their heads at the sound, finally noticing us standing a few feet away from them. There's no music on yet, and we're the only ones here, so the silence is deafening.

"Gentleman," Jake says in a deep, authoritative tone. "Our new bartender is here."

Kade, having only made eye contact with Jake, steps back from his brother and, without another word, stalks off toward the door behind the bar that leads to the storage area and Jake's office. He flings it open, the top of his buckskin cowboy hat disappearing behind the now swinging door.

"Sorry about that," the tall cowboy says after a heavy pause. He removes the black hat from atop his head, revealing short sandy-blond hair and deep green eyes that would make any woman swoon. He takes a step toward me, his bowed lips drawn into a tight smile. He looks embarrassed at whatever it was I witnessed but tries his best to remove the evidence of it from his square features.

"Nice to meet you; I'm Gavin," he drawls, holding out his hand.

Not usually one for handshaking, I force myself to extend my arm so I don't come off as rude.

"Nice to meet you." Our palms meet, and his grip is strong, but it only lasts a few seconds before he's pulling back and planting his hat back on his head.

"You'll have to forgive my brother's behavior." His warm voice vibrates in the space between us, but there's a sadness in his eyes as he says it. "He usually has better manners."

Jake lets out a huff that tells me he doesn't agree. Gavin glares at him, and I shift on my feet, feeling even more out of place. It's always weird being the person that doesn't have the inside info.

I stuff my hands in my apron pockets. "It's alright."

Gavin clears his throat, and then silence cocoons us once more. My brain tries to think of something to say, but now I'm thinking of Kade storming off and remembering the tail end of the argument I witnessed. It was charged, and by the way they were speaking to each other, I felt as if this was a normal occurrence for them. It reminded me of how Derek and I used to fight.

A chill runs up my spine, and I squash my curiosity. I don't need to get involved. I need to keep my head down and stay out of other people's business. I don't want more drama in my life. I came to Randall to get away from it, not find it.

Maybe a small town was a bad choice, then.

"What did you say your name was?"

Gavin's timbre breaks through my thoughts, and blood rushes to my cheeks. Crap, I didn't tell him my name. Two points now for awkward first impressions. Not that it's worse than Gavin and Kade's dramatic entrance.

"I didn't. And it's Presley."

He smiles at my name. I know he's wondering the usual questions. "Were you named after Elvis?" "Were your parents big fans?" "Is that a nickname you picked?" And the answer is no to all of them. My mom doesn't even like Elvis, and my dad didn't like the name. Unfortunately, Presley is a product of Mom going into early labor and Dad being out of town on business. She heard Elvis on the radio in the cab ride to the hospital, and it was all she could think of when they asked for a name.

It's stupid, but I've grown to love my name. It's unique and stands out, something a person needs in the music industry. I also happen to love Elvis, so I guess that's a win for me. *Hooray...*

"Well, it's nice to meet you, Presley."

"Likewise."

He shoves his hands in the pockets of his Wranglers and glances at Jake. "Can I talk to you in the back for a second?"

Jake's eyes bounce between us, and he stays silent for a moment before he says, "Sure thing. Presley, you can scope out the place for a few minutes. If you want, hop out back to get a little fresh air. It's going to be a long night."

I bite the inside of my cheek. I'm going to have to work hard tonight to make a better and less-awkward impression on my new boss if I want to keep this job.

Jake continues, "Once Gav and I are done, I'll send him out to show you the ropes."

I nod. "Sounds good."

Both men smile warmly at me before they walk toward the door Kade stormed through a few minutes before. I take a brief moment to look around the bar and expel a tense breath.

In the silence, my thoughts and anxiety become louder, like pots and pans clanging around in my brain. It leaves me wondering if coming here was a good idea.

You can do this, Presley. You can do this.

CHAPTER 3

Kade

I PRESS MY HEAD against the brick wall. The October sun is still bright, but soon, the sun will start to set, and people will trickle in for happy hour. Which is a funny concept if you think about it. The implication is that you only get to be happy for an hour, or in some cases, a few hours. And that happiness is supplied to you by half-priced alcohol and deep-fried bar food. Or my favorite: all-you-can-eat chips and salsa.

And why is that even more funny to a man like me? Because people wonder why we have so many cases of alcoholism in the United States. We're born and bred to believe our lives should consist of hard work and only hours of happiness. Happiness that is then supplied by alcohol.

I laugh at myself. I'm not even old enough to rent a car yet; I should be thinking about more interesting things. Or happier things, though my thoughts are a product of living in Randall my whole life. I often think that if I hadn't been born here, maybe I'd be fresh out of college or working in corporate America—not that those options are better than shoveling cow shit. In fact, most people around here would say it's more fun to be knee-deep in muck rather than working for The Man as a suit monkey.

I pull my silver flask from my pocket and stare at it for a moment, tracing the engraved Montgomery monogram with my index finger. I carry it out of habit, but after last night, I found myself filling it for the first time since before the accident.

The flask is a family heirloom. Figures that Dad would leave a symbol of his love for alcohol to me while leaving our ranch, the only thing I wanted, to Gavin—the thing he promised me right before he died.

I unscrew the cap and bring the whiskey to my lips.

As I tip it back to take a swig, the back door opens, and I see a flash of blonde. This must be the new hire that was standing with Jake when I walked in. I'm not sure, though, because I didn't get a good look. I was too busy being annoyed with my brother. He'd been upset with me about coming home this morning smelling like alcohol and sex then even more upset I agreed to teach line dancing tonight.

No matter how many times I told him I was fine, that he didn't need to worry, he wouldn't stop pestering me. He wanted to know what happened after my doctor's appointment, where I went, how much I drank, who I was with. None of which is his business—and never will be his business. I'm a grown adult. He doesn't have control over what I choose to do with my life or *who* I choose to do, even though he thinks he does.

"Sorry, I can leave." The velvety sound of my guest's voice has the hair on my arms standing on end. The lush resonance of it reminds me of how a woman's voice sounds when she first wakes up in the morning, thoroughly sated. It grabs my attention in more ways than one.

Ignoring the effect a simple voice has on my groin, I shift my body to look at the girl, or should I say woman, from beneath the brim of my hat.

The first thing I notice is that her hair isn't fully blonde. It's wavy, framing her diamond-shaped face, but what makes it unique is the purple. There are different shades of it, starting lighter near her cheekbones and moving into darker, violet tones at the bottom. The color makes her skin look ivory, as if she hasn't seen the sun in months.

When I meet her eyes, unsure sapphire irises stare back at me. After a brief second, she looks down at her feet then back up.

When she does that a few more times, it becomes clear she's unable to hold my stare for long, as if my eye contact makes her nervous.

"Right, I'll—" She points to the door, turning to head back in. I get a flash of her generous ass in a pair of form-fitting black jeans, which doesn't help the tight-pants situation I've got going on. You'd think I'd be sated after the fun I had last night, but honestly, while the release felt good, it only provided me with a few moments of fleeting pleasure, leaving me emptier than before—like a black void of nothingness. I want to chuckle to myself, because maybe I was wrong and I already have gone numb without the use of my vices.

As the woman is about to open the door, I manage to speak up. "You can stay. This is a free country, after all."

She turns, her eyes moving to my flask before her shoulders slouch and she slips her hands in her pockets. She starts fishing awkwardly for something, her gaze trained on the ground while she pats her jeans and apron pockets.

While she's distracted, I let my eyes wander her pear-shaped body. Besides the unique shade of her hair—that I know is going to garner her quite a bit of attention from the people in this town—she's got a bunch of tattoos inked down her left arm. That's something I never see in Randall. A few of the guys get 'em, but I can't think of any woman I know who has any. If they do, they're hidden. But I like the way the black-and-gray flowers look against her skin. I have the urge to ask her why she chose the flowers that she did. Maybe she has a thing for violets since her hair is violet, too.

When she hikes up her jeans that have slid down her wide hips and puts what looks like a vape pen to her mouth, I stop my perusal.

"You smoke?" I ask, surprised. Sure, she has colored hair and tattoos, but she doesn't strike me as a smoker. But maybe that's why her voice sounds like sex.

Her cheeks blush a delicious pink color, and she pulls the pen from between her lips. "I did for a few years when I was in college. A nasty habit. I quit a few years back."

"Then what is that?"

She eyes the thing in her hand. "It's an inhaler that has peppermint, valerian root, and chamomile in it. It's supposed to calm you."

I press my lips together but can't help the chuckle that escapes. "Okay, that was the most city-girl thing you could have said."

She scrunches her nose. It's cute and reminds me of a bunny rabbit. "Is that a bad thing?" she asks.

"No, not a bad thing." I grin. I didn't know she was a city girl when I said it, but it was easy to guess, and now she's confirmed it.

The woman tucks a strand of her hair behind her ear and takes a drag of the fancy pen. When she exhales, a puff of white dances from her glossy lips. The wind catches it, and I'm hit with a whiff of peppermint and herbs. "Sorry," she offers, swatting the minty cloud like she can force it not to come toward me.

"It's fine." I take a drink from my flask. The whiskey burns as it goes down, hitting my empty stomach and reminding me I haven't eaten since this morning. I should take care of that so I don't end up making a fool of myself on the dance floor.

Without thinking, I hold the flask out to my new friend, if I can call her that.

She takes another puff of her weird stick thing and shakes her head. "I don't think I should drink on the job, especially on my first day. I don't want to get fired."

I tip the flask back and take another small sip. Most of the people who work at Night Hawk wouldn't have refused a drink—clearly this woman is not the usual type Jake hires. Mostly, my coworkers are locals or people who come stay as seasonal ranch hands and want some extra cash on the side. Come to think of it, they're usually men, too.

I let my gaze drag over her ample body once more. She's round and soft in lots of nice places. The Night Hawk T-shirt she wears lays mostly flat against her small chest, and her backside, as I've already established, is more than great. I can't stop my mind from swirling and fantasizing a bit more, wondering what I'd discover under her cotton shirt. How her tits would feel in my palms.

When another cloud of peppermint hits my nose, I realize I've been staring at her chest. I clear my throat and connect with her chiding eyes. *Busted.*

I display my most charming smile, the one that's always gotten me out of trouble or into women's pants. "You don't have to worry about getting fired. Jake isn't that kind of boss. Things are relaxed around here."

She nods, holding the inhaler stick in one hand while she tugs at the short sleeves of her shirt.

I raise an eyebrow at her. "Are you cold?" She can't be cold. It's hotter and muggier than Satan's armpit for an October evening.

Those already pink cheeks of hers turn the colors of strawberries as she stops tugging. "I was thinking I should've worn a wig or something and a long-sleeve shirt."

"Why?"

She nibbles at her bottom lip, her shoulders curving in and chin dipping like she said too much and she's trying to pull into herself. "Just thinking about an earlier conversation with Jake. I'm going to stand out."

While her hair and tattoos suit her, she's right about that. But she'll also bring in some good tips. The men around here like when we get someone new. When you live in a small town, you either get mixed up in the drama of dating someone's daughter or relative or you have to go out and catch a city girl and hope she doesn't leave you high and dry when she figures out marrying a cowboy isn't all it's cracked up to be.

I kick some dirt near my feet and exhale a small chuckle. "Trust me. If you wore a wig and a long-sleeve shirt, you'd stand out even more. Nobody wears long sleeves to a bar, at least not in this town. It gets hot with all the people dancing and drinking."

The woman sighs then takes another drag from her pen. She holds the white cloud in for a long beat then, when I think she's going to swallow it, she blows it out.

"Thanks for the advice—Kade, is it?"

The hairs on my arms stand up again when she says my name with that velvety inflection. "Have we met before, Sweetheart?"

The energy in the air between us goes taut, her shoulders squaring and body pulling tight like a bow string. Her lips part, fists clenching at her sides as she stares directly into my eyes with a hardened gaze. "I'm nobody's sweetheart," she snaps.

Her cold tone feels like a bucket of ice water was dumped over my head, and I hold my hands up in surrender. I know the sound of someone ready to deck me, and that was it. I stand to my full height, trying to present myself in the most non-threatening way—half smile, relaxed shoulders, warm eyes. "I meant no disrespect." And I mean that. Women usually love when I call them pet names: sweetheart, baby, honey, you name it. But I guess not this woman.

For a few moments, we stand there, deadlocked. When I flash my teeth in a wider smile, she finally blinks, snapping out of whatever thought spiral she's having. She inhales and exhales twice before she regains her bearings then puts her pen in her pocket.

"My name is Presley."

"Like Elvis?"

Apparently that, too, was the wrong thing to say, because she cringes. "Just Presley," she bites out. "No P, or Pres, or Lee. Presley is my name. Please only call me that."

My eyebrows lift. This woman is a surprise. Normally, women don't talk to me like this. Maybe my Momma or Gran, but that doesn't count. Evidently, Presley has a spark underneath her awkwardness. It's one that needs to be lit, but I see it there.

"Jake and your brother told me your name," she says. "So no, we don't know each other, but we're going to be working together. Let's put whatever that was behind us, yeah?" She holds out her hand for me to shake—which was the last thing I expected her to do—but she does it in a funny way, as if she doesn't want me to shake it. Her arm is sort of hanging there limply, fingers slightly curled toward her palm.

I study her hand, nails painted dark purple to match the ends of her hair, then meet her questioning eyes again. This city girl is strange, a woman who, without a doubt, has a story to tell. Presley. I like her name. And whether it has anything to do with Elvis or not, the uncommon name suits her.

I remove my hat and place my palm into hers so those curled fingers brush against the back of my hand. Her skin is warm against my palm—almost too warm, even a little sweaty from her nerves and the hot night.

As we shake, her eye contact wavers, her red cheeks getting redder the longer I hold her captive with my stare. It's both sexy and sweet. Presley on the surface isn't the type I usually go for—I tend to like women who aren't shy—but I'll admit she sparks my interest.

I've been with enough girls to know which ones are looking for more, though, and her vibes are screaming that she's the relationship type. I am certainly not looking for a relationship. But despite all this, I like the outgoing rocker-chick vibe she's giving off that's in direct contrast to how she's acted so far in front of me.

Now that I'm seeing her up close, her soulful eyes tell me she's too good for me. The gentle lines on her face, the serious maturity lingering under the surface, and the interaction we've just had all give me the impression she wouldn't give me the time of day. She's polite, but this will be a strictly professional relationship. Which, in the end, is what it should be. I don't need to shit where I eat.

"Yeah," I finally say, shaking her hand one more time before pulling back. I place my hat on my head then take a step toward the door. That step brings me and Presley closer, close enough that I can smell the peppermint on her breath.

Her breathing stops, and she looks up at me from her coal-colored lashes. I don't miss the way those blue eyes flash to my lips, and for a second, I lean in. I'm not sure why I do it, maybe because I know I'll never kiss her. But for this brief moment in time, I let myself imagine what it would be like. The way she'd unfold for me as I backed her against the wall and dove in to taste her like a starving man. I bet, once comfortable, Presley would bloom under my touch. Maybe even beg for it.

When all the blood in my body travels south, I know it's time to end whatever it is I'm doing. I'm not thinking with my brain.

I step around her, leaving Presley standing there. When I turn my head over my shoulder, she's still frozen in time, her eyes on where my lips were.

"See you inside," I say under my breath before opening the door. It's not until the back door closes that I finally inhale and decide it's best to erase that interaction from my memory.

CHAPTER 4

Presley

EVEN WITH JAKE'S WARNING, I wasn't prepared for how busy Night Hawk gets on a Saturday night. The place is wall-to-wall bodies, and from what I've heard, a line has started outside. It's the first time, apparently, and I guess one of the locals volunteered to be a bouncer for the night until Jake could figure out a solution for the future. It's insane.

"Presley, can you run to the back and grab some more limes?" Gavin yells over the roar of the crowd and Garth Brooks singing "Friends in Low Places." It's so loud, my ears are ringing. Makes me wish I could wear earplugs. I've always been sensitive to loud noises, and as a musician, my hearing is everything.

"Yeah, sure," I yell back to him. He gives me a smile that looks exactly like Kade's, and my stomach does a little flip-flop. But unlike his younger brother, Gavin has been nothing but professional with me. Despite it being busy and loud, it's been easy to shadow him, especially since he stopped the endless questions I had to answer at the beginning of the night from the locals. As soon as they started to arrive, the curious bunch sat at the bar and wouldn't stop chatting my ear off.

Polly Carson, a bright-eyed and sweet girl, asked me twenty consecutive questions about my hair color. Then her boyfriend, Tim, a cute red-headed cowboy, asked me questions about my tattoos. It was around the thirtieth question that I really did wish I had worn a wig and a long-sleeve shirt. Probably seeing my annoyance, Gavin made them leave the bar and go find a table. From then on, it's been a complete blur of activity.

At seven, Kade started line-dancing lessons. The small dance floor near the bull swam with women in mostly white cowboy hats and painted-on jeans, including several bridal parties dressed like Jessica Simpson in *The Dukes of Hazzard* circa 2005.

After my interaction with him outside and our…I don't even know what that was, I've tried to avoid looking his way. It's hard, though, especially when I can hear his voice over the loudspeaker calling steps to the crowd and telling jokes. His voice is a strong baritone, not too deep and easy to listen to, like a warm hug on a cold afternoon. He's encouraging to the dancers and definitely the flirt he demonstrated himself to be when we were outside.

When the song changes, and his "yeehaw" reaches my ears, I find the brim of his cowboy hat in the sea of women. He does some complicated move on the dance floor, spinning a girl out and back into his chest. My eyes follow the movement of his hand in hers, and my palm—the one that was against his earlier—tingles.

Before he came inside, I thought he was going to kiss me. Which is ridiculous. And not just because he's handsome with his neck-length dusty-blond hair and tortured hazel eyes, but we're going to be working together, and he's six years younger than me—a fact I found out from a random local. Plus, I do not want to let any man get in the way of my life again. I let that happen with Derek right out of college and with the people who claimed to be "helping me" with my career. I'm not going to let my hormones make any decisions for me.

And did I mention the man is tortured?

If the way he stormed into the bar earlier, angry at his brother—plus the flask—isn't a dead giveaway that he's going through something, his sad, angsty eyes are. I know because I've looked in the mirror every day for the last six years and seen the same sadness. But his look...I don't know, it's more defeated in a way that has me wanting to avoid his gaze. I feel like staring into his eyes will show me a scary reflection of the feeling I ran away to avoid—and the entire reason I came here was to start a new life.

There was also the part of our conversation where he called me *Sweetheart*, which is an immediate no for me. That endearment burrows under my skin like a splinter. It's one that Derek loved to use when he was being condescending, which was most of the time. But then Kade apologized, and I attempted to let it go. I reminded myself that despite his bad first impression, I don't know him. If Jake judged me on my first impression, I'd be screwed—so I wasn't going to judge Kade, either.

"Presley?"

My head swivels to Gavin, and I smile sheepishly. Speaking of bad impressions—he asked me to go get limes, and I haven't moved.

"Limes, got it." I think he chuckles, but I don't linger, already embarrassed I was standing there like an idiot.

As I walk toward the back, the other bartender, Stu, smiles at me, and I give him a little wave. He's been nice to me, too. Really nice. The thought makes my eye twitch because it's funny how much that stands out to me, but it soothes the sadness I've felt inside for so long.

Apparently, people being nice without wanting anything in return is noteworthy now.

I release a long sigh as I enter the back room, stray peanut shells from the bar crunching beneath my feet. With my hands on my hips, I take a look around and wonder where the limes are. I see a door that leads to Jake's office, a door to the alley, and a little table that we can sit at to take breaks as well as little cubbies for us to put our belongings in during our shift.

"Ah, yes!" I say to myself when I eye the rows of shelving with supplies, including bags of peanuts and pretzels, thinking they could be there.

I move through the rows, eyes scanning and hands searching, but I'm not having any luck finding them. I probably should've asked exactly where they were, but I thought they'd be easy to spot.

After another minute, I start to get annoyed. There are lots of different types of mixes for drinks and more pretzels, but I don't see any limes. I move to the next row and keep looking. When I do, I feel my phone vibrate in my back pocket.

I've been feeling it go off all night. I should've just turned it off, and I don't know why I haven't. When it vibrates again, I look around to see if anyone is back here, but I'm alone. So I pull out my phone and glance at it quickly, not wanting to be the girl who leaves her coworkers hanging for too long.

I grit my teeth when I see who it is, even though I knew it was going to be him.

DEREK: Are you going to tell me why you did this?

DEREK: Seriously, P? What the fuck were you thinking?

DEREK: You're ruining this for us. For me. Don't you care?

DEREK: Answer your damn phone.

DEREK: Seriously, WTF! I know you're not dead. Answer the fucking phone.

DEREK: We're going to replace you, then. Is that what you really want?

My eyes sting, and the bridge of my nose prickles. Of course he wouldn't be concerned about my well-being, only his own. And the last text—my stomach turns over, and I feel sick. I put my hand over my mouth and try to take deep breaths through my nose. It doesn't help that the smell of peanuts and stale beer is thick in here, making me feel stifled and hot as if the very air I'm breathing is closing in on me.

My anxiety spikes, tendrils of dread curling in my gut and snaking up my back, causing me to shiver. I squeeze my eyes shut and scold myself. I will not have an anxiety attack in the back room during my shift. Now is not the time to let my stupid ex get to me.

I take my inhaler pen from my jeans pocket and take a long pull of it, the peppermint soothing my frayed nerves before I turn off my phone and shove it back into my pocket. I've been gone too long again. While Gavin is nice, he'll probably start to dislike me if I don't get my shit together.

I tuck the inhaler alongside my phone then take another few deep breaths as I try to focus on the task at hand. Limes. I need to find limes.

But just as I'm about to move, I register the sound of giggles.

I freeze, looking to the side to see Kade and a woman kissing as he walks her toward the back of the room. They're so involved in each other, they don't see me between the shelves.

"We have to be quiet, cowgirl," Kade croons as they disappear from my view, the boxes blocking them now.

"What if I don't want to be quiet?" the woman answers back.

"Then I'll have to gag you."

She expels a high-pitched giggle, and then they start to kiss and groan into each other's mouths. *Jesus*. Why did Gavin have to send me back here for limes?

I stay still, trying to determine if I can get out of here without them hearing me. But I'm screwed, because the moment I move, they'll know I'm here. I guess it wouldn't be that bad if they did, but I can't bring myself to budge. My body is paralyzed by the idea of being caught, even if I'm back here for a reason. I just don't want to embarrass myself further.

The throaty moan of the woman draws my attention to them again, and I shift so I can peek through a space between peanut boxes on the shelf. I mute my breathing, careful not to make a noise as I observe them.

Kade's hand travels up the woman's thigh then disappears beneath the fabric of her dress. When my gaze reaches the top of her head, I notice she's wearing his cowboy hat. It strikes me as odd, but then I remember the saying I've heard while visiting bars around the South: "Wear the hat, ride the cowboy."

The woman writhes against him, her lithe body pressing into his. From this angle, Kade's back is to me. He's built, the kind of built you get from working long, hard days in the sun. I get lost in watching his biceps flex and the way the veins in his tanned forearms are more prominent as he grips the girl's ass.

I bite my bottom lip despite myself. I don't know why I'm watching. I need to leave. I should have gotten out right away, but—

"Yes, Kade!" The woman's head thumps against the wall. He kisses her again, his other hand coming up to grip her neck. My interest spikes as I watch. I've made out, and I've had sex, but only with Derek. And never once did he touch me like Kade is touching this woman, like he's a starved man and he needs her like he needs oxygen. It's...

Hot.

"I told you to be quiet." Kade squeezes her neck, this time a little harder so his thumb indents her skin and she gasps for air. For a split second, I wonder if I should be nervous for her, but he's not gripping her throat in malice. And by the hitch in the woman's cry and the way she grinds into him, she likes it.

I lean forward a bit and tilt my head so I'm still hidden but now I can see more of Kade's profile. His long hair is mussed from his hat and a bit sweaty from all the dancing. The shadow of his stubble on his square jaw is more pronounced in the harsh overhead light, and his cheeks are flushed from their kissing.

When my gaze reaches the sly smile that tugs at his swollen lips, I think about our interaction outside—how I swore he was about to kiss me, the way his hand felt so strong and warm in mine. I press my tongue against the back of my teeth at the sudden onslaught of images that crash into me.

Instead of this random woman against the wall, now it's me. Kade is squeezing my throat and pressing his body into mine. He's using those perfect lips to kiss up my jaw then tease my tongue with his. I can almost smell the saltiness of his skin as I imagine what it would feel like to experience those well-worked hands all over me and what sensations his stubbled jaw would cause between my thighs.

I bite my lip so hard it stings, the action bringing me back to reality. Shame fills me, and my desire to get the heck out of here comes back. I'm a twenty-eight-year-old woman, and this is my place of work. I should not be standing here watching this. I should not be imagining that a younger man, who is also my coworker, is pinning me against the wall about to have his way with me.

I mean, *crap*. Am I this starved for attention that I was basically treating this like my own personal porn show? What is wrong with me?!

I quietly step away from my viewing spot and turn my back to the shelf. I need to get out of this room. Maybe I should consider going to live in the mountains somewhere. It will be me, myself, and my fiddle. A semi-pathetic existence to be sure, but at least I wouldn't have to worry about embarrassing myself or having to deal with people.

"Presley?" Gavin's voice calls. "I need those limes—" The words die on his lips as he enters the back room. From where he's standing, he can see both Kade and the woman as well as me between the shelves. Kade's hookup screeches, and I peer between the open space to find the woman flushing and Kade unbothered. He removes his hands from her body and faces his brother. A wide smile stretches his lips, smeared with pink lipstick. I don't know how to explain it, but he almost looks as if he's glad he got caught.

"Can you cover for me, Presley?" Gavin asks.

I jump at my name and remember I'm still here, still standing in between the storage shelves. My entire body burns with embarrassment as I meet Gavin's eyes, taking several steps toward him until I'm revealed to Kade. I don't know why, but I dare a quick glance at him. The corner of his lip twitches when we make eye contact, and I know he understands I've been here the whole time. Maybe he even knew I'd been watching.

My ears turn pink, and I'm developing pit stains from how much I'm sweating. Thank god this T-shirt is black. When my head turns back to Gavin, he raises one of his light eyebrows at me, and I recall he asked me a question.

"Yes, I'll, um..." I stumble over my words. "I'll go do that now."

"Thanks, Presley," he says. "And you"—he points at the woman as I walk by his shoulder—"please leave. This isn't a space for customers."

I think she whines in protest, but I'm not sure because I'm met with the boisterous sounds of the bar as I hurry through the swinging door. The chaos of the room breaks me out of the bubble I was just in, the one where I'd been imagining Kade between my thighs and his hand pressing into my throat. The one where I'd just watched him make out and feel up another woman when I was supposed to be getting limes. My awkward self has the urge to tell someone "I carried a watermelon," but I doubt anyone would get my *Dirty Dancing* reference.

Stu walks by with a couple of beers and grins at me then eyes the back door. His bearded jaw clenches like he knows exactly what's going on behind that door, which has me wondering if he saw Kade take the woman into the back room. They would've had to come through the bar area, so maybe Kade *did* want to get caught? But why?

"You good?" Stu asks.

"Yeah," I lie. "I'm good." My voice comes out squeaky, but I clear my throat to try to cover it up.

"Hey! We've been waiting for like ten minutes here!" a guy behind us yells. Stu's brown eyes dart to the door then to me, and I know it's time to step up and get my shit together. I need to prove to Jake that I can handle this job. Gavin showed me the ropes—now it's time to sink or swim. This is the life I choose now. Or at least it is for the time being.

"I got it, Stu."

"You sure?"

"I told Gavin I'd cover for him. I'll be fine," I say over the twang of Luke Combs singing "Beer Never Broke My Heart," a song that seems fitting for the place and the people in it. Stu nods his assurance, and I turn toward the man who was just complaining.

I take in his black cowboy hat, the shine of it making it clear he's not an actual cowboy. He's also got on an expensive-looking T-shirt and designer jeans. I've seen his type all over the country, and I know he's wearing this getup because he wants to be a cowboy for tonight and thinks it will get him laid.

I paste a saccharine smile on my face, the one I would placate Derek with all the time, and ask, "What can I get you, Cowboy?"

CHAPTER 5

Kade

I FORGOT HOW MUCH tequila hangovers suck. My head feels like an explosive ready to blow, and I can hear my heartbeat in my ears. My sweat even smells like tequila. And women. Fuck. From now on, I'm sticking to beer and whiskey.

I put the pitchfork down against the side of my horse Willy's stall and look around to make sure nobody, especially one of my family members or Blake, is lurking, then I take out my flask. Hair of the dog should do the trick. The watered-down whiskey makes the eggs I ate this morning threaten to make a reappearance, but it's the only thing that will make this hangover end more quickly. My body isn't used to drinking this much after three months without, and it wants me to pay for it with heartburn and a headache.

I remove my ball cap and wipe sweat from my brow before putting it on backward. It's too damn hot already, the unbearable heatwave only adding to my ornery mood. I start going through the chores I have to do for today and debate if I can grab a dip in the spring later—not only to cool down but also to help clear my mind after last night.

Once Gavin found me and the girl in the back room, he sent her back to the dance floor then proceeded to lecture me about workplace etiquette. Was I an idiot for bringing her back there in the first place? Sure. It wasn't my proudest moment, but it's not the first time I've done it, either. I also wasn't thinking clearly; I drank more than I'd planned. One minute, I was dancing and having fun for the first time in a long time, then the next, I was being handed tequila shots in memory of my dad. I'd been trying to forget that the anniversary of his death passed last week, but this dang town won't let me.

Once that first tequila shot hit my stomach, it was game over. After that, I kept being handed them, and I didn't decline, wanting to erase the grief of losing my dad from my mind for the evening. Erase any feelings whatsoever.

Eventually, the girl ended up putting my cowboy hat on her head, and then I was sneaking her into the back for a little fun. We never ended up fucking, and I left Night Hawk shortly after, hitching a ride home from a local. The girl, while attractive, wasn't doing much for me. I was happy when we were found. I was finding it hard to get into, just like I had the previous night. It felt empty. Her touch was...just that. Touch.

The only thing interesting about that whole situation was the fact that the new bartender, Presley, was watching. That surprised me. I felt more seeing her blush and look away from me than I had getting attention on the dance floor all night. It made me think of our time in the alley, of the way she looked like she wanted to kiss me when I stood over her.

I grunt, my head pounding at all this thinking.

I decide I need another little drink of whiskey to help me out. Just as I swallow, I hear Blake's boisterous laughter from down the barn aisle followed by Gavin's. I slip the flask in my waistband so it's hidden from sight, not wanting them to see it and start trying to psychoanalyze me—though I'm sure Gavin already has in the last couple of days.

I grab my pitchfork again and go back to mucking just as Blake's chocolate-brown curls come into view outside of Willy's stall.

"Kade, you're here!" She smiles, her warm eyes making contact with mine.

"I'm here," I say.

She chuckles, Gavin standing at her side with his arms crossed over his chest. I try not to roll my eyes, but it's damn hard not to when he looks at me like that, as if he's so much better than me. Like he's my dad or some shit.

Blake, her gaze flitting warily between us, says, "Heard it was busy at Night Hawk and Jake had to use one of the Corbin boys as a bouncer."

"Yeah, it was a packed house. I guess people were excited I was back for line dancing."

"As they should be. You're the best of the best."

I tilt the corner of my mouth up. "Thanks. It was fun."

"I'm glad. Well, I just wanted to check in and make sure you had breakfast. Gavin and I decided to splurge and grab something from The Diner for all of us. He went to ask you if you wanted anything, but you weren't in your room and your phone was off."

"Thanks, but I got up early and ate. No need to worry about me."

Blake's forehead creases, and I can tell she wants to comment, probably say something about how she'll always worry about me because she cares about how I feel, especially after saving me that night at Devil's Rock. But she doesn't, because Blake understands me in a way my brother doesn't.

We've both experienced grief and extreme trauma, her more so than me after witnessing her younger brother's tragic death five years ago. More than anyone, except maybe Jake, she doesn't judge me.

She nods. "Good. I don't want you to go hungry." Her phone timer goes off then, and she takes it out of her pocket. "I've got a phone call with a potential new hire to help us with some ranch chores in five minutes. But before I go, is everything good with you? I didn't get a chance to check in after your appointment on Friday. Gavin gave me the bullet points, but I want to hear it from your mouth."

I pat my chest and give her the best smile I can muster. "All clear."

She moves so fast, I hardly have time to react. She steps into the stall, throws her arms around me, and squeezes. I'm still holding the pitchfork awkwardly to the side, but she doesn't seem to care. "I'm so glad, Kade."

After a few seconds, my body relaxes. I can't help but let my guard down a bit with Blake—she cares about me too damn much for her own good. It has my heart squeezing in my chest. That familiar pain in my sternum smarts to the point I want to rub it again like I did at the doctor's office.

Fuck. I don't deserve someone like her in my life, someone who cares so much about a screw-up like me. I pull back, my sinuses stinging with unwanted emotion. Her own eyes shine with tears as she shoots me a knowing look.

After clearing her throat, she says, "I'll leave you boys to it." She kisses Gavin on the cheek then walks down the barn aisle toward an old tack room we set up as an office for us to use. My brother watches her leave like the fool in love that he is, and I use the moment to collect myself.

I fork a pile of Willy's shit into the muck bucket and turn my back to Gavin, my attempt at telling him to fuck off. I'm hoping it sends a clear message that I don't want to talk about what happened last night. But I know my brother, and I'm waiting for the other shoe to drop.

It only takes the sound of the office door clicking closed for him to step into the stall with me, shavings crunching beneath his boots.

When he stops directly in front of where I'm working, I have no choice but to look up at him. His arms are still crossed over his chest, biceps bulging. With Blake gone, he has his "big brother mode" turned all the way on, and I know we're about to get in a fight.

I lock my jaw, hands flexing around my pitchfork. I've been avoiding this confrontation since our conversation on the phone after my appointment, but I guess it's time to face it.

"Can I help you with something, Gav?" I ask after a minute of his staring. He hasn't said anything—he's just stood there with that critical gaze he loves so much. And honestly, I'm sick of it. I throw the last of Willy's shit into the muck bucket then lean on my pitchfork.

"You smell like tequila and one of those perfume stands in the mall," he finally says.

I chuckle darkly. I expected a comment like this from him. Ever since Dad died, he's been on my case about being a "playboy," acting like he didn't sow his wild oats when he was my age. Like he never came home smelling like tequila and perfume from all the women he two-stepped with and probably fucked.

But what makes his comment even funnier to me is that he believes the reason I wasn't in my room this morning was because I went home with someone. What he doesn't know is I slept in the barn loft, not wanting to risk seeing him.

I wipe more sweat off my brow and look him straight in the eye with a half grin on my face, one that says more *fuck you* than anything else. "You go to malls often, Gav? I thought your boots looked new."

Gavin grinds his molars then exhales. "Are you okay?"

The question surprises me. I expected him to give me a lecture right out of the gate. That's been our relationship for the last year. I do something, he lectures. I get pissed, we don't talk. We make up. Then the process starts again.

Right before and after my accident, our communication was slightly better. We'd come to a sort of understanding that we'd both been working through our grief in different ways. But then, over the last few months, my lack of ability to do anything—to work, to get my anger out, to have any meaningful conversations—has faded. Now, my spiraling dark thoughts gnaw at me like a rat on a scrap of food.

The anniversary of Dad's passing didn't help quell those feelings, especially when I kept trying to understand why he left Gavin the Montgomery land instead of me. Why Dad, then subsequently Gavin, didn't just fucking tell me we were struggling so badly.

The more I think about everything that's gone down in the last year, the angrier I get. Gavin likes to pretend as if the sorrys we said to each other after my accident were enough, but they weren't, not by a long shot. I guess I'm just supposed to be okay, move on, build this dude ranch, and act like everything is peachy.

"Kade?" Gavin asks again.

I blow out a harsh breath. "I'm fine."

His eyes flick down my body, his gaze resting on a thin scar I now have on my right arm from surgery. "You know you can talk to me."

"Can I really, though?" I ask before I can think about what I've said.

Gavin visibly bristles. "What do you mean by that?"

I grab the handle of the trolly the muck bucket is on and start to head out of the stall. Gavin blocks me, and the bubbling rage I've tried to tamp down gets the better of me.

"I meant nothing by it," I bite, my head pounding harder.

Gavin's nostrils flare. "I know things have been tough for you, especially with the anniversary of Dad's death, but I thought getting the all clear from the doctor would help. I thought the drinking and the women were in the past. Now, it feels like you're reverting back to how you were before your injury."

"I'm fine, Gav. I'm just having some fun." I think we both know that's a lie, but I don't want to talk about how I deal with my feelings right now. Especially when A, I don't think he really wants to know and B, only his judgment waits on the other side of my truth.

"Kade, please talk to me."

"I said I'm fine!" I yell.

Silence fills the space before Gavin puts his hand on my shoulder. I tense under his grip. "I miss him, too, Kade. It's alright to have feelings, despite what shit he left us in."

While I agree our dad left us in a pile of shit, his statement doesn't placate me. Gavin had a completely different relationship with him than I did. My big brother was treated more like a son and less like a friend while I was the opposite.

The day I lost my dad was the day I lost everything—not just one of my closest relationships but my future, too. Gavin thinks he understands how it felt to lose him, but he doesn't. He can't. And he never will.

"I have work to do." I push past my brother and make my way to the compost bin. I don't have to look back to know he's following me.

"Kade, would you please stop? I just want to talk for a minute. I'm worried about you."

"Are you?" I yell back, not turning to face him. Because I have to wonder if all his mother henning is out of actual concern or if he's just trying to make shit less awkward for him, take the burden of his lies off his shoulders.

"Kade!"

I still don't turn back. There are a few ranch hands around, and they're observing us as if we're two gorillas at the zoo getting ready to fight. That's the last thing I want. I'd rather not have the people we hire thinking we're a bunch of emotional ticking time bombs ready to go off. That's not the way to run a business or get respect. At least that's something Dad taught me.

Gavin puts his hand on my bicep and forces me to turn and look at him. This time, I do pull away from him. "Gav, I said I'm fine." I keep my voice low so nobody can hear me.

"But—"

"If you're concerned about my behavior, try to get it through your head that I had one night out after my appointment and fucked a girl to celebrate after three months of sitting on my ass and twiddling my thumbs. Fucking sue me."

Gavin rubs the back of his neck like he does when he's upset or nervous. "And what about last night, then?"

"I was having fun."

"We were at work, Kade. And you made Presley uncomfortable."

I think back to finding Presley's blue eyes staring between the shelves after Gavin walked in. The thought has me wanting to tell Gavin that I don't think she hated what she saw. In fact, I'd say besides looking embarrassed, she didn't exactly try to stop me and the girl I was with from doing anything. I'm going to guess she watched the whole thing. Which I find interesting.

When I don't answer Gavin's question, he sighs. "I don't want you to move backward, Kade. I love you and—"

"I'm going to stop you," I spit out quietly. "I said I'm fine. You had fun when you were my age, so don't act like I'm any different. Now you're tied down and acting all mature and shit. If you're jealous, just say that." The queasiness from earlier comes back at my words. Despite our differences, I love Blake and my brother. And he very much loves her and is happy with his life. But I'm too hungover and pissed off to feel regret over my words. I just want him to get the hell away from me.

"This isn't you," Gavin says.

I square my shoulders. "Open your eyes, big brother. Maybe this has always been me but you've been blind to it."

"No—"

"See, Gav, this is the problem. You keep telling me who I am. Maybe you should stop and smell the dying roses." With that, I walk away, making a point to go greet one of the ranch hands, Art, with a smile on my face and a joke already leaving my mouth.

Art laughs, and the tension in the air breaks. Gavin is burning a hole in the back of my head, but I refuse to look at him. I have work to do, and I don't want to fight anymore.

"Art, can you finish out the stalls in the back? They just need new shavings."

"Sure thing," he says.

I hand him my pitchfork and dump the bucket. With Gavin's eyes still searing into me like I'm a bug under a microscope, I decide I need a break to cool off from this conversation and nurse my hangover.

"I'll be back this afternoon to finish up that fence in the south pasture," I tell Art.

"Need help?"

"Sure. I'll text you." With that settled, I head toward the house. I know Gavin won't follow me because there's too much work to do.

When we all decided to move forward with Blake's plans for the Montgomery Family Dude Ranch, it was understood there'd be a ton of work to do to get it off the ground in such a short amount of time. Nine months, to be exact. Three of which have already passed.

I said we needed more time, but I was ignored. Not that I could fight much, anyway. For the first month after the accident, I spent my time in bed on pain meds while Momma fussed over me. Turns out broken bones and a broken heart are a complete bitch to mend.

During the second month, I got more involved, but I still found myself being pushed out. Blake did her best to include me, but since I was going to the city for appointments and tests on my heart, again, I couldn't do much.

By the start of the third month, I had mostly given up trying. I started physical therapy for my arm and was allowed to take longer walks by my doctor but was banned from lifting anything. Again, not something easy when your life is working the land.

In a last-ditch effort, I tried to help Blake with some paperwork, calling and negotiating with contractors about the updates we needed to the guest house and such, but I'm not meant for sitting on my ass. I prefer physical work, to feel as if I've earned putting my feet up at the end of the night, to know that I did good work that day, accomplished something.

Not being able to do that has made me feel worthless. I'm hoping now that I'm able to work again, I will feel less of that.

But it doesn't feel that way. Especially after my fight with Gavin.

After a few minutes, I approach the house I've lived in since the moment I took my first breath in this world. My feet stop, and I take in the peeling white paint of the two-story home with the wraparound porch that needs a fresh sanding and a coat of paint. Dad and I would spend hours out here some nights, unwinding after work. Sometimes Gran, Momma, or Gavin would join us. We'd talk about work, mostly, things that needed to be done, cattle that needed to be sold. Nothing too deep but things that were important to our livelihood.

A yearning fills my chest, one for simpler days when Dad was still alive, when I was more like the carefree boy Gavin so desperately wants me to be again. That thought has more memories of my time on the porch flash through my mind, like the day my dad gave me my first drink of whiskey at fourteen years old. The time I realized that my future was this land, living in Randall—not becoming a horse-reining champion like my kid self once imagined.

An intense feeling of sadness hits me like a mallet, and the hair rises on my arms. *Open your eyes, big brother. Maybe this has always been me but you've been blind to it.*

Those words I spoke to Gavin echo in my mind. I said them for a reason, even if I didn't mean to say them out loud. Because despite the memories I have of this porch, my home, the nights spent with Dad, I'm not so sure I was ever the carefree and happy boy my family believed me to be. Because I think I've always felt this crack inside me. This past year has only spread it wider, the pit below it growing and festering.

I reach for my flask, wanting to feel the sting of whiskey down my throat instead of the burn of the feelings I so desperately have been trying to rid myself of for maybe my entire life. My fingers brush the cool metal just as a blue butterfly flutters by.

The insect stops my action, and I blink. I exhale a breath through my teeth and squeeze my eyes shut, trying to rein myself in. Rein my thoughts in. It's too early to get drunk, and even if Gavin thinks I'm like our dad, I can handle my shit without getting buzzed by noon. Or at least, I think I can. I stopped myself from drinking before. I was sober for three months.

I adjust my hat, running up the few steps to the front door and flinging it open. I'm going to grab a few things then take that dip in the spring. I need to get off this property for a bit and clear my head—hopefully press the restart button on this day.

Yep, that's what I'm going to do.

CHAPTER 6

Presley

TEN MISSED CALLS, TWENTY-NINE text messages, and even an email. A freaking email. I tried not to read them—or listen to the five voicemails Derek left, either—but of course I did. Because I'm a glutton for punishment.

My favorite text was: *Why would you do this to me? To us?*

To "us"? There hasn't been an "us" for over half a year. And if I'm honest with myself, there hasn't been an "us" for even longer than that.

I roll over in the twin bed, springs creaking as I press my face into the pillow and scream. Anxious energy crawls in my gut, and I scream again, trying to release some of it. I don't work until later tonight, so the only natural thing for me to do is doom scroll on social media and listen to my ex rip me to shreds.

There's also the fact that I can't stop thinking about the backroom incident with Kade last night. I keep seeing that little upturn of his lips when he found out I was watching him make out with that girl. So embarrassing!

I scream into the pillow again. It's times like these I wish I wasn't such an awkward turtle. I wish I was more confident and didn't care what people thought of me.

I flip over in the creaky bed so I'm staring up at the ceiling. The yellow paint is peeling off around some watermarks I assume came from the roof leaking after some rain, and there's a chip that creates a tiny crack in the off-white ceiling lamp. I fling my arm over my eyes and try to stop myself from crying.

What the hell am I even doing here? Why did I leave my life for this? Why couldn't I just deal with my shitty ex and bandmates? If I could've only been stronger, at least I'd still be playing fiddle, doing what I love, instead of laying on an old bed staring at a ceiling that needs a fresh coat of paint while questioning my life choices.

But I guess in the end, I have nobody to blame but myself. No matter how much I want to blame Derek and every outside force that influenced me in my journey to this moment, *I* got involved with him when my friends were telling me he wasn't a good guy. I let myself get wrapped up in his attention and lead me away from my goals, even if, at the time, I thought he was only helping me. God, I was and am such an idiot.

A cow moos loudly in the distance, like they're agreeing with me. Great. Now I'm taking a cow mooing as a sign of my failures.

A knock on the door startles me, and I wipe my tears away.

"Are you in there, Presley?"

I sit up at the soprano voice of the Delgados' daughter, Lyla, outside. I've chatted with her a few times since I've moved in, and she's the first person I met when I arrived in Randall. She made me feel at home from the moment I unloaded my suitcase.

Not wanting to make her wait, I get up off the bed and open the door to find her standing there, wringing her hands nervously. Since she always appears to be in a good mood, her demeanor has my stomach churning.

"Everything okay?"

She tucks a strand of her dark hair behind her ear. "Can I come in for a quick chat?"

I glance behind me at my mess of stuff on the floor. I didn't have many belongings with me, but what I do have hasn't been put away yet. Not that this little studio has a lot of space for me to unpack—just a small dresser and closet. But I'm determined to make it work.

"Um, sure. It's a mess. I'm still unpacking, but—"

She waves me off, stepping around me to come in before I have time to fully open the door. "It's not a problem. You should see my room!"

I smile a bit and close the door. When I go to shove my hands in my pockets, they slice through air because I forgot I'm wearing leggings. Lyla pretends not to notice, but I can see the amused glint in her eye.

I clear my throat and fold my arms over my T-shirt-clad chest. I should have thought more about what I was wearing before I opened the door. I'm not even wearing a bra. Thankfully, this is when having small boobs is optimal. I don't have to worry about them flopping in the breeze.

"What's up?" I ask, unable to wait to hear what she's going to tell me. By the look on her face and the way she's still fidgeting on her feet, it can't be good.

"I've got some bad news."

I worry my bottom lip, wondering what the hell the bad news could be. I've barely lived here a week, and I paid her my rent for the full month. And I've hardly left the space since I got here besides to work at the bar, so it's not like I've done anything that could label me a bad tenant.

"Okay, hit me." I cringe at my awkward phrasing.

"I really hate to do this. I just feel so awful." She takes out a wad of cash from her back pocket and hands it to me. "I have to give you your rent back."

My eyes bounce from the money to her brown eyes. "What do you mean?"

"I'm so sorry, Presley, but my brother is coming back from Mexico early. He was supposed to be there for another few months, but...well, he had to come home. It's complicated. I'm so sorry. I feel terrible. My entire family feels terrible. We would never have rented this space to you if I thought it was even a possibility."

Bile burns my throat. "Really?" I want to smack myself for that response, but I don't know what else to say. She does seem apologetic, and her body language screams that she's telling the truth. I didn't sign a lease, so it's not like I can take it up with the management company or something. I found this place via a listing on a corkboard at the general store.

"Again, I'm so sorry, Presley. I feel so terrible. We wouldn't have even put the place up for rent if we knew he'd come back this early. But the house is full with some of my cousins here to help with the fall season and..." She trails off, her eyes shining with tears.

I reach out to squeeze her shoulder. I'm not normally one for comforting people, but I can tell she needs it. And she does, because before I know it, Lyla is throwing her arms around me and squeezing me into a hug.

My entire body stiffens, not used to the feeling.

Growing up, my family was more of the side-hug-and-wave type of people. As a child of divorce, my parents didn't even tell me they loved me, say nothing of giving me a lot of affection, and I guess I got used to it. That was one of the things Derek never liked about me. He's touchy-feely, and I tend not to be. I like my personal space.

Yet another reason I've been stuck on thoughts of Kade. Him invading my bubble in the alley and me not stepping back was strange of me.

I pluck that thought from my head as soon as it enters. I shouldn't be thinking about him, anyway, not when I have an emotional Lyla in my arms. I pat her back awkwardly as she cries. Should I say something to her?

Just as I'm about to make a probably weird attempt at an "everything is going to be okay" speech, she pulls back.

Her tan cheeks darken. "Oh my gosh, I'm so sorry. That was so...wow!" She brushes the tears from her face and steps back.

"It's okay."

"I'm known for not having any filter or boundaries. I didn't mean to cry on you—we hardly know each other. You must think I'm nuts."

I shake my head. "No, I don't think that." And I don't. Even though I'm not a touchy-feely person, I constantly do things that make me seem weird, as shown by my behavior last night at Night Hawk. At least I ended the night on a high note—Stu told Jake he was impressed by how I handled the bar when Gavin was saying god knows what to Kade in the back room.

I was proud of how I handled the pressure. I don't really remember the rest of the night because of how busy it was. All I know is that I made some decent tips, and I only had a few people comment on my hair and tattoos after Polly and her friends.

Lyla sighs. "I should be the one comforting you. I'm so sorry, Presley. Really."

With the focus back on me and my new predicament, my heart starts to race, and my palms sweat. I hear myself say, "It's okay, Lyla," even though I don't know how I'm going to be okay with no place to live. "I just hope everything's fine with your family."

"It'll be okay, just a lot going on. This year hasn't been the greatest for the crops with the drought. We got some rain, but—anyway, you don't need to hear about farm problems or family drama, so I won't bother you with it."

"You can if you want."

She throws her arms around me again, and this time, I allow my body to relax as she hugs me. "I knew you were a good one, Presley. That's why we rented you this place." When she pulls away, she's smiling through her wet eyes. "Now, do you want to hear the good news?"

I raise an eyebrow at her, my heart still pounding. "There's good news?"

Lyla rocks on the balls of her feet. "Oh, geez, I should've led with that! Sorry."

My lips press together. Yes, that would have been nice, but now I just want to know what the good news is. "It's okay."

"When I found out my brother was coming home, I knew I couldn't just kick you out without another place to go." She eyes the suitcase on the floor before meeting my gaze again. "You don't have another place, right?"

I shake my head. Without this guest house, my next option is a motel or my car, which is a last resort considering I'd have no place to shower and my car isn't exactly big. This space was perfect because I could pay as I went and I didn't have to make any commitment.

With the size of this town, I'm not exactly sure what kind of housing options they even have on such short notice.

"Great!" she says happily.

I screw my face up in confusion, wondering why that's great.

When she sees my reaction, she huffs a laugh. "That was bad phrasing. I say 'great' because I found a place for you to stay."

That settles my racing heart a bit. "You didn't have to do that, Lyla."

"Pfft! Yes, I did. I told you; I feel terrible."

"Please don't. I understand that things come up." And I mean it, too. She doesn't owe me anything. I'm practically a stranger to her, so it's nice she's even trying to set me up in a new place.

She hums then begins to wring her hands again while looking at the floor.

"What is it?" I ask.

She bites her lip as our eyes connect. "The room, it kind of comes with a catch."

"What kind of catch?"

"There's a big ranch down the road. They went through some hard times in the last year, and they found a way to turn it around by starting a dude ranch."

"A dude ranch?"

She nods, her eyes lighting up. "Yes! It's a great idea. The town thinks the tourism will bring in money for a lot of us, especially in the summer. But they're looking to hire someone to help around the place. The original person fell through this morning, so they're in a pinch. It's not operating yet, but they're getting a bunch of new horses in, and Blake said they could use the help. The job comes with pay and a room."

The name Blake rings a bell, and I remember Jake talking about a friend of his with that name. Then it hits me. She said *job* and a room. "Lyla, you want me to work on a ranch?"

She presses her lips together then speaks. "I don't know if you want another job, but the pay is decent, and their property is beautiful. It's ranch work like mucking stalls, painting, stuff like that. And like I said, it comes with a free place to live!"

I want to say the living quarters are technically not free if I'm working to pay it off, but I don't. Lyla seems very excited about this solution, and I don't want to seem ungrateful.

"And..." She leans in closer to me like she's telling me a big secret. "I know we don't know each other, but between you and me, there are lots of hot single guys over there. If anything, you'll have a nice view when they're shirtless and sweaty. Let me tell you, there's nothing hotter than a cowboy while they're working, especially if they're wearing one of those white tank tops and a ball cap. Phew!" She giggles.

I blink at her, and after a second, I can't help but crack a smile. I admit, she's right about that. Not that I've seen a lot of barely clothed cowboys working on a ranch. None, actually. But I can't help thinking of the image I saw of Kade on social media, the one that got me here in the first place.

Lyla laughs again and gets a dreamy look on her face, her infectious happy nature rubbing off on me a little bit. I like the way she's not afraid to be herself and say whatever she's thinking. It's something I wish I could've done more, especially when I was her age. My early twenties would've been a lot easier if I wasn't always trying to be what others—what Derek—wanted. Now look where I am...about to be a ranch hand?

"What do you say?" she asks when I don't say anything after another moment. "I know it's not exactly ideal, but everyone there is awesome and will welcome you with open arms."

I mull over the idea. Part of me wants to say no, but I *do* need a place to live. And another job will not only help me with my finances but will also fill my days with something other than reading Derek's stupid messages or thinking about how my life has gone completely off the rails.

I twirl a lock of purple hair around my finger and meet Lyla's gaze. "You really think I can work on a ranch? I'm kind of scared of riding horses, and I've never mucked a stall, whatever that means."

She shrugs like that's no big deal. "I think you can do anything you put your mind to, Presley."

My eyes sting, and I swallow down the sadness that clogs my throat. There were so many times I wished my parents would say something like that to me. So many times I wished they'd encouraged me to go after my dreams, that they'd been a solid and supportive part of my life. But they never were. Once my dad moved to California, he hardly had any interest in my life. And my mom and her new husband were quick to brush me aside every chance they got, especially when my half-sister was born just as I turned fifteen.

Lyla cocks her head at me, a look in her eye that says, *Come on Presley, do it.*

And maybe I should. If anything, it's something new. Different. Like when I dyed my hair purple and thought it would lead me to finding a new version of myself after Derek and I broke up. But this time, I'm in a new place surrounded by new people who have no influence over me. Isn't that why I came to this town—to figure out how to start over and not be the same scared Presley I've been for so long now?

I inhale a deep breath and make a decision that might be considered rash, but I'm going to roll with it. What's one more rash decision on top of the ones I've already made?

"Alright, if Blake is okay with a worker who has no experience."

"Trust me, she will be. She'll just be glad for the help on such short notice."

"Then you can tell her I'm interested."

Lyla claps and does a little happy dance. "I'll text her now!" With a grin on her face, she takes out her cell from her back pocket and taps out a text message. She goes back and forth for a minute before looking back up at me.

"Okay! The job is yours."

My eyes widen. "That's it? Does she not want to meet me or anything?"

"I vouched for you, and so did Jake," she says as if it's nothing at all. But I'm glad to hear I made a good impression on them both despite what my inner thoughts made up. "I'll give you Blake's number, and you can chat with her more about the job. If you get there and decide it's not for you, you can leave with no hard feelings, and we'll help you figure something else out."

"This town is really trusting," I say, thinking about how Jake hired me just from a phone interview with limited experience. Now, I'm going to be a ranch hand with no experience. I feel as if I'm living in some weird fever dream. But nope, just a very small town.

"Something you learn in Randall is that we take care of our own. And you, Presley..." She throws her arms around me again. "You're one of ours now."

I gently squeeze her back, tears stinging my eyes at her words. "Thanks, Lyla."

"It was nothing." She pulls back. "Thanks for being so understanding and not getting angry, not that I thought you would. You're too nice!"

She has no idea how true her words are. Even though people in my life have not been nice to me, I have been way too nice to them. It's how I've gotten in trouble and become a doormat. It's how I let people like Derek walk all over me and take advantage of my kindness.

"You don't have to move out right away," Lyla continues. "My brother comes back in two days, but he can stay up at the house on the couch until you figure out everything with Blake."

"Thanks, Lyla."

After she sends me Blake's number and we say our goodbyes, I sit on my bed and open a blank text to my new boss that I haven't even met or spoken to.

I sigh. Am I really going to do this? Work on a ranch? Now I'll be around people all day and night, which wasn't exactly part of my plan. I just hope I'll be able to play my fiddle without people hearing. The last thing I want is for anyone to find out I play right now, not until I figure out what it is I even want.

Gosh, was I stupid for agreeing to this? I don't know if I'm cut out for ranch work. I know it will be hard work, which I'm not opposed to—I love working hard. It makes me feel accomplished. But working outside? Working with farm animals? I also don't do well in the heat and sun for long periods of time. But I guess that's what water and sunscreen is for.

I lay on the creaky twin bed and stare up at the ceiling just as my phone vibrates. I don't have to look at it to know who it is, but I do anyway.

> **DEREK:** The band wants to talk to you.
> You're acting selfish, P.

P. He knows I hate when he calls me that. The freaking asshole. My vision goes blurry, and the feeling of failure, of being unsure of myself, creeps back in—or should I say *intensifies* since I don't think those feelings ever left. Changing my location didn't change my personality.

When my phone vibrates with another message, I don't read it—I simply swipe up to clear the notification then open the text to Blake and send her a message. I can't go back to my old life. I just can't. There's a reason I turned my life upside down and came here. I need to see where this leads, if only to prove to myself that Derek doesn't rule over me anymore.

When my phone vibrates again, thankfully, it's Blake.

> BLAKE: Let's meet Wednesday morning. I'll send you the address.

With a renewed sense of determination, I send her a confirmation message then shut my eyes, holding my phone to my chest. I guess I'm really going to do this. I'm going to be a ranch hand. If only college Presley could see me now.

CHAPTER 7

Kade

I WIPE DOWN A glass and put it in its place under the bar. It's just about six o'clock on a Sunday, and Night Hawk isn't too busy yet—which annoys me.

I wasn't even supposed to be working, but after I finished patching up the south pasture, I took a ride on my horse, hoping it would clear my mind since my dip in the spring and work had failed to do so. But just like everything else, it didn't help. So I came here, praying the chatter of people and maybe a couple of women to flirt with would stop the thoughts that just won't quit. But no luck so far.

I pick up another glass, wiping it down as I stare at one of the neon signs above the bar that says, "Never Stop Lovin' Cowboys." Kind of a funny sign if you ask me, considering people love the idea of cowboys but usually not the cowboy themselves. Or they think a cowboy is the kind they read about in romance novels or see on TV, when in fact there's only a small percentage that make the kind of living people who come to this bar expect. In reality, being a cowboy is hard fucking work, and most of us are broke.

I chuckle sadly, because when I was a kid, I had naïve ideas like that, too. I wanted to be one of those fancy cowboys. I'd often daydream about becoming a reining champion, a competitive Western discipline where a rider takes a horse through a precise pattern of circles, spins, and stops. After I made a name for myself by winning a bunch of fancy titles, I wanted to use those skills to train the next generation of reiners, breed horses, the whole shebang.

In many ways, I wanted to create the kind of life Blake grew up having and build a similar operation to the one her family runs now. I wanted to make the Montgomery Family Ranch a name that people in the sport could trust. A legacy for my children, if I were to have any.

But that dream died. Not because I wasn't good—the opposite, actually—but I learned at a young age that I wasn't meant for silly things like big dreams. Not only did Dad constantly remind me of my responsibilities around the ranch and how my training got in the way of those responsibilities, but my momentum was crushed early on.

I had qualified for a big senior youth competition in Arizona, one that could have put my name on the map if I even placed in the top ten. I had given Dad the paperwork I needed to enter, but he passed it on to Gavin to complete because he was busy. Gavin forgot, and I missed the deadline.

I remember the night I found out so clearly, the utter blood-boiling rage I felt. How I literally could see all my dreams disappearing into the air like my breath on a cold winter night. I think that was the first time I truly lost myself and let my temper get the best of me, so much so that I hit Gavin and we got into a huge fight.

In hindsight, I know missing the deadline was not his fault. Just like me, he had a lot on his plate. Dad had given him more responsibility than he could handle on the ranch, and as I later found out, he was just told he couldn't go away for college. He was needed on the ranch, and if he wanted to continue school, community college was his only option.

The whole ordeal is just another example of our dad not being a great dad. And the more I think about our childhood, especially my teenage years, the more I wonder if Emmett Montgomery was never the man I thought he was.

"Can I get another beer, son?"

I turn to look at one of the locals, Jerry. Like many of the older men in this town, he's rough around the edges. Crow's feet line the corners of his brown eyes, and the skin on his face is tanned and sunspotted.

"Sure thing."

I hand him the longneck after I've removed the bottle cap on the bar top, a bit of a tradition around here. I don't know who started it, probably Jake's Pops. The wooden top has dents and nicks all up and down it. Jake claims that just like the peanut shells on the floor, it gives Night Hawk a certain charm. And I suppose it does. Much like most of my friends, we grew up coming to this bar with our parents since nobody had babysitters. It looks a lot different now, but I like it all the same. Jake's done a nice job creating a place that's welcoming and fun.

I hear a man whistle, and I pop my chin up to the sight of blonde-and-purple hair walking into the bar. I pick up another glass to wipe off as Presley approaches with her head down, eyes cast to the floor. The apples of her cheeks have turned pink from the man's attention, which strikes me as a bit odd, considering everything about her screams for attention—her wild hair, her tattoos, that full bottom of hers in those tight jeans.

When she reaches the bar, she glances those pretty blue eyes of hers up at me for only a second, but it's enough for me to see the stain of her cheeks turn a shade darker. The colors have me thinking about last night, how she watched me feel up the girl in the back room. I wonder if that darker flush means she's remembering it, too, or if it was simply caused by the whistle. Since I don't know Presley that well, I'm finding it difficult to get a read on her.

When I open my mouth to greet her, her head turns to Jerry, who's staring at her—well, more like at her hair and tattoos. She awkwardly waves at him then bolts to the back room before either of us can get a word out. It's a strange reaction, but maybe it's because of me and what she saw last night. Or I could be giving myself too much credit and it's just her general awkwardness.

I run my tongue against the back of my teeth, my curiosity about our new bartender growing. Questions swirl in my head, and there's a part of me that wants to follow her into the back room and ask her why she bolted, how she felt about seeing me in the back room last night, if watching me turns her on. The questions are mostly inappropriate, but for the first time all day, I'm not thinking about my problems. I'm thinking about the mysterious city girl whose appearance begs me to look at her, yet her actions say otherwise.

"Who's that purple girl?"

I snort. "That's the best you can come up with?"

He shrugs and takes a sip of his beer. "Never seen hair like that."

"That's because you don't come here on a Saturday night." Which is true—Presley isn't the first person to come in here with colored hair.

"Too many of you young'uns for me to come on a Saturday. Heard you had a line here last night."

"You heard right."

He grumbles something about times changing just as the back door opens and Presley walks back out. Jerry studies her again, his gruff expression not changing.

"Howdy," I say. The greeting is silly, but working in a place like this, it's all part of the charm—and hard to turn off when I'm within these walls. As I said, the people love the whole Texas cowboy act.

Presley shoves her hands into the pockets of the apron tied around her waist, fidgeting on her feet for a long second before her lips part.

"Hi," she squeaks, her eyes bulging slightly from her clearly unintentional tone of voice before she looks down at her feet again.

I attempt not to laugh while I tuck the rag I was using in my back pocket, waiting for her to look at me. When she eventually does, those sexy sapphire eyes of hers are still unsure, but she manages to keep eye contact with me.

"Jake told me to find you. Said you'd know what to do with me." As soon as the words leave her lips, the flush that had just started to dissipate returns in full force.

I clench my lips together, really trying hard not to laugh now. But hell, I'm not going to lie. Her simple words spark something in my low abdomen. I'm a twenty-two-year-old man, one who uses sex as a way to clear my mind, ease my pain. Girls have always come easy to me, just like ranching, reining, and drinking. This woman? While she might confuse me a bit, I sure as hell would know exactly what to do with her. What I could do *for* her.

My eyes drop down Presley's body, lazily looking her over. The sound of her throat clearing has me meeting her now narrowed gaze. I flash her a flirty smile, one that tells her I'm not ashamed of looking. This only lights a fire in her eyes, just like the one she had last night when she caught me looking at her boobs and I called her Sweetheart.

She cocks an eyebrow at me, and my heart beats faster in my chest. I wonder what it would take to break down Presley's walls, to crack her open and get her to let loose. To fan that flame I see behind her eyes right now. I can think of so many ways, many of which involve that velvety voice of hers crying out my name—

Fuck. I inhale a breath, willing myself to get it together. While being at work has never stopped me from pursuing a woman, I know better than to get involved with a coworker. Like I said, Presley isn't my usual type, and I highly doubt she'd want anything to do with me, anyway, despite our little moment outside yesterday.

There's a reason I have the reputation of Randall's playboy, and I didn't get that name by sitting on my hands. The first time

I had sex, I was fifteen, which isn't uncommon here. Not much to do for fun in a small town, and our high school parties in farm fields often led to kids hooking up—or at least making out. Over the years, my experience grew, and eventually, I got into the kink community online, with rope bondage in particular catching my interest. That led me to taking drives into the city and getting some hands-on experience in clubs after I turned eighteen.

The way Presley fidgets and avoids eye contact reminds me of some women I used to play with when I first started out, ones who take time to unfurl and need a safe place to explore. In the last two years, minus one woman before my accident, I've only hooked up with women who sought me out. These were women I knew could handle my rougher tastes and didn't need to be coddled, didn't ask to exchange phone numbers after, and didn't want to date.

"Kade?" My name on her lips cuts through my thoughts. Jesus, now who's the one staring awkwardly? I need to stay cool, if for no other reason than to simply not look like an idiot. I lessen my smile so it's more friendly and less *let me tie you up, darlin'* and motion for her to follow me. It takes us only a few steps to reach our destination.

"You can set up shop here for a bit," I say, showing her the station I use to slice all of our citrus and refill things like cherries. "It's pretty slow right now, so it's a good time to cut and refill everything we need for drinks." I pick up a lime and toss it in the air before placing it on the counter.

Her eyes watch the action and widen like saucers, her cheeks flaming pink again as if it's their natural color. At first, I have no idea why a lime is causing her to react this way, but then I remember Gavin saying something about limes when he walked into the back room last night.

I can't help the small chuckle that leaves my lips. While I should feel bad, the situation *is* kind of funny. It's also good she understands what kind of man I am. Maybe she will keep her distance, and then I won't have such a hard time trying not to think about all the ways I could make her come undone.

I tap my fingers on the bar. "Think you can handle it?"

"Yeah, I got it."

I nod and step back so she can take my spot at the station. "Great. We should be getting busier in the next half hour or so. On Sundays, it's mostly locals who come around, trying to take the edge off before another long week. We offer half-priced bull rides, and tonight, we have a band coming. They should be here any minute."

Her breath catches in her throat, and a look of panic flashes through her eyes.

"Have something against live music?"

"No." She shakes her head but then asks, "What band?" There's a slight quiver to her voice when she says it, and my hackles rise. I don't think I've ever seen someone get nervous over talk of a band, which adds to my confusion and curiosity about this woman. It has me feeling like I should comfort her, but given our interactions so far, I doubt she'd like that. And I definitely don't need to get involved in her life—that would only complicate things.

"Just some band from a town over," I answer. "He's a friend of Jake's. I should say it's more one guy with his guitar and his friend, a fiddle player who sometimes plays the banjo."

She drags her gaze to meet mine as she picks up a lime. "Do you want me to cut all of these?"

Alright, change of subject. I can't knock her for that, especially since I can relate to not wanting to talk about my feelings. "Just fill up all the containers. Then you can put the rest in the back fridge for later."

The mention of the back room has her pink again. Jesus, this woman. How does she get embarrassed so easily? "Look, Presley," I say, making sure I use her name and not an endearment. "I'm sorry about last night."

She puts her hand up before I can continue. "It's not a problem. I'd rather not talk about it."

I blow out a sigh. "If that's what you want."

She nods, holding my gaze, though once again, I can tell she's struggling to do it. Her pupils bounce around while she clenches her fists, and questions I want to ask her sit on the tip of my tongue. The biggest one? Why does a person who's as shy as she is, who doesn't seem to be one for small talk, move to a town like this and start working at a bar? It's confusing. She's confusing.

Fuck. Maybe I should have a drink. While the thoughts of her stopped my spiral over the drama that is my life, now I'm obsessing over her. I shouldn't care about Presley or why she is the way she is. Yet I can't seem to stop myself.

The boisterous laugh of one of our patrons makes Presley jump, and she breaks eye contact, moving back to the task of cutting limes. I watch her for a minute, her hands delicately grabbing the fruit before she slices into it. Her cuts aren't perfect, and the wedges are all uneven, but she's dedicated to her task. It reminds me of when I started working here and how mine looked even worse.

"I can teach you a trick to cut the wedges evenly if you want."

She stops cutting and looks up. The corner of her mouth twitches as if she's irritated, like I've offended her by offering to help. She places the knife down and wipes her fingers on her apron. "There's a trick to cutting lime wedges?"

I chuckle. I don't know if she meant to, but her tone was flat like she was calling me an asshole without actually saying it. It doesn't bother me, but again, I'm trying to figure out why something as simple as saying I could teach her how to cut limes would be annoying.

"Look, you can cut them any way you want, but Jake had to teach me. Thought I could make it easier on you."

She places her hands on her round hips and steps back. "Show away."

I smirk again, inhabiting the spot she just occupied. When I pick up the knife, I find she's standing off to the side, putting a large distance between us. "Can you see from there?"

Presley blinks, face burning bright again. Only now it's not from embarrassment or shyness but clear irritation. I want to ask her what her deal is because I did nothing to make her angry in the last five seconds except offer her help. Huh. Maybe that's the issue.

Before I can tell her to carry on how she was doing it, she puffs out a breath from between her teeth and steps closer—but still not close enough to see properly.

I grunt, now getting annoyed right back at her. "Get in here, woman. I need you to see what I'm doing."

Her eyes harden. "Did you just call me 'woman'?"

I resist the urge to roll my eyes. Calling her "woman" was a slipup. At least that's what I'm telling myself. "Presley." I say her name in hopes she'll cut me some slack. "Please, I'm just trying to show you something."

Jerry's loud cackle draws my gaze to where he's seated at the bar. I'd forgotten he was there, most likely watching our entire exchange. He tips his bottle at me as if he's saying *good luck with that one* before he takes a drink.

When my focus moves back to Presley, she's got her arms crossed over her chest. "Show me."

With a slight shake of my head, I angle my body so she can see. "First, you want to cut the lime in half."

"I know that. Anything else?"

Laughter bubbles in my chest, but I manage to tamp it down. Despite my annoyance, I like this fiery side of her. It's better than the awkward and shy version. Feels more like I'm actually talking to her.

"Yep. Do you want to know the secret?"

Her foot taps on the floor, and for a second, I think she'll say no. Then she surprises me by nodding.

"You have to cut a slit in the middle. That way, you can put it on the rim of the glass easier." I pick up the lime, and since she won't come closer to me, I hold it up and show her how I do it. "Cool, right? Just make sure not to go too deep so you cut through the rind at the bottom."

Presley watches my hands work, and then she nods. "Got it. Don't go too deep."

I bite the inside of my cheek. Why does everything out of her mouth sound like sexual innuendo to me? Before I can think too much about that or embarrass her again, I place the wedge I sliced on the cutting board. I finish showing her how to cut the lime at an angle so it makes three perfect wedges.

"Simple enough, right?"

"Yes."

I step out of her way again, realizing I'm not going to get anything else from her. She takes her place back at the board, and I hand her the knife with the handle down. When she reaches for it, our skin touches. I don't miss the way her breath hitches at our nearness like it did yesterday when I stupidly wanted to kiss her.

Eyes penetrating into mine, Presley's fingers linger. Everything about this moment makes me feel as if she's trying to see something in my eyes, trying to read me like I've been trying to read her. The thought has a tilted grin pulling at the corner of my lips, and for whatever reason, that snaps her out of whatever she's thinking.

Her fingers brush over mine once more as they go for the knife. When they do, I notice her fingertips are calloused, the texture of them interesting. I look down at her left hand, but she pulls the knife away, trying to put distance between us. That isn't easy, since I'd have to move away for that to happen.

"Thanks, I've got it from here," she snaps.

"You want to try it once—"

"I got it," she says again, defiance in her tone.

"Presley." My voice is quieter, not wanting to draw attention to us. More people have started to come in, and Stu is now at the bar helping customers. "Are you okay?"

She places the knife down, refusing to meet my eyes. "I have to use the restroom."

Before I can blink, she makes a swift exit, and I'm left to wonder what happened. Was it because we touched? Or was it because of our previous interactions?

"Women, am I right?"

I turn my head toward Jerry, who's sipping his beer with a funny look on his face. "You need another one?" I ask, not wanting to get into a conversation about Presley, or any woman for that matter, with him. The man is twice divorced. It was all the town could talk about for a while. I don't think anything he says could help me out.

He looks at the bottle then at me. "Why the hell not?"

CHAPTER 8

Presley

I SPLASH SOME COOL water on my face, wishing it was colder to help calm the burning of my cheeks. My body is still feeling the effects of Kade staring at me as I walked off. I probably shouldn't have left like that, but the moment our hands touched, my anxiety crept in. I had to leave before I cried or yelled at him.

I wipe my hands off with some paper towels and look at my calloused left fingers. I know he felt them when I took the knife back, and I don't know why it set me off. They could easily be from working outside, but my mind went straight to "he knows you play fiddle!"—which is silly. And at the end of the day, would it really matter if anyone knew I played? The worst that could happen is maybe they'd ask me to perform for them.

But if I'm honest with myself, I know that's not why I freaked out.

While my interactions with Kade have been less than desirable, including but not limited to him calling me "woman" just now, I can't help but be attracted to the cowboy. When I'm around him, I feel as if my body has a mind of its own. He pulls me in like a moth to a flame, making my belly flip-flop and my skin tingle—a feeling I haven't felt since I met Derek. Or maybe ever.

I huff out a long breath. Figures this feeling would come now, at the most inopportune time, from a man who's younger than me and very much a playboy. That fact is obvious to me not only from his behavior in the back room last night but also from the gossip I heard while working the bar yesterday.

The biggest topic was Kade's return to Night Hawk. I heard something about an accident, but mostly, they spoke of his penchant for drinking and women. I was too busy to think much of it at the time, but now Jake's comment about him chasing after the bachelorette parties makes a lot more sense.

All this to say I have no business feeling any type of way about Kade. I moved to this town to get away from red flags, not move toward them. I just have to remind myself of that when he's around.

With a deep inhale, I check my appearance, glad I don't look the way I feel on the inside. My skin is a little red and dewy from the heat and the water, but otherwise, I look like me. Wavy, dyed blonde-and-purple hair, black mascara and eyeliner, pink-tinted moisturizer for my lips, small tits, big hips, and clothes that cover all my rolls. Just a woman. Nothing special.

After that great pep talk, I walk back out to the bar. It's gotten busier in the few minutes I've been collecting myself. Kade is serving a new group while Stu pours some shots for a couple of women who look like they're from the city. Even though this is my second shift, I'm learning how easy it is to tell. The locals are dressed more casually with worn hats and boots, their skin tanned or sunburnt from working outside. The "city folk" are dressed as if they're trying to fit in. Their hats and boots are brand new, and their clothes appear fresh off the rack.

I walk over to the bar and take my position back at the cutting board. I don't know if I should still be doing this now that it's gotten busier, but I'm not going to ask Kade. So I get to work and cut the limes and lemons, using the technique he showed me until all of the containers are filled. I hate to admit it, but I'm glad Kade taught me this skill, or it would've taken me a lot longer.

"You cut those like a pro."

I look to my side to see Jake. He's got on his Night Hawk uniform and his red cowboy hat, which I've learned is a signature of his.

Kade appears behind Jake and slaps him on the back. "Showed her what you taught me."

"Ah, the old slit trick." He grins.

Kade snorts. "Please don't call it that."

I scrunch up my nose. "I agree."

Both men eye me like they're surprised I spoke. Have I really been *that* awkward since I've met them?

Yes, yes, I have.

"My Pops taught me that, and it's what he calls it," Jake says fondly. "Just passing it on to future generations."

I snort. "I'm pretty sure I'm older than you."

A boyish grin forms on his features, and I know I'm right. Jake strokes his fingers over his clean-shaven jaw. "Don't let this pretty face fool you. I have good genes. Kade's the twenty-two-year-old baby, but I'm actually eighty."

The reaffirmation of Kade's age makes me wonder how long he's worked here—and if he's been coming here for longer than it was legal.

Kade chuckles. "Don't pay Jakey boy here any mind; he thinks he's a comedian." He goes to say something else, but a customer asks for service and stops him. He winks at the both of us then walks away.

"You doing good, Presley?" Jake asks.

"Yeah, great."

"Good, you think you can handle working the floor tonight? Since it won't be as busy as yesterday, I'll have you go around and take orders at the tables. Then Kade can fix the drinks for you, and you can grab any bottled beer or seltzers. I'll have Stu work the bar top."

I nod. "No problem."

He smiles, his dark eyes glinting. "Alright, then. Did Kade tell you about the band? They'll play for a couple of hours and get drinks on the house."

I force a smile, attempting to do a better job this time of keeping any emotion from my face. While I know the band isn't Derek, it could still be someone I know, especially if they have a fiddle player. I'd rather not have my prior life mixed in with the one I'm trying to build here, at least until I can figure out what I want to do with my music career.

"Yeah, he did."

"Just two buddies of mine. They play here often. You like live music?"

It's harder to keep my face neutral at that question, but I manage to nod. "Who doesn't?"

Jake chuckles and nods like he agrees. "Well, specifically, this is bluegrass."

My smile is tight. Little does he know, that's the majority of what I play. "Yeah, I enjoy it."

"Good, you'll hear a lot of it here. Well, I've got some paperwork to finish up. I'll be back out in a bit, but again, come grab me if you need anything."

"Will do. Thanks, Jake." He tips his cowboy hat and walks off, leaving me to my own devices. I pat the pockets of my apron, double-checking I have a pad of paper and pen in case I need to write something down.

When I gaze out at the floor, many of the tables are filled, and I notice people are looking at me with curious expressions. Once again, I wish I could erase my tattoos and change my hair, but I can't. Maybe I should've asked Jake if I could work the bar instead. Last night felt easier because I was able to get into a rhythm of serving that didn't involve a lot of talking.

A Pandora's box of energy threatens to unleash its contained anxieties inside my stomach, but I force myself to exhale. Since I can't go on a break and take a few drags of my calming inhaler, I start to prattle off a list of things in my head, a trick I learned from a friend to help pull myself out of an oncoming anxiety attack. It also helps me fall asleep at night when I can't shut my brain off. *Chicken, Alaska, fence post, computer, water, bird, coffee*. Each word is carefully selected to be unrelated to the previous one.

I sigh my relief when it starts to work, my shoulders relaxing and the insides of my stomach uncoiling. I don't know why I didn't think to do this earlier, because I'm already feeling better, maybe even better than if I'd taken a drag of my inhaler. After a few more strings of words and another couple of breaths, I plaster a smile on my face and walk up to a table with two women. I hear the tail end of their conversation as I approach.

"I think the anniversary of Emmett's death really screwed him up, especially with only having just gotten better from the accident. That's why he's gone back to drinking and sleeping around," one of the women says to the other.

"Can I get you ladies anything?" I ask, interrupting their gossip.

The woman who was talking turns her gray eyes on me and scans me up and down. The disapproval I feel from her stare is brutal. *Frog, sky, air fryer, trolls...*

"Who are you?" she bites out, her steely gaze slithering over my tattoos then my face.

"Cricket! That's not very nice," the other woman scolds.

I blink at the woman called Cricket and think it's appropriate she's named after a bug. I may not know her, but I would never talk to someone like that.

Cricket's plump lips, painted a bright red, stretch painfully into a tight smile. "Sorry. May I ask your name?" Her tone is saccharine and still not nice.

"Bartender," I answer her. None of us wear name tags, but given the tone of her voice, I don't think she deserves to know my name.

She flips some of her brown hair over her shoulder. She's a beautiful, curvy woman, the kind of Jessica Rabbit curves I'd kill to have. But even before she spoke to me, the way she had her nose turned up and the gossip on her lips told me she thinks very highly of herself. And not in a good way.

"Your name is Bartender?" She giggles condescendingly.

I ignore her question. "What can I get you?"

A beat of awkward silence passes between us.

Her jaw ticks. She's probably not used to people not answering her questions. "Do you live here, *Bartender*?"

"Nobody lives in the bar, Cricket. Except maybe Jake."

The hair on the back of my neck rises as a now familiar warm baritone voice enters our little chat.

Cricket's gaze flicks beside me, her smile becoming so sweet and flirty that it makes me want to puke. "Kade," she coos, batting her eyelashes.

Oh god. I hope he hasn't slept with this woman. I mean, he probably has, seeing as she's gorgeous. But I'd definitely question his taste in women if that were true.

"Howdy, Cricket."

She reaches her arm out and touches his forearm delicately. I'm unable to resist looking at his face out of the corner of my eye. He's smirking as if he likes the flirtation, but I notice the way his molars are clenched and tiny lines have appeared in the corners of his eyes. Most people wouldn't think anything of it, but I've spent a long time pretending to like the touch of someone when I really didn't. And that's not even mentioning the men I've met over the years in the industry who loved to touch me without asking. Harmless touching, mostly, but still touch that crossed personal boundaries.

"I haven't seen you in months," she purrs.

Kade pulls his arm out from under her and tips the brim of the buckskin cowboy hat he's got on, the same one from yesterday. "Been tied up. Or I guess laid up."

She giggles, but I don't think Kade meant that as a joke. Or maybe he did. I don't know him well enough to know.

"You ladies need a drink?" he asks.

Her friend goes to speak, but Cricket cuts her off. "Surprise us with something!"

Kade's jaw ticks again. "I can have our new girl here make something for you. She's really good with limes."

I can't help it; my cheeks stain pink. I'm never not going to think of Kade when I see a lime.

Cricket's eyes narrow at me, but she keeps a smile on her face. "We want you to make it for us, Kade."

"I've got to help the band." He looks to the small stage where I see two men beginning to set up. One has a guitar case and another a fiddle. A tense breath blows quietly past my lips at finally putting to rest the unanswered question I had. Thankfully, I don't recognize either of them.

"Are you sure, Kade? Just one little drink." Cricket pouts.

I roll my shoulders back and turn my attention to this woman again. She reminds me a bit of Derek, someone who can't take a hint.

"City Girl can handle it." Kade smirks.

God, this man sure does love his nicknames. But in this case, I'll allow it since I don't want this woman to know my name. Though it's not like I can hide it. I'm surprised she doesn't already know from town gossip.

"City Girl?" Cricket chirps. "Explains the hair and tattoos." She giggles.

"Hey, now, Cricket. Be nice," Kade says.

She giggles again, the sound grating on me. Kade didn't mean that to be funny, but again, this woman does not know signals.

"It's fine," I interject, not needing him to fight any battles for me. "I'll go make a drink. Something extra sour?" I ask, knowing this girl probably likes her drinks with extra sugar.

Kade's jaw ticks again. This time, I don't think it's from annoyance but because he's trying not to laugh. Now I'm curious what story lies between them, even if I shouldn't care.

"I like strawberry mojitos," she says.

"How *City Girl* of you." It's past my lips before I can stop it. The urge to slap my hand over my mouth is strong, but I can't take it back now. Kade purses his lips, but a bit of laughter sneaks out.

"Kade." Cricket bristles. "Are you going to let her talk to me like that?"

"You asked for it."

Her lower lip shoots out in an obnoxious pout. "Kade," she whines, squeezing his bicep. "I'm not trying to be mean. Can you please make us a drink? You know how we like it." With the lift and tone of her voice, her double meaning was clear.

But Kade doesn't play into whatever trap she's trying to lay. "City Girl can learn how you like it."

Cricket huffs, reminding me of a child who isn't getting their way. "Come on, Kade. I want you to make it. The city girl will screw it up, I just know it."

"The only thing that screws things up in this place is you." His words startle me just as much as they do Cricket and her friend. I bite my inner cheek and stand there awkwardly, waiting to see what happens next.

Cricket's eyes water. "Now, that's not fair."

"And what you did was?"

Her lips part to answer, but she doesn't get the chance.

"That's enough, Kade."

Cricket's back stiffens at the deep tone of a new voice. Gavin is now standing at the table with a hard expression on his face, and Kade clenches his fists at his sides and stares at his brother. The chatter around us has quieted, and when I dare to look beyond the spectacle we've created, the people seated at the surrounding tables have stopped to watch and listen. They may have been watching the whole time.

Kade doesn't say anything to Gavin. Instead, he walks off to the bar, and I'm left standing there, trying to figure out what's going on.

"Gavin," Cricket says. "I thought you wouldn't be here tonight."

My eyes bounce between the two of them, the tension palpable. Now I'm wondering if the brothers have both slept with her. That would be a cause for awkwardness for sure. But I don't stay to find out.

I quietly back up and leave, and no one at the table seems to take note of my exit. When I step behind the bar, Kade is fixing a cocktail. He puts the metal shaker over the top of the glass, forearms flexing as he shakes the drink. He's glaring at the back of Gavin's head, the flirty and carefree demeanor he had before now gone.

"Are you okay?" I ask, not understanding why I suddenly care how he feels.

"Leave it be, City Girl," he snaps.

That's all it takes to make me remember why I shouldn't care. Why I shouldn't have even asked. "Right, then."

"Just go do your job, and stay away from anyone who looks like Cricket."

I stare into his hazel eyes and know I should leave this conversation because he's in a mood, but I can't help myself.

"What's your issue?" I place a hand on my hip.

That little smirk of his pulls at the corners of his lips, but it's not flirty this time. "I don't have an issue, Sweetheart."

My stomach turns, and I'm left speechless. I'm confused as to why he's upset with me and intentionally pissing me off—I had nothing to do with whatever happened at that table. Besides, a minute ago, he was trying to defend me. This man is so hot and cold, and I'm questioning even more now why I ever found him attractive.

Kade puts the cocktail on the bar top, adding one of the limes I cut up to the rim.

"Take this to Cricket," he says, sliding it toward me.

"What is it?" I ask, the pink drink bright in the glass.

"Tell her I call it 'The Cheater.'"

Then he walks off, leaving me baffled.

CHAPTER 9

Kade

ANOTHER DAY, ANOTHER HANGOVER. If I wrote a story about my life, I think that's what I'd call it. Or *How to Fuck Up 101.*

Last night, after I was a complete asshole to Presley for no reason, my flask and I became best friends. I tried to resist, but the whole situation with Cricket pissed me off. And now, my new coworker probably thinks I dated Cricket and she cheated on me. In actuality, I was standing up for my brother. He had dated Cricket before he met Blake, and she'd cheated on him after Dad died.

The kicker is, I have nobody but myself to blame for last night. Before my accident, I gave Cricket some mild attention to piss off my brother, and she's been trying to get in my pants ever since. She's probably also trying to piss off Gavin and make him jealous, which will never happen since he's utterly head over heels in love with Blake.

What really sent me over the edge was not just the fact that Cricket was being rude to Presley—I still don't understand why that pissed me off—but that when Gavin came in, he acted all upset that I was even getting on Cricket's case. It proved to me that I can do no right when it comes to him, even when I'm trying to be a good brother.

"Are you going to stare at your coffee or drink it?"

I lift my eyes from the coffee in question, which has probably gone lukewarm by now, and meet the honey-brown eyes of

Momma. She's wearing her favorite pair of worn jeans and a rose-colored long-sleeve sun shirt Blake got her for her birthday, her silver-and-blonde hair tied in a loose ponytail.

"I thought you'd be out in the garden already," I say, taking a sip of the bitter liquid that indeed has gone cold.

She walks over and pours herself a cup before sitting next to me at the kitchen table. "Slept in a little."

Momma tucks a strand of hair behind her ear and smiles, the morning sun creating a halo around her head. The picture she makes has me thinking of Dad. He always called her a natural beauty, the girl that everyone wanted in high school but he got lucky enough to have. Now, in the year since his death, grief has aged her. She's still beautiful, but more lines have appeared at the corner of her eyes and around her mouth, and there's a slump to her shoulders I've never noticed before.

Guilt gnaws my gut, because I know my actions have given her many of those lines and wrinkles. I've contributed to the sadness in her eyes.

I take another sip of my coffee. "That's good. Glad you got some rest."

She nods, silence settling around us so all we can hear is the old clock ticking in a staccato cadence. The longer we don't talk, the louder the ticking seems to get. I tap my fingernails on my mug, the lack of words between us leaving me to my thoughts.

I used to talk to Momma all the time, and I never had a problem thinking of what to say. Even before my accident, I could charm the hell out of her. She knew I was drinking, seeing girls most nights, but she never tried to stop me or said anything about it. Gavin attempted to get her to scold me, but she brushed him off. It was one thing I appreciated, that she was letting me have my space to grieve my way. To figure things out.

But after that day at the cemetery and the accident, our relationship shifted. Now, I find it hard to talk to any of my family members, especially Momma. I know she's in pain. I can see it on her face every time she looks at me. I know she regrets not trying to talk with me before the accident, but I imagine finding out the love of her life had been keeping secrets from her for years wasn't easy, either.

In a lot of ways, I think we can relate to that disappointment. Dad was my best friend, and I loved him. We may not have talked about our feelings, but we talked about everything else. Except the truth, which is what mattered most.

Given all of that, I'd have thought talking to Momma about everything would be easier, to talk about the pile of shit Dad left for us. How he betrayed us with his lies, how Gavin continued that lie. But speaking about big things, being vulnerable, it's not something the Montgomerys have ever been good at. It's not something anyone in Randall is good at. Life is hard out here. You simply learn to pick up the pieces when shit goes wrong and move on. You don't have time to glue them back together.

"Kade," Momma's timid voice says.

I blink, unsure of how long I've been staring at my coffee again. I meet her eyes, my caffeine- and alcohol-filled stomach turning over at the concern I see in them. I know she says she's forgiven me for punching Gavin at the cemetery and for getting myself hurt at Devil's Rock, but I don't believe her. I know she's disappointed in me, and I'm positive Gavin's made her aware of my behavior the last few days since my doctor's appointment.

"Are you alright, Kade?"

I grip my hand around the mug. I should be glad she's asking me how I am now. I know she cares for me, but her question just adds to my growing anger because I'm sure she's asking because of Gavin.

"I'm fine."

Her eyes scan my body, stopping on the center of my chest like she's trying to see if my heart's beating. I clench my jaw, and that stabbing pain in my sternum returns. I know she's thinking of the day Dad died from his heart attack, the day he went off to till the soil and never came home. Momma was the one to find him, and it still crushes me that she had to see that.

I reach my hand across the table and place it over hers. "My ticker is fine, Momma, I promise." She brings those comforting brown eyes of hers to mine, blinking away the tears that threaten to fall.

"Good. That's good," she says, as if trying to reassure herself. With a tight smile, she pulls her hand out from under mine. I think she's going to sit back, but instead, she grabs my hand and squeezes.

"You're so much like him, you know? Look just like him, too."

I bristle, my features turning hard. I was not expecting her to say that. She hardly talks about Dad now, and I can't say that I blame her. And while once I would've loved to be compared to Emmett, that's changed. I should probably just leave this conversation now, but my curiosity gets the best of me.

"How so?" I remove my hand from hers to sit back.

She looks disappointed to lose contact with me, but I push any feelings I have down. I want to know how I'm like the man who lied. Who ruined this family.

"Well, you've got the same eyes." She smiles. "Same hair."

"You know that's not what I meant, Momma." I sit a little taller in my chair. "I want you to tell me how I'm like the liar who ruined our lives." The last part comes out with fire, fire I didn't initially intend to have behind my words.

Her eyes widen, and her nostrils flare. "You don't talk about your daddy like that, young man!"

"I'm only speaking the truth, and you know it."

"He was a good man, and he taught you to be better than this."

I slam my eyes shut. Her words sting my body like acid rain, burning away at my skin and eating me alive. While Momma is right, that he could be a good man, she doesn't know shit about what he taught me. Yes, he did teach me manners among other important life skills like a damn good work ethic, but he also gave me my first drink when I was fourteen. He taught me the different notes of a good whiskey when I was sixteen and how to flirt with girls.

I suck in a tense breath through my teeth and smack my lips. "He taught me to be exactly who I am right now, Momma." The angry truth of it spills out of me.

"You're not acting like yourself," she says, hand gripping the table.

I want to laugh, because she sounds exactly like Gavin. The urge to throw my coffee mug from the table hits me like a freight train—it's time I leave this house before I do something I regret. I don't want to hurt Momma any more than I already have, and right now, I'm not in control of my words. I stand up from the table and push in my chair.

"You're going to leave?" she asks.

"Yep. I don't want to say more. Trust me, you don't want to hear it."

She stands and faces me. I've got a lot of height on her, but she's always been intimidating for a small woman with her strong shoulders and strong will. "Say what you want to say, Kade. I can take it."

I walk to the sink and thunk my mug down into the basin before I grip the countertop, knuckles turning white as I try to force down my anger. But no matter how many breaths I take, I can't stop the events of the past few days, of the last year, from rising to the surface.

I turn back to face her but keep my distance, saying what's been weighing on my heart. "You think I'm like him because I drink too much and I have a temper. Not because he was a good man."

She shakes her head. "Emmett didn't have a drinking problem."

"You're delusional if you think that."

"Kade!" she chides again, her voice louder now.

"You said you could take the truth, so I'm giving it to you. That man was not who you thought he was. He's not who any of us thought he was. He drank like a fish, and he fucked up this family. He almost lost us our home, our land!"

"He was doing the best he could!"

"And you never questioned him about anything. Just like you never questioned Gavin. Just like you never questioned me until now. You just let things happen, Momma. You just stood by while Dad royally screwed things up and then Gavin took his place. If you want to compare the glorious Emmett Montgomery to anyone, maybe compare him to my fabulous big brother that you love so much!"

"Enough!" Gavin's voice bellows from the door.

"Speak of the fucking devil." A chuckle of disdain spills out of me as I throw up my hands. "You're always coming in to save the day, Gav. Do you have everywhere I go bugged?"

My big brother steps into the kitchen and goes straight to Momma, ignoring me. "Are you okay?" he asks her.

She brushes a tear that's escaped from her eye and nods. "Fine. We're just having a conversation."

I shoot my brother a long and hard stare. "You think I would purposely hurt our mom? She wanted to know the truth, so I'm giving it to her."

Gavin narrows his green eyes at me, and for the first time, there's something akin to hatred in them. I've seen a lot of looks from my brother, but nothing like this. Maybe I've finally tipped him over the edge.

"There's a way to speak to people, and this is not it. You need to take a step back and figure your shit out, Kade."

"Are you for fucking real right now?"

"Watch your language," he scolds, like he's my fucking dad.

I point an angry finger at him. "I don't understand you, Gav. I don't understand any of you. You want me to talk. You want me to tell you how I'm doing. Then when I'm honest, I'm the one who gets looked down on. I'm the one you get angry at."

"You know that's not why we're upset with you."

"At least you admitted you're upset with me instead of just trying to disguise it with concern."

"Kade, we only want to help," Gavin says.

"Help me with what?"

"Dealing with what happened."

"Maybe y'all need to deal with it. I'm dealing with it just fine." My esophagus burns with acid, and my mouth feels heavy with my lie. But I'm sick of this conversation, sick of being looked at like I'm the problem. I'm not the goddamn problem.

My family just wants me to talk about my feelings, to apologize and say that I'm the one who causes all the issues so they can feel better about all their sins. Then I'm supposed to smile and be happy, to keep my mouth shut and act like I'm okay with everything. Not just the lies and deceit, but everything that's happened since.

They want me to just accept that our family's ranch is being turned into a tourist attraction to save it, to accept that the only reason that's happening is because we got a loan from Blake to dig us out of a hole. But I'm not going to. And I'm not going to play nice anymore or hide my true feelings. I don't care if they don't like it.

"Kade." Gavin sighs. "Stop pushing us away. We're your family. We care about you—"

"If you cared about me, you would've given me the land like Dad wanted. You would've listened to me months ago."

"Young man," Momma says, stepping up next to a now silent Gavin. "You know that's not Gavin's fault. He didn't know—"

"He didn't know then, but he knows now." I glare at my brother, and his eyes are dark, his jaw set in a hard line. He needs to know how I feel, that I still think it's all bullshit.

"I thought we settled this," Gavin says. "I thought you'd moved on."

"You thought wrong."

"Then you should've talked to us about it. Instead, you're taking your anger out on Momma and me, and you're drinking yourself silly."

There are a million things I could say right now. Many of them I have, but he never gets it. He thinks because Blake found a solution by turning our place into a dude ranch and paying off our debt that suddenly I don't care about him getting the land. He thinks that since we're working as a family, as a team, to save the Montgomery family name, that I feel like the land is also mine.

But that's all horseshit, because it's not mine. It's never been mine. But Gavin's too dense to see that, to understand what that feels like on my end. To have nothing and nobody who understands you. To have lost the only person you thought understood you only to then find out you were the one to not understand them. To not know them.

I step back from Gavin and Momma, grabbing my hat from the table. "I've got work to do."

"We're talking here," Momma says, her voice desperate.

If I were a better man, I would stop and try to talk. But maybe she's right. Maybe I am more like Daddy than I ever thought.

"I'm done." I turn and step toward the doorway, truly meaning my words.

"Don't walk out that door, Kade," Gavin says in a warning tone. "Don't do this to us again."

To us. Fuck, that hurts. What about what they're doing to me, what they've already done to me?

With a sad chuckle, I continue to the front door. "I'll do whatever the fuck I want, big brother," I say over my shoulder, "just like you do."

He calls after me as I walk away, but I don't turn back. I have work to do and, most likely, people to piss off. Just another fucking day in my life.

At least now I can stop holding myself back.

CHAPTER 10

Presley

GRAVEL SPITS OUT FROM the wheels of my car as I drive the long road to the Montgomery ranch. I have my minimal stuff in the trunk, so if Blake doesn't end up hiring me, I guess I'm sleeping at the tiny motel I saw when I first drove into town. It gave me Alfred Hitchcock's *Psycho* vibes, though, so I'd rather not.

The sounds of "Man of Constant Sorrow" covered by Alison Kraus & Union Station fill my car from some random radio station I found. I can't help my smile at how appropriate it is for my current situation. But that's one of the things I love most about music. Somehow, the songs I hear always seem to be the soundtrack to whatever is going on in my life.

I glance in the rearview mirror at the case of my Antonio Strad Heritage violin. It's my single prized possession in my pathetic existence, and it stares at me from the backseat as if it has eyes. Very judgy eyes. Eyes that say, *Why did you run, Presley? You gave up the opportunity of a lifetime, Presley.* Or maybe that's just the echo of Derek's incessant texts that haven't stopped since the moment I left.

I nibble on the inside of my cheek, focusing back on the gravel road. My violin is a physical representation of my life story. Of me. I worked my ass off in high school to buy it since my parents wouldn't, and it's my heart and soul. It represents my dreams, fears, and failures. Which is why I haven't taken it out of its case since I ran away last week after our meeting with the record label. When I blew up my life.

It's the longest I've gone without playing since I was five years old. I can't deny that I've been itching to play—it's probably why I've been so grumpy. Added to that, my whole interaction with Kade on Sunday night keeps popping up in my mind.

After he was overtly rude, I took the drink he made to Cricket, but I didn't tell her that he named it "The Cheater." Gavin was still at the table, talking to her in hushed tones while her friend looked on. I set it down and then hightailed it to the other tables. Eventually the band played, and I let the man's decent fiddle playing get me into a rhythm of serving, pretending like my interactions with Kade hadn't gotten under my skin.

Since then, I've tried to ignore him, only speaking to him when necessary. The space has given me time to observe him, to see what kind of person he is. What I've found is that while my experience of him has been hot and cold, he's well-loved by the locals and customers. He and Jake are also very close, always laughing and talking together when the place isn't swimming with people.

But one thing that's really stood out to me is his frequent drinking. Not just from the flask he carries—he never turns down a free drink from a customer, either. I've also heard a lot more chatter about his accident and overheard locals asking him how he was doing and if he was okay.

While I still don't know what happened to him, I can't help but be curious. Maybe my short time in a small town has already rubbed off on me. Soon, I'll be asking people for the latest gossip. That thought makes me chuckle, because it's so not like me. But neither is agreeing to work as a ranch hand.

I grip the steering wheel as I pass under a peeling wooden sign that says "Montgomery Family Ranch," the top of a modest white house coming into view. Lyla wasn't kidding when she said this place is huge. I'd think this land belongs to multiple houses, not just one, but I don't see another home around for miles, just gently rolling plains, cows, and corn. A true Texas setting.

I can't believe I'm even considering this. I've never even picked up a shovel. But it's too late to turn back now.

When I pull up to the house that sits on a small hill, I see a curly-haired woman standing near a black truck. She waves, pointing to the open space next to the vehicle on the wide gravel driveway. I park where she indicated, smiling at her through my windshield.

Not wanting to mess this first impression up, I give myself a quick pep talk before getting out of the car, pulling at the hem of my simple black T-Shirt and tugging up my black jeans. It's the best I could do for now since I don't have a lot of ranch-friendly work clothes. Most of what I have in my suitcase are a few casual outfits and my favorite stage clothes in a style my bandmates say reminds them of a more conservative Cher from *Clueless*. That was one of the nicest things they ever said about me since it's one of my favorite movies. And my personal style is more '90s grunge, or at least it was before last week. Now I've been living in jeans, T-shirts, and my pajamas.

"You must be Presley! I'm Blake," she says cheerfully, holding out her hand.

"That's me," I say, subtly wiping my hand against my jeans, not wanting it to be sweaty. Then, I once again find myself partaking in this stupid human custom. I think I hate it because not only do I have to touch someone I don't know, but I also never know if I'm going to get a firm handshake or a soft one. It's so weird to go in strong and then their hand is like a wet noodle. Thankfully, Blake's is firm and short, matching mine perfectly.

She tucks a curl of chocolate-brown hair behind her ear then places her hands on her round hips, ones that rival mine. "It's nice to finally meet you. Lyla's been texting me a bunch, telling me how great you are and reiterating how upset she was to kick you out. She wanted me to tell you she's sorry again."

I let out a sigh. "She's sweet, but there's no reason for her to feel bad. And I think she's told me she's sorry at least a million times by now. Among other things," I add, thinking of the tangents that girl can go on.

Blake laughs, the sound light and almost comforting. "Lyla is a total chatterbox."

"That's an understatement," I say dryly. My eyes widen when I realize I've said that out loud.

But before I can get too embarrassed, Blake chuckles again. "I like you already, Presley. It's nice when people say what they're thinking."

I stick my hands in my pockets and smile at her. I want to say I normally don't, but maybe my earlier observation was right, and this town has rubbed off on me. Or maybe the change is because I've completely uprooted my life and now I'm a bartender and soon-to-be ranch hand instead of an up-and-coming star fiddle player.

That same feeling of an anxiety attack coils in me, like a jack-in-the-box ready to pop open. Since I'm not going to pull my calming inhaler out in front of Blake, I list off random items in my head. *Happy days, birds, teddy bear, fan, fork*—such a funny word, *fork*.

"You okay?" Blake asks.

I look into her brown eyes, ones that remind me of light roast coffee, and thankfully find no judgment in them. Gosh, I can't believe I did the quiet staring thing *again*. I wonder if Lyla warned her about me being so awkward.

"Yeah, I was just wondering why you'd want to hire someone with no ranch experience." My statement is partially true, because even with what Lyla told me, it doesn't make any sense.

Blake's round face is sunny as she says, "As long as you don't mind working hard and getting your hands dirty, you can do this work. The only thing I'm concerned about"—she looks at my feet—"are those tennis shoes. We'll need to get you boots for working, especially around the animals."

I look at my feet then back up to her eyes. Despite what my shitty ex-boyfriend would say, I don't mind working hard. And I can handle being dirty, even if it's not my favorite. That's why hot showers exist.

"I'm not afraid of hard work," I voice to Blake. "And I can get new shoes."

She grins. "I'm sure we can find you a pair of boots around here, and I didn't think the work would phase you. Gavin said from what he's seen at Night Hawk, you'll be just fine here. It might even be easier since you don't have to deal with town gossip or people who drink too much."

My stomach churns a bit at the mention of Gavin. I knew this town would talk about me, but it's one thing to think it and another to hear they actually are. "You know Gavin?"

Surprise colors her features for a second, like I should know that. "You could say that." She smirks. "Come on, I'll show you around."

I nod, curious if Gavin is like her brother or something. But they don't look related, so that would mean she's...his girlfriend? I wonder if she knows about the situation with Cricket the other night. I get the urge to tell her, but for all I know, Cricket and Gavin don't even have a past, and they were just talking about Kade.

Oh god, I hope Blake's not friends with Kade then, too. I'd have to see him even more than I already do at Night Hawk. Jake said he's decided to pick up more shifts, which means I'm going to have to deal with his antics more than just on the weekends. I exhale a breath and try to focus on things that do not involve the sexy cowboy I hardly know, like making a good impression with Blake. If Kade comes here often, I'll just have to deal with it like an adult.

"Sounds good," I finally say.

"Great!" She motions for me to follow, and I fall in step beside her. Just like the Delgados' ranch, it's quiet out here. The Texas plains provide only the sounds of nature with the occasional moo of a cow in the distance. But as we get closer to a big red barn, I hear men talking and the sound of hammers and other tools.

"We're in the process of remodeling this barn," Blake says, raising her voice. "This one hasn't been used for the last couple of years. Nothing too major, but it can get kind of noisy. We're in crunch mode since we've got about ten horses coming soon."

I gape at her. "Ten?"

She nods. "We'll get more next month, but we're going to get them ready in batches. Can't have a dude ranch without safe trail horses."

"I don't know much about dude ranches, but that sounds like a must-have."

"Have you ever been to a ranch?" she asks.

"Until last week? No."

Blake opens a sliding door to the big red barn, and the noises get louder. "Are you from Texas?"

"Born and raised."

"Whereabouts?"

"Lynn. Do you know it?"

"It's outside the city, right?"

I nod. "Yeah. It's kind of small but not nearly as small as this place."

She snickers. "Nothing is as small as Randall. At least it feels like it sometimes." She pauses for a second and turns to appraise me. "You've really never been to a ranch until last week?"

"I really haven't."

"That feels so odd to me since this is mostly all I've ever known. Minus five years in Tennessee." She says the last part almost sadly.

I lick my lips. "Like I said, maybe I'm not the best person to hire. Aren't ranch hands supposed to know ranches?"

Blake waves me off, a smile returning to her face. "You'll learn. And I'm sure Lyla told you, but I had someone lined up, and they fell through. They got a better-paying job at a dude ranch in Montana. I know we're not offering much, but the living quarters aren't bad, and you're more than welcome to daily breakfast and lunch up at the house."

I want to tell Blake that even though I've been questioning her choice to hire me, nothing she could say would make me leave. She told me over the phone I'd be making minimum wage, but if I'm not paying rent, I'm not going to complain. And the tips at Night Hawk have been good. I've made more at the bar than at a lot of the gigs we played, which surprised me for such a small town.

"Sounds great," I say. Because while this isn't the work I'd pick for myself, I've been enjoying the quiet of the Delgados' ranch. And when people aren't hammering, I'm sure this place is peaceful. Maybe even too peaceful.

For the next hour, Blake shows me around until my feet begin to hurt from all the walking. They have three barns: the one that houses their current horses, the one being remodeled, and one that stores supplies and hay. There's also a big shed close to the main house and guest house where they keep ATVs and other things, which is being reorganized. She said she'd eventually take me out on one of the ATVs and show me more of the property.

By the time we get to the hands' quarters, I'm feeling a little better about my choice to come here. While I haven't done any work yet, Blake's made me believe that I can do what she'll be asking of me. I really like the ranch, and everyone I've been introduced to has been just like most people I've met since I arrived here: nice.

Blake holds out her arms, giving her best impression of Vanna White. "This is where you'll be staying." She grins. "Just painted it myself."

I study the white rectangular building with green shutters and multiple doors that indeed has a fresh coat of paint. It reminds me of pictures I've seen of kids' summer camp quarters except a bit larger. A long porch that looks freshly painted connects all the doors—I count eight of them. We walk up a few steps, and Blake goes to the one in the middle.

"This is the main living area," she says as she opens the door. "Right now, you're the only one here—the rest of our workers live in town, so they don't need the space. Eventually, guests will stay here, and then we may move you or keep you here depending on how many people we get. Hopefully, we sell out." She chuckles.

I feel a warmth in my stomach as I realize she's already considering the possibility of me staying for an extended period, to the point where she'd have to think about my accommodations when they have guests. And from what I understand, that won't be for another six months or more. Though I shouldn't be surprised by her thoughtfulness—over the last hour, I've learned that Blake really cares about this place and the people here.

We've only chatted about little things, like how much she likes my hair and how she's always wanted to get a tattoo but her dad would kill her. I've been able to avoid questions that feel too personal, though I think she can tell I'm not really one to dump my life story on just anyone.

At least not like some of the people I've met at Night Hawk. The other night, I listened to a man named Jim tell me about how he spent all his money at the race track last week and his wife kicked him out for the night. He even started talking about the bunions on his feet until Jake saved me.

"The TV doesn't work yet," she says as we stand in the middle of the room, "but Gavin said he can fix it for you."

I press my lips together when I see the old boxy TV, the kind from the '80s and '90s. I'm not really a TV watcher, so that's not a problem.

I follow her as she strides to a small kitchen area with a fridge. "We don't have the gas hooked up yet for the stove, but we can get you a hot plate if you plan to do any cooking. But the microwave and the fridge work."

"I'm not much of a chef, so the microwave is fine for now."

"As I mentioned before, we provide breakfast and lunch. If you need dinner, June makes enough food that you could come up to the house and eat whenever you want. Honestly, if you don't, she'll bring you food anyway. That's the kind of family the Montgomerys are."

I purse my lips after hearing her statement. She's done that a few times, referred to the Montgomerys like they aren't her family. "June's your grandma?" I ask, finally curious enough to voice my questions. "Or does she work here?"

Blake crosses her arms over her chest and faces me. "Did Lyla not tell you anything about this place? I would have thought she'd give you all the history and the family trees of every person in Randall."

I shake my head. "It never came up."

Blake stares at me as if something has finally clicked in her mind. "Gavin is my boyfriend, and this is his ranch. I'm not a Montgomery." She says the last part playfully, which leads me to believe she will eventually be one.

I fiddle with the silver ring on my finger as I look into her friendly eyes. When I replay the information she just gave me, my blood goes cold. *Oh no...*

"This isn't your ranch?" I ask, my voice high and uneven.

Blake stuffs her hands in her pockets. "It isn't."

"Don't say that, Blake. This is *your* dude ranch."

My head turns toward the haughty male voice, and I can't stop the full-blown shiver that races up my spine. Kade strides in from an open bedroom door, a grin stretched across his face as he meets my eyes. Under his attention, I swear my stomach feels as if it's going to drop right onto the floor, like I'm on one of those scary drop rides at a carnival.

"You know that's not true," Blake replies, disappointment clear in her words though I can tell she's trying to keep a smile on her face as she says it.

He shrugs, his hazel eyes not leaving mine. "What are you doing here, Lemon?"

"Lemon?" I ask, unable to stop myself.

He clucks his tongue against the back of his teeth. "Lime is a silly nickname. Figured Lemon has a better ring to it."

I try to keep the blush off my cheeks, but I fail. My skin burns as several questions spark in my mind, like: Why does he have to keep bringing up the back-room incident? And why give me this nickname at all? Does he think I'm sour? But I don't ask anything, because while I'm curious, I don't want to know the answers. I also don't want to further my embarrassment.

Blake's voice interrupts my thoughts. "I didn't know you were down here, Kade."

Kade finally stops looking at me, hazel eyes meeting hers with a half smile. "Gavin told me a new hire was going to be staying here and asked me to make sure the bed didn't squeak."

A short and awkward laugh leaves Blake's lips. "Such a funny guy today."

"You know me, Blakey girl. I'm full of fun times and laughter."

Blake's body language swiftly changes at his words, her sunny demeanor from before now cloudy and dull, face crestfallen and shoulders tense. I stand there, unsure of what to do, as the pair silently stares at each other. A silent conversation that doesn't look pleasant passes between them. Eventually, Blake tips her chin down, and I think I see tears shining in her eyes.

Unable to handle the tension, I clear my throat. "I can leave."

Blake focuses on me and blinks a few times. Yeah, those were tears. "No, that's not necessary. Kade was just leaving."

Kade's narrowed gaze stays frozen on Blake's profile. But after a long moment, his face visibly softens, the furrow of his brow relaxing and shoulders drooping. It doesn't take a genius to know what's going through his mind: regret. A whole lot of it. But instead of addressing it, he seems to shake it off, his attention moving back to me.

A flirty grin pops back on his lips as he sticks his hands in his jean pockets. "You're the new ranch hand, Lemon?"

"My name is Presley."

He chuckles. "Right. I guess we'll be spending a lot more time together." His eyes rove over my body like they had that first night outside of Night Hawk until they land on my sneakers. "You sure you're up to this job, Presley?" he asks, popping the P of my name.

I fight the urge to hide my body from his gaze and push my shoulders back a bit. I'm not sure that I can handle this job, but I'm also not going to let Kade make me squirm. If he wants to be a jerk, then I'm going to be a jerk back.

I turn to Blake, and her lips tip up as if she's encouraging me to say yes. I take in a breath and meet Kade's hazel eyes again. That boyish glint I saw last night before the whole Cricket situation is back.

"I am, *Kade*." I make sure I punctuate the K and D of his name.

He rocks on the balls of his feet and hums. "I guess we'll see about that. Chores start at five-thirty tomorrow."

I try not to flinch at the time. I've never been a morning person, and I feel like he knows that. It's going to suck when I work at Night Hawk in the evenings. I guess I'm going to have to say goodbye to sleep most nights. But if Kade and Gavin can do it, I can, too, right?

"You don't have to get up that early, Presley," Blake interjects. "Kade is just yanking your chain."

He smirks. "I wasn't, actually. Nobody gets special treatment around here." The way he says it makes me think it carries a double meaning.

"Kade," Blake tries again, frustration building in her voice.

"It's okay, really," I say, not wanting to see another fight in front of me. I've witnessed enough of Kade's hot-and-cold antics already. "I can wake up then."

Kade looks like a fox in the henhouse. "Make sure you set at least three alarms." He tips his hat. "See you later, Lemon." Then he walks out the door, whistling what sounds like "Hurricane" by Luke Combs.

When I'm pretty sure he's gone, Blake takes a step toward me. "I'm so sorry, Presley. I don't—I'm not sure why he was like that. Kade must've woken up on the wrong side of the bed this morning." She tries to be playful, but there's worry behind her words.

I try my best to comfort her. "It's alright."

She closes her eyes and lets out a long sigh. It reminds me of when I'm trying to stop an anxiety attack. Whatever just happened between her and Kade has done a number on her.

After another few breaths, she opens her eyes and attempts a smile. "Are you sure you want to work here after that?" Her tone is semi-teasing, but I know she's afraid I'll say no.

"If you'll have me. I still don't know if I'll be good at it, but—" I scan the room, taking a closer look. The living room isn't that large, but the sage-painted walls and beige couches and chairs give it a homey sort of feel. I haven't seen the bedroom yet, but I'm sure it's fine. A bed is a bed as far as I'm concerned. "I think I'd like to try."

Blake claps her hands together excitedly. "That's great, Presley! I know you're going to do just fine here. I mean, you can handle Kade. If you can do that, you can do anything." She laughs.

I want to tell her I'm not sure I can, but I hold my tongue because regardless of if I want to be around Kade or not, I do need a place to live. "I'll sure try."

Her brown eyes light up, and she holds out her hand. "Welcome to the Montgomery Family Ranch, Presley. I hope you'll stay awhile."

Before the words can really sink in, I'm shaking her hand again. But this time, I find that it's not as awkward.

CHAPTER 11

Kade

THE OLD MUSTY BARN loft is quiet as I stare out at the dusty plains lit by the warm glow of the setting sun. My mind races with a million thoughts as usual, thoughts that plague me every time I'm not distracted and sometimes even when I am. I exhale a long sigh as I grip the splintered wooden railing.

Why is it that a day can't just be normal around here anymore? Before Dad died, we'd wake up, I'd fetch some eggs from the coop for Momma or Gran to fix up, then we'd sit at the table for an early "shovel down" as we liked to call it. We'd devour our eggs, bacon, and toast, then we'd head out for work.

That included mucking, feeding, and moving cattle. Then of course tending to the crops and fixing anything else that needed fixing. If we didn't have school, we'd usually have a lunch of sandwiches, then in the evening, we'd all sit back down together for dinner and figure out what needed to be done the next day. After that, Gavin would usually go off and hang out with his friends, and I ended up with Dad on the porch where he'd sneak me some whiskey after Momma and Gran went to bed.

It always seemed fucked up to me that I had just turned twenty-one when he died. I could finally drink legally with him, and that night, we went to Night Hawk to celebrate with Gavin, Jake, and his Pops. Dad even rode the mechanical bull. Old man didn't stay on that long, but we all had a good laugh about it. It was shortly after that, the night before he died, that he divulged to me that he planned to change his will. That he was going to leave the family ranch to me. At first, I felt guilty, like I should've asked him to leave it to both me and Gavin, but the more I thought about it, the more I wanted it all to myself.

Some may think that's selfish, but it wasn't. We all knew if Gavin had the option, he would leave Randall. While I know he loves this place, our land, our home—he isn't meant for a small town, and I mean that in the best way possible. Despite my differences with him, Gavin is larger than life. He may be the silent type unless someone gets him talking or when he's up onstage, but he's always deserved better than a town of five thousand people. He's smart and charismatic, and he excels in everything he does. If Dad hadn't guilted him to stay home and go to a community college, he would probably be working at some fancy job right now or traveling the world like he always wanted.

But when you live in a place like this and you grow up in a family of ranchers that know nothing else but a hard life, dreams are stupid. Not only were mine crushed that day when I missed the reining competition deadline, but I also had a front seat to Dad breaking Gavin. I watched how he slowly squeezed every dream he had out of his head till he was all work and no play.

That's why when Dad said he'd leave me the ranch, in a way, I felt and still feel like it would've been his greatest gift to Gavin, for him to be free from this place. There was also a small, tiny part of me that wondered if I could at least turn the Montgomery Family Ranch into a shadow of what I had dreamed. While I wouldn't have been a reining champion, I could have implemented some of my ideas, none of which would've included turning it into a tourist attraction.

But like I said, dreams are stupid here. And I didn't know how badly Dad left the ranch in debt, either. So while a dude ranch isn't what I wanted, I've honestly tried to be okay with it. At the end of the day, this is still my home. It's still the place I love, the place I never planned to leave outside of death. Though with everything that's happened over the last six months, I'm not so sure anymore. I can't help but feel like a fish out of water now.

Gavin has Blake. Momma and Gran are always together and doing their thing. But what do I have? Whiskey and women. At this point, I'm simply a trespasser on my family's own land. Hell, they don't even tell me who they're hiring anymore, for god's sake.

I blow out a breath, my eyes finding Willy grazing with a couple of our other horses. The setting sun has turned the Texas skies a burnt orange mixed with pinks, blues, and yellows. The beauty of it doesn't stop me from wanting to reach for my flask, to drink its contents and drown out the world. But I resist, still trying to prove to myself that I don't need it to get by. I did it before; I can do it again. However, I'll admit it's hard not to after today's argument with Momma and Gav and the nice follow-up with Blake and Presley.

The city girl's blue eyes invade my mind like they have quite a few times since I've met her—more than I care to admit. I tried to blame it on not sleeping with anyone since my doctor's appointment last week. But that was idiotic because I can go without sex for more than a few days.

I think of our interaction mere hours ago and want to kick myself for it. I not only made her feel as if she wasn't welcome on our ranch, but I also gave her another nickname I knew she'd hate, even if it does suit her. I'd like to say I know why I continue to annoy her, but I'm not exactly sure.

It could be because I have the tendency to be an asshole to push people away, but I don't think that's it. The better answer is that I enjoy how her subdued sapphire eyes light up when I get to her. How that fire, that spark, ignites, if only for a moment

I think there's a part of her that enjoys it, that craves me as the spark to her flame. I'm not blind. I've noticed the way her eyes find me at Night Hawk, how the skin of her cheeks flush every time I'm near and she holds my eye contact a little longer than she does for other people.

A lukewarm breeze ruffles my long hair, and I inhale the smell of earth, rust, and hay as I grip the railing so hard my knuckles turn white. It's funny—I've attempted to stay out of Presley's way since the Cricket incident, keeping to myself at work and only talking to her when needed. But then today, I walk in to find her with Blake, hired as our new ranch hand. A new ranch hand who will be living on our property.

While my reaction to the situation could have been better, it was the culmination of everything that's been going on with my family and in my mind. That still doesn't excuse it, which is why I've been debating for the last couple of hours if I should seek out Presley and apologize, but in the end, I think it would be a moot point. The words were said, and she accepted my challenge. I can apologize in the morning.

The person I should be running to and begging for forgiveness is Blake. What I said to her has been festering in my stomach like garbage in the hot sun. I called her Blakey girl, the name her late brother, Reed, used to call her.

The nickname slipped past my lips in the hospital after she saved my life. I was out of it when it did, and later, she told me she believed it was Reed letting her know he'd been there with us that night, leading her to save me. I had no fucking right using that nickname again—especially in that way. I knew it would hurt her, but I chose to do it.

I pat my pocket for my flask but stop myself again before I can pull it out, feeling the urge to hit something. I know alcohol won't take away my pain, just like I know fucking around with women won't help, either. I've tried it, and it's not working like it used to.

"Kade." Gavin's stern voice comes from behind me.

I suck in a deep breath and roll my shoulders back. I was so absorbed in my thoughts that I didn't hear the barn door open or him coming up the steps to the loft. I should've known it was only a matter of time before he came to find me, to scold me about how I treated Blake. Not that I can blame him.

"Hey, big brother," I say, but I don't turn to face him. I keep my eyes on the colorful sky, on my favorite horse grazing, willing my mind to stay calm. I'm focusing on allowing myself to have a civil conversation, praying for it not to escalate like the last several we've had.

The wooden boards of the loft creak with Gavin's approach before he stands beside me. Out of the corner of my eye, he leans his tanned arms on the railing and follows my gaze to the pastures. For a long while, we stay silent, the sound of the breeze rustling trees and the occasional groan of the floor beneath our feet the only noise between us.

Eventually, Gavin lets out a long breath. "Blake told me what you said."

There's no anger in his tone, which is unsettling because I was sure there would be.

"For a few hours, she wouldn't say what was eating at her, why her whole mood had changed since I saw her last. But I finally got her to tell me."

I still don't speak, thinking it's just like Blake not to run off and blab to Gavin about what I said. She's got more pride than that.

"If Blake hadn't made me sit and cool off, I would've made a run at you. I wanted to—" He stops. I turn my gaze to his, noticing his jaw is clenched as he finally looks at me.

"You wanted to what?" I ask.

He swallows, Adam's apple bobbing on his stubbled neck. "I wanted to hurt you, Kade. I..." His voice cracks. "I've never wanted to actually hurt you, but—I wanted to throttle you for using Blake's brother that way and embarrassing her in front of Presley."

He shakes his head. "I don't recognize you anymore. You're—" His voice cracks again. "You're not the brother I grew up with."

The sharp pain in my sternum comes back, like my heart was put in a vice and someone turned the handle. My hands grip the railing so hard I wonder if the old wood is going to snap in half. We've had similar conversations before, but this feels different. Everything about our relationship feels different.

"I'm sorry," I say, not sure what other words I can come up with. We've had this discussion before. He speaks the truth: I'm not the brother he used to know. But he's not the same, either. How could we be when so much has happened?

Gavin stands to his full height and faces me. I expect to at least see a flash of anger in his eyes, but I don't. Just defeat and disappointment. My stomach churns, and my mouth waters from the nausea I feel.

"I'm sorry, too, Kade."

I stare at him quizzically. There's been a lot said between us the last year, so I don't know what he's apologizing for. I lick my lips. "What for?"

Gavin takes a small step forward, his arm moving as if he wants to put his hand on my shoulder, but then he stops, putting it in his pocket instead. "I'm sorry because I thought you had gotten better. I thought you were over the drinking and the women. I thought you were managing your..." He stumbles over his words.

"My depression?"

Gavin's eyes widen, as if the word I uttered was the worst thing to have ever come out of my mouth. I may be a small-town country boy, and I may not have gone to college, but I know what I've been struggling with. It became even more clear to me that day in Dr. Ellis's office.

And it's not like Gavin hasn't struggled with it, either, or Momma or Gran. Fuck, Dad sure as hell did—I know that now. Living in a town like this, it's natural to get depressed. Most people here are depressed. Some deal with it by drinking, others are able to ignore it, some hide it. I'm just not hiding it anymore, and it's making him uncomfortable. It's making my entire family uncomfortable.

"Kade, if you need help, I can get it for you. There are things that—"

"Don't," I snap. "Please don't talk at me like that."

He closes his eyes and inhales through his nose. "I don't mean to talk at you or lecture. I swear I'm just trying to talk to you. I've been trying."

"No, you haven't. All you've done is talk at me. That's all you've done this past year. You tell me what you think I need—to go slower, to go along with your dude ranch plans, to not drink, to not flirt. It's always talking *at* me like I'm a little boy who needs to understand. I'm not your baby brother anymore. I'm an adult."

"If you started acting like an adult, this wouldn't be an issue."

"What's that supposed to mean?"

"You know what it means. Christ, Kade, can't you see how much you've changed? We can't even speak more than a few words without fighting."

"You know what I think, Gav?"

"No, I don't."

I shake my head, my temper rearing its ugly head. "I think you're upset that you've changed and I didn't come along for the ride. That you haven't been acting like an adult with all your fucking lies. That you've given all your care and attention to Blake and now your precious dude ranch. I think you feel insurmountable guilt because the place you didn't want is yours now. That you took it from me and haven't looked back."

He has the audacity to look hurt and semi-shocked by my words. "We talked about this." He huffs.

"No, you talked *at* me. You apologized, sure. But all you've been doing is telling me what's going to be done. You told me how it would all work. You told me when you planned to open, how many horses we need, the renovations being done, what my jobs will be."

"I was asking for your opinion the entire time. I tried to involve you as much as possible these past months, but you never seemed interested."

"I was injured! And I was in a lot of fucking pain some nights, if you don't remember."

He grimaces. "I *do* remember. I was trying to give you space. I was doing the best I could, and you never said you felt this way. I thought we were trying to move on."

"You should've asked me! We talked in the hospital, and you just took my apology to mean everything was hunky-dory."

"That's not fair, Kade. We talked as a family, and we agreed to move forward with this idea."

I think of the first few nights after I came home from the hospital, how we sat down for a family meeting in the living room. My arm was killing me, I was still getting out of breath just walking from one room to the other, and I was craving a drink of whiskey I wasn't allowed to have because of my pain meds.

"I agreed because there was no other choice," I spit. "And even if there was, you were so stuck on the idea. Not just you, either, but Momma and Gran, too."

"If you didn't want the dude ranch, you should've said something. It's too late now, Kade. We've spent too much money. We have to see it through."

"Which is exactly what you and Blake want."

Gavin rubs the back of his neck again, the tell that says I'm stressing him out. "I thought you loved Blake. And after all she's done for you—"

"I never asked her to save me!" I bellow. The words seem to ring through the loft even though there's no echo. "I never wanted…"

I spin myself back to look at the landscape. The sunset is far too beautiful for how ugly I feel on the inside right now. The walls I let down for a moment build back up, and by the time Gavin speaks again, I'm no longer willing to listen.

"You never wanted what, Kade?"

"It doesn't matter," I say quietly.

Gavin steps closer, and this time, he does place a hand on my shoulder. I shrug it off and turn so we're facing each other again. The pain in his eyes is almost too much to bear. It reminds me of looking in the mirror, and for a heartbeat, I feel bad for how I've been treating the people I love. But that bad feeling doesn't last, because my own pain is a bigger burden. It's blackened my insides, and now, it's all I feel.

"Kade, let us help you," Gavin pleads.

"For the last time, I don't want your help."

"That may be the case, but you need it. We can all see that you need it. I don't know what triggered you after your doctor's appointment, but whatever caused this setback, we can figure it out. We can help you get back to where you were."

I want to laugh in his face. My family is more oblivious than I thought. They really didn't notice how miserable I was the last three months? How much I've been pretending to be okay while I really wasn't? How hard the anniversary of Dad's death hit me?

They say they care about me, but do they really? It sure as hell doesn't feel like it.

I let out a low chuckle. "You know, Gav, I was thinking for a bit that maybe you weren't such a selfish asshole, that I got you all wrong." He looks confused, but I continue. "But once again, you proved to me that you are."

"Kade, for Christ's sake, please stop trying to turn this on me. We aren't talking about me."

"Because we're never talking about you! You can just lie and then think everything has been fixed because Blake figured out a way to save the day and you said sorry. Life doesn't fucking work like that. Blake may be able to forgive you, but I can't."

"I thought you had! Where is this coming from, Kade?" he begs.

I want to scream at him and ask him why he's so dense. I don't want to be helped by my family or Blake—or anyone, for that matter. I want my family to really listen, to fucking ask themselves why I'm so upset. I want Gavin to make things right. I want Dad to come back from the dead to explain to me why he did the things that he did.

But I stay silent.

I stare out at the pasture. The sun is gone, though there's enough dusky light to see the horses. Must be nice to be completely unaware of the drama that just unfolded between me and my brother, the one who keeps staring at the side of my head, his eyes like lasers.

After a minute of charged silence, he exhales a long, tense breath. "That's it, then? You're not going to talk anymore?"

I don't turn to answer. I don't even blink.

"Do you want me to give up, Kade? Because I will. I'll give up."

My insides roll at his words. Gavin isn't one to give up on anything. He never has been. But the tone in his voice isn't one I've heard before, either. Still, I stay quiet.

"I'll leave you be, Kade. But so help me god, if you use Blake's brother to hurt her again or explode on Momma, I'm done. And if you have any decent bone left in your body, you'll put your stupid pride down and apologize to them."

I hear his words. While I know he's right, I think I'm done, too.

Gavin stands there a minute longer, and I can practically hear his silent plea for me to say something, to tell him I'm sorry and to not give up on me. But that's not going to happen. For the first time, a part of me wants to just get in my truck and drive away. I don't know where I'd go, but I feel like I'm suffocating. This land, my home has never felt like this before—and I don't fucking like it.

Gavin exhales again, and the floor creaks as he walks away—but not before he gets in some last words. "Be good, Kade. And never forget that I love you. We all do."

The sound of his footsteps fade into the night, and I'm left alone with my thoughts. The overwhelming feeling of regret washes over me as I reach for my flask, the cool metal on my fingers as Gavin's words replay in my mind.

Be good, Kade.

Fuck being good.

CHAPTER 12

Presley

WHY ARE PEOPLE AWAKE this early? That's what I want to know. The sun hasn't risen yet, and the roosters aren't even awake.

I turn my head to look at the digital clock on the small nightstand next to the twin bed. I have about ten more minutes till I need to be at the barn to meet Kade for chores at five-thirty am sharp like he so nicely "requested."

Last night, as I was falling asleep and questioning my life choices, I almost decided to just get in my car and leave. After the adrenaline and bravery wore off, I had to ask myself why I needed to show Kade I could do this work. It's not like I have anything to prove to him. But there's just something about this cowboy that makes me want to show him that he's wrong about me. Had he been Derek, I would've just admitted defeat before I even tried.

I chalked up my desire to stay to the fact that I have nowhere else to go. Maybe Nashville, but I'd run out of my money even faster there, not to mention the much stronger possibility that I'd run into Derek or someone I know—which I'm not ready for. I don't know if I'll ever be ready for that.

I tie my hair into a ponytail and look down at my attire, jeans and a men's T-shirt with an MTV Spring Break logo from the '90s on it that I bought from a thrift store.

I let out a breath, and my lips flap comically. I need to put on some clothes that make me feel more like me eventually. I'll probably have to go for a night out to another town to wear them so I don't stick out even more.

Once I've pulled on the pair of old cowboy boots Blake gave me, I'm ready to go.

I turn off the light to the modest room with green walls and two twin beds then close the door. Nobody's staying in this place but me, but I feel weird leaving it open, especially with my violin in there. Not that I think anyone would steal it, but I'm still not ready to let people know I play.

Once the door clicks shut, I walk into the small living area that has the TV and kitchen. I wonder if there is any food stocked in the pantry. I doubt it, since the gas isn't even turned on for the stove, but I may as well look. There's no way I'm going up to the house like Blake said to get breakfast. Normally, I wouldn't want to eat this early, but I forgot to eat dinner last night because of all my overthinking. By then, it was too late to try to figure something out, so now, my stomach is growling.

I take a few steps toward the kitchen when a soft snore stops me in my tracks. The hair on the back of my neck rises, and I turn my gaze to the couch. My eyes are just adjusting to the dark, but a large lump is definitely there, one the size of a man. Blake didn't mention anyone else sleeping in here, and she doesn't strike me as the type not to tell me.

I stand as still as I can, trying to determine what to do next. I could scream, but the main house is a good distance away, and I don't think anyone would hear. I look around the space, but I doubt they have a baseball bat.

Just as I spot a fire poker near the old fireplace, a sleep-filled voice fills my ears and makes me jump. "You didn't strike me as someone with somnophilia, Lemon."

Somno-what? What the heck? "Kade?" I question, my normally low voice high-pitched with lingering fear.

He groans and sits up. "The one and only, City Girl."

I see we're starting early with the nicknames. How is his brain even functioning enough to be snarky? "What are you doing here?"

He moves and puts his booted feet on the ground. How did he fall asleep with those clunky things on? Then he reaches over and flips on a table lamp, making both of us squint at the light. Once my eyes have adjusted, I see he still has his clothes on from yesterday, a pair of dirty Wranglers and a white T-shirt that's smeared with dirt.

"Well?" I ask him again. "Don't you have a house to sleep in?"

He looks up at me through sleepy eyes and long lashes, eyelashes that any woman would kill for. How have I not noticed them before? Oh yeah, because he's generally been an asshole to me despite how handsome he is. In this light, he resembles Brad Pitt in *Legends of the Fall*. My mom used to love that movie.

Kade narrows his eyes at me, and I'm reminded that ogling him isn't what I should be doing right now. Or ever.

"I'll be staying here from now on," he says.

My mouth drops open. "What? Why?"

He stands. At his full height, he's got several inches on me, but I try not to cower. I don't feel unsafe around him, just small, which is a rarity for me growing up in a larger body. I can't help but notice he smells like alcohol.

"Lemon, I don't think I have to tell you what I do on my own property."

"But Blake said I'd have the place to myself."

"She was wrong. I'm staying here."

"On the couch?"

He smirks at me. "What, you want me to stay in your bed? We could see if it squeaks."

I scoff. "You're gross."

He chuckles. "I've been called many things, but that's not one of them."

"Seriously, Kade," I huff. It's too early to be having this conversation, and I just want a straight answer from him. Which is apparently hard to get.

He crosses his arms over his chest, and I attempt to keep my eyes off the way I know his veins are bulging on his forearms. I've watched them while he makes drinks at the bar, and I know their power—and I refuse to fall prey to them.

"As much as I know you're wishing I was sleeping in your bed, Lemon, there aren't any mattresses in those other rooms. I'll get one today."

"My name is Presley."

Kade's eyes smile. "So you've told me."

"Then why don't you use it?"

He shrugs and turns to walk away.

"Hey, I asked you a question." Without thinking, I reach out and grab his elbow to stop him. A zap of static electricity hits me, and I yelp, pulling back. I look down at my hand then up to a chuckling Kade.

"Well, look at that, Lemon. I think we just had one of those romantic moments in movies."

I want to ask him what romcoms he's watching, but that's not important right now. "It's called science, you idiot."

His lips press into a hard line at the barb, but then he collects himself. "If you say so. Or maybe we're just electric."

"More like a dumpster fire."

He lets out a laugh that hurts my ears. Again, it's too early for this.

"You're funny when you talk, Lemon."

I release a quiet sigh, resigning myself to the fact that Kade is never going to stop calling me nicknames. Given how I've felt about nicknames in the past, I could make a real fuss about it and put him in his place, but something holds me back. A part of me feels like I'd miss the banter it sparks between us.

When he calls me Lemon, even though it stems from my embarrassment over the back room, I like that it's personal, that it was created just for me. It's not a generic "sweetheart" or a lazy variation of my name. If he tried to call me Pres or P, I might knee him in the balls. Or at least, that's what I'm going to tell myself.

"We're late," I say to change the subject, pointing to the digital clock that now reads five-forty.

The smile doesn't leave his face as he says, "Gavin and I start earlier than everyone. The hands get here at six-thirty am for chores."

"You told me five-thirty."

"I wanted to see if you got up."

"I got up before you."

"I woke up just when I meant to—didn't know you'd be staring at me when I did. Did you like what you saw?" He traps his lower lip between his teeth and gestures to his body.

I roll my eyes. Does this man ever not make things sexual? I suppose it fits with what I saw in the back room this weekend and all the chatter I've heard about him being a playboy. I guess he's consistent—I can handle consistent. It's the chameleons that throw me off my game, like a certain ex I have.

"Can we just get to work, please?" I ask.

He eyes me up and down like he did yesterday with Blake. When he catches my cowboy boots, he grunts. "You may have the right shoes now. But let's see if you last the day." Those flirty hazel eyes connect with mine, and he winks.

The urge to stick my tongue out at him like a child is strong, but I manage to remind myself to be an adult, even if he's not acting like one. I want to tell him that he underestimates me, that just because I'm from the city doesn't mean I can't work hard. The work I do looks different from his, but playing the fiddle day in and day out, being onstage, and constantly traveling to catch gigs isn't easy.

"I'll be fine."

"If you say so, Lemon."

"I do."

He chuckles. "Alright, then. I look forward to seeing you eat those words. But first, I need some fucking coffee."

Kade walks toward the door, ass flexing in his too-tight Wranglers that make me once again wonder how he fell asleep in them. I'd feel like an anaconda was suffocating my thighs.

When he notices I'm not following, he stops and turns. Before I can move my gaze, he catches me. I blush and try to act like I wasn't just staring at his ass, but he couldn't miss it. "I know it's fun to watch me walk away, but we've got coffee to drink and work to do."

Then he's strutting outside, once again whistling "Hurricane" by Luke Combs.

My stomach grumbles, and I stare at the kitchen. It looks like it hasn't been used in years, so I doubt any food is there. I guess coffee will have to do for now. I just hope I can stomach Kade on no food and bitter liquid.

Turns out, I can't handle Kade on an empty stomach. After he took me to a mud room in the main barn where a pot of coffee sat brewing on a timer, he got me started on our chores. He's having me work beside him, though I think he just wanted to annoy me while I muck crap.

"You missed a spot."

We're in another one of the horse stalls. I don't know how many we've mucked because I lost count. At first, I didn't mind it—it was kind of meditative. But one thing kept ruining my groove: Kade.

For a man that I'm assuming is hungover considering how I found him, he sure isn't functioning like I would be. His mood has also changed greatly from when I saw him yesterday. He seems lighter, happier. Which again, weird, especially for a dude who probably got a few hours of sleep on a couch after drinking.

Maybe he got laid, or maybe it's because he's young. Before I turned twenty-five, I could sleep in awkward positions without needing a chiropractor afterward, though I've never been great at tolerating alcohol. I may be a bigger girl, but a couple of drinks, and I'm three sheets to the wind.

"Did you hear me, Lemon?" he chirps.

I look to where he's pointing, a spot I just cleaned, and put my hand on my hip. "There's nothing there, Kade."

He chuckles. "Just keeping you on your toes."

I sigh, wiping sweat off my forehead. It's hot for the morning, which means it's only going to get sweltering as the day goes on. Freaking heatwave.

I fight the urge to close my eyes as a wave of dizziness hits me. My blood sugar is low, that much I know. But I'm not going to give Kade the satisfaction of making the "city girl" ask for her break on the first day. If I sneak another cup of coffee, I could at least dull the hunger pains. Too bad humans can't eat hay, because there's plenty of that around.

I ignore the stabbing pains in my stomach and pick up more horse poop. This stall is a mess—there's crap everywhere, and it's all mixed in with the shavings. Until today, I had no idea people used shavings for horses. I thought they were just for gerbils and hamsters.

I scoop up more poop and go to dump it in the muck bucket when Kade's hand on my wrist stops me. I shift my gaze from where we're touching to his eyes.

"There are good shavings in there," he says. "You need to sift it."

He pulls his hand back and picks up some of the muck with his pitchfork.

"This horse is what we call a *tornadoer*." He shakes the fork so the shavings start to fall to the ground. Eventually, all he has left is poop before he throws it into the bucket. "If you don't sift, then it costs us more money. Which is never a good thing on a ranch."

I salute him. "Save the shavings, got it."

He cracks a half smile as a bead of sweat trickles from beneath the band of the backwards cap he's wearing. Lyla said there was nothing hotter than a cowboy working in a white tank and a ball cap, and now I understand what she meant. While Kade isn't wearing a tank top, the white T-shirt he's got on does the job. I've had to stop myself several times from drooling. I'm going to blame my hunger for making me look twice. But with the way his shoulders bunch beneath his shirt as he works, I can't help imagining what his broad, sweaty muscles look like sans clothing.

I swallow and get back to mucking, my mouth as dry as a desert. Yep, I'm definitely blaming this weak moment on no food and a lack of water. Otherwise, I wouldn't be thinking of Kade in this way. I wouldn't be thinking of him in a nice way at all. The man is annoying. We don't get along. And he's a walking red flag. I can't let my hormones and delirium change my opinion of him. Right?!

Kade clears his throat.

"What now?" My question comes out exasperated, and not just because of my prior thoughts. If he tells me I'm still doing it wrong, I may scream.

He starts to point to a spot on the ground, and I snap. "I didn't miss a spot! I'm still working."

He stifles a laugh. "Your weird hippie nicotine vape fell out of your pocket."

Heat licks up my neck. I forgot I even put it there this morning. I haven't been using it as much in the last few days, relying more on my random word reciting to get me through my anxiety. "It's not nicotine."

"Whatever you say, Lemon."

I sigh, bending over to pick up the pen. "It's not. I told you; its peppermint, valerian root, and chamomile."

He cocks his hip and props himself against his pitchfork. "Can I try it?"

I scrunch my nose at him. "You think I'm lying?"

He expels a breathy chuckle. "Just wondering what you like about it."

I stare at the pen then look back up at him. For a second, I debate if I should let him. This interaction leans toward normal conversation between two people who are getting to know each other. Usually, every other word out of his mouth is him telling me how I'm doing something wrong.

"I swear I don't have cooties," he chirps.

I shake my head but decide to let him try it; this conversation is better than him annoying me. I hold the inhaler out, and he smirks as he takes it. His work-calloused fingers brush mine as he does. While there's no zap of electricity this time, my stomach flips despite my desire to be irritated at him.

Kade pulls back with the inhaler in his hand and an even wider grin like he knows I felt something when we touched. I try to remain neutral, but my eyes track his movement as he brings it to his lips, mouth wrapping around the small cylinder before he sucks. My breath hitches in my throat as his cheeks hollow, and my grip on my pitchfork tightens. I think my body now lacks any moisture at all.

When he removes the pen, my heated gaze meets his amused one, and I feel like a kid being caught with their hand in the cookie jar. I've never been good at being subtle. He holds the vapor in, and while I expected he would cough, he doesn't. When he exhales, peppermint mixes with the scent of hay and horses, making my nose tingle.

"That," he says, handing the pen back to me, "is the weirdest shit I've ever put in my mouth."

I huff a tense laugh, wanting to shake the feelings coursing through my body. "Something tells me you've had weirder."

He quirks one dark-blond eyebrow at me. "What do you think I've had in my mouth, Lemon?"

"I don't know. Rocky Mountain oysters?"

Kade barks a laugh that vibrates down to my toes. "See, I knew you were funny. I told Jake you were just hiding your personality from us."

His comment makes me anxious, and that flip in my stomach turns to rocks tumbling around. I suppose it's not hard for the people around me to notice that I haven't exactly been forthcoming about myself. I've done that intentionally. But even with that, I'm not the type of person who shares or relaxes until I feel comfortable. And nothing about my spontaneous move to Randall is comfortable. Nothing about my life right now is.

I bring the pen to my lips and inhale to tamp down some of the anxiety. Kade goes silent as he watches me take a drag of my "hippie pen." Gooseflesh breaks out over my arms as I observe the way he licks his lips, his gaze trained on my mouth as I inhale. Maybe it's his comment that makes me do it, but I hollow my cheeks a little more than necessary. When I exhale the minty cloud, I put the pen back into my pocket and face Kade.

"Does it work?" he asks, making me blink. I would've thought something sexual would come out of his mouth after my blatant tease.

"What do you mean?"

"Did it actually help you quit smoking?"

More surprise fills me, and I don't answer right away. Instead, I try to figure him out. Everything about the question—the way he said it, the curiosity in his hazel eyes—tells me he genuinely wants to know the answer. Which I find curious.

"It helped, but it was a process," I say truthfully. "I did the patches and even tried hypnotherapy, but I still needed something to do with my hands, and the inhaler helped. Probably still bad for my lungs, but I don't use it that much anymore unless I get too—I mean, at least it's not nicotine, right?"

"Unless you get too what?" he digs.

I should've known he'd never let me get away with that. "It helps me with my anxiety attacks." I tell the truth because—well, honestly, I don't know why. But he seems to really want to know. And maybe I told him because this is the first serious question he's asked me all morning.

Kade stares at me thoughtfully, his usual grin a pensive line and shoulders relaxed. It's a far cry from flirty Kade, and the intensity of him has me wanting to know what he's thinking.

"Kade?" I ask after another moment of him staring. He blinks, and I watch his body go from relaxed to tense. Was I too honest?

But before I can think much on it, he cracks one of his dimpled smiles and points behind me. "You missed a spot, Lemon."

Right. I guess serious Kade is gone now. With an internal sigh, I turn to the spot and see there's nothing there. *Fucking Kade.*

His laughter sounds behind me, and I don't satisfy him by looking back. Instead, I try to ignore my hungry stomach and the sweat now trickling down my back then get to sifting.

CHAPTER 13

Kade

THIS MORNING HASN'T BEEN half bad. So far, Presley has proved me wrong, impressing me with her gumption. I would've thought she'd give up by now. I knew she could work, but this kind of work is different—not everyone can handle it. I've seen grown men complain and give up after a week, especially when they get a whiff of the pig pen. But Presley hasn't quit, hasn't complained once. Sure, she's rolled her eyes at me, but that's because I'm annoying her.

At first, it started off as a way to have a little fun after last night's "talk" with Gavin and a way to loosen her up a bit—she's been so quiet and uptight. I'd say she even rivals Gavin in that department. But despite that, I'm learning that I like Presley. She may be sour, but once I got through that first layer, I found she's more interesting than anyone I've met in recent years.

That makes me hate that she found me hungover and passed out on the couch this morning even more. I didn't plan for her to see me like that, sprawled out in my day-old clothes and boots, but I drank a bit too much with Jake. Not a bit too much. A lot too much. I honestly don't remember much about last night besides asking Jake to drop me off at the hands' quarters rather than the main house so I could avoid my family. The woman must sleep like the dead, because I don't think I was very quiet when I stumbled in after two in the morning.

Speak of the devil, or should I say Lemon, Presley stops shoveling dirt and wipes a bit of sweat from her forehead with the collar of her T-shirt. The action lifts the hem of the fabric just enough that a small sliver of skin peeks out.

We've moved on to clearing some debris from the construction of an indoor/outdoor lounge area behind the barns, a place Blake wanted to build for guests to sit, watch the horses graze, and have bonfires. It'll be a great spot to get out of the sun.

Presley wipes more sweat away with her shirt, and I bite the inside of my cheek when I see the skin of her stomach again. I wonder if it's as soft as it looks. When she notices where my eyes are trained, she tugs at the hem so she's covered again. Her cheeks turn red, redder than they are from the heat and physical strain, and she shoots me a sour look.

"Do you always stare at people for prolonged periods of time?" she asks, leaning on her shovel. Her words are funny considering I've caught her staring plenty of times. Just this morning, I could feel her eyes on me while we mucked stalls.

"Do you?"

She purses her lips together as another bead of sweat rolls down her forehead. I watch it travel down the side of her face and over the smooth column of her neck before falling against her shirt. I'd like to say that my thoughts don't go to the gutter, but they do. Hell, who am I kidding? They've been in the gutter since the moment I met her. And now, working with her all morning, hearing her soft grunts and moans while she's exerting herself, has only made the images I've been dreaming up of her more vivid.

My desire to know what she looks like in my ropes, making the sounds she's making, sweat dripping between the valley of her breasts while she comes, has increased tenfold. When I try to stop them, they only seem to get worse, even when I remind myself that Presley should be off-limits. I tell myself that she's my coworker, now technically my employee, and she lives on my property. I even tried to remember that she isn't the type I normally take to bed, that there are a lot of women I could play with who are not her—ones who would literally jump between the sheets if I asked. But none of that matters.

Presley tugs at her shirt again then trains her eyes back to the dirt pile. "Just stop staring," she says under her breath, wiping more salty water from her eyes.

Ignoring her request, I flick my gaze down her body. But this time, I study her for other reasons. She's very sweaty, and now, I get concerned.

"You're looking flushed. Do you need to stop for a lemonade break?"

"I'm fine," she snaps before turning back to the dirt pile to shovel again.

"I'm being serious. If you need a break—"

"I said I'm fine."

I hold my hands up in surrender, and she continues to shovel, mumbling something under her breath. Deciding to leave her be for the moment, I pull out my cell from my back pocket to see we're getting close to twelve. I've got a missed text from Jake but none from Gavin. By this point in the day, he's usually messaged me a few times, but after last night, I can't be surprised that he hasn't.

> JAKE: You alive after all that whiskey last night?

I chuckle to myself before typing out a text.

> KADE: Been working since before 6.

JAKE: I would say that shocks me, but it doesn't. How's Presley doing?

KADE: Why do you ask?

I glance at Presley, who's working away, but the more I watch her, the more I notice she's slowing down. Her movements aren't as powerful as they were when we first started. *Bzzz. Bzzz. Bzzz.* I look down at my phone.

JAKE: You don't remember?

KADE: Remember what?

JAKE: After you went on about Gavin, you wouldn't shut up about her.

I wrack my brain, trying to remember last night. Jake and I grabbed a bottle of whiskey from Night Hawk and sat in the back of his pickup to shoot the shit, something we did more of before Dad died. Yes, I wasn't of legal drinking age, but most people around here believe that if you can go to war and die at eighteen, you can make the choice to drink. If you had asked Emmett Montgomery, he'd say you can drink as soon as you can do a full day's work. But that's an idea of his I'd rather not unpack.

Bzzz. Bzzz. Bzzz.

> JAKE: To quote you: "I wonder if she has tattoos under that shirt."

> KADE: I did not say that.

> JAKE: You did. You turned down every woman who asked for your number after we went back into the bar. In all the years I've known you, I've never seen you do that before.

I understand why I turned women down—I was not in the mood after the fight with Gavin. But has Presley really gotten under my skin so much that I spoke about her to Jake? It's one thing to think my own thoughts about her, to be attracted to her, but it's another to speak those thoughts out loud to my friend, especially when drunk.

Bzzz. Bzzz. Bzzz.

> JAKE: Did you die from embarrassment?

I huff to myself before typing out a text.

> KADE: Me? Embarrassed?

> JAKE: I feel like if anyone can embarrass you, it's your "Lemon."

Your Lemon. What the fuck? Maybe I should've taken one of those girls' numbers, because I have no business calling her my anything. I hardly even know her.

I start to type out a nice "fuck you" text to Jake when my eyes catch movement. I glance up just in time to see Presley almost drop to the ground. I shove my phone in my pocket, and in a couple of strides, I'm behind her. I place my hands on her waist, and she jumps, attempting to move away from me. But when she does, she sways on her feet.

"Presley." My voice is laced with concern. I know something is wrong because she doesn't push me away this time. My heart beats loudly in my chest, and I feel like I want to stab myself in the gut for not forcing her to take a break—and for not thinking of giving her one sooner.

"Now you call me by my name?" she teases weakly.

I chuckle at her answer but then her body goes limp, shovel falling to the dirt with a thud. At the sudden shift in weight, I almost crash to my knees but manage to keep us from falling to the ground.

"Presley!" I shout, but she doesn't move. Panic wells in my stomach, and my eyes scan our surroundings to find anyone to help, but I don't see a soul.

Before I pocketed my phone, I saw it was nearly twelve, which means a lot of the workers probably went to eat lunch. The thought makes me remember that we haven't eaten, either, and the last thing I saw her drink was coffee right before we came out to shovel.

Jesus, no wonder she fainted. I'm used to working on a hangover and hardly anything in my stomach. Not that it's good for me, but Presley doesn't have that kind of tolerance built up.

I lower us to the ground as carefully as I can, placing her head on my leg before I feel her forehead. She feels clammy, her skin wet with sweat. I take off my cap and hold it over her head to shade her eyes from the sun then use my other hand to tap her cheek a little.

"Presley," I say. "Come on, open your eyes."

She doesn't move. I tap her cheek again and still nothing. Dread fills me, and my hands shake. I take a deep breath, willing the curling black tendrils of fear to leave me. Now's not the time to let how I felt the night of my accident resurface. I need to help Presley, and I can't do that without a level head.

I place my fingers on her neck. Her pulse is a little slow, but I think she just needs shade, food, and water. I set my hat back on my head and lean forward so my lips are against her ear, my nose tickling the shell.

"Presley, darlin'. Please open those pretty eyes." I shake her a bit. "If you don't get up, I'm going to have to spray you with the hose," I tease. Just as I'm about to make good on that promise, she groans, her nose scrunching up in the way she's done before, like a bunny.

"No hose..." She moans.

I let out a relieved chuckle, though inside, I feel like I want to hurl. The Kade before the accident would've never freaked out over someone passing out—he would have patiently waited until she woke up. This was an entirely new experience, one I never want to feel again.

For a fleeting moment, I think this is what Blake must have felt like the night she saved me. Helpless. Afraid. Like the world is closing in and you'll do anything to grasp onto a lifeline. But I push that out of my mind, swallowing it down with a smile.

Presley's lids flutter open, her heavy eyes meeting mine. They widen, then, in a flash, she's trying to sit up. It happens so fast she almost whacks our foreheads together. "Whoa, there, easy now." I grip her arms to steady her.

"Kade, let—" Before she can finish the sentence, she's leaning over and dry-heaving onto the ground while trying to shove out of my grip. I cringe, holding her tight in a very awkward position as her body tries to vomit nothing, reminding me yet again I'm an asshole for not making sure she ate and drank water.

Presley groans, her shoves becoming weaker. I attempt to keep her hair back from her face, but in an unexpected burst of strength, she pushes me. Taking the hint, I let her go as she holds herself up on the ground, another heave leaving her lips.

"Let me help you," I say.

After another heave has subsided, she takes an inhale, her face screwed up in pain. "I'm good. Please leave me alone here to die from embarrassment," she manages weakly.

I tilt my head. "Why are you embarrassed?" I'm genuinely curious, because I've been in worse shape than her in front of others, said and done a lot of crazy things, like apparently calling her "my Lemon" last night. Seriously, what the fuck was that?

She lets out a long and painful groan. "Please, leave me here to die."

I stare at the strange girl with purple hair who always surprises me with what she says and does. It only makes me want to know her more, to unravel her, to figure her out.

Fuck. Maybe I *do* want her. How did that happen?

How the hell did I *let* that happen?

When she groans again, I curse under my breath. "You're not going to die. We need to get you up and in the shade, then I'll get you some food and water. Can I please help you?"

Presley stares at the ground where there's a tiny bit of her bile in the dirt. I don't miss the way her face burns at the sight of it. Her arms shake when she tries to get up, her body weak enough that she can't do it on her own. After another long moment of her struggling, she finally looks at me and nods.

With a breath of relief I stand, staying behind her so I can pull her up under her armpits. I try to keep the movement slow so she doesn't pass out again. When she's on her feet, she sways a bit, so I act fast, tucking her into my side.

"Put your arm around my waist." She grumbles at the request, and I smirk. "Has anyone ever told you you're as stubborn as a mule?"

"Has anyone ever told you that you're annoying?"

I let out a sharp laugh to cover up how grateful I am that she's okay. "Glad to see you're feeling better, Lemon."

Her eyes narrow at me, but she does as I asked. Once she's settled against me, I place my arm around her shoulder and make sure she's secure. For a brief second, I relish the contact, reveling in how her soft body feels against mine, how she fits perfectly into my side. It's...nice. More than nice. But I don't have time to think much on it because the sound of dirt crunching has my focus shifting to meet the assessing gazes of Blake and Gavin.

Great. Just fucking great.

My brother and I make eye contact. He looks from me to Presley, and the nice feeling I had fades. I know that look on his face—he thinks I've hit on her, that I've got my arm around her for reasons that he'd rather not know about.

Not that I care. After last night, he can think what he wants. I hope the gossip mill told him about me getting drunk with Jake. I hope he thinks I fucked half the bar. At this point, I think Gavin would believe anything anyone told him about me.

"What's going on?" Blake asks first, rushing toward us. Gavin's tense features start to relax, as if his brain is recognizing that, from the tone of Blake's voice, this is not what he thinks it looks like.

"Presley just needs a break," I answer.

Blake goes into mama-bear mode and puts her hand on Presley's forehead before her feet have even stopped moving.

"Did you eat this morning?"

My gaze moves to Presley's profile, and I don't miss the way her hand grips my waist a little tighter.

"I had a little something."

I swallow, knowing she's lying. The question is why—is it because she's embarrassed?

"Kade, have you given her breaks?" Blake asks, her stern stare boring into me. The normal warmth is gone. I can't help but notice she's sporting dark circles under her eyes, as if sleep has been evading her. Are they because of me?

Presley turns her head briefly toward me, her dry lips pressing together. I feel terrible for not taking better care of her and try to convey that through my gaze. I swallow and open my mouth to answer Blake, to tell the truth, but Presley beats me to it, her eyes making direct contact with Blake and Gavin.

"He has," she says firmly.

Blake deflates, the scolding she had ready to give me leaving her body.

"Presley," I find myself saying. My brain is trying to figure out why she's lied both about eating something and about this.

"I just need a little more food and some water. Not used to all this manual labor in the sun," she says through a breathy laugh.

Blake studies her, Gavin's protective gaze watching over us like the mother hen that he is.

"I'll take you up to the main house," Blake says. "We were just coming to tell you both to come to lunch, anyway."

"I think I'd like to go back and rest," Presley answers. "If that's okay."

Blake smiles at her. "Of course. I can take you back."

"I've got her," I say, almost too fast. My fingers press into the soft skin of her shoulder. "You can go grab us some food."

The already muggy air becomes suffocating, and it feels like Presley and I are in a standoff against Gavin and Blake. When Presley leans heavier into me, I go on high alert, gripping her tighter. I don't want her to pass out again.

When I take a step forward, Gavin holds up a hand. "I want to talk with you. Let her go with Blake."

It happens in a flash, but the warmth of Presley leaves me, and then she's leaning on Blake. For whatever reason, Presley's sapphire eyes look apologetic when they meet mine. I wonder why, because it's not like she can know what's happening. I know she saw Gavin and I argue the first day we met, but she has no idea of the true nature of my family drama unless someone at the bar has told her. Which is possible, I suppose.

"I'll see you back at the house," Blake says to Gavin. I see her check in with Presley to make sure she can walk, and then they're taking off toward the hands' quarters, leaving me with my brother. I can't shake my thoughts about last night. Maybe I should just leave this place altogether. I have no idea where I would go, but it would be better than this. Better than the judgment and the tension.

"What did you do to that poor girl?" Gavin asks as soon as Presley and Blake are out of earshot. I flex my jaw as I bend to pick Presley's shovel up off the ground and start to walk away.

"Kade," he calls after me. "Please tell me what happened. She's our responsibility."

I stop and spin to face him, not liking that he just assumes that whatever was going on with Presley was my fault. I should have gone easier on her; I know that. I'm already feeling like an asshole, so I don't need to add Gavin's shitty opinion of me on top of it.

"I don't have to answer to you anymore, Gavin. You gave up on me, remember?" I drop the shovel on the ground and let my anger come out. "Unless you changed your mind in less than twelve hours?"

"Kade." He sighs. "I was upset when I said that."

I stare into the eyes of my brother—the man I once looked up to—a million things I want to say on the tip of my tongue. But it's not worth it. It will just end up like it always does. I turn my back on him and walk away.

"Where are you going?" His exasperated tone follows me.

I whistle the melody to "Here for a Good Time" by George Strait before yelling over my shoulder, "Didn't you know, Gav? I've got women to corrupt and booze to drink." The first part is a lie. The second part is not. I think I deserve a drink after this. Blake will take care of Presley and make sure she eats and drinks.

Right now, I just need to be alone.

CHAPTER 14

Presley

DEREK: Presley. Cut this shit out. You're ruining everything.

DEREK: We really are going to replace you.

DEREK: If I don't hear from you by tomorrow morning, I'm going to call your Mom and say you're missing.

ONE MISSED CALL FROM *Mom.*

Anger and sadness lodges in my throat as I stare at my phone next to my bowl of chili and cornbread on the small kitchen table. Leave it to Mom to call me only when she thinks I'm murdered or missing.

I spoon the beanless meat mixture before letting it plop back in the bowl. I haven't had much of an appetite since I fainted yesterday, but if I don't eat, either Ruby, June, or Blake will force-feed me. Maybe not force-feed me, but they'd probably make me eat in front of them.

I groan and push my bowl away. I can't believe I passed out—and in front of Kade, no less. I've never passed out a day in my life. It made me question if the cowboy was right in his assumption that I couldn't handle being a ranch hand. But Blake would hear none of my apologies, telling me how she did something similar earlier this year when she got heat stroke. It was nice of her to try to make me feel better, but I still feel guilty for not completing my first day of work. On top of that, when I woke up this morning, Kade was nowhere to be found. I half expected him to be asleep on the couch again, but he wasn't there, and unless he slept in one of the rooms not connected to the living room, he didn't come back at all last night.

I'm trying to figure out why I felt disappointed when I didn't see him or why he didn't come check on me after everything happened yesterday. He seemed genuinely concerned when I passed out, which is part of the reason I lied when Blake asked me if he'd given me breaks. He hadn't, but I'd also been irresponsible. I should've told Kade what I needed, but my desire to prove myself won out over my own safety.

Kade only shocked me further when he offered to bring me back to the house, his arm tightening around me as if he didn't want to let me go—a feeling that made my stomach flip-flop in ways it shouldn't. His desire to care for me was sweet, albeit strange, after all the shit he'd been giving me.

The logical side of my brain tells me I shouldn't like him, but after spending time with him...I don't know. He's confusing. Which makes me want to understand him, get to know him and this caring side better—

No. I can't let myself go there. He has issues. I do, too. And while I can't lie that my body is attracted to him, he's not a person I should get involved with. Especially because he's a playboy who drives me nuts half the time.

But then my mind wanders to the look on his face when I opened my eyes—there was fear there, real fear. It brings my curiosity back about the rumblings I've heard at the bar, why he was off work for three months, the accident I keep hearing about. Did something happen to him or someone he loved?

Ping!

I jump as my phone chimes and vibrates on the table. It's Derek. You'd think it would be my mom, that she'd be concerned I still haven't returned her call. But no, I guess my shitty ex cares more about me than she does.

The vibrating stops, but before I can turn the phone off, it starts again. Derek's name flashes across the screen.

I put the spoon back in my bowl of chili and debate my options. If I don't answer, will the cops show up looking for me to get proof of life? The idea of that happening in front of any one of the Montgomerys or people at Night Hawk makes me nauseous, though I find it hard to believe anyone in my life back home cares that much.

As a teen, there were times when I would test my mom. I would stay overnight at a friend's place without asking, thinking she'd call worried, wondering where I was or why I didn't come home. But that never happened.

Then when I turned fifteen and she had my half-sister, Desi, I became a complete and total afterthought. Not that I wasn't before, but it only got worse. The new baby made me nonexistent. Which I understood at first, but over time, I realized my own mother had replaced me with a shiny new baby, a child she liked better. One would think she'd have had space in her heart for both of her children, but that wasn't the case. She put all her focus on Desi. Last I heard, she was entering her into beauty pageants.

It figures because she always wanted a little girl who would be the cheerleader and homecoming queen. That was never me. I was just her weird, orchestra-nerd daughter who could never lose weight. When she got what she wanted with Desi, that was the end of me.

And don't get me started on my dad, who only texts me on holidays and on my birthday. It's not like he'll be calling me anytime soon.

Ping!

Screw it. I can't have the cops showing up to make sure I'm alive—or Derek. With shaking hands, I tap the screen to answer the call. I don't say hi, and I don't need to.

"Presley! What the fuck?"

I cringe at the tone in his deep voice, the voice I used to love. Now it only gives me goosebumps—and not the good kind. "Well, hello to you, too."

"Cut the cute shit, P. Where have you been?"

"I left you a note," I say. I knew that note would never be enough for him, but it was all I could do when I left. I wasn't going to risk speaking to him and having him convince me to stay.

"Are you fucking kidding me with this shit? We have a record deal, and you don't show up to sign the contracts? Do you know how bad that made us look?"

I feel like that viral sound: *Well, if it isn't the consequences of my own actions.* I shouldn't have picked up.

"It wasn't my intention to make you look bad," I say honestly, and it really wasn't. I just wanted to get out of the city fast.

He mumbles a few curses under his breath then huffs loudly. "We've already been auditioning fiddle players. They're better than you."

Tears sting my eyes. I should expect nothing less than Derek taking a dig at me where he knows I'm most insecure. It's his favorite thing to do. I blink and clear my throat as best I can, trying to hold myself together. "Then why are you calling me?"

"Because I wanted you to know."

"You've been texting. And my mom, really? You didn't have to call her."

He chuckles snidely. "I couldn't get a hold of you. I thought you may be dead. How was I supposed to know you were reading them?"

The chili in my stomach revolts, and acid burns my throat. "Please stop calling and texting me. If you're replacing me with someone better, then it doesn't matter."

I hear him crack open what I'm guessing is a beer before he says, "I just wanted to tell you how disappointed I am in you, that I never should've gotten involved with a loser like you. You've ruined all our lives, and for what?"

I go still, processing his words. Derek used to be sweet—at least, he was when I first met him. He saw me play at a bar in Boston and seemed to be enamored with me. He was the first guy who ever approached me in a bar to hit on me, the first guy to pay attention to me instead of the hot women in the bands I played with. It felt nice, as if I was finally special to someone. And I fell for him and his pretty words hook, line, and sinker.

It wasn't until we were dating for a year that he began to take digs at me. It started with little comments like how I should dress differently for gigs, that the food I ate wasn't good for me. Then he would start on the quality of my fiddle playing. I don't know why I stayed with him for as long as I did—five-plus years of my life—but I did. And I regret it.

And I regret that I picked up the phone after finally having the courage to walk away. Not just from him but from my toxic band.

"Did you hear me, P?"

"You know I hate it when you call me that."

I hear him throw something that crashes against a wall. "You ruined everything! We're never going to forgive you for this. You made me look like a fool. A fucking fool, Pres."

"Please stop calling me. We're done."

"No, I get to say when we're done. You fucked *me*."

"No, *you fucked another woman*," I spit out, unable to contain my anger any longer.

"Is that what this tantrum is about, Presley? That I fucked someone hotter than you?"

"Screw you, Derek!"

"Don't you dare hang up on me. You need—"

I end the call and throw my phone down on the table. Tears spill from my eyes, and I pull at the collar of my T-shirt, trying to breathe, but the air just won't seem to come. More acid burns my throat, and I force myself to breathe through my nose. "Don't let him get to you, Presley," I say under my breath. I reach into my back pocket and grab the calming inhaler. It's almost gone, but there should be enough to help me through this anxiety attack.

I wrap my lips around the mouth and breathe in. The familiar taste of peppermint and chamomile coats my tastebuds, and my heart rate slows slightly. As I pull it from my lips and exhale, I stare at the little stick. Behind my eyelids, an image of Kade appears from yesterday when he'd wrapped his lips around the same opening. I take another drag of it and hold in the vapor before exhaling again.

"How did you end up here?" I ask myself, wishing I could answer, wishing I knew why I let someone like Derek screw up my life so badly. I wonder why I answered the phone. Even if Mom did think I was dead, would it be so bad? I could live my life how I want to, pretend my past doesn't exist.

In a lot of ways, I've already gotten a head start by moving here. Nobody knows me in Randall, and they don't know anything about me. I'm just an awkward city girl who's a half-decent bartender and now a bad ranch hand.

My phone pings again, and I let out a frustrated sound, grabbing it off the table. Derek's text lights up the screen:

> DEREK: You were never good enough, anyway.

You were never good enough, anyway.
You were never good enough, anyway.
You were never good enough, anyway.

Tears well up again, and I almost choke on the emotion clogging my throat. Never good enough? I'll admit that I let Derek get in my head about my talent, but I'm a good fiddle player. More than good—I'm one of the best in Texas, but I let my ex's own insecurities and hurtful comments make me think otherwise. I let him influence my life and the choices I've made. I let him worm his way into every part of my mind, making me question who I am and every dream I've ever had.

My phone buzzes with another text, and all my muscles bunch in my body.

"Screw you, Derek!" I scream.

"Who's Derek?"

I scream again, this time from surprise as Kade strolls through the door from the other connecting bedroom.

"Kade!" I place a hand over my heart. "You scared the crap out of me!"

He steps up in front of the table, and I stand, my entire body vibrating. His hair is wet from a shower, and he's got on his Night Hawk T-shirt and a pair of jeans with boots. For a moment, I forget about my anger and the fact that I have tears in my eyes, because I swear every time I see him, he gets more attractive.

Kade's gaze narrows as he looks me up and down. The intensity of it makes my stomach muscles clench and my body tingle. I swear he looks concerned again—like he was when I fainted.

"What happened?" he asks.

I shove my phone in the back pocket of my jeans and take a breath. I realize it sounds shaky, but I've never been a good actress. "Nothing."

Kade steps into my space like he did the first day I met him, and he brings his thumb up to wipe a tear from my cheek. My entire body freezes at the tingling sensation the brief touch left in its wake as blood rushes into my ears. He studies the wetness on his thumb, observing it as if he's never seen tears before.

"Doesn't look like nothing, Lemon." His hazel gaze flicks to me, our bodies so close that I can see they're mostly green with little flecks of brown and gold in them. I think I even see a little blue. They're beautiful.

"What did this Derek do?" he asks.

The breath that I've been holding breaks free at the sound of Derek's name on Kade's lips. I blink away the tears and step back, folding my arms over my chest.

"Personal space much?"

The corner of Kade's lips turn up into what I can only describe as a rogue smirk. "You want me to punch his lights out for you? I'm not above wiping the floor with an asshole."

I stare at him, this man who doesn't know me, who has done nothing but confuse and arouse me since the day I got here.

"I have to leave for work," I say, ignoring his question. I would love to see someone punch Derek in the face, especially this handsome cowboy, but I don't need a man defending me. Kade doesn't even like me—though maybe that assumption is wrong given our interactions over the last twenty-four hours.

He lowers his hand, the smile from before still on his face. "You're good at keeping the focus off yourself, aren't you?"

Not wanting to get into this now—or ever—I step back from him. I walk away, grabbing my keys and small purse from the kitchen counter. When I turn around, Kade is standing right there again, his tall body in my path.

"Who's Derek?" he asks.

"I'll see you later." I move to step around him, but he blocks my path.

"We can drive together. I'm working tonight."

"I'd rather drive alone."

"Well, see, that's impossible."

I cross my arms over my chest and chuff in annoyance. "Why is that impossible?"

"Because your tire is flat."

My eyes widen. "You're lying."

"Not lying. I was going to offer you a ride."

This time, he lets me step around him as I walk outside to where I have my car parked. Sure enough, I have a flat tire.

"Really?" I stare up at the sky and groan. I feel like the universe or some cosmic being is trying to screw with me.

"You need new tires."

I turn to face Kade and glare at him. "Thank you, Captain Obvious."

He shrugs, whistling a country song I don't recognize. "Come on, Lemon. My truck is comfy and has tires that aren't flat."

I sigh, squeezing my eyes shut and asking whoever upstairs is playing a cruel joke on me to at least grant me strength. Because I guess I'm riding to work with Kade Montgomery.

CHAPTER 15

Kade

HAVING PRESLEY IN MY truck feels oddly nice, natural even. There's been several times where I've almost laid my hand on her thigh because of how natural it feels. But while tempting—very tempting—Presley would probably deck me, maybe even curse me out.

Though now that I think about it, maybe she wouldn't curse. I haven't heard a bad word out of her mouth yet. Makes me wonder if she's one of those proper city girls or used to be a pastor's kid who rebelled by looking different. The corners of my lips tug up as I think of the word *fuck* leaving her lips while I parted those pretty thighs currently filling out my passenger seat—

Ping!

I blink at the sound of the phone and return my full attention to the road. In my peripheral vision, I see Presley shift to take her cell from her back pocket and glance down at the screen. She tries to hide whatever reaction she has to the message, but she doesn't do a very good job. Her body goes tense as her hands clench around the device.

I wonder if it's Derek. I shouldn't care who Derek is or if she's upset. I shouldn't care about her at all. Yet for the last twenty-four hours, Presley's been all I can think about, taking up every nook and cranny of my mind.

I gave her space after she passed out since I wasn't in the best mental place after my most recent argument with Gavin.

I ended up spending the night at Jake's, then this morning, I didn't see Presley during chores. Blake must've told her to take the morning off after yesterday or had her doing something far away from me.

Yet while Presley wasn't physically in front of me, I felt as if she was. Her blue eyes were stalking me from behind my eyelids.

I turn my head a bit to see her better as she puts her phone back in her pocket. Her lips move, and I swear I hear her listing off groceries or something under her breath. When I go to ask her about it, she turns her hardened gaze to me.

"Watch the road."

I grin at her bossy tone but do as she said, even if I could drive to Night Hawk with my eyes closed. "I should've known you were a passenger-seat driver."

"I'm not. But I don't want to die."

I chuckle. "I'm not going to kill you, Lemon. I wouldn't be able to annoy you."

I think she's going to scold me for saying that, but instead, I spot the ghost of a smile on her lips. It's not a full one, but it's nice. That's another thing I have yet to see her do: really smile or laugh. She hasn't even done it with a customer.

I haven't thought much about it until now.

"What would you do with your life if you couldn't be annoying?" she asks.

A belly laugh erupts from my lips, and she jumps a bit at the sound. "You're always surprising me."

She screws up her face. "Why do you say that?"

"Why wouldn't I?"

"We don't know each other. In theory, wouldn't I always surprise you?"

"That's fair. I just thought I knew your type."

Her gaze is fully on my profile like she's trying to burn a hole in my face with laser-beam eyes. "My *type*? What do you mean by that?"

I shrug again and turn left down the town's small main street. There's not much out here—the bank, Allen's General Store, The Diner, a couple of bars, and a Mexican food joint. Night Hawk is just on the outskirts of town.

Sometimes I joke Randall isn't even a town, more like a blip on the map. A town everyone would look over if they were passing through unless they really needed to stop and use the bathroom.

"Tell me," she prods. "What's my type?"

I glance at her before looking back at the road. Her voice has an edge, and I know I'm going to have to tread carefully. "I mean no offense by this..."

She offers a derisive chuckle. "If you need to start with that, it's going to be offensive."

Yeah, this is not a good idea. I should've kept my big mouth shut. "Forget I said anything."

"No. You don't get out of a statement like that. I want to know what you see when you look at me."

I grip the steering wheel and shift in my seat. I like this demanding side of her; it has me wanting to see more of it. I speculate if it would show up while in my bed or if it would take some coaxing. I bet—*Jesus*. I run my tongue against the back of my teeth and grip the wheel harder.

I need to stop imagining Presley as anything more than a friend—a distant friend—or I'm not going to be able to stay away. But the devil on my shoulder wonders if that would really be a bad thing. We work together, now practically live together, and she doesn't really know me. It could be nice, though, to start semi-fresh with someone.

I've begun to think that she's like me in some ways. She's dealing with something—that much was obvious when I walked in on her crying earlier. And she overcame her smoking addiction, or at least found a way not to rely on it.

"Kade."

I blink a few times, loosening my grip on the steering wheel.

"Are you really not going to answer me?"

"Sorry," I say truthfully. "I don't want you to get angry."

"You haven't let that stop you before."

She's right there. I collect my thoughts and blow out a breath. "When I first saw you, I thought you were another one of the city folk we get in here, people running from their life or wanting to escape for a bit. And with your purple hair and tattoos, I thought you were looking for attention, maybe someone or something to take your mind off things. But you surprised me, and you keep surprising me. Nothing I've thought about you so far has really been the case—except that you *are* a little sour." I wink at her, trying to keep what I just said light.

Presley stays quiet, her chin dropping to her chest and hands clutching her black-fringed purse. Any lightness in the air has been sucked out, and the tension radiating off her has the hair on the backs of my arms standing on end.

"See, I told you I should've kept my mouth shut."

She stays silent as I pull into Night Hawk. After I've parked, I think she's going to jump out and run as far and fast as she can from me, but she doesn't. I remove my seatbelt and turn toward her.

"Presley, I'm sorry."

The sound of her name has her looking up at me. "What do you think of me now?"

My eyebrows raise. "Honestly, I don't know. You've not given me a chance to get to know you."

"And if I told you that you were right?"

My curiosity sparks. *Is* she running from something? Maybe this Derek guy? The idea has me feeling sick. "Then you would surprise me again," I say.

Her searching eyes stare into mine, and the tension between us grows. But this is a different kind of tension, the kind right before something good or exciting happens. It has me even more tied up by whatever is going on between us...or *not* going on between us.

Just as our bodies move toward each other—as if an invisible rope is pulling us together—a sound makes Presley jump, her head whipping toward the disruptive noise.

"It was a car door," I say, my voice quiet.

She licks her lips and unbuckles her seatbelt. "Thanks for the ride." She turns her body and opens the door, hopping out of the truck so fast I swear I see a streak of purple in her wake.

I take a long inhale before blowing it out. I don't know if she's mad at me for what I said, but it seemed more like she was afraid, afraid that I'd figured a part of her out.

And now I have a million questions. I want to know if it's Derek she's running from. I want to know where she came from and why she picked Randall. I want to know everything.

Ping!

My gaze falls to the seat Presley just vacated to see her phone. I pick it up only to find the screen isn't locked and there's a text from this Derek guy. I shouldn't look. I should respect her privacy. But I've never been good at doing what I should do.

> DEREK: This is your replacement. I just gave her the job.

Replacement? What job? I tap the phone and see an image attached, an attractive blonde woman in a selfie with a man I assume is Derek. He's got dark-red hair and tattoos up his neck and piercings on his face. He looks like a total douche with a smarmy grin and fake smiling eyes.

A new message comes in, and now I'm too curious to stop looking.

DEREK: You should hear her play.

DEREK: You fucked up the chance of a lifetime, Sweetheart.

I feel queasy at the *Sweetheart* nickname. I remember how she reacted when I called her that the first day we met, and now I understand why. God, I was a dick to her. Granted, I've been a dick to everyone lately.

I press the side button on her phone so the screen locks. She'll probably know I've looked, but it's too late now. Shame hits me, and I have the urge to come clean to her about what I just read.

I turn my focus to Night Hawk and see a group of people filtering in, the typical crowd that comes in for line-dancing night: women from surrounding towns and the city dressed in their shortest shorts and tightest tops with cowboy hats and boots. Normally, I look forward to these nights where I can dance and flirt and maybe get a horizontal partner for the evening. But that's not anything I want right now.

I want Presley back in my car so we can talk. And not just surface-level chatter, either, but real talk about things that matter. I don't know if I've ever wanted that with a woman. At least not in a long time.

How's that saying go? Curiosity killed the cat? I hope I don't end up going through more of my nine lives trying to figure out this city girl.

I thread my hands through my hair that's in serious need of a trim before grabbing my hat from the backseat and placing it on my head. When I look in the rearview mirror, my hazel eyes stare back at me, and I fix a smile on my face, one that will get me through tonight.

I put my hand on the door handle to hop out of my truck, but then the passenger door flies open, and Presley climbs back in. Her wide eyes see her phone in my hand, but she doesn't say anything about it. Instead, she closes the door and then stares straight ahead. After a few breaths of silence, I start to get worried.

"Presley?" I ask. "Everything okay?"

She turns her head to me like she forgot I was even here. "I can't go back in there."

I think of the texts I just saw. "Is it something to do with this Derek guy?"

She blinks, her eyes darting to her phone in my hand then back to me. "Did you read my messages?"

I hold her cell out to her, and she snatches it. "Just the newest ones," I admit. "Your phone was unlocked, and—*fuck*, that's no excuse, but I looked."

Her brow pinches as she taps in her password to see the messages. Her body stills, going silent like the trees before a big storm.

"Presley?"

She squeezes her eyes shut then mutters something under her breath. It sounds like another grocery list—I think I heard *chicken*, *dinosaur*, then *baseball bat*. Her body only grows stiffer, the hand around her phone turning white before she reaches into her purse to pull out her hippie vape thing. She inhales then holds the vapor in before exhaling it out again. The smell of peppermint hits my nose, making it tingle a bit. She inhales another drag, then another, before she finally seems to calm down.

"Do you want me to take you back to the ranch?" I have no idea what happened inside Night Hawk, but it must have triggered the anxiety she mentioned to me yesterday. The texts only seemed to have sent her over the edge.

"We can't leave Jake. He'll fire me."

I shake my head. "He won't fire you. If he fired people, I would've been fired a long time ago."

"I don't want him to think I'm lazy."

"You're not lazy. I saw you work yourself to the point of passing out yesterday. I'd hardly call that lazy."

She shifts uncomfortably, probably remembering how embarrassed she was by the incident. *Way to go, Kade.* I hold back a sigh and take my phone out to make a call.

"Wait, what are you doing?" she panics. Her hand flies out to land on my forearm. I try to ignore how nice it feels to have her touch me as Jake's voice comes through on the other end.

"Should I be worried you're calling me?" Jake asks.

"Can you cover for Presley and me tonight? She's not feeling well, and I'm going to take her back to the ranch."

Presley's nostrils flare, and she looks equal parts relieved and pissed.

"You've got it bad," Jake chuckles.

"Never you mind," I snap. He hasn't stopped ribbing me since the whole drunken "my Lemon" thing.

I'd hoped Presley wouldn't have heard that through the phone, but by the confused look on her face, she had. Fucking great.

"You owe me, man," Jake says, though his tone is playful.

"Yeah, yeah. I'll work all next week so you can go do whatever the hell it is you want to do."

"Deal."

"Want me to call someone to cover? I can hit up Tim; he mentioned he wants to help more."

"I got it handled."

"Thanks, Jake."

"Tell Presley I hope she feels better."

"Will do." I hang up the phone and turn my attention to Presley, who still has her hand on my arm.

"You didn't need to do that," she says.

"It's fine."

"But you could come back and work."

"Presley, relax. Let me take you home."

She pulls back her hand as if she's been burned, the opposite of relaxing. God, this woman drives me nuts.

I don't know what's going through her mind, and I want to know what happened inside Night Hawk. So as I turn the key to start up my truck, an idea forms in my mind.

"You wanna have some fun, Presley?"

Her head snaps to me. "I'm sick, remember?" she snipes. A sly smile takes over my lips—I'm glad to see some of the fire peeking back through.

"Trust me."

She crosses her arms over her chest and glares at me. Her body language tells me everything I need to know about how much she doesn't trust me, which is fair.

I let out a long breath. "I know we don't know each other well, and you probably don't think I'm a good man, but I swear I would never hurt you." I pause. "Unless you ask me to."

When the words have finished echoing between us, I wonder if I've gone too far, revealed too much about myself with that add-on. But...

If it wasn't quiet in my truck, I would've missed her sharp intake of breath. I keep my eyes on her, and she shifts as if—is she *turned on* by that?

Jesus, I need to stop that. No fucking Presley—she's going through something. *You're going through something*, a little voice in the back of my brain says, but I ignore it.

"Come on, Presley. It's rare to get a night off around here, and you deserve to have a little fun. Everyone does. Just trust me, even if it's only for one night."

She stares at me, unblinking, which is different from her normal avoidance. I watch as her pupils contract, lips twitching as her brain works overtime to make her decision.

After another long pause, her shoulders relax, and she tips her chin. "Okay," she mutters. "Just don't take me to a bar."

I smile, a true one this time. "Wasn't planning on it."

CHAPTER 16

Presley

WHEN KADE PULLS UP to the Montgomery Family Ranch, I'm surprised. I thought he'd take me somewhere else. I don't know where, but when he said he wanted me to have fun, the ranch wasn't the first place I had in mind.

I play with the fringe on my purse and gaze out the window at the golden plains. While my anxiety attack has ceased, my heart is still racing from walking into Night Hawk and seeing Marié, the lead singer of my now ex-band. When I spotted her lithe frame and long brown hair standing at the bar, I immediately turned and ran out. If she saw me, she would've told Derek where I was.

The entire ride back to the ranch, I quietly scold myself for not picking a town further away from the city, but I didn't think she'd ever come to a place like this. She likes upscale restaurants and VIP clubs, not bull-riding bars in small towns.

Crap. At least she didn't see me—well, I don't think she did. I was only in the bar for a second before I turned and ran at the sight of her. So there's that.

"Do you have a hoodie or something?" Kade asks.

I turn my head to look at him. He's parked outside the hands' quarters and has just killed the engine of the truck. Now, he's waiting for my answer.

"Why?"

He smirks. "In case you get cold."

"Please tell me we're not camping. I don't camp."

"You really are a city girl, aren't you?"

"I just like beds."

That makes his smile grow wider. "We have that in common."

I raise my eyebrow at him. He really wants to go there right now?

"Presley." He sighs. "Just get into something comfortable. We're not going camping."

Presley. He hasn't called me Lemon or any other nickname since I got back in the truck. It strikes me as strange and a little off-putting.

Wait, am I upset he's calling me by my name? My heart skitters to a stop in my chest. Is there something in the water that's making me like his nicknames for me? Maybe I'm still sick from fainting. I should go to bed instead of hanging out with a person I don't even like. Or think I don't even like.

"Kade—"

"Nope." He cuts me off. "You're not getting out of this. Fun is going to happen."

I sigh as he unbuckles his seatbelt.

"Go get changed. I'm going to grab a few things. I'll come get you in ten."

Kade exits his truck and jogs away toward the main house, leaving me to my own devices. With an exasperated sigh, I get out of his truck and head to the quarters, making a mental note to figure out how to get new tires as I pass my car. Just another thing I'll have to dig into my savings to pay for.

Once I'm inside the safety of my room, I take out my phone. There are more texts from Derek, but I don't look at them. I turn my phone off and put it in the bedside table drawer. He's already caused me enough pain; I don't need to think about him or that selfie he sent me with my replacement...or the fact that Kade saw the messages and I had an anxiety attack in front of him!

My life is so screwed up right now. Kade's assessment of me was right, too—I *am* running from my life. Though the second part of his assumption made me reevaluate what I came here looking for.

Did I come to Randall for someone or something? Do I want attention?

I walk into the bathroom and grip the sink, taking a deep breath. Maybe I need to try to see a therapist again. They offer free sessions at a clinic in Lynn. I thought I was managing my anxiety attacks, but they're coming back full force with all the changes in my life.

I splash some cool water on my face and stare in the mirror. I look tired, sad, and lost—a far cry from the girl I was before I met Derek. I didn't have anxiety attacks like this then. I had normal anxiety like any person living in this day and age does, but not like this.

I take a few minutes to clean up my face then reapply a little bit of mascara to my lashes and some pink-tinted moisturizer to my lips. It doesn't make sense, but I kind of want to look good for him instead of showing up as some weird gremlin girl. Not that it should matter.

I search the small wooden dresser between the room's two twin beds and find a pair of high-waisted black leggings, a loose-fitting white shirt with bell sleeves, and an oversized tan-and-white flannel button up. I tug them on, tying the flannel shirt around my waist and then putting on a pair of white off-brand sneakers I got last month. They will probably get dirty, but I don't feel like wearing cowboy boots. They're not that comfortable on my wider calves, and he told me to be comfortable.

Fine with the way I look and feeling a little more like myself, I walk out into the living area just as Kade strides in through the front door. He stops and smiles when he sees me, letting out a whistle.

"You look good in white. Though your shoes are gonna turn brown." His words echo my earlier thoughts.

"It's fine," I say, ignoring the fact that he complimented me. I'm sure he was just being a flirt like he is with everyone.

"Alright, then. I got provisions." He has a bulging canvas bag in one hand and a blanket over his other arm. "Follow me."

He doesn't give me time to think before he's walking out the door. I follow less reluctantly than I thought I would. Despite how Kade and I first started out, something about him draws me in, makes me want to follow him instead of protest. That has me putting one foot in front of the other to go have "fun" with him.

The gravel and dirt crunch under our shoes as we walk, and Kade slows down a bit so we're now side by side. He has to intentionally shorten his stride so we're moving at the same pace—I'm not that short, but he's got long legs. It's kind of funny to watch him try to stay beside me.

"Are you feeling better?" he asks.

I study Kade's side profile, his five-o'clock shadow coming in strong. The sun is setting, and the orange hues of the sky make his suntanned skin almost glow. He's beautiful.

I clear my throat before he can comment on my silence. "I'm fine."

He scrutinizes me but doesn't say more, pointing to the big red barn ahead of us. I haven't been inside yet, but Blake told me it's where they keep all their hay stores and some equipment. She said one day they'd like to renovate it for events like weddings, which would make a killing in a setting like this. I can see the photos brides would get with the tree-dotted plains rolling expansively in the background. It would be stunning.

"We're going in here."

My interest piques. When he said we'd be having fun, I didn't picture going into a barn. But I reserve judgment, thinking there must be something more to it.

Kade slides open the door, and my attention moves to the way the veins in his forearms bulge and how his glutes flex inside his Wranglers. My cheeks flush at the sexiness of it, and I look away to try to school my features, not wanting him to catch my reaction to his body this time. Thankfully, he doesn't look at me as he walks inside, flicking on a light. I follow him silently.

Once we're both in, he slides the door back in place, and I look around. The overhead lighting isn't super bright, but it's enough to illuminate the hay inside and the particles of dust and feed floating in the air. The barn is huge, and the vaulted ceilings are high, making it look even larger.

"Up the stairs you go," Kade quips. He's smiling wide, dimples showing, as he points to a staircase toward the back of the barn.

I head that direction with him hot on my heels. When we reach the steps that will presumably lead us to the barn loft, I put my hand on the railing at the same time Kade places his on the small of my back. I tense at the unexpected touch, and he pulls back.

"Sorry, I should've asked," he offers sheepishly. "These stairs are old, and I didn't want you to trip."

Warmth fills my chest. I can't remember the last time a man, let alone any person, was concerned about me unless they needed something from me. Like Derek being fake concerned about me being hurt or murdered so that I would pick up the phone.

"It's okay." I nod, and Kade takes that as permission to put his hand on my lower back again. I try to relax then take my time walking up the steps, and I'm a little winded when I reach the top.

I suck in a shallow breath as Kade drops his hand. I'm not going to lie; I miss the heat of it. The security of it.

Taking another short breath, I force myself not to think of that and observe my surroundings. Like downstairs, the light up here is dim, but the sunset from the open loft door casts an orange-and-yellow glow around us. I walk toward the opening and wrap my hands around the wooden railing, looking out over the plains and pastures. The beauty of it steals my breath.

"Wow" is all I manage to say. The sunset paints the sky, almost like it's been photoshopped—reds, oranges, and yellows streak in almost broad brushstrokes across the landscape as the sun slowly sinks behind the horizon. Horses graze in the distance, and the sound of cicadas surrounds us, Yes, I've seen sunsets before, but not like this. Not on an open plain with no light pollution to hide its true beauty. Now I get why Kade was excited.

"Mother Nature is putting on a show tonight," he hums, stepping up beside me. "When I saw the way the sky was turning, I had a feeling it would be a good one."

I gaze at his profile again and take in his genuine love of what he sees. I don't think I've ever seen a man appreciate nature like this before. It's endearing, a side of Kade I never expected to see.

Lately, though, he's been showing a different side of himself—his question about why I quit smoking, his concern for me after I fainted then again when he found me crying. I also can't ignore that he gave me a ride to work because of my tire and took me away from Night Hawk after my anxiety attack. And now this, an attempt to get me to have fun. Maybe he's not as bad as I thought?

I turn my attention to the skies, and we quietly watch the colors of the sunset and the breeze blow across the plains before he steps back and motions for me to follow. Then he points to where he'd set down the canvas bag and blanket he brought.

"What is all that?" I ask.

He smirks. "What? Did you think the fun was just looking at the sunset?"

He bends down to grab the blanket then hands it to me. Our fingers touch when I take it, and much like the first time, electricity passes between us.

He lifts one of his dark-blond eyebrows at me. "Are you really going to tell me that's just science?"

I huff. "I have dry skin."

He laughs, pulling his hand back. "Spread that out for me, Presley. *Please*."

"Wow! My name *and* a please. What did I do to deserve this?"

Kade runs a thumb over his stubbled cheek, his eyes locked on mine. "I guess you've been a good girl."

The coyness in his baritone voice has me shivering and my stomach filling with butterflies. I swallow for no reason. In an attempt to ignore his burning stare, I spread the blanket out then stand to my full height only to find his eyes haven't left my body. His hazel gaze is softer than it usually is, and I think he's trying to get a read on me.

After a second, he kneels on the floor and grabs the canvas bag, pulling things out and setting them on the blanket. A bag of chips, two bottles of water, a deck of cards, two shot glasses, another blanket, and a bottle of whiskey.

For a fleeting moment, I wonder if he should be drinking. But while he's young, he's an adult who can make his own choices. And even though I don't know Kade that well, I know that people who live hard lives mature faster than others. Sometimes I don't even feel like I had a childhood since my parents were so absent. I had to learn how to take care of myself, be my own boss—that changes a person. I don't have to know Kade to know it's been the same for him.

"Are you going to sit?" he asks before taking off his cowboy hat. He sets it next to him and extends his booted feet out in front of him, his palms propping him up.

Even though I am still unsure of how this is going to be fun, I shove away my thoughts and sit, crossing my legs underneath me as I look back out at the darkening sky.

"Are you sure Jake is okay? I feel bad."

Kade nods. "You worry too much. He's fine. I'm sure Stu helped him. And Jake can dance, he just doesn't like to teach if he doesn't have to. He also says if I'm there, I get more tips for us all and people spend more money on drinks."

His statement makes me feel worse. "You can go back, you know. You don't have to stay with me. I'm fine."

Kade lets out a rumbling sound. "Presley. It's okay. I want to be here."

His words stun me into silence, but I don't know how to respond to that. Thankfully, I don't have to because he sits up and takes the bottle of whiskey in his hands.

"You drink?" he asks.

"A little. Socially, when I'm—" I stop myself from saying playing gigs, though I suppose if he saw those texts, he knows I play something.

"When you're...?" he asks, not letting it go.

I sigh. "Just pour me a dang shot, Kade."

That has him smiling again. "I like when you're bossy."

I ignore his flirting and take the offered shot. It's been awhile since I've done a shot of any kind, especially whiskey. I normally go for watered-down sugary drinks or a margarita on the rocks, but I guess this will have to do. After the last week, it'll be nice to let go a bit—even if it's in a barn loft with Kade.

"Cheers," he says, lifting his shot glass to mine. We clink, and then I put the cool glass to my lips. As soon as the liquor hits my tongue, it burns, so I gulp it down as quickly as I can and reach for the bottle of water. Kade chuckles to himself while he watches me wash the horrible taste from my mouth.

"How do you drink that?" I cough.

"Have you never had whiskey before?"

"I have, but did you make it yourself?" I cough again.

He shakes his head, lips pressed into an amused line. "Just cheap shit."

He puts the cap back on the bottle then opens the bag of chips. He offers me some, and I shake my head.

His eyes crinkle at the corners. "Eat some. I don't want you passing out on me."

"I had dinner."

"You ate a little of it. The bowl was still mostly full."

A tingling sensation tickles deep within me when I realize he noticed that, but I ignore it by grabbing the bag and stuffing a chip in my mouth. "Happy?"

He smiles in satisfaction. "Very."

We munch on chips for a minute, and I think of how different this situation would've been with my ex. Derek would have rather let me pass out than offer me chips. He was always on me about my appearance, especially when we started booking bigger gigs. He wanted me to look like all the other women around us: thin, attractive, and fashionable.

I brush my hands clean of chip crumbs and reach for the bottle of whiskey. Kade watches me as I pour myself one then fill his glass, too.

"Trying to get me drunk?" he asks, a playfulness in his tone.

"I'm trying to get myself drunk." Then I knock back the second shot.

CHAPTER 17

Kade

I THROW DOWN MY cards in front of my crossed legs. "Full house."

Presley stares at me with a half smirk, one that's wicked. I know before she puts her cards down that I've lost.

Again.

"Royal flush."

I groan, putting a chip in my mouth before pouring myself another shot of whiskey. She's lucky I hold my liquor well, or I'd be on my ass already.

"Okay, new game," I say.

She almost cackles. "I didn't know you were such a sore loser, Kade."

"Yeah, yeah. I should've known you'd have a good poker face."

That smile tugs at her lips again. It's been peeking out here and there as we've played the last couple of games, and I'm determined to get a full-blown one at some point.

"What do you want to play, big boy? Go Fish?"

"Man, Presley. You really know how to bust a man's balls, don't you?"

She shrugs her shoulders all cutely. "BS?"

Maybe it's the alcohol talking, but I don't want to play a card game anymore. "How about Never Have I Ever?"

Her eyes widen a bit. "You want to play that with me?"

"Why not? It's a fun drinking game, and you need to catch up," I say, thinking there's no way she's done more than me. When she doesn't answer, I raise an eyebrow at her. "It's either that or Truth or Dare."

She puts the cards down and crosses her arms over her chest. "Why are those my only two options?"

"They're the most fun."

She sighs, taking a swig of whiskey directly from the bottle. I don't think she'd normally do this sort of thing, but the more she drinks, the more playful and comfortable she becomes. And I'm not going to lie, watching her lips wrap around the bottle as she takes a sip is sexy as all get out.

Presley puts the bottle down then tips her head up to the loft ceiling. After a pause, she looks back at me. "Fine. Never Have I Ever. But I get to go first."

I give Presley a once over, my gaze lingering on the flushed skin of her neck and the way the purple ends of her ponytail brush against her collarbone. She clears her throat, and I smirk when it meets my eyes. I'm not going to lie; I'm shocked that she said yes to the game. I thought she'd leave and go to bed, but I'm glad she's decided to stay.

"Deal." I'm happy to let her go first.

Presley fills both of our whiskey glasses, giving me another opportunity to drag my gaze over her alcohol-flushed skin. When she's satisfied with her pours, she puts the bottle down and stretches her legs out in front of her.

"Never have I ever—"

I tut. "I didn't tell you the rules yet."

Her mouth drops open. "I know the rules. If you've done it, you drink. If you haven't, you don't drink. Now let me ask you, Montgomery."

I snort. This woman. I love that I'm getting to see her personality, and I'm pretty sure I'm the only one who's seen it so far. I like how playful and snarky she is. I also like how she said my last name. I want her to say it again.

"Alright, ask away."

"Never have I ever made out in the back of a storage room."

"Dang, girl. That was a cheap shot."

She smiles proudly with her shoulders back and a bit of straight white teeth showing through her pink lips. It's a look I've yet to see from her, and it makes my heart beat faster in my chest. It's even closer to a true smile, which has me wanting to try harder to make that happen, to see her smile with her entire being until happiness shines through every part of her like bursts of sunrays through the clouds. I know it will be beautiful.

With that goal in mind, I take a shot of whiskey then continue to play.

"Never have I ever moved somewhere new."

Her mouth drops open. "And you called *mine* a cheap shot?"

"What goes around comes around, Presley." She bites her lower lip, but her eyes remain playful as she downs another shot, coughing and sputtering once it slides down her throat.

"Easy there, don't choke." I lean forward to pat her back.

I don't know if it's the alcohol that's made her more comfortable, but she doesn't shy away from my touch. I clap her back a few more times before pulling away. Her cheeks are red from a combo of coughing, alcohol, and, I'm guessing, embarrassment.

I hand her a water, and she takes a sip before sitting back with a long exhale.

"You need a break?" I ask.

She shakes her head. "Nope." Then she taps her chin, a tiny smile on her lips as she eyes me. "Never have I ever ridden a horse."

I almost tease her for choosing another easy one, but then curiosity fills me. "Wait, you've never ridden a horse?"

She shakes her head. "Riding kind of scares me."

"You realize you took a job as a ranch hand, right?"

"Yes, Kade. I don't necessarily have to ride a horse to do that."

My chest shakes with laughter. "We'll have to change that."

"I'll stay on the ground, thanks."

"We'll see."

"Take your shot."

I do as she says, realizing that maybe this was a dumb game. We need to slow down so we don't get blackout drunk. But I want to play one more round.

Without pausing, I say, "Never have I ever played in a band."

Her breath hitches, and her eyes turn to the ground. Fuck, maybe I shouldn't have gone that far—I let my curiosity get the best of me. But then Presley exhales, her hand moving to pour another shot before she swallows it down.

So she was in a band. I wonder what she plays, or maybe she sings or plays guitar—maybe both? When she lifts her gaze back to mine, her eyes are set with determination instead of anger, fear, or sadness like I would have expected.

"Let's play a different game," she says.

I nod, happy she suggested it. We need a little change of pace after I brought the mood down. "True or Dare then?"

"I don't know if—"

"If you don't want to answer, you drink. You don't have to do anything you don't want or say anything you want to keep to yourself."

She tucks a strand of hair behind her ear, thinking over my rules. After a moment, she nods, and I can't help the relief that floods through me. I don't want this night to end yet, and by her agreement to play, I don't think she does, either.

"How about you go first," I say.

She places her shot glass back down then shifts so she can remove her flannel shirt from around her waist before setting her blue gaze on me. "Truth or Dare?"

"Truth," I say, liking that her action leads me to believe she's making herself more comfortable to stay awhile longer.

Presley's eyes narrow as if she's puzzled that I chose truth, but she doesn't miss a beat. "Why don't you and your brother get along?"

My chest stings. "You don't ease into anything, do you?"

She eyes me like I've got her totally wrong. But from what I've seen so far, she doesn't seem like the type of person to think things through. The fact that she moved to a small town like Randall then took a bartending and ranch hand job with what sounds like little to no experience—that's rather impulsive to me.

Not that I'm much better. I don't often think a lot of things through.

"You drinking then?" she taunts.

I lift the corner of my mouth. "I don't back down." Her lips mirror mine as I collect my thoughts to answer. After I take a sip of water, I look her in the eye. "Gavin and I—it's complicated. It's not that we don't get along, it's that he doesn't listen to me. He doesn't *try* to listen to me. He likes to lecture and talk at me instead."

"That doesn't answer my question," she says.

I sigh. "You really want to get into this?"

She leans back on her palms, her handful-sized breasts becoming more prominent so I can see them outlined under her white T-shirt. "You wanted to play," she says softly. "You chose truth."

She's right on both counts. I puff out a breath through my teeth before I begin. "My dad died last year from a heart attack. He left the ranch to Gavin after he said he'd leave it to me."

Presley stays quiet, her focus on me and her eyes soft. I lick my dry lips and take another sip of water.

Once I find my voice again, I let the story spill from my lips. I tell her about the lie Gavin told and how the dude ranch came to be, but I leave out the parts about my fight with him at the cemetery and the accident, because that has nothing to do with my relationship with him currently, not really.

When I'm done, Presley stares wide-eyed at me. "I'm sorry, Kade. You didn't deserve that." Her tone is so genuine, so real, it makes my chest smart. I don't think I've ever had anyone side with me, had anyone apologize—*really* apologize. And she doesn't even have anything to apologize for.

I clear the emotion now clogging my throat. "Thank you." I set my water bottle down before I ask. "What about you—truth or dare?"

Sensing that I need to change the subject, Presley sits a little taller. That almost full smile comes back to her lips. "Dare," she says.

I should've known that's what she'd pick. My brain sorts through different dares, ones I've made my friends do over the years. When an easy one comes to mind, I eye the open loft door. "I dare you to moon the cows."

She snorts. "You're serious?"

I shrug. "You wanted a dare."

She blows out a sharp breath but gets up off the ground, walking over to the open loft door before turning to face me. "Are you going to watch?" Her skin flushes.

"I have to make sure you do it. Remember, you can always drink," I hold up the half-empty bottle of whiskey.

She glances at the bottle then puts her hands behind her. She pulls her leggings down and up so fast I almost blinked and missed it.

I snort. "That was more like a crescent moon." Presley huffs and sits back down, crossing her arms over her chest.

"It was a stupid dare."

"Okay, smarty pants. I pick dare. Give me your best one."

She squints her pretty blue eyes in thought and strokes her upper lip like an evil scientist with a mustache. Her eyes open comically wide as if she's had a lightbulb moment, then she flushes bright red.

"What's the dare?" I urge, now more curious.

Her gaze darts to my lips and then to my eyes again. My heart rate picks up. She's not going to ask for a kiss, is she?

When she doesn't say anything, a smile spills across my features. "What's your dare, Presley?" My voice is testing. Teasing.

She licks her lips and shifts, recrossing her legs under her. It's a sign that she's turned on. I've been with enough partners to know the tells a woman gives when she wants me to do something to her body. And while Presley is normally guarded, the alcohol is opening her up like a book, making it easier to read the pages. If she wants me to kiss her, I'm not going to question it.

"Why did you stop calling me Lemon?" she asks.

My eyebrows shoot up to my hairline. Okay, maybe I was wrong about the kissing.

"That's not a dare," I say.

"Can you just tell me?"

Her voice is so full of pleading that I relent. "When I looked at your texts earlier, Derek, whoever he is, called you 'Sweetheart.' I don't know, I just—I didn't want to hurt you more than you were already hurting."

Her body jolts like I've shocked her with my words. I shift, moving closer to her when she doesn't say anything, my mind analyzing why she asked the question in the first place. Wanting to test a theory, I lower my voice and say "Lemon" in a hushed tone.

Presley's arms break out in goosebumps, and her breathing picks up. My hunch confirmed, I dare to move even closer to her until our crossed legs are only inches apart. "Do you like it when I call you Lemon?"

She doesn't speak, but she nods ever so slightly.

"Tell me why you like it."

She exhales a tense breath. "It's your turn."

I shake my head. "You asked me something; now I'm asking you."

"That's not—"

"Tell me, Lemon." I lean the top half of my body closer. "Why do you like it?"

Her eyes track to my lips then back up to my eyes again. "It feels special," she says, her voice almost a whisper. "I know it was meant as a joke, but—nobody has ever given me a nickname that means something only for me."

My heart aches at her words, but what she's saying makes sense. Everyone likes to feel special, to feel as if they mean something. To feel as if they mean something to *someone*—even if it's as simple as being called by a nickname.

"You deserve special, Lemon," I voice, not missing the way her eyes get glassy when I say it. "And the nickname isn't a joke—or at least, it's not to me, not anymore. Understand?"

She nods, blinking away the wetness in her eyes.

"Now, tell me your dare."

Her chest rises and falls underneath her shirt at a more rapid pace, and I find myself placing my finger under her chin so those beautiful pools of blue are looking straight into my eyes.

"Tell me your dare. Don't make me spank it out of you."

Her pupils expand, her nostrils getting wider, and the sudden heat in her gaze causes my blood to rush south and the front of my jeans to become uncomfortably tight. That comment aroused her just as much as it did me.

"Do it," she says, her words rushing out like a waterfall.

I swear my heart stops in my chest. "You want me to spank you, Lemon darlin'?" The endearment slips out attached to her special nickname, but before I can apologize, the smallest of moans escapes her lips. Clearly, she didn't mind this time. Maybe it's because of the closeness of this moment, or maybe it's because she knows I'm speaking it just for her.

I shift myself again so our crossed knees are touching, the heat of her body transferring to mine and setting me on fire, making my cock twitch.

"Presley." I run my finger down the soft skin of her cheek. "If that's what you want, I'll give it to you. But just know, there's a lot about me you don't know. I like this kind of thing. I like it a lot. I'm good at it, too. If you let me touch you in that way, if that's what you really want, I'll give it to you. But you have to want it."

Her eyes lock onto my mouth, her hands fidgeting in her lap. The evening sounds seem to deafen as I wait for her answer. Just when I'm about to call it quits, she lifts her chin so our eyes lock. I expect to see fear or unease—but instead, I notice a strength I've yet to see from her.

"I dare you to spank me, Kade."

A smile overtakes my lips, causing the dimples on my cheeks to form. I tuck a stray strand of frizzy blonde-and-violet hair behind her ear.

"Then get over my knees, Lemon. Let me teach you how to be a good girl."

CHAPTER 18

Presley

THIS IS WHY I shouldn't drink. I get myself into crazy situations. The last time I had too many margaritas, I slept with my boyfriend. See, crazy.

Kade moves slightly away from me to get more space then sits with his back straight, extending his legs so there's a place for me to lay over his lap. "You wanted this, Lemon. I'm waiting."

There's a teasing lift in his tone, but mostly, it's a command. The sound of it sends tingles down my spine and has my toes curling in my shoes. I didn't think I would be into this kind of thing, but Kade—I don't know. He's made me feel at ease, more comfortable than I have in a long time, if ever.

"I want to keep my clothes on," I rush out, the reality of the situation setting in. I don't know if I'm supposed to get naked for this, but it's the first thought that came to my awkward mind. I haven't been naked in front of anyone for a while now, and I've only had my clothes off in front of one man my entire life, so I don't want to go that far.

Kade keeps his eyes on mine, a gentle smile on his lips. It's the kind of smile someone gives when they're trying to soothe a person, as if they're worried they'll startle them.

"I didn't ask you to strip—I asked you to lay over my knees."

My cheeks burn, and my panties become wetter than they already are. From the moment we started playing poker, I found myself getting hot and bothered. The way he joked with me the whole time made me feel comfortable. How he whined about losing, but I could tell he was secretly impressed I'm such a good player. It was fun, the most fun I've had since college. Just like he said this night would be.

I survey his long jean-clad legs and then my own body. I'm larger than him. My rolls may be hidden by the loose shirt I'm wearing, but they're not gone. Derek always used to keep me on the bottom, and usually, we had sex with the lights out. While this isn't sex, I don't know how I feel about laying over his thinner legs, no matter how strong they are.

Kade's finger comes into view, and he's lifting my chin up again so our eyes lock. His hazel gaze is stern but still manages to be gentle.

"Presley," he says, his tone laced with such care that it stuns me for a moment. "Whatever you're thinking right now, stop. I want you over my knees. And if you aren't in the next five seconds, then I'm going to take that as a no, and we'll both walk out of here and go to bed. But if you want this, then get over here and offer me that beautiful ass of yours."

I don't know if it's the whiskey or the way he called a part of me beautiful, but my body starts moving. I get on my knees then crawl a bit, gracelessly I might add, until I'm over his legs with my forearms still propping me up so my weight is not on him.

"That's a good girl," he praises, his voice a low purr that sends shivers down my spine.

I'd never been called a good girl until Kade muttered the words earlier. And now hearing them once more only reaffirms that I like it. I want to hear him call me that again.

"Now lay down, and relax into me," he says.

My body tenses at the idea. I want to ask if I can stay like this. He could still get the job done, right?

"Can I touch you?" he asks against my ear. His calm tone eases my mind a bit, and I think of his hands on me. I agreed for him to spank me, so I basically asked him to touch me already. But the rest of my body? I inhale a breath, and then I remember the way it felt to have the warmth of his palm on my lower back earlier.

"Y-yes." I stumble over my words. "Just not my stomach."

Kade freezes but recovers quickly, letting out a breath as he moves. He puts his left arm under the space between my forearms so that the top of my breasts and collarbone will lay on top of it then presses his other hand between my shoulder blades. He runs his warm palm down my spine, moving slowly. When he gets to my low back, he applies gentle pressure, helping me ease down.

"Exhale, Lemon. Put all of your weight on me. Let me hold you."

Tears sting my eyes at his gentle words, words that mean more to me than he'll probably ever know. I blink away the emotion so I don't lose it and release the tense breath I've been holding. My stomach and pelvis relax into him as my chest presses into his arm under me. My knees are still gently bent to keep me steady, but I'm as relaxed as I can be in this position.

Kade slides the hand from my low back to my outside hip, gently tugging my body into his. With this movement, I can feel all of him, including his own arousal. It shocks me—but not only the hard length of it, more that he's turned on. I didn't expect it.

"That's it," he soothes. "You did that so well."

The combination of how he feels and his gentle praise has those dang tears threatening to come back. I try to hold them in, but I'm failing. Why is this so emotional? I'm going to blame the whiskey because this shouldn't be making me cry. This should only be hot. I mean, it is, but why do I feel like I want to cry at every word he says? At every touch?

"Lemon," he says gently. "Look at me."

I squeeze my eyes shut, hoping that what I'm feeling doesn't show before I turn my head to him. He shifts his arm under my chest so I'm more supported, the small movement doing nothing to help keep my emotions at bay.

"Feel whatever you need to feel. Let me take care of you."

Now Kade is the one surprising me. Isn't something like this supposed to be a few swats, then it's over? Why does it feel like so much more than that when we haven't even started?

Despite the swirling thoughts in my mind, I nod.

"If I spank you too hard, tell me to go lighter. If you want me to stop, I'll stop. Do you understand?"

I nod again, but apparently, that's not good enough for him.

"Use that smart mouth of yours, Lemon. Do you understand—yes or no?" He grins, his eyes smiling with it.

I instinctively squeeze my thighs together at how he speaks to me. It's still commanding, but the light flirting I've come to know as uniquely Kade is there, too. It lightens the mood a bit, making everything we're doing more comfortable.

"Yes."

"Good girl." He squeezes my hip then moves his palm to my ass, holding it there. "I'm going to start light. Breathe through it, and just let yourself experience it. Don't think so much. You understand?"

"I'll try not to." His palm comes down on my ass lightly, and I jump in surprise. His hand under my chest holds me tighter.

He swats me again. "Only try, Lemon?"

"Okay! I won't think so much." I squirm, every nerve ending in my body buzzing.

He rubs his hand over my legging-clad ass and hums. "Attagirl. I like it when you follow directions." He lifts his palm off my ass, and I think he's going to spank me, but then I feel his fingers lightly stroking over my covered skin in a teasing motion. "Fuck, your body is so beautiful. This ass." He punctuates his point by squeezing it a bit. "It's a work of art."

Blood rushes to my cheeks. Oddly enough, I find his compliments more embarrassing than what we're doing. I want to protest his words, to tell him he doesn't have to lie to me, but when his hand comes down on my butt again, he swings it in an upward motion so only part of his palm spanks me.

I cry out, but before I can recover, he does it again and again, switching cheeks as he swats. The barrage of sensations clears all my thoughts from my mind until all I can think about is the way his hand feels against my body and how his erection gets harder as I shift against him from the force of his spanks.

I'm not sure how many he's done—and they aren't very hard—when he suddenly stops. After a pause, he lays his hand on my heated backside, causing me to jump, but instead of spanking, he goes back to rubbing his palms over the stinging skin.

"How was that?" His voice sounds different, huskier. My thighs rub together of their own accord, and I can't help but notice how wet I am. I hope I don't leave a wet spot on his pants—that would be embarrassing.

A strike on my ass, one a little harder than before, has me turning to meet his intense gaze. His hazel eyes are almost brown in the darkened loft as he waits for my answer.

"I liked it."

A sly grin plays at the corner of his lips. "Do you want more?"

"Yes," I say, not having to think about it. Maybe it's the endorphins talking, but I want whatever he'll give me.

Kade hums, the hand under my chest moving. His forearm now rests between my breasts, and his rough hand comes to gently grip the column of my throat. The action has me thinking of what I witnessed in the back room, how he'd held that woman's neck as he kissed her.

It turned me on then, and now that it's me, more arousal floods my sex. I become highly aware of every inch of my body. My nipples are hard, pressing against the thin cups of my bra. My breasts feel heavy, like they're aching to be touched, and the same goes for every inch of my skin as if all of my nerves are on fire and only Kade can put them out. Even my clit pulses with need, a sensation I've never had.

"Is this okay?" His fingers press softly into my neck.

"More than okay," I breathe out.

He hums again, and I swear he looks proud of me. His chest is puffed and broad, and a sure, closed-mouthed grin is on his lips. His eyes are soft and sparkling.

"I'm going to go harder this time. Do you want that, Lemon?"

I nod, and that earns me a spank that is indeed harder. "Yes! Please, Kade. Go harder."

His mouth drops to the shell of my ear, and he runs the tip of his nose over the sensitive skin. I shiver as he says, "You're a quick learner. I like it."

He pulls his lips back and sits up, his grip on my throat tightening as his palm comes down on my ass. This time, he doesn't tease; he spanks me with more force like he promised. He uses his whole palm now, and because I'm so turned on, I feel every hit more strongly. His smacks are firecrackers on my skin that spark and smart, causing me to squirm against him and cry out with soft sounds of pleasure mixed with pain.

Kade stops his spanks, and his grip on my throat becomes heavier. He adjusts us, his body moving underneath me so I can feel even more of his very hard length digging into the skin of my low stomach.

His mouth returns to my ear. "If you keep squirming, I'm going to have to get out my ropes."

Ropes? I've seen rope bondage on the internet before, but I guess I never thought someone like me would be into it. Apparently, that's not true, because the image of me tied up over his lap has a moan I didn't plan to utter bursting from me and bouncing off the walls of the loft.

An amused chuckle escapes him. "Good to know for next time." I don't have time to think about what he said because he brings his hand down on my ass again. "Now breathe, darlin'. Remember what I said. Feel what you need to feel."

My body immediately relaxes at the way he says *darlin'*. This man and his nicknames. But just like with Lemon, the way he says it with his sweet Southern drawl has me feeling special, like he's saying it just for me.

There's also the fact that he stopped using the nicknames after the texts he saw. Despite my desire to smack him for invading my privacy, I understand why he looked. Maybe it's silly that I had a change of heart about it all, but these nicknames are different. They aren't said to be condescending or generic; they're said for me. They're a part of who he is—and I'm starting to really like this man.

A strong spank to my left ass cheek has me releasing a groan.

"Stop thinking. Let that mind of yours be free, Presley."

Tears that had gone threaten to come back, and I clamp my eyes shut. He spanks me again and again, and I exhale through the pain.

"That's it, my good girl. Just feel what I do to you. Let this beautiful body of yours take over."

A tear leaks from the corner of my eye, and I drop my upper body into the pressure of his hand around my neck and his forearm between my breasts.

"You're amazing," he purrs between swats, his fingers stopping to tease the sensitive skin now and then. "Thank you for trusting me. Thank you for trusting me with your body and your mind."

My chest tightens, and I think I'm starting to understand Kade more, why he likes this—the control, the trust—especially given what he told me about his family situation earlier.

Smack. Smack. Smack.

"Oh my god, Kade!" A cry leaves my lips, and I can't take it back, so I turn scarlet. I never make sounds.

Kade notices my reaction. "Be as loud as you want. Let it out." He tightly holds the heated skin of my ass then smacks the cheeks harder this time.

"Oh, fuck," I groan. It's starting to really hurt now, but to my shock, I like it even more. The pain gives me a certain sense of freedom, of release, like he's been wanting me to have.

Kade chuckles, so I open my eyes. His teeth are showing as he smiles down at me. "I was wondering if I could get you to swear." He hits me again, and I curse again. "I like this side of you."

He's right; swearing has never really been my thing. I always figured there was no reason for it, but it feels appropriate considering how he's making my body feel right now. I couldn't hold back even if I tried.

Kade stops his spanking and glides his hand up my spine until his fingers reach my hair. He tugs on the ponytail a bit, and a keening noise unfurls like a curl of smoke from my lips. I swear I feel Kade's cock jump beneath me, and without thinking, I rub my aroused sex on his thigh. I gasp from the short relief then freeze when I realize what I've done.

He tugs on my ponytail again, and at the same time, the hand on my neck applies a pinch of pressure, his thumb digging into my thrumming pulse point. Kade turns my head. "Do you want something from me, Presley?"

My full name on his lips has me squirming again. He's done what I dared him to do; he doesn't have to do any more. But I'm feeling bolder with the alcohol and endorphins coursing through my blood—plus, the way he's been praising my body has given me a high, even if I'm not sure he meant it.

"It's your turn," I say.

He looks confused for a moment, but then his eyes light up. His hand grips tighter on my ponytail as he hovers his mouth above my ear and takes the lobe between his teeth. He bites down hard enough that I gasp, my sex rocking against his thigh.

"Truth or Dare?" Kade's breath against my skin is hot and sensual, and I swear I'm going to combust. I haven't had an orgasm in...a long time, and I've never felt like this, like if I don't get some relief, I may just cease to exist. Is this even normal?

"Truth," I manage to say.

"Do you want me to get you off, Presley?" Kade takes the lobe of my ear between his teeth again.

"Yes, Kade." His erection throbs against my clothed skin, and I bet if we weren't dressed, it would burn me.

"Say please," he commands, his nose teasing the shell of my ear.

A bead of sweat drips from my forehead, and I want to curse this man for making me speak as much as he is, for making me plead. But I do it anyway. "Please, Kade. Please touch me."

A growl comes from his lips as he pulls back. His hand leaves my ponytail, and I think he's going to touch me where I most want him, but he spanks me instead. I gasp, and he keeps me still with a gentle squeeze to my neck. He spanks me a few more times until I'm crying out, the sting of my skin almost unbearable. Just when I'm about to tell him to stop, he does on his own, rubbing his palm over each burning cheek.

"Such a good girl. You're taking my hand so well."

Kade continues to praise me as he rubs the skin, his hand moving lower until his fingers reach the heated skin of my sex.

"Put your ass up for me a bit, Lemon darlin'. I need better access to that dripping pussy."

His dirty words wash over me, the heat of them making my clit pulse and heart beat loudly in my ears. As if my body is a puppet just for him, I dip my stomach into him as much as I can so his hard length presses further into me and my ass rises higher.

"Perfect," he whispers. "Just perfect."

I close my eyes as his fingers return to my cheeks. I hiss a bit as he teases the flaming skin under my leggings.

"You're not going to be able to sit down tomorrow, Lemon. But I like that you'll be thinking of me all day." His comment only adds to my need for him to touch me. I grind into him as best I can, and he chuckles. "Such a needy girl. You want my fingers on you, don't you?"

"Yes, please. Please, Kade. I can't—"

Finally, he gives me what I want. He maneuvers his hand so he's cupping my sex, slightly lifting my lower body. The pressure has me cursing again, much to his delight.

He squeezes my pussy at the same time his hand grips my throat. With how tight my body is strung and the aroused whimper that leaves me, he has to know it's not going to take much for me to come.

Kade lets up on the pressure and lowers my body back down so he can press two of his fingers right where my clit is. My arousal-soaked clothes only add to the much-needed friction I desire, though now I'm wondering what his bare fingers would feel like. How would his work-calloused skin feel stroking me?

He removes his hand and spanks me once more before placing it back on my folds, pressing into my clit again.

"Oh, yes, that feels..."

"Feels what, darlin'?"

"So damn good."

I said the swear word on purpose, and when I feel his cock jump under me, I know it had the desired effect. He moves his fingers over my swollen clit in firmer strokes, and I shift forward, seeking more pressure from his hand around my throat. When he figures out what I'm asking, he doesn't hesitate to give it to me. His grip tightens so it constricts my breathing just a tiny bit, sending even more wetness between my thighs.

Kade pulls back the pressure and spanks me again at the same time. I cry out, feeling my orgasm just at the brink of exploding. My body shakes as so many emotions take over—arousal, fear, anger, happiness, pleasure, sadness...all of it.

"That's it, Presley, let go. I've got you." His fingers circle my clit, and the pressure on my throat returns.

"Yes," I cry softly. My spine tingles as he gives my swollen nub a firm stroke, finally sending me over the edge. My vision blackens, then fireworks explode in a million different colors behind my eyelids as I come completely undone, spiraling down into a pit of pleasure as my body shakes and trembles while being held firmly by Kade.

I've had orgasms before, but this? I don't know what it is. I'm faintly aware that my cries are no longer just cries of pleasure, but relief. The pain I've been carrying expels from me, and my body almost flops against Kade's, but his strength doesn't waver. He's still there holding me, helping me ride the emotional waves as I fly high and then start to plummet back to earth.

With heavy breaths, I faintly hear Kade telling me to breathe. I do as he says, my shaking body easing into small sparking aftershocks as I feel his hand brush a tear I hadn't known escaped from my cheek, then another one. Am I really crying?

Kade presses a light kiss to my forehead. "You're unreal," I think I hear him whisper, but I could've easily imagined it with how high I feel right now.

"Presley," he says, his voice loud enough that I know he's speaking this time.

I pry open my wet eyes to stare into his hazel ones and find them softer now, not hard and demanding like they were before. "How are you feeling?"

I open my mouth, but it's dry. Kade must've noticed or expected it because he shifts, still keeping me over his lap as he grabs his water bottle. He holds it to my lips, and even though this moment feels too vulnerable, I take the offered water.

He brushes a strand of hair back from my cheek after I've finished drinking. "Was it too much?"

I finally manage to find my voice. "No. It was..." I stare into his eyes, trying to convey to him that it was one of the most profound moments of my life. That seems silly given it was nothing I ever would have seen myself doing, but I feel lighter, like a weight has been lifted from my shoulders.

Kade nods, giving me another sip of water. "Thank you for sharing that with me, Presley. You were so brave and open." His thumb brushes over my tear-stained cheek before he pulls his hand back. "Thank you."

Confusion must show in my eyes because he smiles gently. "We can talk more about it later, but we should get some rest. We have chores in the morning."

The air around us seems to shift, and while I was expecting it to be awkward after what we've just done, it's not.

When I go to move off Kade's lap, he stops me. "Where do you think you're going, Lemon?"

My brow furrows, and a light chuckle leaves his lips. "I thought we were done."

I don't miss the way his gaze drops to my mouth before our eyes connect again. "Let's lie down for a moment. That was a lot on your body and mind. Rest a bit, and then we can head back down."

My cheeks flush as I stare into his caring gaze. He's serious about his request, and I can't help but think this feels like a lot more than just a dare between friends...coworkers?

Gently, Kade helps me off his lap so I can lie down beside him. A part of me wants to argue and retreat to the hands' quarters, to process what we just did. But if I'm being honest with myself, I'm not ready to leave yet. To leave him.

I lie down on the blanket and try to hide my flush that seems to be a constant around him. Kade takes a sip of water then moves to lie down beside me. I think he's going to keep distance between us, but then he pulls me into him so my head rests against his chest.

"Relax, Presley," he says as he tugs the extra blanket he brought over us. "Remember not to think so much."

I try to do as he says and settle against his warmth. I inhale a few breaths, allowing his steady touch and the sound of his thumping heart to ease both my mind and my still-thrumming body. I breathe a satisfied sigh, and my eyes begin to droop.

As I drift off toward sleep, I swear I feel Kade press a soft kiss to my forehead.

But maybe I imagined it.

CHAPTER 19

Kade

IN MY DREAM, I'm warm. I'm content. It smells like fresh berries and a summer breeze. I inhale again and something tickles my nose.

My eyes open at the sensation, and I realize I'm not dreaming. A smile plays at the corner of my lips as I take in the scene.

The upper half of Presley's body is laying over me, acting as my own heated blanket. Her head is resting in the crook of my neck, putting the top of her blonde head near my nose.

That explains the smell of fresh berries and summer. It must be her shampoo.

I check my watch, careful not to disturb her sleeping form. It's just about five, which means I have to wake her soon, but I let myself indulge in her presence before I do.

The soft yellow light we left on in the barn allows me to see her even though the sun hasn't risen yet. She's gripping the fabric of my shirt in her hand like it's a rescue rope. My gaze drags up the black and gray flower tattoos on her arms, and if she weren't asleep, I'd give in to the itch to trace the fine lines of them, each and every petal. They're beautiful, just like her.

A soft sound escapes her slightly parted lips, and I study her face. Unlike when she's awake, her features are relaxed now, making her look younger and softer. When I see the bit of mascara smudged under her eyes from her tears last night, my chest aches for her.

Whatever our "game" helped her release, it felt important. And I meant what I said—I was grateful she'd shared it with me. But while I learned more about her last night than I knew before, it did nothing to quench my thirst for getting to know everything about her; it only fueled it. I want to know her past, her present, what makes her smile, blush, and curse...what she released last night that made her cry. I want to know it all.

I gently brush a lock of hair from her cheek and twirl a soft strand of it around my finger. Since my doctor's appointment, I've experienced a whirlwind of emotions. I've been hurt, and in turn, I've hurt a lot of people I love. But there's been one consistent thing: Every time I'm around this woman, I feel something other than rage and hurt.

And after what we shared last night...

I squeeze my eyes shut and try to be a gentleman while she's sleeping, not wanting to make the morning wood situation I've already got going on worse. Instead, I think of what I experienced beyond the sexual nature of it.

I've done spanking sessions like hers before. When I was starting to explore kink, spanking was one of the first things I discovered outside of rope bondage. I enjoyed it right away. The control I feel, helping the person I'm partnered with explore the pain and giving themselves over to it, and the trust. That's my favorite part of kink, and it's been too long since I've gotten to really explore that aspect of it. Lately, everything has just been a way to get my own release, to be free of the ache in my heart. To numb the pain.

If I'm being honest with myself, last night was the first time I've felt this connected to one of my partners, like what she experienced transferred to me. Because despite the fact I have a hangover from the whiskey we drank, I feel...lighter. Like today may be a little easier than yesterday. The idea has my heart aching in my chest for an entirely different reason.

Presley shifts, snuggling deeper into me like I'm her own personal teddy bear. I grin into her hair and press a kiss to it softly. When she sighs, that contentment in my chest grows. Is it possible to feel this way about someone you haven't even kissed? That seems irrational.

I'm sure if I would ask Gavin, he'd say I've never been good at being rational, but I disagree. He sees my anger as immaturity, but he doesn't understand, not really. We've both lost. We both have insurmountable grief and have been through hard times. But he thinks my age makes me fly off the handle more quickly and make poor decisions. And while I have made poor decisions, so has he. I don't think he truly gets that, even if he says he does.

Presley sighs and stirs again, her body waking up. I reach for the almost empty water bottle, wishing I had brought more with me. Normally, after what we did last night, I would have taken her to bed and made sure she had a full stomach and lots of water, even given her some ibuprofen. But we'd both been exhausted and fell asleep. I'm sure she's going to feel a lot of things today, many of which are not pleasant. The thought makes the bit of sadism in me preen. As I told her last night, I like that she'll feel me all day and be reminded of what happened between us.

I glance at my watch again and decide we do need to get up. I have an idea brewing in my mind—one she'll probably hate—but I think, in the end, she'll love it. I know we've both got shifts at Night Hawk tonight, too, which means we have a very long day ahead of us.

"Open your eyes, Lemon darlin'." I smile to myself at the nickname, taking more pleasure in it now that I know she likes it.

Her eyes snap open, and she sits up way too quickly for someone hungover. She groans, pressing her hand to her forehead as her eyes close. I sit up and rest my hand on her shoulder to steady her.

"Drink this." I hold the water bottle to her lips as she opens her eyes. She's blinking rapidly, her brow furrowed, probably confused after waking up so suddenly. For a second, I think she's going to refuse or try to grab the bottle from my hand, but she puts her lips to the plastic, letting me tip the liquid into her mouth. Her nose screws up, and she puts her hand over where I'm holding the bottle so I can't give her more.

"It's warm."

I chuckle. "It's been sitting in this muggy loft all night. If we get moving, we can get a good breakfast and cool water before chores."

Presley's eyes move to her hand over mine, then she pulls hers away as if she was burned. I try not to take it personally since she just woke up from a brand-new experience and is hungover. She clamps her eyes shut again, and as if she's watching a movie, I see her replay last night in her mind. Her skin flushes, and then she grimaces at the movement of her butt on the floor.

"Are you okay?" I ask.

When her soulful blue eyes look into mine, they seem darker than usual in the low light. She purses her lips then takes in a breath. "I feel..." She pauses, looking down at her body then back to my eyes again. "...different."

I school my expression to appear neutral, happy she's not just running out of the barn embarrassed. That is what I would've expected from the woman I first met in the back alley of Night Hawk. But she's right, she *is* different—or maybe she's just more comfortable.

She rubs the back of her neck and stretches it from side to side then closes her eyes. She processes for another moment before she meets my stare again. "I...I, um..."

I quickly come to her rescue. "You don't have to say anything right now, Presley—just let yourself have a moment. It's normal to feel different after a big emotional release. Not to mention, you're hungover and running on hardly any sleep. You should shower, get some food and water. Then, if you need to, we can talk more about how you're feeling."

She tucks some loose hair behind her ear and nods in agreement, her body easing at the affirmation from me that she doesn't need to figure everything out right now. She can just be.

I stand first then hold out my hand to help her up. Presley shakes her head, refusing my assistance. Still stubborn, I see. But maybe another session or two will help her realize that she can accept help, even if she doesn't technically need it. It's obvious to me that whoever was in her life before didn't give a rat's ass about her or her feelings. They tore her down. Her comment about staying fully clothed—and specifically the one about me not touching her stomach—has left a simmering rage in me since she uttered them. I'm surprised it hasn't burned a hole in my gut.

Once Presley's standing, she winces again, bringing one of her hands to her butt. She hisses when her palm meets the fabric, and I have the urge to kiss it better.

"I have some balm that will help with the soreness."

Presley's head whips around to look at me as if she forgot I was standing there. If I had a wish, I would want to hear what's going on inside her head right now.

"Thanks," she mumbles, clasping her hands in front of her body.

I give her a firm nod before I collect the things from the ground with her help. Once everything's secured in the canvas bag, I turn my focus back to her. "Let's go before Art or one of the other ranch hands finds us up here, yeah?"

She gasps, covering her mouth with her hand. "Oh my gosh. I didn't even think about that last night. Do you think anyone heard or saw us?" Her voice is high-pitched with worry, and her body goes taut.

I close the small distance between us and tuck a piece of hair behind her ear. She tracks the movement of my hand, licking her dry lips as if she's imagining them somewhere else—maybe on her pussy again. The idea of it has the blood returning to my cock. I clear my throat to try to will that image away; we have work to do. Later, we can play if she'll allow it.

"Don't worry." I pull my hand back. "Nobody comes here except me at night. Everyone is usually in bed by nine, anyway."

She exhales her relief and bites her lower lip.

"Come on. Let's get going."

I hold my hand out for her to take, the action surprising not only Presley but myself. I've never really been a hand-holder, unless you count the girlfriend I had in my junior year of high school. Presley regards it curiously, as if she's never held a hand, either, but then, after a short moment, she places hers in mine.

As soon as our skin touches, the ache in my chest that seems to persist most days eases. My shoulders I didn't know were tense sag, and I squeeze her hand in mine as if it's a tether to reality. It shouldn't feel this easy with her, but I don't want to question it.

I tug her hand and lead her out of the barn.

"I'm not riding a horse," Presley objects, hands on her jean-clad hips.

We've finished morning chores, which took longer now that we have an extra ten stalls to clean and horses to feed. Then I made sure Presley and I had a snack and some water before our next task. This one is more fun—at least for me.

"We need to start testing out the horses and evaluate them for guests."

"You're going to use me as a test dummy?"

I chuckle. "Of course not."

The sound of hooves and footsteps approaching reach my ears, and I glance toward the barn to see Art with a tacked-up bay gelding.

I turn back to Presley. "I'm going to ride him first, and you can watch. But all the horses we bought are seasoned trail horses, so they're safe. Some might have a little more spunk than others, and we'll try to save them for the more experienced riders, but even that level of spice isn't very spicy."

"Howdy," Art says, tipping his hat to us both. "This is Big John."

Presley eyes the horse up and down. "You want me to get on a horse named *Big John*?" The squeal in her voice has Art and I stifling a laugh. "This isn't funny! What if Big John gets mad and I die?"

"Lemon." I step toward her, not caring that Art is here, and place my hands on her shoulders. "Take a breath."

She does as I ask, and it makes me feel great. Before yesterday, she probably would've ignored me and said she was fine.

"You're not going to die," I assure her. "We were told this horse is great for kids. I'll ride first, and then you can get on him. Think you'd be willing to try?"

Her blue eyes close for a moment, and she sucks in another breath. When she opens them, she seems calmer. There's even a small glint in her eye.

"I wouldn't hold your breath," she chuffs.

Art laughs, and I shake my head at her, clicking my tongue against the back of my teeth.

"Such a smart mouth." Then I lean in closer to her ear and whisper, "But we'll work on that."

I wink and step back to face a very curious Art. He's got an eyebrow raised at me that says, *What the hell was that?*

I ignore it, taking the split reins from his hand and thanking him. "Can you bring another one of the horses out for me in forty minutes? Maybe that palomino they said was for experienced riders?"

Art, still eyeing me, nods. "Sure thing, boss."

I roll my eyes at him. He knows I hate when he calls me that—especially since I hardly have any pull around here. The only reason I know anything about the new horse is because this is one of the tasks I was given by Gavin during a short conversation that was only about work and lasted all of five minutes. He'd handed me a packet of papers with a profile of each horse and the information we were given on them from their previous owner, then he told me to ride them and get a feel for each one.

Once Art's gone, I turn back to Presley. She's staring at Big John like he's going to eat her. The horse is just standing there, his tail swishing at flies and ears twitching.

"Come over here, darlin'."

Presley's eyes snap to mine at her nickname, and one of the hands on her hips shifts to reflexively rub at her butt through her black jeans. I can't help the sly grin that appears on my face because I know she's thinking about the first time I called her darlin'.

"You feeling okay?" I ask.

Presley glances at her hand on her ass, her gaze sheepish when she focuses on me again. Her hand moves back to her hip, and she blushes. "I'm fine."

"Mm-hmm. Do you need more balm?"

She shakes her head, cheeks turning pinker. "I'm good. It doesn't hurt."

"That's good to hear." I look around to make sure nobody is in earshot before I murmur, "That just means next time, I'll have to go harder."

Presley's mouth drops open, but I don't say anything else. I step back and throw the reins over Big John's head, looping them over the saddle horn before I mount. He's a big boy, probably over sixteen hands, but he's gentle. I don't have to be told that to see it.

The gelding hasn't moved a centimeter since Art brought him out, and I didn't see any crazy in his eyes, something I always look for. It's easy to tell sometimes, like a twinkle in their soulful gaze that says, *If you screw with me, I'll buck your ass off.* Big John has none of that.

The Texas sun beats down on my back as I stare at Presley from beneath the brim of my cowboy hat. She's wearing her typical T-shirt and jeans with the borrowed pair of boots, ones I've noticed she keeps pulling at around her calves, signaling they're too tight. I make a mental note to try to find her a different pair. She's also got on one of my Texas Longhorn ball caps to protect her eyes from the sun. I really like seeing her wear something of mine, and I'd be lying if I said I didn't already dream up images of her in the cap, naked and on my lap with her head thrown back as she rides me.

I clear my throat and shift in the saddle. If I think about her naked any longer, this will be an uncomfortable and embarrassing ride.

"I'm just going to do a little warm up and test him out. Then I'll get you on."

"Kade," she whines. "I don't think that's a good idea."

"Just watch me, okay? Then you can decide." I mean it, too, because at the end of the day, I'm not going to force her to do anything she doesn't want to do.

"Okay, but I'm not making any promises."

"I wouldn't expect you to, Lemon. Now watch me ride."

CHAPTER 20

Presley

WATCHING KADE MONTGOMERY ON a horse is...

Wow.

I think I've developed a cowboy kink. Or a Kade kink. Am I into kink now?

I feel hotter than the sun as memories of last night make their way into the forefront of my mind *again*. Not that I've been able to forget—it's all I can think about.

I may have fibbed a little when I said I wasn't sore. While it's not bad, occasionally my jeans and underwear rub against my skin just right, and it burns a bit. But I like it. Because he's right—it reminds me of him and what we did. And while I didn't think I'd want to be reminded of being spanked, fingered, and brought to tears fully clothed over his lap, I find I'm not that embarrassed. At least, not in the way I thought I would be—it's more so because I liked it.

"Presley," Kade calls to me from atop Big John. I'm standing outside the gate of what he called a "round pen." Which is literally that: a circular pen made with metal piping. "Are you hearing anything I'm saying?"

I smile bashfully. "Um, can you repeat it?"

He shakes his head, but I can see he's amused. "One of the most important things is to stay relaxed. Keep your heels down, your hips open, and your seat"—he points to his ass—"in the right position. We don't want you to be pinching your knees." He shows me what he means by gripping the horse with his knees, making his heels pop up. Then he puts his heels down and relaxes again. "See?"

"I see."

He continues to walk the horse around the circular pen. "Big John here won't give you any trouble, but it's important not to be tense while on a horse. They respond to your seat, to your emotions. If anything were to happen, if they were to get spooked, the best thing to do is to try to remain as calm as possible."

"You're not making me want to get on him."

That throaty chuckle of his reaches my ears. At one point, it would've annoyed me, but now his laughter sends tingles up my spine.

"Just watch me a bit more, Lemon. He's harmless. I would never put you in danger."

His words wrap around my heart, and I feel another one of my walls start to crumble. How is this man getting into my system so quickly? Should I be worried?

Trying not to think too much—like I normally do—I focus on Kade.

As he walks Big John around the pen, he tells me more about the basics of riding. How to steer the horse, how to use my legs, different vocal cues. One thing *does* become clear: Big John seems like a good boy. I have to admit he's kind of cute, too. He's a dark reddish-brown color that almost looks mahogany in the right light, and I like his long black mane and tail. My favorite part, though, is that he's got a white marking on his forehead that looks like a heart.

Kade clucks to the horse and tells him to trot. At first, Big John doesn't listen, so Kade gives him a little tap with the spurs he put on his boots earlier. The horse finally picks up speed, but it's slow.

Kade laughs, the sound carefree and light. I like seeing him like this, so unlike the man I first met.

"Well," he calls, "nobody will be winning any barrel races with this guy, but he'll do fine for what we need him for."

I don't know what he means by any of that, but I watch Kade for another ten minutes, enjoying the way he works with the large animal underneath him. He talks to Big John a lot as he rides, patting his neck and moving the horse around like he could do it in his sleep. I allow myself to forget about anything and everything and let watching him become an almost religious experience. He's good at this. *Really* good at this.

Yep, I definitely have developed a Kade kink.

After a while, he brings Big John to a stop near where I'm standing—still safely outside the pen—then hops down. "Your turn."

"I don't know if that's a good idea."

Kade unlatches the gate and opens it with the hand not holding the reins. "Come in here, and we'll go slow."

I stare at the horse then into Kade's soft hazel eyes. "Please don't let me die."

He purses his lips as I step into the pen, closing the gate behind me so I'm trapped between him, the horse, and the metal piping. "I promise," he says, his voice low and sincere. "Nothing is going to happen to you. Trust me, Lemon."

"I trust you," I say without hesitation. Not only because I want to say the words, but also because it's true. After last night and how he went out of his way this morning to care for me—making sure I ate, drank, and took ibuprofen and giving me that mentholated balm—I feel as though I can trust him, no matter how stupid that may be, especially considering my past. But I have to go with my intuition on this one, and it's telling me that, despite the rocky start we had, I can trust him.

When Kade's eyes light up and his entire face softens, as if those three simple words had a profound effect on him, I know I've made the right choice. He squeezes my bicep gently before he pulls back, motioning for me to stand at Big John's neck.

"Stroke his neck and shoulder; chat with him for a bit."

Even though I watched Kade talk to him, it feels silly to talk to a horse. I tentatively press my hand against the beast's warm neck, his soft hair tickling the skin of my palm.

"Breathe, Lemon. Remember, horses feel your emotions. They're sensitive animals, but you have no reason to be scared of Big John here."

I do as he says and exhale, stroking down the horse's neck. "Hi, Big John. You're a big boy, aren't you?" As soon as the words are out of my mouth, I feel heat creep up my neck. Why is this embarrassing?

"That's it. You're doing great."

His praise has me flushing harder as I remember him praising me last night. For crying out loud—I've turned into a horndog after one intimate moment with him. Well, more than a moment.

But if Kade notices my reaction, he doesn't say anything about it.

"Do you want to try to sit on him?"

I stroke Big John's neck and look into his soulful brown eyes. "Don't hurt me," I tell him. The horse snorts, and I jump back, bumping into the wall of Kade's chest.

"That was his way of saying he's not going to hurt you," he says, his mouth now near my ear. I allow myself to stay in his warm embrace, relishing the way I can feel his chest rise and fall as he breathes. Just as I'm about to step back, Kade leaves a lingering kiss on the top of my head like he did as I was falling asleep. I tilt my chin up at him, and he looks almost as shocked as me that he did it.

He recovers after a second and smiles so his dimples are showing. "You can do this. I know you can. I'll be right beside you."

I nod. "Let's do this before I change my mind."

The look of pride he gave me last night returns, and I can't help but feel fueled by it. Nobody has ever looked at me like that. Not my parents, not Derek, no one.

"Okay. I'll give you a leg up. We don't have mounting blocks around here, but I'll be sure to get one for the future." Kade has me follow him to the center of the pen then adjusts the stirrups for me so they're shorter. Once he's done, he motions for me to stand near the saddle.

"You're going to put your left leg in the stirrup and take hold of the reins and the saddle horn with your left hand. Then I'm going to help swing you over by supporting your right leg and pushing you up."

I shake my head at the thought of him lifting me up in any capacity. "Kade, no. Isn't there a rock or something?"

"Lemon." He lets out a sad sigh. "I don't know what's going through that pretty head of yours, but whatever you're thinking, stop. Let those thoughts go, or I'll spank them out of you again." He taps my butt to emphasize his point, and I jump. Then he brings his lips to my ear. "Now put your foot in that stirrup, and let's get you on this horse."

My gaze meets his. He looks like he did last night before he spanked me, all authoritative and sexy. I find myself nodding and doing as he asks. Kade stays at my back as I wrap my left hand now holding the reins around the horn, my body tensing as I realize this is actually happening. I'm about to get on a horse.

"Just breathe through your fear, darlin'. Remember, I got you."

I exhale the rigid breath I've been holding as he bends down to grab my booted calf.

"Bend your knee, and then when I count, you jump on three. Got it?" he asks.

"Got it," I answer, bending my knee.

"Good girl." His words send shivers up my spine as he starts to count. "One...two...three." I jump on three, and Kade hoists me up with strength I didn't expect. I let out a squeal as I awkwardly flop on top of Big John, who, to his credit, doesn't move an inch.

"Look at you, Cowgirl."

My thighs grip the large animal as my hands turn white around the saddle horn. It's high up here, but at least I'm not afraid of heights, just mechanical failure. Or in this case, Big John failure.

Once I get my bearings, I relax my hands a little and stare at the horse's ears flicking back and forth. It hits me then what I'm doing, and a feeling of pride begins to swell in my low stomach. I'm facing a fear of mine.

"Holy shit—I'm on a horse!" I exclaim.

Kade releases a deep belly laugh. "You're on a horse. And you swore again."

I smile down at him, a wide smile that has my cheeks starting to hurt. A sensation that feels an awful lot like happiness spreads through my body like wildfire.

Kade stares up at me with a look of wonder on his face, like this is the first time he's ever seen a smile before. His hazel eyes are gentle, and after a moment, a grin to rival mine appears on his lips. The way he beams has the sensation of pride in my stomach turning into an entirely different one—one that feels an awful lot like a thousand butterflies.

The hand that's still on my calf tightens, and he licks his lips. "Feel okay?"

I take another breath and nod. "Yeah, better than okay."

He squeezes my calf one more time then pulls his hand away. "Good. Now put those heels down and relax your legs. You're telling him to go right now. You're lucky he's lazy."

I immediately do what he says, willing my legs and thighs to relax more. As soon as my butt sinks deeper into the seat of the saddle, the burn left over from Kade's slaps becomes more prominent. The sensation has me biting the inside of my cheek to stifle a small groan, and my brow furrows.

When my gaze meets Kade's, he looks like the cat who caught the canary. "So you *are* feeling it, huh?"

"It's not bad."

He tsks, tapping my thigh. "You'll pay for that, Lemon darlin'. But let's get you moving. We'll talk about that later."

"Move?!" I squeak, making Big John's ears flick at me.

"You can't just sit in one spot. It's time to practice riding now. Unless you'd rather ride me." He winks.

I'm unable to stop the huff of laughter that leaves my lips—there's the Kade I first met. But this time, I think he means it. My nipples harden beneath my bra, and I try to clear my mind of the images he put there. He may be flirting with me, but it's not like we're going to take this further or do something like date. I can't date right now, and he doesn't do serious relationships—at least from what I've heard. It would be silly of me to think otherwise, right?

I blow out a long breath. "Okay, let's try it. But don't leave me, please."

The words come out more pleading than I expect, and Kade's eyes soften. "Like I said, I'll be right here."

"Okay." I nod.

"Okay." He grins, patting the horse's shoulder. "Let's turn this city girl into a cowgirl, Big John."

CHAPTER 21

Kade

I REACH INTO THE freezer and grab a flexible ice pack with Velcro, strapping it to my forearm, right where the break from my accident was. I've felt great since getting the all clear from my doctor, but all the ranch work and sleeping on the loft floor last night has my muscles aching.

It was worth it.

Presley went to shower and get ready for her bar shift tonight, and I came up to the main house to not only grab the ice pack but also to get some snacks and things for the hands' quarters since I haven't had a chance to go to the store yet. I made sure Gavin's and Blake's trucks weren't outside before chancing it, and I knew Momma and Gran had a meeting in town today to talk with someone about paint colors for a new guest quarters they want to build.

I have no idea how they're affording all this construction; I guess Blake gave us more money than I realized. I let out a sigh as I fill the canvas bag over my arm with chips, crackers, and a few granola bars. After I take some fruit, I stop at the fridge to grab some pre-wrapped sandwiches I know Momma makes for any of our workers when they need some extra fuel. I get one for Presley and myself then make my way toward the door.

As I walk by the kitchen table, a pile of papers catches my attention. I slip the bag I'm holding over my shoulder and pick them up. As I read them, anger starts to heat at the back of my neck. Before my accident and finding out about the situation

Dad left us in—back when I thought we were just a big ranch with money troubles due to the drought—I asked Gavin if there was any way I could help get our ranch back on its feet.

I researched ideas like leasing out land to cattle ranchers in Mexico and other nearby ranches that need land for their herds at specific times of year then told Gavin about it. At the time, he shot my ideas down, but apparently, he's changed his mind.

I flip through more of the pages and see various contracts. I don't understand why my ideas weren't good enough then but they are now. And what pisses me off even more is that it wasn't just Gavin—nobody in my family, not even Blake, told me about these plans.

From the dates on the pages, this has been in the works for months now, going back to when I was healing from my accident. Some may say I should be happy they used my ideas, and I would be—had they included me. Instead, this only makes me feel more like an outsider.

I exhale a heated breath, the anger I'd managed to turn down to simmer after my time with Presley returning to a boil. I wish I had one of those sticks she likes to suck on, but since I don't, I turn my thoughts to her. I think of her beaming face when she sat atop Big John today. How I got to see her truly smile, a smile that showed her teeth and lit her sapphire eyes like the sun shining on spring water.

She was so proud of herself, and I couldn't help but be proud of her, too. It was nice to be part of the reason she smiled like that, to see her conquer her fear and do it with trust for me in her eyes.

I place the papers back on the table, and for the first time in a long time, I don't have the desire to drink or drive into the city to find someone to scratch an itch. I just want to go back to Presley. Come to think of it, I left Dad's flask on the dresser in the room after I'd showered yesterday and forgot about it.

"Look at what the cat dragged in."

My short-statured Gran walks into the kitchen with a sense of determination, Momma right behind her. Gran's expression looks neutral, while Momma's pink lips are pursed, and her eyes are sullen as if she wants to cry or yell at the sight of me. Neither of which feels great.

"I was just leaving," I say, moving to walk past them, but Gran grabs my bicep. She's strong for a woman in her eighties and has never been the type of woman to back down. I've always admired her for it, and our relationship was good until the night of the accident, when she, too, took Gavin's side. Or at least she made me feel that way.

We talked and played cards while I was on the mend, but just like with most of my family, our conversations did not get that deep. And she hasn't tried to speak with me since my doctor's appointment last week. To be fair, I haven't sought her out, either, but I knew our conversation would go nowhere and I'd end up with another family member pissed at me.

Gran's hazel eyes stare softly into mine for a moment, then she moves her focus down to the ice pack on my forearm.

"Are you hurt?" She crosses her age-spotted arms over her chest, and Momma makes a little noise of concern at her question, tucking a piece of silver-blonde hair behind her ear.

"I'm fine," I say honestly.

"You're overdoing it," Gran chides.

"It's only muscle pain. Really, I'm fine."

The women who have always been two of the most important people in my life stare up at me with doubt in their eyes, and I know they don't believe me. While small, this interaction reminds me why I can't stay in this house, why I like to drink and be numb. It's not a good feeling knowing my family never takes me at my word, that they always think I'm just a young kid who doesn't get it. They think I lie and do what I want without considering the consequences for others.

They've been so blinded by my brother and my dad before him, by their "honest country boy act," that they don't see I've always been the one telling the truth. I've never tried to hide who or what I am. They just don't like what they see all the time.

"Please tell me you're not overworking that city girl, too," Momma says. "Gavin told me she fainted when she first started."

I suck in a breath through my teeth, her comment shooting an arrow through my heart. On a different day, maybe I'd fight back. But I don't want to fight with my family any more, and I don't want my temper to get the best of me.

"Presley is fine, too." Their disapproving gaze has me wanting to reach for the bottle again. It's my cue to leave. "You may have already figured it out, but I'm staying down at the hands' quarters. I'll be there if you need anything from me." I take a step back to tap on the papers on the table. "But it seems like you've already got everything handled."

"Kade." Gran sighs, running an exasperated hand through her short gray hair. "Don't try to force the puzzle pieces together. Let's sit down and talk so you don't end up thinking things that aren't true."

"Maybe if I had all the pieces, I'd be able to put the puzzle together. Can't do that when they're being withheld from me."

"Kade, please, let's sit."

I shake my head, knowing that if I sit down, I'll either end up saying more things I regret or find myself at the bottom of a whiskey bottle. This time, I give myself a wide berth to exit around them so they can't stop me.

As I walk back toward my new quarters, nobody follows. Nobody calls after me. And I can't decide if that's what I want or not.

CHAPTER 22

Presley

NIGHT HAWK IS BURSTING at the seams, just like I expected it to be. Kade is teaching an early line-dancing class while the band that played last week is here to provide live music. Later, they're doing late-night bull rides.

I feel better equipped to handle the very enthusiastic crowd this shift, and Stu is working the other end of the bar while a new guy named Dan is on tables. He's only here for the fall—someone's friend from a neighboring town—and Jake roped him in to help.

Jake checks in on me now and then, but otherwise, I'm on my own and doing great. The comforting sound of the fiddle player and the smooth baritone of the lead singer's voice helps me keep a nice rhythm. The tempo helps ease the anxiety I felt returning to work after yesterday. Thankfully, I haven't seen Marié, though I didn't think I would two nights in a row.

I tap my foot to the fiddle player's version of "If You're Gonna Play in Texas (You Gotta Have a Fiddle in the Band)" by Alabama—a classic for a place like this, a fun one people like to dance to. I serve a customer their gin and tonic then pour multiple tequila shots to a group of women who are talking about Kade. His Southern drawl—which he's laying on thick for the crowd—reaches the bar as he calls out dance moves into a microphone.

A blonde woman in the group squeals. "I stuffed my number in the back of his jeans pocket."

Her friend whacks her on the shoulder. "Oh my god; I did, too!" They both dissolve into buzzed giggles.

"Did you see his ass in those tight Wranglers?"

"Girl, if he asked me to go out to his truck right now, I would."

Their tinkling laughter grates on my nerves as I push the shots toward them. "Here you are. Do you have a tab?"

"Yes, under Annie."

I nod, and they lay down some cash for a tip before she distributes the glasses to her friends. They clink their glasses and down their shots before going back out to the dance floor.

Kade is surrounded by women, but they manage to work their way back in. I expect Kade to throw his arm around one of them or shoot them a flirty gaze, but instead, his head lifts, and our eyes lock.

He winks at me, and I think my heart stops in my chest. Was he looking for me? No. Why would he? We're just—I don't know what we are. But I don't think we're seeing each other.

It's not like we've had a chance to talk about last night that much. After we finished our horseback-riding lesson, Kade exercised a few more horses while I watched, then we helped with the early-evening clean and feed of the horses.

He disappeared after that while I took a shower and got ready for work, but when he came back, we rode together to Night Hawk, and he was quiet the entire ride. I wanted to ask him if he was okay, but I got the vibe he didn't want to talk about it. I wondered if it had something to do with what he told me about his relationship with his brother. Maybe they got into an argument or something else happened when we were apart for those couple of hours.

The blonde woman, Annie, throws her arms around Kade's neck, and his body wavers under her weight. I bite the inside of my cheek, my hand gripping the bottle of tequila as my stomach sours.

Am I jealous? That can't be what I'm feeling. I don't have any claim on him. I shake my head and let go of the tequila bottle, not wanting to address that thought. After I've sucked in a calming breath, I walk over to the POS system so I can add the shots to Annie's tab before I forget.

"Hey, Stu, do you mind if I borrow Presley for ten minutes?" My head pops up to see Kade in front of me. He's grinning from beneath the brim of a dark-brown cowboy hat, the white T-shirt he's wearing instead of the usual black Night Hawk uniform clinging to his muscles. The sweat he's accumulated from teaching line dancing for the last hour only accentuates his lean form. My mouth goes dry, and thoughts of other women hanging on him go out the window.

"Yep, I'll get Dan to cover," Stu yells over the noise, grinning while he looks between me and Kade.

"Come on, Lemon," Kade says. He's standing next to me now, holding out his hand.

"Why?"

The words are out of me before I can think it through, and Kade chuckles. "I need a dance partner."

I scan all the women on the dance floor before my eyes land on Annie, who is shooting me evil daggers with her dark-brown eyes. "You have lots of women to choose from."

Kade crosses his arms over his chest, and I watch the way his forearms and biceps bulge. It has me thinking of what they looked like as he spanked me, as he held me by the throat, gently squeezing. I inhale a sharp breath, as if I can feel his hands on me again right now, and my eyes close.

"Presley," Kade says, his mouth closer to my ear now. "Are you thinking about our time in the barn loft?"

My eyes fly open, and embarrassment floods me, but I don't step back. "No."

He raises one eyebrow. "Hmm, another fib to pay for. Now, come on. Let's dance."

This is the second time now he's said something about paying for my little white lies, but he grabs my hand and tugs on it so I can't think too much about it. I tug back. "Kade, I'm not a good dancer. You have other options."

He stops and turns to face me. "I don't want other options."

His words freeze my heart again, and my stomach flutters. My ears don't—can't—believe the words that just came out of his mouth. Then the two-man band starts to play a slow song, "Something in the Orange" by Zach Bryan, and I hear a few groans.

"Trust me." He smiles so I can see a tease of his dimples. "This will be easier than riding Big John." I relent and mirror his joy. It's nice to see him acting more like the Kade I know after that quiet car ride.

"Okay, fine."

He whoops a silly holler and tugs me to the floor. There are a few couples dancing, but Annie and her friends have grouped off to the side. They're still staring at me.

"I thought this was line-dancing night," I say quietly, watching the couples dance around us.

"I'm done for the night. Now it's free dance before we do bull riding at ten."

My eyes widen. "Then why did you ask me to the dance floor?"

He pulls me to him in a confident hold, his left hand gripping my right while his other hand takes mine, placing it on his shoulder. Then he moves his arm to my hip and places his right hand on my lower shoulder so we're in a basic dance position.

"I told you. I need a dance partner."

I puff out a breath. When he asked me to the floor, I thought it was to help with some dance moves or something, not just to dance with me for fun.

"Kade, we're supposed to be working."

He shrugs nonchalantly. "You needed a break."

"And you thought I'd want to dance on my break?"

He chuckles and pulls me closer. "You really don't want to slow dance with me?"

My skin sings under his playful gaze. "Kade," I try again, though my voice isn't chiding anymore. "I don't want to get fired."

"For the last time, Jake isn't going to fire you. Especially for taking a ten-minute break."

I huff. "You're annoying, you know that?"

"Good. I like annoying you. Now let's dance, Lemon."

I try to stop the anxiety curling inside me from rearing its ugly head—not just from Kade asking me to dance but from all the women who wanted to go home with him tonight and are mentally murdering me right now.

Even though we've just begun to dance, I'm waiting for one of them to cut in, but I hope they don't. Because despite how obnoxious he can be, it feels nice to be in his arms. It feels even nicer that he chose me out of all these beautiful women, ones who were literally shoving numbers in his pants all night. The only time I ever felt chosen was the night I met Derek, but I think that was all a lie. He was just using me. Even then—

Kade puts pressure on my shoulder and squeezes the hand he's holding so I focus back on him. "Stop thinking," he reminds me. "Just feel the music. Transfer your weight from foot to foot, and I'll lead you."

"Okay." I exhale and start to list off things in my head, trying to clear my mind as we begin to sway to the music. *Happiness, New Zealand, eggs, baseball...spanking.* My cheeks flush.

He cocks his head to the side. "Where did you just go right now?" He leads me around the dance floor as we fall into step with the other couples.

"Um...well." Heat rises up my neck. "I kind of list things off sometimes to help me when I'm anxious or nervous."

His face brightens as if I've clicked something into place for him. "Is that why I thought you were talking to yourself about groceries yesterday?"

I bite my lip. "Sort of. You list things that don't have association with each other. It helps when you're spiraling. Sometimes, if I'm having a hard time falling asleep, I use it then, too."

"Does it really work?"

"Most of the time."

Kade uses the pause at the end of my sentence to push me out gently so there's space between us then turns me under his arm. I go off-balance a little but then he pulls me back in. I fall into his chest, laughing at my clumsiness.

He smiles down at me. "Are you thinking anything now?"

I peer into his hazel irises and find myself smiling so that my eyes crinkle around the corners. "You," I breathe out. "I'm thinking about you."

I know I could have lied and said I was thinking about nothing, but I'm sick of lies and being fake. I just want something real.

Kade's features relax, and he doesn't say anything. He just pulls me closer so our bodies don't have space between them, and I feel his lips touch the crown of my head as he lays a kiss there. I tense and try to pull back because we're in public—and at work—but Kade is quick to stop me.

"Don't, Presley," he says. Begs. "Please. Just stay for this dance."

The pleading in his voice makes me give in, letting myself indulge in the way he clutches me like I'm a slat of wood floating in the ocean, like a life raft for him to grab onto. Nobody has ever held me like this. Come to think of it, nobody has ever *danced* with me like this. Or even asked me to dance. I inhale a long breath through my nose before exhaling, allowing my muscles to relax against him, to soak in his strength and to feel wanted.

"Isn't this cute."

I pull back from Kade at the deep, mocking male voice, and he jolts at the jerky movement. The hairs on the back of my neck stand on end, the turkey sandwich I ate earlier threatening to make a reappearance.

I clench my fists at my sides, anxiety licking at the base of my neck like hot flames as I stare into the slate-gray eyes I've come to loathe. I guess Marié saw me yesterday after all.

Eff my life.

Though I'd rather run the other direction, I turn to face my ex-boyfriend. "What the hell are you doing here, Derek?"

He smirks, the kind of slimy grin that makes my skin crawl as if it's covered in a thousand spiders. "I've come to talk to you, P. We have business to discuss."

Chapter 23

Kade

When I hear the name Derek, I think of some rich boy douchebag who takes his daddy's car for joyrides or a guy who plays video games all day in his mom's basement. Presley's Derek paints a completely different picture, one I couldn't fully see in the selfie on her phone.

He has dark-red hair and a tall, lanky body covered in tattoos, and he's sporting a nose ring that I have the desire to yank out. He's not ugly by any means, but he looks like someone who is very punchable.

Presley shifts nervously next to me, and I debate what to do. My immediate reaction is to step in front of her and tell this guy to fuck off. But from what I've learned about her in the short time I've known her, she doesn't want to stand out, at least not in social situations.

Getting her to dance just now had been hard enough, especially since she'd been so worried about what Jake would think. At a regular job, she'd probably be right in her concern, but at Night Hawk, we don't exactly run like a normal establishment. I've covered for Jake on plenty of occasions when he's needed "breaks," and he does the same for me. Now Presley is included in our little bar family—it's just how things go in a small town.

I also saw the way she was looking at the women who'd been throwing themselves at me. It was part of the reason I asked her to dance. When I made eye contact with her from across the room, I felt giddy at seeing the jealousy in her eyes. I had the overwhelming urge to run across the room and kiss her, to tell her that I'm not interested in any other women.

That thought had shocked me, punched me in the gut so hard I just about fell over. Before I met her, I would have never pictured myself in this situation, but here I am. I've been hit by Hurricane Presley, and my life is never going to be the same.

Presley crosses her arms over her chest. "There's nothing to talk about, Derek," she finally says in answer to his statement. "Please leave."

Douchey Derek looks her up and down with a type of evaluation that screams critical judgment. The intensity of it has Presley shifting closer to me. I want to pull her into my body, but I know that wouldn't help her right now.

The asshat turns his steely rat gaze on me, but his clear disapproval of me doesn't bother me in the slightest. I'm used to looks like that from not only my own family but also from people I've grown up with my entire life. What does bother me, though, is the way his eyes narrow and his pointy shoulders straighten. How he turns up his nose as if he's better than me.

"We have lots to talk about, Sweetheart."

My throat burns, and my fists clench. How can a sweet nickname sound so disgusting coming from this man's mouth? I understand even more now why Presley wasn't into nicknames at first. But I will admit it makes my heart swell knowing she likes *my* nicknames, that she asked me to call her by them.

"No, Derek, we don't." Her anxious eyes dart around the room. Several people have stopped what they're doing to watch this interaction. And while the band is still playing, and a few people have started to dance, the tension between the three of us is obvious.

This guy sticks out like a sore thumb amongst the sea of cowboy hats and Wranglers. His piercings, white T-shirt, leather jacket, and overly baggy pants scream for people to look at him. His tall height and smarmy face don't help him, either.

Douchey Derek reaches out to grab Presley's arm, and this time, I don't stop myself from stepping in. My fingers wrap around his wrist before he can touch her, and I give a warning twist—not very hard but enough to sting.

"I don't know where you were raised, but out here, we don't touch a woman without asking."

Derek yanks his arm back, and I let it go without a fight. I watch as he babies his wrist like I broke it. "Don't touch me, you damn hillbilly. My hands are worth a lot of money."

One of our regulars, Tim Corbin—who's sitting at a table near us on the perimeter of the dance floor—hears Derek's words and lets out a hoot of amusement. It's enough to make me grin.

"You need help knocking this city boy out, Kade?" he asks.

I tip my hat at him as Derek scoffs out a sound of protest. "We're good, Tim. Derek was just about to get in his car and go back to where he came from."

"If any of you touch me, you'll hear from my lawyers."

Presley puts her hand on my back and applies gentle pressure. I move to the side so that she's facing him, whoever this man is to her.

"What do you want, Derek? Tell me quickly, then please leave." Her eyes dart around the room again, more frantic this time. She crosses her arms over her chest, and I watch as the woman who had just started to blossom begins to close up again. I don't fucking like it.

"Marié said she saw a fat girl with purple hair and flower tattoos here last night. Not many people we know with that description. I had to come see for myself if it was true, if you were slumming it in the sticks."

I step forward again, the simmering anger inside me that is always waiting to boil spreading heat through every part of my body. The reasons Presley wanted to stay clothed, to not have me touch her stomach, why she was worried about her weight on my legs and me helping her on the horse today—it all makes perfect sense now. I want to beat this guy's face to a pulp.

Presley tugs on my bicep, but it doesn't stop me from getting in his face. "Watch your fucking mouth," I seethe.

"Step the fuck back," Derek barks, drawing more attention to us. He's taller than me, but I've got a lot more bulk on him. And now that I'm this close, I know he's drunk. I can smell alcohol and what I'm assuming is weed on his breath.

"Make me," I say.

"I'm talking to my girlfriend. This is our business."

I try not to flinch at the words coming out of his mouth, but he notices my reaction.

"This bitch not tell you?" He cackles like a wicked witch.

I grab him by the collar of his shirt, and his body jostles from the force. I'm blinded with rage now, a rage I've only felt once before: the night I found out Gavin had been lying to us. But the rage isn't because he called her his "girlfriend"—it's because of how he's speaking about Presley overall. Whether they're in a relationship or not, I'm going to stand up for her. She doesn't deserve to be treated like shit and called disgusting names.

"Kade!" Presley cries quietly, pulling on my arm again. "He's not worth it."

The pleading and desperate tone of her voice manage to worm their way through the ominous emotions coursing through my veins, helping me remember where I am and who I'm with. If Presley doesn't want me to pummel this douche, I won't.

I relax my fist and release my hold on him. As soon as he's free, Derek steps back and fixes his shirt, brushing at it like he's wiping away dirt. The band keeps playing despite the drama unfolding. "The Devil Went Down to Georgia" by The Charlie Daniels Band is fitting for this moment.

Derek eyes the stage then glares at Presley. She looks smaller and meeker than the woman I've come to know. Despite her awkwardness at first, she's never been meek with me. That was what drew me to her in the first place.

Derek rubs his hands together excitedly like he just won the lottery. "I'm glad I came to see this. I knew I wouldn't be disappointed."

Presley swallows, following Derek's gaze—he's eyeing the fiddle player—before she looks back at him. "To see what?" she asks.

I hate how scared her voice sounds. It makes me want to pull her in my arms and hide her away from the world. Especially from this piece of shit.

"To see how far you've fallen." He smirks then takes a step back. I think he's going to walk away, but then he makes a big show of pointing at Presley and raises his voice. "This woman right here, Ladies and Gents, is one of the best fiddle players in the country, and she threw it all away for some cowboy's dick!"

Several people gasp, and the band stops playing at the commotion. I'm faintly aware of the sound of chairs scraping against the wood floors and Tim moving out of the corner of my eye, but I don't think for another second—I just send my fist flying into Derek's face. To his credit, he doesn't go down like I thought he would, but the force of it has him stumbling back.

"Oh my god, Kade!" Presley cries.

Derek's hands fly up to his now bloody nose. His feet move to charge at me, but Tim and Jake are suddenly there, grabbing the lanky man by the arms.

He struggles against them. "Let me go! He assaulted me, for fuck's sake!" Derek screams.

Chants of "Throw him out!" travel through the crowd as he continues to fight against my friends' hold. The veins in his neck bulge from the effort.

"You both okay?" Jake asks. He holds on to Derek tighter, his face neutral as if he's not holding back a struggling man.

I shake out my hand as I check on Presley. I expect her to look embarrassed, but instead she looks livid, eyes full of fire and jaw like marble. But her gaze isn't directed at me—she's glaring at Derek.

"Presley?" Jake asks.

She doesn't answer him. Her furious stare is now locked with Derek's as he continues to squirm like the worm he is.

"Presley," Derek says, his voice gentler now. "Tell these bastards to get their hands off me. I'll take you back home. You can fix this."

I watch the scene unfold carefully, ready to step in if she needs it. But by the way she squares her shoulders and the determined shine in her eyes, I think she's got whatever she's planning handled.

With two short strides, she's in front of Derek.

In a bold move, the asshole smiles at her sweetly, gaze softening, as if he thinks that will manipulate her into doing whatever he wants. Presley leans forward so they're close, a smirk on her lips that, if I were Derek, would send alarm bells dinging in my brain. But the asshole has the audacity to look as if he's won, like her closeness means she's going to kiss him.

"How many times do I have to tell you, Derek?" she spits, her voice unlike I've ever heard from her. Gone are her velvet tones, and in their place is a raspy anger. "I'm not your fucking girlfriend! You are a lying"—she stabs her pointer finger into his chest—"cheating"—she pokes him again, so hard he groans—"piece of shit!"

Then she pulls her finger back, but instead of stepping away, she winds up and socks him right in the gut.

The Night Hawk crowd erupts in cheers as Derek groans and slumps in Tim and Jake's grasp. Presley steps back, exuding the same confidence I witnessed earlier when she sat atop Big John. She glances at Jake with that same assurance.

"I think Derek needs a good night's rest in a holding cell to sleep off all the alcohol he drank."

Derek grunts.

"Oh, and Jake?" Presley taps her chin. "Isn't the recreational use of weed illegal in Texas?"

I press my lips together as I try not to snort. My Lemon is savage, and that is sexy as hell.

"You'd be right, Ms. Presley." Jake grins.

"You bitch!" Derek spits, struggling again.

"Alright, someone call the Sheriff so we can stop listening to this asshole," Tim says, shaking Derek a bit.

"He's already here," somebody calls from near the door.

Jake chuckles. "Gotta love small towns, huh, asshole?"

At the mention of the Sheriff, Derek's energy shifts, fear riddling his busted face. "Presley, come on! You'll ruin my life," he pleads, but she doesn't react, only stands there with her lips pressed in a hard line.

Jake glances between Presley and I while he and Tim continue to hold Derek tighter.

"Why don't you two get out of here for the night," Jake says. "Stu, Dan, and I will manage. If we need more help, Tim can step in. Right, Tim?"

"At your service," he nods.

Presley blinks, snapping out of whatever she's thinking. "No, Jake. That's not necessary."

"It's all good, Presley."

"Presley!" Derek's whiny voice cuts in.

"Oh, shut up," Tim mimics in the same tone. "Let's take him out to the Sheriff," he directs at Jake.

Jake nods, turning his attention to the stage. "Start up the music, boys!" he yells to the band. Then he looks out at the crowd. "And let's get those drinks flowing. It's now officially power hour!"

The people in the bar cheer at the mention of cheap beer, and the place starts to liven up again as the fiddler plays. I turn to Presley, her focus on Jake and Tim as they drag a sulking Derek out of the bar.

"Are you okay?" I ask, taking her hand.

Her blue eyes flutter up to meet mine. I stare into the depths of them, and my heart beats faster in my chest. God, she's beautiful, so beautiful, and I hate that she doesn't know it. That this asshole made her feel any less than perfect the way she is.

Presley's gaze volleys to my lips then once again to my eyes. "Kade," she breathes out, my name sounding like a prayer on her lips.

"What do you need, Lemon?" I ask, my head lowering of its own accord. The sounds of the bar and the lingering stares of those around us fade, and I feel like we're the only ones on this dance floor.

The words she wants to say rest on the tip of her tongue—I can see it. I bring one of my fingers up to brush across the soft skin of her pink cheek before I press my thumb into the flesh of her lower lip. Her breath hitches, and I'm faintly aware that my knuckles are bloody from the punch I threw, but I couldn't care less about my hand right now.

Presley blinks, sucking in a breath as if she's gathering courage. When our eyes connect, I see a heat in them now, a raw desire I saw earlier when we flirted, when we were both thinking about what transpired between us last night.

"Lemon?" I ask again. This time, my tone is light and teasing as I drag my hand down the column of her throat, pressing my thumb against her fluttering pulse point. "What do you need, darlin'?"

My words are enough to finally shake her from her thoughts. Presley licks her lips then exhales, her warm breath skittering across my face. "I need you, Kade. Just you."

I lean forward and press a kiss to her forehead, my soul soaking up her words like a sponge. What she said, the meaning of it—I don't even know if I can grasp it right now. I only know I wanted to hear it, *needed* to hear it.

"Then let's get out of here."

CHAPTER 24

Presley

KADE'S HAND RESTS ON my inner thigh as we drive back to the ranch. It feels foreign to have a touch that's both safe and gentle yet possessive on my body. His fingers dig into my skin every now and then like he's either remembering punching Derek or wanting to punch him again.

I need you. My words on the dance floor ring in my ears. *I need you.* I can't believe I said those words out loud, but it was true. I did need him. I *do* need him. And sitting in the truck with him right now, driving down the dark roads, feels good. Right. Even if it doesn't make a lot of sense.

I look down at his raw knuckle and cringe. "You should ice that."

He flashes me a cheeky grin. "You worried about me, Lemon darlin'?"

I flush at his question, the color of my cheeks answering him. I fix my gaze on his hand and study the marred skin. I debate touching him then decide *screw it*. I've already done so many things unlike myself in the last twenty-four hours, I might as well add more to the list.

I trace my finger over his bones, making sure I steer clear of any open wounds. When we go over a bump in the road, I must hit a sore spot, because he hisses.

"Sorry."

I pull away, but he grabs my hand before I can get too far, gripping it with reassurance. "Don't be. It's just a little sore, but it'll heal quick. It's not the first time I've punched someone." His tone is playful, though I wonder if that's to cover up the emotions that come with those memories.

Kade places our entwined hands on my thigh, his thumb brushing over my knuckles. The truck is silent save the sound of the road beneath the tires and the wind against the windows. I close my eyes, indulging in the sensation of Kade's hand in mine and the warmth of his touch.

In the quiet, my mind wanders back to the altercation with Derek. I've never laid a hand on anyone in my life. I can't say I want to do it again or that I would normally condone violence, but Derek deserved it. He honestly deserved more than that given the things he said—and in a small town in front of the people I work with, no less.

I'm sure what happened is already being gossiped about and spreading like wildfire. So much for staying under the radar. In a way, I feel free, freer than I ever have before. But that doesn't mean I don't regret what happened tonight.

I gently squeeze Kade's hand. "I'm sorry."

He looks at me briefly as we pull down a road close to the ranch. The sound of the gravel beneath the tires is now familiar and comforting. I used to find it almost irritating.

"For what?" he asks.

"For what happened and for your hand. Derek has always had a temper, but I didn't think he'd get drunk, show up here, and make a scene. And I'm sorry he got you involved."

"First, you have nothing to be sorry for. You can't control the actions of someone else; only Derek is to blame for what happened."

He pauses, like whatever he said is applying to more than just this situation.

I watch him swallow, his Adam's apple bobbing before he continues. "Like I said, my hand is fine. I'm just glad I was there." He lifts our joined hands and kisses the back of mine so tenderly it almost makes me weep. *Who is this sweet cowboy, and where the hell did he come from?*

"Kade," I whisper. "Derek's not my boyfriend. I mean, he was, but—"

Kade places our hands back down on my thigh as we pull into the ranch's driveway. "You don't owe me an explanation."

"No, I want you to know." I swallow, willing my now nervous stomach to settle. "We broke up after he cheated on me—on Valentine's Day, no less. But we were in a band together, which forced me to be around him almost every day, even after the breakup. He's obviously very angry that I left, and I can explain that, too, if you want. But I need you to know that I'm not with him. He doesn't mean anything to me, and I'm so sorry that he even came here tonight. The awful things he said he—"

"Presley." Kade stops me. "Take a breath." He removes his hand from mine to turn off the ignition, and I see we're parked in front of the hands' quarters. He unbuckles his seatbelt before scooting across the bench seat and taking my face in his hands. Then he inhales with me. "Flowers, whiskey, football," he says.

I can't help but smile.

"Now you do some."

"Birds, T-Rex, blanket, stars, horses, marker...lemons," I finish. My lips curl into a soft grin.

He brushes his thumb over the apple of my cheek. "Feel better?"

I nod, leaning my head into one of his calloused hands, soaking up his strength and comfort and letting it seep into my body. My eyes fall closed as I take in another breath. Then another.

Kade moves the hand on my other cheek down my neck, sliding it back until he's threaded his fingers in the hair at the base of my neck. I shiver from the sensation on my scalp and open my eyes to find him watching me carefully. When he tugs the hairs gently, a gasp escapes from my parted lips.

"You're so responsive, Lemon." He leans in closer so his breath skitters across my face. "*Fuck*, I want to kiss you. More than I want anything else."

I lick my lips, and that feeling I got the first day we met settles in my body. I wanted to kiss him behind Night Hawk, even if I didn't want to admit it, and now that desire is back and completely overwhelming. I don't want to imagine what his lips will feel like or taste like anymore—I want to know for real.

But there's one thing stopping me.

"Presley," Kade questions. "Did I misread this?"

I place one of my hands over the one he has cupping my cheek. "No, you didn't. I'm just..." I collect my words. "Out of practice."

Kade sighs a breath of what I'm assuming is relief, lips tugging at the corners. "Then practice on me."

I smile back at him, something I've been doing a lot more of in the last day. It's a miracle I'm even smiling at all, especially after what happened with Derek and the things he said tonight. But Kade makes me happy. He puts me at ease. He helps erase all the negative self-talk simply by looking at me the way he does—with so much desire it makes my head spin.

He massages the base of my skull, clearly waiting for my answer. His gaze flicks from my eyes to my lips, and I have absolutely no doubt about how much he wants to kiss me.

"Yes." I exhale. "Kiss me, Kade."

In a lighting-fast move, he throws the hat he's been wearing to the back of the cab and closes the gap. He plasters his body against mine so my back hits the door, my hair brushing the window. When I feel the pressure of his left thumb on my cheek, my mouth parts. He uses the opportunity to connect us further, his lips exploring mine as I let out a small gasp. The grip on my skull tightens as our mouths mold together, and he groans into me, vibrations shooting through my body and lighting me on fire.

My chest heaves, breasts pressing against his chest as my hands grip his waist. His lips turn demanding, crushing into mine at a devouring pace. With how gentle he's been with me today, kissing my hair and holding me while we danced, I thought this would be a sweet kiss. I was wrong. This kiss holds the same intensity of his stare when I've caught him watching me. The same intensity I felt last night as he spanked me. He puts his all into it but still makes sure my head is supported as he runs his tongue along the seam of my lips.

I open more for him, and he licks into my mouth as my hands explore along his waist. I like the way his muscles contract and tremble under my touch; it makes me feel powerful. His tongue slowly strokes against mine, rough and hot, and I do my best to keep up with him.

I moan as his minty taste bursts along my taste buds and a guttural sound leaves him. He presses his body further into mine so my back digs into the armrest on the door, and I kiss him harder. When his hand on my neck starts to move south, I exhale into his kiss, letting the feeling of his lips, the masculine smell of him, like salt and leather, invade every fiber of my being.

Kade sucks on my lower lip, both of us gasping for air before he kisses me again. The strokes become firmer and even more demanding. His hand traces over the tops of my breasts and down my ribs, but he doesn't go low enough to touch my stomach. Tears sting my eyes when I realize that he cared enough to remember what I told him last night. I pull back just slightly, and he nips at my lips, resting his forehead against mine.

Kade's hand softly tickles my upper ribs before he moves to trace my clavicle. "Is this okay?" he asks, trailing his fingers a little lower.

"Yes," I say. "Touch me, Kade." *God, I want it.*

"Thank god." He exhales. "And Presley?"

I stare at him through my hooded gaze, waiting.

"You're not out of practice." He dives back in before I can answer, his lips attacking mine with fervor as he cups one of my breasts, squeezing and thumbing my nipple through my bra. I moan at the feeling of the tight bud being teased while I drag one of my hands up to rest on the muscle of his shoulder, digging my nails in just slightly. Kade must really like that, because he squeezes my pert breast tighter.

He continues to tease and explore my chest over my clothes, and my body starts to sweat as the truck heats up from our labored breathing and raised body temperatures. I don't know how long we kiss, but my entire being is screaming for more than just a hot and heavy make-out session.

I pull Kade as close as I can, tugging his shirt from his pants and running my nails along the lower muscles of his abs, my fingertips brushing the coarse hairs of his happy trail.

"Jesus Christ, Presley," he groans. He kisses down my neck, and his hands drift to the space just under my breasts.

"Don't stop," I exhale. The huskiness of my own voice surprises me. I've never heard myself sound so desperate and turned on, not even while he spanked me. I feel as if another woman has possessed my body, the kind of woman I've always wanted to be but have been too scared to set free.

Kade kisses back up the column of my throat until our eyes meet. It may be dark, but I can see how worked up he is. His lips are swollen, his cheeks are flushed, his pupils are dilated, and the outline of his erection is prominent under his jeans. My clit thrums at the sight of him, and I'm hungry for his fingers between my legs again.

"Tell me where else I can touch you." His voice, too, is deeper than normal, and it sends shivers up my spine.

"Everywhere."

He looks stunned for a second, and I understand why. I bring my hand to his cheek.

"I trust you, Kade. You make me feel safe."

A warm smile lights up his face, and he delicately kisses my nose then my lips, sipping at them as if they're a fine whiskey. When he meets my gaze again, his eyes are shining with that intensity of his, the same as when I asked him to spank me. It has my body humming, my heart racing, and goosebumps breaking out over my arms in anticipation.

"Can I try something?" He strokes my cheek.

"Will it hurt?" I turn sheepish as soon as the words have left my mouth because I didn't mean it in a bad way. I liked the pain he caused me last night, and I want to experience it again.

Kade takes his hand from my chest and grips my thigh. "Do you want it to?"

If it was bright in here, he'd see me turn into a tomato in front of his eyes. I purse my lips, my mind racing because I'm unsure of what to say.

Kade lands a gentle smack to the inside of my thigh, and I gasp in surprise. "Don't think so hard about the answer, Lemon. Tell me: Do you want it to?"

I stare into his eyes and remember I don't have to feel afraid with him. I can say what I want. "Yes. But I also want to feel good."

He smirks. "Of course you do." His tone is teasing, so I swat him in the chest. He grabs my hand and kisses my fingers. "I can make it hurt, Presley. But I can also make it feel better."

His words strike me in a way I don't expect. My stomach clenches, and I try to ignore the part of me that says I shouldn't like this. I should be a normal, boring girl like my mother always wanted me to be. But then again, I've never had a normal life, and I never truly wanted to be a normal girl.

I've never done what's expected of me or even tried to fit in with the crowd. Even if my career hasn't worked out for me, I went against the grain and followed my dreams despite the cards being stacked against me. And yes, I let Derek screw up my life, leading me to where I am right now. But as I look into Kade's teasing hazel gaze, I realize there's nowhere else I'd rather be.

"Then do it, Kade," I murmur. "Make me feel everything."

My words transform his features into a sweet gaze. His expression is soft and vulnerable, but his eyes are sparkling as if I've given him the perfect gift on Christmas morning.

"If anything is too much, Presley—if I touch you in a way you don't like, tell me to stop. Just like with the spanking, you're in charge here. Understand?"

"I understand."

He smiles, running his thumb over my thoroughly kissed lips. "Good girl. Now, give me your wrists."

CHAPTER 25

Kade

To Presley's credit, my request doesn't cause her to falter. She holds out her wrists to me like a good girl, and the action goes straight to my cock. I don't know what I did to deserve this woman walking into my life, because I sure as hell haven't been on the nice list recently. Or ever.

I shift back in my seat, the coarse fabric of my clothes irritating the skin that feels as if it's been set ablaze. If I was a less-practiced Dominant, I would have had her lips wrapped around my cock by now. But Presley, she needs time to explore, to settle into her beautiful body. And over the past couple of years, I've learned to get pleasure in many other ways that don't involve getting my dick wet.

Like with Presley. I want to see her open like a rose in spring under my touch, to start asking for what she wants and following my direction. I desire her to crave the rougher aspects of me while trusting me enough to let that part of me unleash itself on her. Experiencing her submission isn't something that's just pleasurable for me—it's a gift from her, one I'm going to cherish for the rest of my life.

Her trusting eyes look at me expectantly, and I bring myself back to the moment. I grin slyly as I unbuckle my belt, the jingling sound of the metal buckle echoing throughout the cab. I keep a close eye on her to gauge her reaction, but she looks calm, despite her heady breaths that match my own. I pull the worn brown leather from the loops and then take her wrists in my hands, kissing each pulse point before I meet her gaze.

"I'm going to secure your wrists with my belt. Are you okay with that?"

She nods. "Yes."

My cock twitches again at her breathy response, and I don't waste time getting to work. I flip her hands so her palms are together then make quick work of binding her, looping the belt so it forms handcuffs around each wrist.

I learned long ago that the key to this is to make sure I leave enough space for her wrists to breathe, otherwise I risk damage, which is the last thing I want. Once I've tested it out and made sure everything is to my liking, I place her hands on her lap for a moment while I make more space for us. Using the lever on the side of my seat, I recline the bench seat back so I have more space to move, and Presley can rest easier. Then I get on my knees to reach into the back where I have an extra set of clothes. I grab a flannel and fold it before scooting back to the woman watching me.

Her eyes are half-closed, and her breathing has gotten faster. She looks on the verge of orgasm already, and we haven't even started the real fun yet. The devil inside me grins at the picture she makes in the bindings while I place the flannel behind her on the door.

"Lie back."

She follows the direction, then I take the tail of the belt and lift her arms up. She watches with rapt attention as I secure the belt on the "Oh, shit!" handle, which is exactly what I plan to make her scream out tonight. Once I'm done, I grab the blue handkerchief I keep in my back pocket and open it up.

"Are you comfortable?"

She moves against her bindings and shifts her delicious heart-shaped ass against the seat. A bit of it hovers over the edge, but she's secure with her feet still on the ground. We'll change that in a minute.

"Yes." She nods again.

"How are your wrists?"

She tugs a bit, and a tiny groan leaves her mouth. "They're good."

"Not too tight?"

"No. But, Kade?"

"Yes, darlin'?"

She nibbles on her lower lip. "What if someone walks down here?" Her cheeks flush, but I see the way her nipples pebble at the idea of it. I store that information in my mind for later and rub her knee gently.

"I doubt anyone will. They have no reason to."

That placates her, and she dips her head once more, so I lift the handkerchief. "I'm going to blindfold you with this."

Her eyes widen, and I see the tiniest bit of panic cross them. I let my hand drift from her knee to her thigh and stroke gently.

"You think too much, Presley. This"—I hold the fabric closer to her—"will keep you in your body. It will let you feel everything I do to you."

She swallows, licking her lips as she thinks it over. For a moment, I wonder if she'll say no, but then she nods. "Okay."

I smile warmly at her. "There's my brave girl." She blushes as I reach over to tie it around her eyes. She keeps her blue irises locked on me until the moment I cover them up. I let the warmth of her body seep into me as I take my time, knotting the blue fabric before sitting back to admire my work.

Holy Christ, she's hot. Between the belt and the blindfold, she's completely at my mercy. I'm not going to sugarcoat it—it's one of the best things I've ever seen, and I've seen a lot. But I have to say this is the first time I've done anything like this in my truck.

"Remember, if I go too far, you say stop."

"I will."

"Then relax. I'm going to make you feel good." I gently stroke her jean-clad leg then lift my hand, bringing it back down to strike the inside of her thigh. The skin jiggles, and she expels a cry from the sensation. I do it again and then strike her other thigh twice as I watch her struggle against the bindings.

"Kade!" I do it twice more on each thigh before I press two fingers against her sex. "Oh my god!" she keens.

"That was just a little reminder to always tell me the truth, darlin'. When I asked you earlier if your ass hurt, you told me no. What do you say for lying to me?" I swat her again, a little harder this time.

"I'm sorry!"

I strike her on the other thigh, this time closer to her pussy. "Will you do it again?"

"No!" She half moans, half cries her answer.

I stop the swats and shift back on the seat. "Use the bindings to steady yourself; I'm going to move your legs. Don't worry about the handle breaking. I don't care if it does."

She nods and relaxes into the belt around her wrists. I lift her sneakered feet, glad she's not wearing the boots that seem to give her calves trouble. These are far easier to remove.

As I arrange her the way I want her, I can't help wishing we'd gone somewhere with more space so I could've stripped her bare. But undressing her lower half will give me more than enough access to do what I have planned.

I keep my gaze on her as I untie her sneakers then drop them to the floor. She squirms a bit as I remove her socks, and I grin because she's just given me vital information. I tickle the soles, and she squeals, kicking at me.

"Wow, Lemon. You're ticklish." She squirms as I continue my assault. She laughs and yells my name as she tries to get away, but she has nowhere to go. When she's about to slide off the bench seat, I stop, situating her again as I chuckle. "Consider that punishment for when you said you weren't thinking about me at Night Hawk. Because you were, weren't you?"

Presley takes a deep inhale before she answers with a breathless "Yes."

Satisfied with how this is going, I skate my hands up her round calves and thighs until I reach her waist. I stop when I get there, letting my hands rest on her low belly, keeping the lightest pressure I can. She sucks her stomach in beneath my hands, and anger rises in me—not at her but at Derek and the world that made her believe she's not good enough.

"Take a deep breath in and out, Presley." Once she exhales, I move my hands again, bringing them to the snap of her jeans. "Just keep breathing." When she lets out another breath, this one sounding calmer, I undo the snap then bring her zipper down to expose her soft midsection. I don't stop as I push my fingers into the band of her pants and start to pull down.

"Lift that sexy ass up now," I coax. Once I have the space, I pull down her pants, taking her underwear with me. I think it's better this is done all at once; that way, she doesn't have time to get into her head.

Once her pants are all the way off, I drape them over the seat and look at her. Her shirt still covers her upper half, of course, but now her most private part is exposed to me.

"Remember what I said: You need to tell me if it's too much."

She bites her lip and exhales another breath before answering. "Yes, I remember."

With her verbal confirmation, I click the overhead light on to see her better. She must recognize the sound because she goes still. "Kade," she whimpers, shifting to try to cover herself up by squeezing her legs shut.

I move into action, pressing my palms on her knees to keep her spread open. "You're beautiful, Presley. Trust me when I say that." I stroke the skin of her thighs softly. "But do you want me to stop?"

She shakes her head, a quiet "no" leaving her lips. I knew it was a risk doing that, but I needed her to know I want and desire her, all of her. I don't want to keep her in the dark—this woman is meant for the spotlight, and her socking Derek in the stomach only proved that to me. I sure as hell don't need to know her life story to see this woman is not only beautiful but also special.

I shift on the seat, spreading her legs wider so that I have room to get between them. It's a tight squeeze, but I make it work. I run my palms up the skin of her legs, the stubbly new hair growing in prickling me.

"I didn't have time to shave," she blurts.

Even though she's not able to see it, I grin. I slide my hands over her legs again to make a point, groaning as I massage her thighs and her calves.

"I don't care about any of that," I assure her. "You're sexy as hell just the way you are." Then I give in to my urge to bite the dimpled skin of her inner thigh.

"Kade!" she cries.

"Just relax." I grip her thighs, shifting myself as best I can as I place her right foot on the ground while draping her left knee over my right shoulder to give me more room to feast on her. I'm in a weird position that's probably going to leave me a little sore tomorrow (not that I give a rat's ass). I position my mouth over her pussy and inhale the smell of her. My mouth practically waters, and all I can think about is drowning in her heady taste.

"Kade." She stills. "I need to tell you something."

The muscles in my shoulders go stiff as I push my right forearm into the seat to look up at her blindfolded eyes. "What is it, darlin'?"

She worries her lower lip. "I've never had someone..." She takes a breath. "I've never had someone do *that* before."

Alright, I didn't expect those words to leave her mouth. I shift my body to get up, but she traps me between her thighs. The movement brings her sweet cunt closer to me, and I groan, my hips thrusting automatically. My cock wants inside of her, but that will have to wait.

"No." She shakes her head. "Please don't stop."

Her plea only makes my cock harder, and I gently pry her legs from around my head to kiss the skin of her thighs, sucking lightly until she moans and her muscles ease.

"I won't. Just tell me if you don't like something."

"Kade," she whines. "Please, just get on with it!" Her hands struggle against my belt, and her hips lift. I chuckle and bite down on her skin again, enough to leave a small mark. She gasps then curses my name.

"Such a brat sometimes," I tease, blowing on her sex. "But I like it. Now relax your legs for me; I want to taste your sweet cunt."

Instead of being stunned by my dirty mouth like she had been at first in the loft, she does what I ask, relaxing her body so she's open for me again. Her arousal coats her inner thighs now, and I'm glad she's blindfolded because she's left a wet spot on the fabric of my truck. I smile at the trophy I get to keep and kiss my way up her stretch marks until I reach her dark curls.

"Please, Kade," she begs.

I debate teasing her for a while longer, but I'm selfish, and I want to have a taste. I want to be the first man to ever kiss and lick between her thighs.

I drag two fingers through her wet pussy, parting her lips so I can see her swollen clit. She squirms, and the belt makes noise as she tries to move her hands, no doubt to put them in my hair so she can press me into her. I want to feel her grip my hair while I make her come, but we can do that another time—this is all about her right now.

"So beautiful," I say, making sure she can hear it. Then I place my lips to her clit, kissing it gently to test out her response. She expresses an animated sound, and I smile against her sex, opening my mouth so I can suction the sensitive bundle of nerves. Her tangy flavor coats my taste buds, and I moan at the same time she does. My hips seek relief for my cock as I grind into the seat.

"Kade," she croons. "That feels amazing."

I accelerate my movements, licking and sucking and lapping at her arousal until her body starts to shake from the myriad of sensations. I'm still trying to get over the shock, the privilege, of being the first one to taste her. But I'm glad, because from what I saw of her ex, he doesn't deserve any part of her, especially the most intimate and vulnerable parts. I like that I'm the only one who has gotten to see her like this, taste her like this.

I pull back, and she whimpers, the needy sound of it going straight to my cock. I bring my fingers to her soaked entrance, and I tease her there, dipping inside slowly before pulling them back out. I repeat the action in a steady pace, fucking her slowly and gently with them.

Fuuuck. Images of my cock replacing my fingers fill my mind. I want to watch my length disappear inside her pussy. I want to feel her tight heat gripping me as she comes again and again while being held by my ropes. My cock pulses at the thought, and I fuck her a bit harder with my fingers. *Soon*, I assure myself. At least, I hope.

"Kade, please."

"Please what?"

She doesn't immediately answer, so I pull back and slap her clit. The force isn't hard, but she jumps from the surprise. I do it again, and she cries a string of curses that has me grinning like I won the lottery.

"Remember, Lemon darlin'. Use that smart mouth of yours, and tell me what you want."

"Please, Kade." She pauses to gather her courage. "Please, I want your mouth on me."

"That's my girl." I reward her by sealing my lips back over her clit, but now, I use my fingers at the same time, thrusting them inside her as I lick and suck.

"Yes!"

I hum around the nerves and plunge my fingers deeper into her tight heat. I can feel her walls starting to flutter, and I know I don't have much more time before she comes. I gently bite at her clit and curl my fingers until I feel the rough patch of skin I'm looking for.

"Oh my god!" she cries.

I thrust my fingers faster now, her arousal slick on my lips and hand as her thighs tremble from her impending orgasm. I lift my mouth and keep moving my fingers against her G-spot, and her cries become louder as I dig my blunt nails into the outside of her thigh.

"I can feel you about to come. Do you want me to make you feel good?"

"Yes!" Her chest heaves, and her wrists strain against the bindings.

I work her harder so I can hear her wet arousal through the truck cab, then I remove my hand and slap her clit again. Her body jerks, and I replace the sting with my lips, sucking on her swollen bud as she tries to ride my face by lifting her hips up.

I press into her and give her what she craves. That's all it takes for Presley to fall over the edge, and I slide my fingers back inside her so I can feel her orgasm squeeze them like she would my cock. For a moment, I allow myself to fantasize about what my cum would look like dripping out of her while her thighs shook. That image has me almost coming along with her, but by some miracle, I don't.

I let her ride out her orgasm for a minute longer until I feel her body sag with post-orgasm exhaustion. I sit up and see her hands turning slightly white from the full weight of her tired body, so I spring into action.

I wipe my hands on my jeans before removing the belt from the handle then free her wrists. Once that's done, I sit back down next to her and remove her blindfold, watching her as her eyes adjust to the dim light in the cab.

Before she can start to think about the mess between her legs and what just transpired between us, I take her chin in my hand and kiss her. My lips are still wet with her arousal, but it doesn't seem to bother her. She sighs into my mouth as I work my hands down her shoulders and her arms, restoring any circulation that was lost while I played.

"You okay?" I pull away to study her.

A giggle leaves her, and while the sound is new and surprising, it warms my heart and fills my chest cavity with butterflies.

"You could say that," she says.

I kiss her forehead, smiling against her crown. When her hand starts to creep up my thigh toward my straining length, I lay my hand over hers to stop her ascent.

"It's okay, Lemon."

She presses a kiss to my lips and tries to move her hand again. "But I want to."

I pull back and look into her eyes. The desire in them has me questioning my decision to say no. "This was for you." I tuck a strand of hair behind her ear. "We've had a long couple of days and need some rest. After that, if you still want to, I'll give you anything you want."

She blinks at me, almost as if she's trying to wake herself up from a dream. Then I think she looks a little hurt.

"Hey, now," I soothe. "I don't expect a tit for tat here. If someone taught you that, they can kick rocks. I enjoyed what we did, if you didn't notice." I grin slyly. "You giving yourself to me was enough. Please know that."

I kiss her to punctuate what I said before pulling her pants off the back of the seat. "Now, let's get inside before someone comes down here and thinks my truck is about to combust," I tease, pointing to the fogged-up windows.

She blushes and takes her pants, the real and genuine smile I worked hard to get on her face settling something in me. I don't know what it is, but I feel calmer, not as restless as I usually do. I hold on to that feeling, hoping it doesn't go away.

Chapter 26

Presley

I SIT ON THE edge of my twin bed with a permanent flush on my cheeks after last night with Kade, the sun casting a warm glow across the small room. There's not much decoration, but the walls are painted a warm green, and the white comforter and sheets are soft, giving the place a cozy feel. And while the hands' quarters don't feel like home, it's comfortable.

When I think about it, I've ever been in a place that feels like home. Not even my own home felt like a home. Neither of my parents' homes did, either, for that matter. I always just felt like a seasonal decoration, one someone likes for a short time and then puts in a box and forgets about for most of the year, if not forever.

Ping!

I pick up my phone, glad for the distraction. There's a message from Jake, letting me know that Derek is still being held at the Sheriff's Department. I was concerned that he would press charges, but it's been almost twenty-four hours, and so far, he hasn't, which goes against his character. He's the type of guy who would sue a coffee shop for their coffee burning his tongue. Regardless, I hope he got the message to stay away.

My phone pings with another message from Jake, and I open it.

> JAKE: Gavin's covering for you tonight. Please take the night off.

My stomach rolls. I'm the worst employee ever. I know Kade says Jake would never fire me, but I would fire me. I suck. I quickly type a message back.

> PRESLEY: I can come in. It's not a problem.

> JAKE: Nope. I won't hear it. However...

As I wait for his next text to come in, my mind races with all the things he's about to say, a product of my never-ending anxiety. But despite last night, I've felt a lot calmer recently. And I know who I can attribute it to.

Ping!

> JAKE: I couldn't help but overhear you play fiddle?

I bite my lower lip and chew on it. Out of all the things Jake could ask me, I'm surprised I didn't think that this would be one of them. I thought he'd ask me to work more shifts to cover my absence or prove Kade wrong and fire me, not ask me about playing fiddle.

I mull over my options. It's not like I can lie because Derek screamed it to the whole bar. Kade told me this morning while we were doing chores that what happened last night had already spread through the Randall gossip mill. Blake even came to me first thing this morning while I ate breakfast to make sure I was okay.

I couldn't help but notice that the whole time she was there, Kade kept glancing at her like he wanted to say something to her. But every time she'd look his way, he'd turn back to his food. I wanted to ask him more about why their relationship is strained, too, but we had a lot of work to do today, and there were far too many people around helping with their yearly cattle vaccinations and weighing.

My phone pings again, and I look down.

> JAKE: Did I scare you away? I shouldn't have said anything.

Great. *Now you made it weird, Presley.* With a sigh, I decide it's time to stop running from this. It's not like I don't want people to know I play fiddle, and it's not like I don't want to play. My hands have been itching to, especially since last night. The memory of Kade's mouth between my legs, his hands on my thighs, and the way he took care of me and made me feel good about myself and my body come to my mind. How he helped me feel...*free*.

Just as I feel when I'm playing music.

> PRESLEY: No, you didn't scare me away! I do play fiddle.

> JAKE: Would you be open to playing at Night Hawk sometime?

I think of standing on their small stage and playing for a crowd of people on a busy night with Kade in the audience. I know he'd be front and center, dancing and cheering me on—that's the kind of man he is. I've never had someone in my life like that before, and even though I don't know him super well, I do know he would be there.

I look across the small room to the other twin bed. My violin case is sitting on the flowered comforter, its metaphorical eyes staring at me, asking me to play—*begging* me to play. My hand clenches around my phone, and I let out a long exhale, finally making a decision.

> PRESLEY: I think I can do that.

> JAKE: Hell, yeah! Let's chat next time I see you, and we'll figure it out.

> PRESLEY: Sounds great.

> JAKE: Now go enjoy your night off ;)

The winky face throws me off a bit. A winky face implies something, right? I almost ask if he meant something by it, but instead, I tell him thank you and put my phone back on the nightstand. While I'm annoyed he gave me the time away—not only because I could use the cash after all my unplanned nights off but also because I'm the one who caused all the problems and shift shuffling the last two days—I'm thankful for the rest.

Ranch work is exhausting. I don't know how Kade and Gavin have done two jobs for so long. They operate on so few hours of sleep that it can't be healthy. I've had to drink an obscene amount of caffeine to function on a daily basis, especially after the last couple of late nights.

I blush from head to toe. The effect Kade has on me...

He's everything I thought he wasn't and more. When we first met, I assumed he was just the immature town playboy, a man who was set on getting on my nerves. But the more time I spend with him, the more I realize that he's sensitive, caring, and protective. Both times we've been intimate together, he's taken care of my needs. Which was never the case with Derek.

Sex with him was always about a quick release. *His* quick release. Looking back, I one-hundred-percent believe he was cheating on me the whole time. I question if he was ever attracted to me, especially considering how he's treated me since I stopped letting him use me for my talent.

I forget about how tired I am and stand up from my spot on the bed, walking over to my violin case. I run my hand along the black fiberglass before touching the latches. How many times have I opened this case? Thousands?

After my longest break from playing ever, I click open the latches then remove the soft cloth to reveal my beautiful instrument. I keep it pristine, taking the best care of it I can. Derek said I baby it like a real child, and in a way, it is. I love it, and it's always been there for me—not just this specific violin but every single instrument I've played before it.

Tingles spread through my body, and a smile curls at my lips when I remember the first time I ever held a violin. This small wooden instrument represents a lot of moments in my life. The first time I fell in love with music, the first time I found something just for myself that made me happy, the first thing I ever felt I was good at. The first thing that ever made me feel seen, heard, and appreciated.

I swallow down the emotion gathering in my throat, undo the Velcro strap holding in my violin, and pick it up. I release a long breath and shake my shoulders out to relax. Earlier, I thought I didn't have a home, but in a way, this violin *is* my home. That may be a weird thing to say, but I imagine it brings me comfort like a home would. It's dependable and reliable, and if something breaks on it, I fix it. When I'm holding my violin, nothing else matters.

Every fiber of my being is chanting at me to play now. If my violin could talk, I think it would be yelling at me, too. Jake has given me the night off, and Kade is somewhere on the ranch, so I might as well use the time alone to my advantage.

Decision made, I tuck my violin under my chin. My body breathes a sigh of relief as the wooden instrument finds its place, fitting perfectly as if it was always meant to be there. I pluck the strings, the steel digging into the pads of my fingers as I tune the instrument. The familiar A, D, G, and E notes wash over me like a balm to soothe all hurts.

Once that's done, I put the violin down to prepare my bow and then stretch out my body. It's sore from ranch work and nights with Kade. I beam to my empty room at the memory of his hands on my body, the way he held me while we danced, and how he comforted me as I cried after he spanked me.

Like drawing water from a well, I pull up all the different emotions I've felt so deeply in my body—in my soul—since moving to Randall. I gather each memory and feeling of pain, confusion, pride, happiness, lust, and pleasure and hold them close. I need them for what I'm about to do next.

I pick up my violin and bow and get into position. A perfect song comes to mind, a cover I never got to play with my band. They preferred to stick to original songs—or at least Derek did. This song never felt right to play around him or my band, anyway. But now, Kade's hazel eyes appear behind my eyelids, and for the millionth time today, my heart beats faster. I close my eyes and inhale before I start to play.

The rich, expressive tone of my fiddle filling my ears after so long makes me shiver, and I lose myself in the notes of "Biblical" by Calum Scott. The first time I heard this song, it resonated with me and my feeling of being isolated by Derek and my band. I so desperately wanted to connect with anyone, with anything, and be loved—and not just romantic love, but any kind of love. I just wanted to have someone who cared about me enough to ask me if I was okay, to ask me how my day was.

I pull the bow across the strings, my body swaying with the soulful notes as I take every emotion I pulled from deep within me and pour them into the song. I absorb every resonate vibration of the instrument, hear every lyric in my mind, feel every stinging press of steel into the pads of my fingers.

Tears flow down my cheeks, and I soon forget where I am, forget about everything in my life, and become a vessel of music and emotion. The song crescendos, and I think I let out a sob, but I don't stop. I feel, and I feel, and I feel, and I play my heart out.

When the song ends, the last E echoes through the small room until it fades into the air like a wisp of vapor along with my exhale. I stand there in silence for a long moment, wiping the tears from my cheeks as I process what I just experienced: my heart coming home.

It isn't until I hear a throat clear that I spin around, my gaze connecting with the eyes I can't stop seeing in my mind.

"Kade," I whisper. His stare is soft, and I can't miss the tears that stain his cheeks. I set my instrument on the bed and take a few steps toward him. He hasn't moved, and he hasn't tried to hide the fact that he's emotional.

"What's wrong?" I ask when he doesn't say anything. My hands itch to touch him, to hold him, but I don't know what I'm supposed to do in this situation. We're not dating—at least, I don't think so. But calling us friends sounds even stupider.

He opens his mouth but then closes it, as if he's speechless. Insecurity washes over me like a tidal wave, and my cheeks burn. "How long have you been standing there?"

He answers by crushing me into his body, wrapping his strong arms around me as he buries his face in my hair. I let him hold me, his warmth seeping into my bones and cocooning around me. A blank space inside me fills, and I try to remember the last time I was hugged. It's been a long time, and I've never been hugged like this, in a way that's all-consuming. I don't know where he ends and I begin.

I squeeze him harder, and he lets out a shuddering breath. "Lemon, that was..." He squeezes me tighter. "...unlike anything I've ever seen or heard." He runs his hands down my back and takes a long, shaky inhale before relaxing into me. "The way you play, it's—beyond words."

I pull back from his body and stare up into his shining eyes, wiping a tear track from his stubbled cheek. He looks so young and vulnerable in this moment that my heart aches for him, for the sadness I see in his eyes that his usual boyish flirtation hides.

Kade takes my hand from his cheek and kisses my palm. "Do you think you could play another one for me?"

Excitement flutters low in my belly at the joy I hear in his voice when he asks. "Don't you have to work tonight?"

"No, I wasn't scheduled."

I think of that winky face in Jake's text, and things click into place.

"You asked Jake to give me the night off, didn't you?"

I should probably be embarrassed that Jake knows Kade is spending time with me, but I'm surprised to find it doesn't bother me. It makes whatever is happening between Kade and I feel a little more real and not just a lot of confusing thoughts in my head.

"I did," he answers.

"Why?"

He pulls me tighter into him. "Don't act like you don't know, darlin'." The teasing tone of his voice lightens the mood in the room, and I clamp my lips together, trying to hide my own smile.

"I wanted to spend time with you," he continues. "Not mucking stalls. Not doing chores or tending bar. Just time together."

The clear desire in his voice only intensifies the feelings I've started to have for him. "What do you have in mind?"

That sly grin of his takes over his face, and he presses his hips forward so I can feel the heat of him. I bite my lower lip to keep back the whimper that tries to escape, but it doesn't go unnoticed. "Play me another song first, then I'll show you."

I laugh. "You drive a hard bargain."

He pouts his lower lip like a puppy. "Please, Presley?"

I shove his chest playfully but nod. "Since you called me by my real name," I tease, "sure. Have any requests?"

Kade grins wider then runs his nose along the shell of my ear, and I shiver and clutch my arms around his waist tighter.

"Surprise me," he whispers.

I pull back, happiness filling me from head to toe. "You got it, Cowboy."

CHAPTER 27

Kade

"Didn't I say I don't camp?" Presley eyes me warily as we get closer to Devil's Rock. I debated long and hard about bringing her to the canyon, the place of my accident and so many other good and bad memories. But after our nights together, it felt right to share this place with her.

I chuckle. "For the millionth time, we're not camping. We're hanging out."

She stares at me, like the concept of hanging out is foreign to her. Maybe it is, given all that I've been finding out about her.

"Okay, but there are a lot of rocks here." She looks out the windshield of the truck with a frown on her face. "And nothing for miles." The tone in her voice would have someone believing we were on a new planet and not a couple of miles into the Montgomery property.

"Calm down, City Girl," I tease. "I thought you weren't afraid to get a little dirty."

The suggestive tone of my statement makes her squirm. It's so easy to rile her up, and I love it. I bet she's getting wet for me already. My eyes glance to the towel I laid on the seat to cover her mess from last night. Images of her coming on my tongue while restrained fill my mind and make me half hard.

I bite the inside of my cheek and grip the steering wheel to try to chill, not wanting tonight to be about sex. I told her we would hang out, and that's what I plan to do. Not to mention, this is the first time I've been back here since my accident.

I've managed to keep how I'm feeling hidden, not wanting Presley to worry, but my stomach has been a ball of nerves. Not because I'm afraid to bring her here or that I'm scared of Devil's Rock, but I have no idea how I will actually feel when I'm standing in the same spot where I almost lost my life. I inhale a shallow breath and will myself to remain steady and calm.

"We're here," I say, stopping a short distance from where we'll set up for the evening. Normally, I'd ride horses to the canyon, but Presley wouldn't have been comfortable. She's got a long way to go until she'll ride at more than a snail's pace, which means it would've taken us over an hour to get here. And riding back in the dark would've been even more of a challenge.

Once I throw the truck into park, I turn to her. "In all seriousness, I promise, no camping. But someday I'll get you to camp, and I'll even bring a bed for you to sleep on."

That makes her laugh and smile wide. "Isn't that against camping rules?"

I match her mood, secretly happy that she didn't balk at me talking about future plans. I put my hand on her thigh and squeeze. "I'd go against all the rules for you, if it makes you smile like that."

Presley glances down at my hand, turning shy. We'll need to work on that. I always want her to be comfortable looking me in the eye, especially when I'm saying something that pertains to the good things about her.

"Come on," I say, reaching over the back seat to grab the things I brought. "I want to catch the sunset. The canyon lights up this time of year."

Supplies in hand, we both hop out of the truck, and I breathe a sigh of relief that she didn't try to lock herself inside the cab instead of joining me.

Presley walks around the vehicle to stand in front of me, her hands in the pockets of her usual black jeans. It's windy tonight and a little colder now that the heatwave has broken. Her blonde-and-purple locks whip around her face, and the oversized black-and-purple flannel ripples in the wind around the curves of her body. Against the backdrop of the canyon, she looks a little out of place. Her grunge vibes don't quite match the vastness of south Texas, yet somehow, she fits.

Presley's lips tip up at me as she tries to keep her hair from flying in her eyes. "If a storm comes and a tornado picks us up, you have to protect me from the Wicked Witch when we get to Oz."

I snort. "Didn't picture you as a *Wizard of Oz* girl."

"I like musicals. And Judy Garland was a beast."

I step up next to her, slinging the backpack I have over one arm and putting a canvas bag of food in the same hand so I can put my arm around her shoulders. "I can't disagree with you there," I say.

"Do you like musicals?" she asks.

"I can't say one way or the other. I didn't watch much TV or movies growing up. At least not the kind you want to tell your friends about." I wink at her.

She screws up her face. "Seriously, Kade?"

I chuckle, taking my arm from her shoulders to grab her hand. "I'm just teasing."

"Sure you are."

I bump my hip against hers as we walk through the rugged terrain, a change from the mesquite-dotted plains surrounding our immediate property. I enjoy the way things have become easy between us. I wouldn't have guessed this happening the first time I met her, but now I find she's the easiest person in my life to be around. That's another reason I decided to bring her here.

After we walk for five minutes, we climb up a rocky incline then come to a stop at the top of the granite rock formation. Both of us are breathing a little harder from the effort.

I drop my items on the ground and tip my head back, inhaling the fall air. It smells like Texas sage and dirt, a smell that's familiar to me after so many years of coming here. That smell triggers a lot of memories, some good and some bad, though I find the scent calms my nerves instead of aggravating them. I take that as a good sign.

Presley looks around, tucking more of her hair behind her ears. "What is this place?"

I put a hand on my hip, pressing my ball cap down on my head with the other so it doesn't fly away. The wind isn't as bad now that we're protected by the small canyons and scattered red- and rust-colored rock formations of varying sizes, but since we're still in the midst of the plains, it's got some power to it.

This"—I point to one of the formations that resembles a horned figure—"is Devil's Rock." I try to keep any emotion or lingering nerves out of my voice. As far as I'm concerned, she knows nothing about my accident. Even if she did, she wouldn't know where it took place. But I woke up this morning wanting to bring her here, to show her the place that, until not too long ago, was a place of solace for me. It was always a place to sit with nature and clear my thoughts, to shoot the shit with Dad and Gavin and talk to each other, work through our differences.

Not only that, but after hearing Presley play her violin, the desire to share such an integral part of my upbringing, of my home—of my *soul*—felt right. Needed, even. Because after witnessing the way she played with every part of her being, I think a part of me that was left in this canyon that night began to heal. The part of me that died here.

I swallow the emotion fighting to come out of me, and I wish I had already told her about what happened here. Then I wouldn't feel the need to hide what I'm feeling now. I wouldn't want to grab her and hold her against me, thanking her for something she's not even aware she's done. But I'm hoping to change that tonight, because she deserves to know more about me. She deserves to have a piece of me like I now have a piece of her.

"Is the rock supposed to look like devil horns?" Presley's velvety voice breaks me from my thoughts.

I clear my throat and look at her profile. She squints her eyes and cocks her head all cute, hand planted on her hip. It makes a smile return to my lips. "Yep, that's how it got its name."

She stares at it skeptically then shrugs her shoulders. "I'm not so sure I see it, but whatever floats your boat." I bark a laugh, and she turns to grin at me. "It's beautiful, though. I can see why you like it."

I grab her hand and kiss the back of it. "I brought some food. I know it's a little windy, so if you want to leave, we can."

She shakes her head. "I'm fine." She looks to the western sky at the setting sun. "I want to see that sunset you promised."

I nod, glad she wants to stay, then I jump into action. Much like our first night in the loft together, she helps me spread out the blanket I brought, then we weigh the edges of it down by placing some rocks on the four corners. Once that's done, I hand her a camping pillow to sit on before laying out the food. It's just a couple of sandwiches and random sides I got at the general store right before they closed.

I had called Jake in a panic, asking him what to bring on a picnic, and he'd laughed at me. But if we're getting real here, I've never taken a woman I like out for a picnic. I've never even packed a picnic, and it's not like I was going to ask Gran or Momma for help. I ignore the sting in my chest I feel thinking of them and sit down beside Presley before passing her a can of soda.

She stares at it then at me. I know what she's thinking, and I can't blame her for that. "Sorry." I rub the back of my neck. "I left my flask back in my room. I thought we'd stay sober tonight, if that's alright."

Her face softens as she tucks her hair behind her ears again, but it just flies in front of her face. "It's perfectly alright." She takes the can and sets it next to her. When her hair blows in front of her eyes yet again, blocking her view, she lets out a huff of frustration.

"Sorry, Lemon. We can go eat in the truck."

She stops me with her hand on my arm. "Not a chance. I'll be fine."

A light-bulb moment strikes me, and my eyes light up. "I have an idea!"

Presley watches me with curiosity as I take my pocketknife out of the back of my jeans.

"Um, Kade? Cutting my hair is not the answer."

I shake my head. "I'm not going to cut your hair." I pull out a piece of twine that was used to secure one of the cheeses I bought and cut off a small piece. "Scoot up a bit so I can sit behind you," I say.

Presley looks at me funny but does what I ask anyway, and my heart palpitates from the display of continual trust she's shown me. I place my own camping pillow behind her then get into position so she's sitting between my legs.

"Hold this for me," I say, giving her the twine. Once my hands are free, I bring them up to her scalp and drag my fingers through her wind-blown locks, gently working through the tangles. A small sigh leaves her lips, and then she stiffens.

"What are you doing?"

I continue to work my fingers through her hair. "I'm braiding your hair for you."

I imagine if I could see her face right now, it would be confused, but I continue with my task.

"You're braiding my hair?" she asks. Yep, she's confused. I guess I would be, too. I'm sure that asshole ex of hers wouldn't know how to braid hair. Even if he did, his fragile masculinity would be reason enough for him to never admit it.

"That I am." I start to work the sections down her head, gathering more in each one to create a French braid. It won't be the best in the world, but it will keep her hair out of her face while we're here. She sighs as my nails drag across the sensitive skin of her scalp then again when I tug the pieces tight.

"How did you learn to braid hair?" she asks after a moment, her body relaxing against mine as the breeze blows around us.

"I braided my horse's hair for rodeos when I was younger. Then I started to braid my own rope as a hobby when I would get bored."

"I see." I can hear the smile in her voice as she says it. "What did you do at the rodeo?"

I lean close so my lips are against her ear. I enjoy the way she shivers when she feels my breath there. "Roping," I say, letting my lips kiss her now exposed neck. "But mostly reining." I ask her for the twine and make sure my fingers drag over her hand as I take it in mine. Satisfied with the way the braid looks, I tie the end then give it a little tug. "All done."

To my surprise, Presley doesn't move. Instead, she leans back into me. I stroke my palms from her shoulders and down her arms, stacking mine on top of hers so that our fingers entwine. She turns her head and tilts her chin up so she's looking at me then removes her hands and directs mine so that they're sliding over her stomach.

Even though her body tenses, she holds eye contact with me as she does it. My heart swells with pride, and a tingling warmth spreads throughout every crack and crevice in my body. Not only did she share her violin playing with me earlier, but now she's conquering one of her biggest vulnerabilities.

This is a big moment for her. For us. Bigger than anything we've done so far.

With a smile tugging at her lips, she places her arms over mine and entwines our hands once more over the middle of her stomach. I lean down and hover my lips over hers, the breeze gently blowing between us. As I'm about to close the distance, she does it for me, pressing her lips to mine.

The kiss is short and chaste and the most intimate I've ever had. When Presley pulls away, she sighs happily and leans back into my chest. Our eyes turn toward the sunset, but I'm not paying close attention to the burning orange and yellow colors in the sky. I'm much too focused on the woman in my arms—how her weight feels against me, the way the berry scent of her hair tickles my nose, and that every minute we spend together, I feel as though something foundational in me shifts like a tectonic plate.

"It's beautiful here," she says. "Do you come here a lot?"

I start to play with her fingers before I press my cheek to the side of her head. It's my way of seeking comfort, even if I don't want to admit I need it. Especially since she's asking questions that will get me closer to revealing why I wanted to bring her here.

"I haven't been here in almost four months. But I would come quite often before that—though not as much as before my dad died. He used to bring Gavin and I out here quite a bit, especially if there was something we had to work through or something he wanted to talk to us about. Then there were times Dad and I would come out here together as well."

Presley lets me trace the lifelines on one of her palms as she says, "Tell me about him."

"My dad?"

She nods. "You told me about why you and Gavin have been having issues, that he lied about the situation you were in a few months back and that your dad left him the land. But I don't know much about you, Kade. I feel like you know too much about me at this point."

I shake my head. "I want to know everything about you."

She rolls her eyes. "You can be really cheesy sometimes."

"You haven't seen anything yet, Lemon darlin'. Stick around long enough, and there'll be so much cheese, you can make nachos."

"Okay, now you're just being weird."

I squeeze her again then pull away so I can sit next to her instead. She looks at me funny, but I gesture to the food. "Let's eat before we lose light."

She crosses her legs and looks at the food then at me. "Are you trying to avoid my request?"

"Maybe." I chuckle. While I do want to tell her about my dad, the words feel like peanut butter on the roof of my mouth.

Presley knocks my shoulder with hers. "You don't have to tell me anything, Kade. But I'm here to listen."

I expel a small breath then hand her a sandwich wrapped in tinfoil. It's not the most romantic, but I tried. She takes it from me, opening it slowly while I do the same with mine.

"My dad was complicated," I say eventually, after I swallow a bite of ham and cheese. "He was a good man, but he had some issues. He drank too much and probably acted more like a friend than a father most of the time, but I loved him, and he loved me. He loved our family. The old man always made sure we knew that, even if he didn't outwardly show it with hugs or words. He liked working the land, and he loved Randall. He never left Texas—not once. And he hardly ever left Randall unless he had to."

Presley's eyes bug out of her head. "Seriously?"

"It's not uncommon for people from a town as small as this to never leave. Sometimes it's for financial reasons, and other times, they just don't want to. The latter was the case with my dad. Like I said, he loved this place, this land, and Texas. He passed that love down to me."

"Are you saying you've never left Randall?"

I take a sip of soda and shake my head. "I did a few youth rodeos a couple of hours north of here that Momma or Gran would take me to, and of course, I've been to the city. But I've never left the state of Texas, if that's what you mean."

"Never?!"

I laugh. "Pick your mouth up off the floor, darlin'. Like I said, it's not uncommon around here. I almost left once for a reining competition in Arizona, but it didn't work out. After that, I've just never had a reason to." I can't help the wave of sadness that crashes in my chest when I think about my answer. It's just another reminder of the dreams I once had that were crushed.

Presley cocks her head. "If you had a reason to leave now, would you?"

I puff out a breath. "If you would've asked me that question three months ago, I would've said no. But now, I'm not so sure." I brush the crumbs off my lap and stare into her questioning sapphire eyes.

Presley puts down her sandwich, mirroring me. "What happened three months ago?"

My gaze lowers to my lap before I look out at the sky. I brought her here to not only share Devil's Rock but also to tell her about my accident. I wanted this moment to happen. She deserves to know about it, especially if this goes further between us—whatever "this" is—and I hope it does. It's another surprising thought I never would've had before, but I'm not mad about it because it excites me more than anything ever has.

"Have you heard anything about me?" I ask before I blab something she may already know. "The gossip is strong here, if you haven't noticed."

She huffs a laugh. "I've noticed. But I haven't heard much, just people talking about an accident. And there was that night with that woman, the one named after a bug."

"Cricket." I smirk.

"Yes, her." Presley scrunches up her face. "She said something to the effect that you weren't the same since the anniversary of your dad's death and the accident."

"I was never with Cricket, by the way. She cheated on Gavin before he met Blake."

She waves her hand like it's nothing, but I grab it in midair and squeeze. "She likes to come into Night Hawk when he's not there and flirt with me. She thinks I'll sleep with her to hurt him, but I won't. I'll admit, I've led her on a bit to piss off Gavin, which isn't right, either, but I have never and will never do anything with Cricket."

She squeezes my hand back. "You didn't have to tell me, but thank you. I'm glad you didn't have sex with a woman named after a bug."

I laugh with my whole chest. "I'm glad, too. My brother was not so lucky."

This time, she laughs as I let go of her hand, taking another sip of my drink.

"So you got in an accident?" she asks once we've settled again, our food now forgotten at our sides.

I look around the canyon. I was right that the sunset would be beautiful. The rocks seem to glow in the warm light, but that warmth does nothing to quell the anxious energy curling inside me as the memories of that night start to flood back.

As if she can sense I need her closer, Presley scoots over until our thighs are touching and she can rest her head on my shoulder. The gesture is grounding and gives me what I need to continue.

"The night of my accident, I came here after I'd fought with my family. I was angry and drunk. It was stupid of me, but I—" I swallow. "I was blinded by my anger—anger at my brother for his lies, anger at my dad for *his* lies, anger at my family for their judgment of me and for always siding with Gavin or ignoring me altogether. I realized that they never took me seriously, even if they pretended to."

Presley holds my hand, her thumb gently brushing over my still bruised knuckles.

"What made that day worse was it was the anniversary of Blake's brother's death, who died in a horseback-riding accident years ago. They hold a remembrance at the cemetery each year, and after I found the business plan that Blake made for the dude ranch, I flipped, thinking she was trying to buy the ranch out from under us to help expand her family's business. I went to the cemetery, confronted Gavin, sucker punched him, then drove to a bar and got into a physical altercation over a woman I was seeing at the time."

I dare a glance at Presley, hoping I haven't shared too much information. Given how our relationship started and what she's heard about me through gossip, I know it's not a surprise for her to hear that I was with another woman.

Presley's eyes are nothing but soft and understanding. She squeezes my hand. "I'm listening."

Those two words sink into me, words I've wanted to hear my family say for a very long time now. I blink back the sting in my eyes and exhale. "I went back to the house, and my family was there with Blake, smiling and laughing and eating fucking barbecue, and I—all I saw was red. I took a bottle of whiskey to the barn loft and drank until I couldn't see straight. Next thing I knew, I was getting on an ATV with plans to come here. Blake tried to stop me, but I told her off. I don't even know how I made it here without crashing."

Presley strokes her thumb over the top of my hand, but she stays quiet.

"I walked up to this spot." My eyes stay trained on the sunset, but my body feels as if I'm in that moment again. "I went to the ledge and stood there for a while. Then the rain started coming down, and it got slippery, like standing on an oil spot. I started screaming at the top of my lungs, pretending my dad could hear me. I wanted him to know how much pain I was in, how much shit he was putting us all through by not telling us the truth. I—" My voice breaks.

"Kade," Presley soothes. "You don't have to tell me this if you don't want to."

I shake my head. "No, I need to tell someone. I never—Presley." Her name spills from me like a frantic call for aid. She clasps my hand harder at the sound of it. "I don't think I stepped off the edge. The doctor told me I had an adrenaline-induced heart attack, and that's probably how I fell. But..." I exhale. "I don't know. I might have stepped off before then, or I slipped. I can't remember. I was so angry, and I felt like my heart was going to explode in my chest from the weight of it all."

I sighed. "I woke up on the ledge below this one with Blake crying over me and pain riddling my body. We were both taken to the hospital, and after I underwent surgery on my arm, they checked my heart to make sure I didn't have any blocks. That was a blur, too. I mostly just remember waking up in my hospital room and telling Gavin the whole thing was an accident. But, Presley—" My voice breaks again, chest tightening and that pain flaring in my sternum. "Presley, I don't know, I don't remember, I might've—" I lose my words, my lungs stinging as if the air I'm breathing has turned toxic.

Presley shifts so she can face me, her hand gripping my face that's wet with tears for the second time today. "Kade, you need to take a breath for me, okay?" she asks. "You're panicking."

I jerk my head in a nod, attempting to focus on her calm features. She inhales, and I follow her, sucking in a breath. My lungs take in the air, but all I feel is pain. Pain in my lungs, pain in my chest, pain in my heart and soul. Pain I've tried to numb and keep from spilling to the surface. A lot of good that did me, because now it feels as if I can't stop it.

"Remember how you helped me last night?" she asks, still no judgment in her tone. I find myself nodding as I suck in another sharp breath. "List off random things. Like penguins, cowboy boots, roses."

I do as she says, trying to think of random words. "Laundry, football, raccoons, reins, peanuts," I say, breathing between words. I don't know how it works, but the pressure in my chest starts to lessen.

"That's it." She smiles. "Again."

"Dancing, dogs, banjo, tractor, violin." I exhale, my hands now steadier and my breathing more even. Her eyes soften, and she has me do another list and then another until my heart no longer beats in my ears.

"Better?" she asks.

My body is still tense, but I can't deny that I do feel better. "That really worked."

She manages a small smile. "Sometimes I can be helpful."

I stroke her cheek, more grateful for her than I think she'll ever understand. "Not just sometimes." If it wasn't darker now, I'm sure I'd see her blush at my words.

"Want to lie down? That helps me, too."

I nod, and both of us start moving the food and everything else out of the way. Once we're settled on the blanket, we stare up at the sky. I pull Presley into my chest, and she nestles her head into the crook of my neck. I inhale the scent of her and let it calm the remaining thrum of energy coursing through my body.

"You know," Presley says after a while. The sun is completely gone from the sky. "When I was a junior in high school, I was in a bad place mentally."

I look down at her while stroking her flannel-covered arm. "You were?"

"I've always struggled with being awkward and having anxiety attacks, but that year was bad for me. For backstory, my parents divorced when I was five, so I took turns at each of their houses. But my junior year, my dad completely checked out and decided to move to California. He didn't even offer me the chance to move with him. To top it off, my mom had a new daughter with my stepdad, and their focus was all on her. I felt replaced, like I didn't matter. And at school, I was the weird, nerdy, chubby girl who wore all black and preferred playing her violin to hanging out with people. I had a couple of friends but never super close ones."

I mull over her words. Everything I know of Presley starts to make more sense, like the tiles of the Rubik's cube of her have finally all aligned.

"I started to think the world would be better off without me. It wasn't like anyone would notice."

I don't miss the way her voice wavers. I squeeze her tighter to me then and play with her braid. I've only known her for a short time, but it's hard to imagine a world without her in it.

"What made you better?"

She lets out a sad sigh. "I don't know if that's the right word, but music saved me. Music has always saved me...or I should say, my orchestra teacher did. She noticed something was off with me, and I ended up talking to the school social worker once a week. I fueled all my pain and hurt into music. She reminded me I'd be going to college soon, that my life would change. She was right—it *did* change. And it was better for a time, until after college."

"What happened then?"

She plays with the fabric of my shirt. "Derek happened."

His name from her lips makes me want to deck the guy again. "Can I ask you a question?"

She looks up at me at my words, her hand coming to rest over my heart. Her touch is tender, and I can't stop myself from placing my hand over hers.

"You can ask me anything."

"How long were you with him?"

"I met him not too long after I graduated from college six years ago. We broke up earlier this year, so just under that."

I'm glad it's dark so she can't see the tightness in my jaw. "What made you stay with him?"

She chuckles. Her tone is both sad and angry. "That's a good question. I'd like to say I don't know, but he was the first man to see me. Or at least I *thought* he was. Turns out, he just saw my talent and wanted to use me for it. I stayed because he was the first consistent thing I had in my life besides school. For a while, it seemed like he cared, and I had never gotten that from my parents. He gave me a family with the band, too. Were they the best family in the world? No. But they were better than what I had. At least I was wanted and useful to them."

I stroke my palm down her arm, so many things I want to say in response running through my brain. That she deserves better than a mediocre group of people who use her for their own personal gain tops the list. But like me, I know she wants someone to listen, to be there for her without judgment.

"So why did you leave?"

Presley tenses but doesn't make a move to get up. "We got offered a record deal. I was supposed to sign on the dotted line the day I came here. That's why Derek was so angry. But Kade, I couldn't." She takes a deep inhale. "I couldn't do that to myself. I just kept imagining the rest of my life with that band, with Derek constantly putting me down and telling me that even though I was one of the best players he'd ever heard, I was still replaceable. He knew that was my biggest fear, to be tossed aside like yesterday's trash. That's why he sent those pictures that night of my replacement. He was hoping it would make me come back, some fucked-up power play to get me back in the band."

The rage I felt when I punched him zings through my body, my sore knuckle throbbing from the memory of connecting with his smarmy face. This beautiful woman didn't deserve anything that happened to her.

I kiss her forehead. "You did the right thing by leaving."

She shifts so she can look at my face again, her gaze penetrating into mine even in the darkness. "Really?"

"You stood up for you, for your life. You're incredibly talented, Presley. When I saw you play today...fuck, darlin', it was beautiful. *You're* beautiful. You deserve to be heard and appreciated. Not just your music, but you."

"Kade." She sighs, her head dropping to my shoulder at the compliment.

"Look at me, Presley." When she eventually does, I tuck a piece of hair that's come loose from her braid behind her ear. "You're not replaceable. You're remarkable." She bites her lip at my words but continues to look at me. "Believe me when I say that. There's a reason you stand out—and it's not because of your hair and tattoos. It's because you're you. I know it may not mean a lot coming from a fuckup like me, but believe it. The people who don't see that, they're the replaceable ones."

Presley sits up, and for a moment, I panic that she's going to leave. But then she's pulling me up and throwing her arms around my neck. I feel wetness from her eyes on my throat as she hugs me. "You're not a fuckup, Kade. You're human. And you're not replaceable, either."

I hug her tighter to me as I try to take in her words. "I think my family would disagree."

She shakes her head before pulling back. "You fight with them because you love each other. I've seen the way Gavin looks at you, the way Blake did at breakfast. I can't speak for your mom or your gran, but from what you've told me, I'm going to say they're in pain, too, and don't know how to communicate with you."

I stare at Presley's hands as she continues to speak. "You said something to me last night in the truck, that we can't control the actions of someone else. That only Derek was to blame for what happened last night. Do you remember?"

"I remember." I remember because as soon as the words were out of my mouth, I felt like a hypocrite. But I hadn't wanted to think about it.

"I can't speak for you, Kade, and I can't speak to your situation, but I do know my own. If I had a family who loved me as much as yours does, I'd do everything I could to make it right with them." She squeezes my hand. "And I'm not saying that has to be now or that they don't need to take responsibility for their part in all this, but they couldn't control the actions of your dad. They're just trying to pick up the pieces, too. Like you are."

"He left the land to the one person who didn't want it," I say, exasperated—not at her but at the part of me that wants to cling to my anger.

"Is that really what this is about?"

I look from our entwined hands to her eyes, the moon and the stars illuminating her features.

She brings her hand to my cheek. "You're still young. You had to grow up fast, and I can relate to that. But when we were talking about you never leaving the state of Texas, what did that feel like?"

I swallow, saying the first word that comes to mind. "Sad."

She runs the pad of her thumb over my lips as the wind picks up around us. "There's a whole world outside of Texas, outside of your ranch."

"What are you saying?"

"Do not limit yourself to what you think you need to want, what you think you need to be. It sounds like you have the opportunity now to do something else if you want."

My thoughts from earlier this week spring to mind again, of what it would be like to leave. My muscles grow tense, and an innate part of me that was bred to live and die on this ranch screams that it's not an option. But the rational part of me knows she's right. My brother and Blake could handle this ranch, no problem. They don't need me.

"You've given me a lot to think about."

"This"—she looks around—"isn't going anywhere. But you can, Kade. You can."

I pull her back down to the ground with me, and we stare up at the smattering of stars across the cloudless sky. The wind is starting to get stronger, and I know we should head back soon, but there's a part of me that doesn't want to, that wants to stay out here holding Presley forever. That's easier than facing reality.

"And what about you?" I ask after a few minutes, my hand rubbing down her back as I find the North Star by following the handle of the Big Dipper.

"What about me?" she asks.

"Are you going anywhere?" There's a vulnerability in my tone I didn't expect. While this thing with her is new, and I don't know where it's going, a nagging voice in my mind says I would be heartbroken if she left.

I feel her shift, and then she's looking into my eyes. "Not right now."

Her words soothe the voice temporarily, and a smile lights up my face that she matches with her own. I kiss her forehead then hug her body to mine. "Good. Because I don't want you to."

CHAPTER 28

Presley

You know that feeling you get when something is going so well that you're waiting for it to blow up in your face? That's how I feel right now, but I've been trying to ignore it because I want to bask in the excitement of things finally going right after so long.

Kade smiles across the barn aisle at me, his ball cap turned backward on his head as he whistles a country tune along with the radio like he normally does while working. It's been almost two weeks since our night at Devil's Rock, and to be honest, I'm a little worried about him. He's been...

Chipper.

When I first met him, I wouldn't have used that word as a descriptor for him. Flirty? Yes. Annoying? Yes. Mostly salty and sweet? Yes. But chipper?

I'm not complaining that he's happy—I want him to be happy—but sometimes I wonder if his new attitude is a way for him to mask all the pain and emotions he has inside him. Especially since I haven't seen him touch a drop of alcohol recently, the crutch he tended to use before.

Again, I'm not complaining. I just know that talking about your problems once doesn't solve them.

I've gently tried to speak to him about it, but he insists he's fine, that he feels better than he has in a long time. He said that if he needs to talk he will, and I have to respect that, especially since he respects me in the same way.

A small smile tugs at the corner of my lips when I think about how patient and caring he is with me. He's even gone out of his way to do things he knows will make me feel safe and comfortable, like buying me the brand-new pair of wide-calf cowboy boots that are currently on my feet. I cried when he put them on me—nobody has ever done something like that for me or gotten me such a thoughtful gift. They weren't cheap, either, so knowing that he spent his money to make me comfortable is something I don't take lightly.

To top it off, he started carrying an extra one of my calming inhalers in his pocket in case I forget to bring one with me or lose the one I have. But like Kade not drinking, I've found I've been using it less and less, to the point I've gone days without. Last night was the only exception.

When Jake asked me last week to play a gig with a few of his friends for their costume event tonight, I said yes. I was excited at the prospect of being onstage and playing my fiddle for more than just Kade. But the more I thought about it, the more anxious I got. Then, while I was practicing last night, my anxiety got the best of me, and I used the inhaler to stop the onset of an even bigger attack.

Kade asked me what I was so nervous about, and I couldn't answer. It's not like Night Hawk is the Grand Ole Opry. It's a small gig in front of locals and customers; I shouldn't be freaked out about it. But it'll be the first time I've played in public since leaving the band, and I want to do a good job.

"Are you thinking about the gig tonight?" Kade calls over to me.

The sounds of other ranch hands and country music whooshes back into my ears, and I'm reminded of where I am. I also realize I've been sifting the same pile of shavings for probably five minutes now.

I smile sheepishly at him as he walks—with a pep in his step—across the aisle and props his pitchfork on the doorframe so he can put his hands on my shoulders. He's sporting a lopsided grin on his face, and there's light shining in his hazel eyes. Like I said, chipper. But who knows? Maybe I am overthinking his new attitude. I'm not used to being around happy people. I'm not used to being happy myself. And Kade, he makes me happy. Really happy. Maybe this attitude is because I make him happy, too.

He shakes me playfully, and my cheeks flush. "Sorry, I was thinking about it." *Among other things.*

He chuckles, squeezing my shoulders. "You have nothing to worry about, Lemon. Even if you got up on stage and completely bombed, which we know you won't, everyone will love you."

"You're ridiculous, you know that?"

"Not ridiculous—I'm just speaking facts. You're going to do great. I can't wait to cheer you on."

I blush, a permanent side effect of being around Kade, and picture him front and center tonight wearing this goofy smile of his.

Like he knows what I'm thinking, his grin gets wider. "You know, I have an idea about how to take your mind off it for a while."

I quirk an eyebrow at him. "What is it?"

He steps back and rubs his hands together excitedly. "It's time to go eat lunch before we preg-check some heifers!"

I groan. He's way too excited about eating food then going to check cows for pregnancy. "I thought you were joking about that earlier."

His eyes shine with laughter, and he shakes his head. "Ranch life isn't glamorous, darlin'. Sometimes you gotta stick your arm up a cow's ass."

Just as Kade finishes, Art walks by with a wheelbarrow full of muck. "You're a kinky motherfucker, Kade," he says, shaking his head with a grin.

"You have no idea, Arturo." Kade winks and turns back to me. The heated look in his eyes now dark with lust has me forgetting about ranch life and clenching my thighs together. Only Kade could make me do a one-eighty like that.

It also has to do with the fact that we haven't had more than make-out sessions and heavy petting since that night in the truck. Not only has ranch work increased significantly, but Jake also asked us to pick up extra shifts at Night Hawk. A social media post went viral, and we've been slammed with wedding parties.

It didn't help that Gavin took a break from his shifts to focus on the dude ranch as well. Kade said he expected that news at some point, but I could see it shocked him. Not because of the reasoning, but because he learned it from Jake and not from Gavin himself. Kade divulged to me that it hurt his feelings to find out that way, but when I suggested he speak with his brother, he said he wasn't ready to go there yet, that he was still thinking about everything we talked about at Devil's Rock.

I think a part of him also wants Gavin to be the one to break the ice. At this point, it feels like a vicious cycle that someone needs to break, but I'm letting Kade work through his feelings because I know he's been pushed enough.

I just hope he talks to Gavin soon so it's at least less awkward between them. When they see each other, they keep things strictly business, but I can tell that they both want to say something and are too prideful to do it.

"Presley." My name brings my attention back to him. "What are you thinking about?"

I brush my more serious reflections away, my eyes moving to his mouth. My lips part, and when I meet his gaze again, his pupils are darker, and the way he's focused on me makes goosebumps pebble across my skin despite the warmth of the day. Now I'm only thinking about what his lips feel like on mine and how his hands feel on my body.

"Kade," I say, the arousal evident in my voice.

"Tell me what you're thinking about," he repeats. His tone is commanding and heady this time, but before I can answer, the distant sound of Art and the other ranch hands talking outside reaches my ears.

While Kade and I haven't exactly hidden our attraction to each other, we haven't publicly made any sort of declaration regarding our budding relationship or kissed in front of anyone. Jake is really the only one who knows exactly how much time Kade and I spend together outside of work. But the rumor mill has spun their theories since the night Derek came to Night Hawk, enough that Blake and June tried to ask me if there was something going on between us one morning over breakfast, but I played coy, not wanting to dive into it with anyone when Kade and I haven't even talked about it. That fact would have given me anxiety in the past, but after going through my last toxic relationship, it's nice to just take things day by day and spend time together when we can.

Kade encroaches on my space, backing me up until I'm against the stall wall. "Lemon," he whispers. "Do I need to take you over my knee?"

I suck in a sharp breath and study the planes of his square features. My nipples go hard against my bra at the suggestion. "I was thinking about you," I finally say. "About us and how much I miss you."

He grins, knowing exactly what I mean. "Then what do you say we spend our lunch break getting a little up close and personal."

I lick my lips as he takes the pitchfork from my hand, propping it next to us before pressing his warm body into mine. It reminds me that we've been working all morning. "We're all sweaty—and anyone could walk by."

He waggles his eyebrows. "Even better."

I swat his chest playfully, but I'll admit a part of me loves that he doesn't care about showing public affection for me or that I probably look like I rolled around in shavings—two things my ex would have balked at.

Kade tucks a piece of hair behind my ear. "I know it's been hectic lately." He nips at my lips. "So let's be a little reckless, darlin'. Let me kiss you"—his lips move to my ear—"touch you a little."

I stifle a groan from his hot breath on my ear and grind my hips into his.

"Presley." He runs his hand up my neck, thumb pressing into my pulse. "Can I kiss you?"

I look into his eyes and think how the old Presley would've never considered making out with a guy in a horse stall with people nearby. But Kade has made me more than just happy—he's turned me into a woman I hardly recognize. But I can't say I don't love it.

"Yes."

Not wasting another moment, he grips the back of my skull and crushes my lips to his. I open my mouth with practiced ease, letting him lick inside so our tongues tangle together. I moan into the feeling and taste of him, the sounds of the barn and my worries about our coworkers fading to the back of my mind.

He keeps one hand in my hair then runs the other down my side and over my stomach, still being careful not to press too hard and make me uncomfortable. The thoughtfulness he shows, even in our heated moments, has me wanting to tear his clothes off. That image has been running through my mind more and more each day.

When my nails dig into his biceps, he groans into my mouth and presses his cock against me, moving his hand to my thigh so he can hitch my leg up over his hip. The new angle has my sex right over his length, pressing the seam of my jeans into my clit. I let out a cry into his mouth, thankful it mutes the noise.

Just as I tug the damp strands of sandy-blond hair at the base of his neck, a throat clears.

I let out a squeak of surprise and pull back. Kade doesn't jump away quickly like I would've if I was in his position.

Instead, he releases my leg and kisses me on the nose before turning to tip his hat to his brother.

"Gavin."

I think I turn the color of a firetruck. I knew someone seeing us was possible, but I thought if anyone did, it would be Art or another one of the hands. Gavin is usually with Blake doing office work or watching over the new builds and repairs.

Seeing him, the man who's technically my boss, after making out with his brother is awkward. This also means that if Gavin thought Kade and I were just a rumor before, we aren't anymore. Now he's seen us together, and he knows it's real. We're real.

Gavin stares at Kade, his brow pinched and lips pressed together. "Can I talk to you for a minute, Kade?" he asks.

Kade puts his shoulders back, the ease and playfulness he had with me gone now.

"Presley and I have somewhere to be," Kade says.

Gavin looks away from his brother's steely gaze and turns to me. "You can have the rest of the afternoon off, Presley."

I take a step forward from where I'd been frozen on the wall. My mind is still reeling with the realization that Kade and I are real. I think I knew it before, but this has just solidified it for me. Our relationship is not just something Jake knows anymore, not just a rumor going around. And while being together, or whatever it is we are, complicates everything—including what our futures may hold—I can't help but feel excited, even in this awkward situation.

I make eye contact with Gavin, my mouth opening to argue that I can stay and help, but the stern look on his face makes me think twice.

I turn my focus to Kade, and he shakes his head at me. "You can stay," he says.

"That's not necessary," Gavin retorts.

"Presley is helping me today."

"I think she's helped enough." As soon as the words leave Gavin's mouth, I feel insulted and embarrassed by them. The urge to run out of the stall and never come back takes over me, but I don't. Presley from her first shift at Night Hawk would have, but after everything that's happened, I don't want to leave Kade alone.

I open my mouth to say something, but Kade beats me to it. "Fuck you, Gavin."

Both Gavin and I stiffen at the intensity of his words, but they seem to snap Gavin out of whatever made him say that. The cowboy's face relaxes, and his eyes soften. "I'm sorry, Presley. That was extremely rude and uncalled for. Please, I would just like to talk to my brother in private."

I don't move from my spot, instead glancing at Kade to see what he wants me to do. He tries to give me a weak smile, but that pain I've seen lessen in his eyes since I've met him starts to come back, as if speaking to his brother transforms his entire personality. That makes my decision for me. Maybe Gavin will fire me, but I don't want to leave. Not right now, not when Kade has been doing so well.

I square my shoulders and make sure I'm maintaining eye contact with Gavin. "I think I'll stay."

Gavin's nostrils flare in surprise. I know I haven't given him the impression that I would ever stand up for myself, and even if he heard about me punching Derek through the grapevine, he doesn't truly know me. And he doesn't know anything real about my relationship with his brother.

Putting the pieces together in my mind now, I think it's probably easy for Gavin to assume that I'm just another one of Kade's conquests and nothing more than that. It makes my heart hurt for Kade a little more, seeing how misunderstood he is by his brother.

"Presley—"

"Whatever you have to say, Gav, you can say it in front of her."
He pulls my hand into his, and I squeeze it, trying to give him
some strength.

Gavin's Adam's apple moves tightly in his throat as he
swallows. His eyes dart to our hands, causing more surprise to
permeate his expression. It confirms what I just thought about
his opinion of us. "This is family business, Kade. It will just take
a minute."

"She's staying," he says more firmly.

Shock zaps through my body as if I've been struck by
lightning, and my heart beats faster in my chest as I tilt my head
to meet Kade's gaze.

He smiles at me softly even though his eyes are stern. "You're
staying," he reiterates.

I try to swallow the emotion in my throat as he squeezes my
hand. The implication of his words truly settle into my bones, so
heavy with meaning that I want to cry. Does Kade consider me
family? The thought alone causes the bridge of my nose to sting
and my palms to sweat. He knows I've never felt like I belonged.
That I've never felt like I've had a family.

I press my lips together and try to keep my composure as
Gavin looks between us. He takes a moment to collect himself
then rubs the back of his neck. "Alright." He exhales. "Kade, I
want you to come up to the house tonight for dinner. We need
to discuss more ways to sublease our land. I thought you'd want
to be a part of it and give your input, especially since it was your
idea."

Despite the tense emotion of the moment, my shoulders
relax, and I feel relieved. I half expected Gavin to yell at Kade for
kissing me in public or say something about us being together
in general.

I look back at Kade, who's still holding my hand. His jaw
is clenched, and I can tell he's fighting with himself because
he thought the same thing. What Gavin implied about me was
rude, but I can understand it was said in frustration. It's not like

these brothers are good at communicating; that much is clear. But this could be the moment I think Kade's been waiting for: his brother reaching his hand out again. I just hate it started off the way it did.

There's silence for a moment before Kade says, "I'm working tonight. But most importantly, Presley is playing her fiddle with the band. I'm not missing it."

Gavin is quiet at his words, his brow raised in silent question. My heart aches more for Kade. I almost can't believe that his brother is having such a hard time believing Kade would say no because he wanted to support me instead.

But then my mouth drops open. I stare at Kade, gripping his hand so tightly it's probably cutting off his circulation, when I truly realize what that means: He's willing to miss dinner with his family for me. Gavin just offered what he's been asking for on a silver platter—to be involved with the dude ranch, to be actively asked to participate and be heard. Yet he's willing to give that up for me, to see me play my fiddle. For him to do that, it's—I can't even put into words how that makes me feel.

"Kade," I say softly, trying not to cry. "It's okay. There will be more."

He shakes his head firmly. "No, I told you I'd be there. I want to be there, Presley."

Gavin clears his throat. "You'll still have time to get to Night Hawk for the show."

"It's fine, Kade," I say, urging him to take this opportunity, to have his family hear him out, especially Gavin. I just hope they'll listen to him this time. "You can do both."

Kade studies me as if he's trying to see if I'm serious. I nod again, and he finally turns to Gavin. "Okay."

The brothers' eyes lock, and a silent conversation passes between them. Eventually, Gavin says, "Dinner is at five."

"I'll be there," Kade answers.

Gavin curtly nods and presents a half smile before he walks off, leaving Kade and myself alone in the stall once more. We just stand there for several seconds, our hands still joined and Kade unmoving.

"Are you okay?" I ask when the silence becomes too much.

Kade turns so we're facing each other, then, without another word, he kisses me. His mouth is almost brutal against mine as he backs me up into the wall. My hands fly to his neck, grabbing on for balance as he delves into my mouth, his palms gripping my ass. He does this for a while, as if he's drinking me in, memorizing my lips and my taste. By the time he's finished with me, I can hardly breathe.

He rests his forehead against mine. His cap must've fallen to the stall floor at some point during our kisses.

"Kade." I exhale, my chest heaving.

He kisses my lips softly again before cupping my cheek so we're looking into each other's eyes. "Thank you."

"For what?" I ask, still breathless.

"For staying. For standing up to my brother."

I place my hand over the one he has on my cheek. "You needed me."

He lets out a tense breath and closes his eyes, his forehead still leaning into mine. "Later," he says, after another beat, "before the show. Let me show you how much I need you."

Kade strokes my cheek, pulls away slightly, and opens his hazel eyes, his gaze boring into mine. The promise in his stare, telling me exactly what he wants from me, makes my entire body tingle. The promise of doing more than just using our hands and mouths to explore each other is impossible to ignore.

"Will we have time?"

That makes him chuckle. "I'm trying to be romantic, and that's your question?"

A laugh bubbles out of me, and I kiss his cheek before he steps back a bit. I bend down to pick up his ball cap, dusting off the shavings and then placing it on my head.

He looks at me in question as my lips tip up in a smile. "What's that saying?" I tap my chin teasingly. "Wear the cap, ride the cowboy?"

Kade's eyes dilate at my words, and he presses his body into mine again. "Careful, City Girl."

"Or what?" I ask, his lips hovering near mine.

"Or I'll turn you into a cowgirl."

I close the distance between us and kiss his lips with a short peck. "Is that a promise?"

"It's a fact." He punctuates the T as he says it then adjusts his cap on my head, pulling my ponytail through the hole in the back. "Now let's get to work. We've got a busy night of roping and riding ahead of us."

Roping?

I want to ask what he means, but he's already walking away. However, I think I know. All of his threats and mentions of "his rope" come to the forefront of my mind.

My body hums as anticipation fills me. Tonight is going to be a good night.

CHAPTER 29

Kade

IS IT POSSIBLE TO go from feeling nothing to feeling everything all at once? To feel as if you can finally breathe, like everything that was colorless is now technicolor and everything that was tasteless is now the most delicious thing you've ever eaten? Because that's happened to me. And it's all because of the woman standing in the bathroom in front of me.

Presley's skin is dewy from her hot shower after a long day's work. She doesn't notice me as I stand in the doorway quietly, watching her for a moment. She's scrunching her wet hair with some mousse that looks like whipped cream. Part of me wants to stop her to tell her that she'll be showering again before she leaves for Night Hawk, but where's the fun in that?

What's more, I like that she's taking time to get ready for me. I expected nothing less given how she reacted when I felt the stubble on her legs in the truck and her general shyness. That's why I wanted to give her a bit of warning about what I've been dreaming up for us. I hadn't planned for us to have sex for the first time tonight, but after what happened in the barn earlier with Gavin and the fact that I can tell her anxiety is still through the roof about playing tonight, it seemed appropriate. And I think introducing her to my rope will help ground her.

I wish we had all night, but the next hour or so will have to do.

When Presley finally notices me standing in the doorway, her skin, already flushed from the humid bathroom, turns pinker under my intense gaze.

"Hey, Lemon." I look her up and down as she turns toward me. She's wearing a pair of black leggings and an oversized T-shirt with a graphic on it I don't recognize. She's makeup-free, but it looks like she's put on a bit of lip moisturizer because her lips are shiny.

"Hey," she says, her voice shy.

That shyness just won't do. I take her by the hips and pull her into me, our bodies colliding. My cock is already at half-mast beneath my jeans, and she gasps when she feels it, her hands flying up to grip my biceps.

"Someone's excited." She runs one of her hands through my damp hair. Despite my plans to get dirty with her, I didn't want to smell like a cow while I worshiped her body, so I showered, too.

"Aren't you?" I ask, though I know she is. I can practically feel her soft body vibrate against mine, though I'm sure some of it's from nerves leading up to our first time.

She takes a moment to answer, her eyes darting to the ground. I quickly place a finger under her chin and make her look into my eyes. "None of that, darlin'. You're going to look at me tonight. I want you to watch everything I do to you."

A spark of fire lights behind her irises as her mouth parts. Not wanting to waste another second of our precious time together, I seal my lips over hers. A small moan escapes from her, and I absorb it into me, groaning into the kiss as our tongues tangle in a now familiar dance.

When we first kissed, Presley said she was out of practice—but that's never proven true. She's an amazing kisser and plays me like a fiddle, knowing exactly how much pressure to give and when I need more or want to take control. As far as I'm concerned, she's a master, and I can't get enough of her.

If we'd had more time lately, I would've done more than kiss, cuddle, and grind on her like a horny teen. But with Lemon, I've been able to be patient because I know she's worth the wait. She needed time to get used to me—to us—as well, but she's ready. We're both ready.

I force myself to pull back, our lips swollen and breathing labored, then I take her hand and tug her toward the room I've been staying in—or sort of been staying in, since a lot of nights, Lemon and I end up falling asleep wrapped in each other on her bed or the couch.

With her hand gripped in mine, we cross the short distance to the door, and I step back to let her enter first. I know what she's going to see, but I don't want to blindfold her for any of this tonight. She needs to have every sense available to her.

Once she's in, I close and lock the door behind us. I locked the front door, too, not wanting a repeat of earlier in the barn. Not that Gavin would come looking for me here—he's pretty much left me alone until today, making good on his word of being done with me. It's something I didn't truly think he'd do, which is why today's invite to dinner was surprising. We've only spoken to each other when needed lately, mostly about chores.

That little fact has left a nagging voice in the back of my mind that's got me wondering if tonight is about involving me more in the dude ranch and finally addressing the papers I found in the house or if the invitation is for something else entirely. It's not like Gran or Momma have sought me out since our blowup, either, though that was probably at Gavin's instruction. But that just makes me even more suspicious about tonight.

"Kade." Presley grips my hand, and I put my full attention on her, leaving it there. I don't want my lingering problems to taint tonight. She deserves for all of me to be here and present.

"Yes, darlin'?"

"That's a lot of rope."

I follow her gaze to the two twin-sized beds I've moved together, where coils of rope and other supplies sit on top of the dark-blue duvets. I plant a smirk on my face and step in front of her. "Did you think I was just tying your hands up?"

She cocks her head, eyes wide. "Aren't you?"

I shake my head, watching her carefully to gauge her reaction. The news surprises her, but the red stain on her neck that's rising to ghost over her cheeks tells me whatever she's thinking excites her.

I cup her face in my hands. "I'm going to undress you. Then I'm going to do a chest and waist harness."

Her body tenses, and I see slight worry flash in her eyes. Since that night in the loft, I've been slowly working to help her become more comfortable in her skin. Not just by touching her where she's comfortable but with things to help build her confidence, like riding lessons on Big John and teaching her how to change the flat tires on her car.

But given her history with her asshole ex and how people in her life have treated her, I'm fully aware that being completely nude in front of me might be difficult, which is why I formed this plan.

"Naked?"

I brush some of her damp hair behind her ear. "Do you trust me?"

Presley's wide eyes soften at my words, and she leans her cheek into my hand. "You know I do."

"You're beautiful, Presley. I want you to believe that." Her eyes turn glassy, and I lay a soft kiss on her lips. "But if this is too much, we don't have to do this. We can—"

"No." She shakes her head. "I want to."

Her confirmation allows me to breathe again, and I kiss her once more before I pull away. The blinds and curtains are drawn, but I've kept the lights on in the small room. It looks like the one Presley's staying in but with sky-blue walls.

If I had more time, I would've found some candles and put the lights on dimmers, but I like that it's not dark. I want her to know I see her—and that I like every part of her. More than like.

"I'm going to undress you now. Is that okay?"

She chews on her lower lip and nods. I tsk. "Remember what we've talked about? Use your words, darlin'. I want to hear that beautiful voice of yours."

"Yes, please undress me."

Warmth blooms in my chest, and my heart rate picks up. "Good girl." I maintain eye contact with her as I trail my hands down her arms, enjoying how the soft hair tickles my palms. When I reach her hands, I squeeze them gently before taking the hem of her T-shirt. "Remember, if at any time anything becomes too much, you say stop. Understand?"

"Yes," she exhales, her voice heady.

"Lift up your arms for me."

She nods, following my request. My heart beats louder in my ears as I focus on my task. I tug the cotton up, my lips parting as I become mesmerized by the sight of her. Inch by inch, her round belly and heaving chest is revealed to me, like a curtain rising on a stage and Presley is my star.

I've imagined this moment on nights I couldn't sleep and mornings in the shower, wondering how she'd look under the baggy clothes she wears or her Night Hawk uniform. But nothing could prepare me for the real thing.

I throw the shirt away and let her stand before me in her simple black bra and leggings, giving her time to adjust. Just as I thought she would, she moves to cover herself under my gaze, but I gently take her wrists in mine.

"Don't cover up what's mine," I growl. "You're fucking perfect." There's no anger in my voice, just heat. I want her to know how much I want her. How much I desire her. "Just breathe, yes?"

She relaxes in my hold, and once I'm sure she won't try to cover herself up again, I release her arms.

"Can I continue?"

"Yes, Kade."

My cock jumps in my pants. God, she's perfect, like an angel sent from heaven just for me to corrupt, to cherish.

With my eyes still on hers, I reach around her back, finding the clasp of her bra. I undo it with ease, tugging the straps down her round shoulders to reveal her perky breasts. Her dusky nipples are tight buds, ready for me to bite and suck, but I hold off. Good things come to those who wait.

I smile to myself as I throw the bra on top of her discarded shirt, then I use my pointer finger to trail a line from her neck to her navel. She shivers at the featherlight touch, and I remind her to breathe again. When she does, I continue to move my finger over her stomach in small circular patterns, waiting for her to relax and enjoy the feeling.

Since Devil's Rock, Presley has initiated my touches to her midriff, and she's been letting my hands wander more and more, encouraging my caresses to become stronger strokes. But now, I want to take this slowly, get her used to the sensations. That way, when the rope is wrapped around her, she'll be ready for it.

I trace more circles, increasing the pressure then moving up higher before venturing down to the band of her leggings and around her navel. When her breathing evens out, I see her eyes have grown darker, telling me that she's enjoying my touch. I work my way back up again, drawing circles around her budded nipples then brushing the tips of each. A small whimper escapes her lips as her eyes start to close, signaling that it's time to move on.

I pull away from her breasts, and she watches with hooded eyes as I finger the elastic of her pants. "Remember what I told you, Presley." I kneel in front of her, taking a small risk—though my heart tells me she's ready for this.

Her lips part as I curl my fingers into her waistband, tugging the fabric down as I begin to pepper varying types of soft and open-mouthed kisses on the skin of her stomach.

She gasps. "Kade!" Her hands fly to my hair, fingers curling around the dusty-blond strands. For a split second, I think she may tell me to stop, but she only adds pressure to my head, urging me on. Relieved that my risk is being rewarded, I continue to gently kiss the curves lined with faint stretch marks as I push her leggings down her body.

I groan when I'm met with her pussy instead of underwear. The tuft of hair covering her sex is freshly trimmed, and she's already wet and glistening for me. I don't know if it's from everything she's feeling or from what I just did, but either way, the fact that she's enjoying this makes me immeasurably happy.

"Always surprising me," I murmur, glancing up to meet her glassy gaze filled with what looks like awe. I decide right here and now that I want to see her look at me like this all the time. I want her to always feel cherished and special, to know that she deserves to be treated properly like the amazing woman she is.

With that thought warm in my gut, I help her step out of her leggings. I ghost the pads of my fingers up her calves and thick thighs, watching goosebumps fan out as I do. Unable to resist, I kiss the rounded flesh at the top of her pretty center before I stand.

Slipping my finger under her chin, I catch her gaze to check in with her. "How are you feeling?"

"Exposed."

I nod and stroke her heated cheek. "Is that okay?"

"Yes," she says. Her voice is more level than I expect it to be, and my chest fills to the brim with pride. I'm happy that she can feel that way with me and be okay.

"Can I continue?"

"Yes, Kade."

I hum my approval, her words going straight to my already hard cock as I pull my plain white T-shirt up and over my head, tossing it beside her clothes. Her eyes drink me in like I'm water in the middle of the desert, and I realize this is the first time she's seeing me without clothes on, too. She swallows, her heated gaze meeting mine when she's had her fill.

"You like what you see, Lemon?"

"Very much."

A smile tugs at my lips. The woman I met in the back of Night Hawk wouldn't have been forthcoming with that information, but it's written all over her face right now, anyway.

"Good." I drag my knuckles down her neck and chest. "Because I like what I see very much, too."

Presley's irises turn bright at my compliment, and she returns my small smile. I reach up to caress her nipples, and when she gasps, I capture the reaction with my lips in a short kiss.

Knowing that if I keep kissing her, we'll never get to what I have planned, I pull back and walk to the beds. Presley's eyes remain focused on me as I pick up two long coils of tan-and-red two-ply jute rope that I've conditioned with food-grade mineral oil.

It's funny how my entire body relaxes as I grip the rough-textured ropes in my hands. It feels almost like coming home or seeing an old friend and settles the deep need for control I have inside me—the need to direct, manage, and take good care of the things I love.

When I'm tying someone up, it's not only challenging, requiring my mind to be focused on my partner, but it's also fun and intimate, too. Just like with spanking and other forms of kink, rope is a way to connect with someone on a deeper level, to learn trust through being vulnerable and open. That's the real reason I've chosen this for us tonight, going beyond my desire to simply see Presley in my ropes.

I take a deep breath and center myself, moving to stand in front of her willing body that looks more beautiful than even my best fantasies imagined. "I'm going to start tying you now," I say, holding up the rope.

Presley eyes them and licks her lips, curiosity sparking in her gaze.

"It's called a four-braid harness, and it's meant to be a little uncomfortable, to bring you into your body and push you a little, like spankings."

Presley bites her lower lip, and I know she's thinking about that night in the loft.

I brush my finger down her cheek. "I think you'll enjoy it. Are you ready?"

"Yes, I'm ready."

I press my lips to hers for a kiss to ground and connect us, exploring her mouth that tastes of mint toothpaste and something that's all her own. When I pull back, she's gazing at me with adoration, trust, and an ease I know reflects in my eyes, too.

"Good girl," I croon. "Now, stand up straight, and let me take care of you."

CHAPTER 30

Presley

KADE HOLDS THE LONG red-and-tan coils of his rope, his workman's hands gripping it gently as he steps forward to drape them behind my head. The moment the coarse-textured material lays on the back of my neck and drapes over my bare chest, I break out in goosebumps from head to toe.

I can't believe I'm doing this—standing in a room, with the lights on, fully naked, while a man I once considered too hot and young for me ties me up with rope.

Rope.

I'm being tied up with rope.

"Keep breathing, Presley. You're doing so well," Kade's baritone voice soothes as his hands work methodically, veins and tendons bulging while his fingers move with practiced ease.

I inhale a long breath then exhale, watching as he braids the four sections of rope at the base of my neck then stops above my breasts. Once he's satisfied, he has me lift my arms up so he can walk behind me and bring the sections around my back. I feel the rough touch of the material on my skin, and then he's back in view, weaving the rope over my breasts.

As he works, his knuckles brush over the hardened skin of my nipples, and I can't stop the gasp that leaves my lips, making Kade smile slyly. I'm already wet from him undressing me, but more arousal floods between my legs.

"Beautiful," he mutters, admiring his work.

I can't see the full picture, but from what I do see, I'll admit it looks pretty. I've never seen anything like this, rope woven on top of skin. But I like the way the red and tan colors cross over my pale neck and chest like a decoration.

"I'm going to lay the rope then pull it under your breasts now," Kade says. His eyes are warm with reassurance as he does the action, his calloused fingers sweeping over the sensitive skin as he once again walks behind me so he can cross the rope in the back. When he puts tension on the ties, they dig into the top of my ribs and my chest, forcing me to push my breasts out.

When I look down again, I see that the rope acts like a bikini top, framing my small boobs and making them appear larger. My mouth goes dry when Kade caresses my ribs and arms before appearing back in front of me with hungry eyes. "You look perfect like this, Presley. Your body was made for my ropes."

I shiver, and my toes curl against the soft cream carpet from his praise. Had he said any of this a couple of weeks ago, I wouldn't have believed it. But Kade isn't a liar—that I know. And the visible outline of his cock pressing from behind the placket of his jeans only further proves how much he desires me, how much he enjoys what he sees. I don't even need his words to know that.

I bite my lower lip, my core fluttering as I imagine what he's going to feel like inside me.

"You're liking this, aren't you?" Kade smiles with flirty eyes, tugging my lip from my teeth with his thumb.

I start to nod, but then I remember my words, knowing how much he likes and wants to hear me verbalize my thoughts and feelings. "Yes, I like it."

He runs his palm down my side, and I don't flinch this time. His touch anywhere near or on my stomach is not a care in my mind as he gets closer to my pussy. Just as he's about to descend on the seam of my sex, he drags a finger over the top of my mons in a teasing manner.

"Kade," I whisper. "Please."

He lets out a low chuckle. "You want me to feel how wet you are for me, darlin'?"

"Yes, *please*."

He puts his lips to my ear, giving me what I want—what we both want—as he glides two fingers through my soaked folds. I lean into the sensation, wanting more, and release a soft cry when he skims over my clit.

"Fuck, Lemon. You're so sexy like this."

"Keep going," I plead.

He tugs on my earlobe with his teeth. "Be patient. I'm not done with you yet." Then he pulls away, his hand leaving my sex as he goes back to weaving the ropes.

I bite my lip again to stop a needy groan at the loss of his touch where I want it most. He looks up through his lashes all innocently, but I can see the cocky glint in his eyes. He enjoys teasing me. I can't say that I mind.

I give him a gentle smile, and we both turn our focus back to his hands as he works the ropes on my body. The moment he starts to loop one over my stomach, he slows his motions and looks into my eyes again as if to ask if I'm okay. I push away any negative thoughts and offer a silent nod.

He loops one of the red ropes over my round middle and slowly walks behind me again. I sink into the sensation, inhaling with the feel of it against me. Then he tightens the rope, the material digging into my fleshy, stretch-marked skin, and I tense, sucking my stomach in.

A momentary flare of panic ignites inside my chest as I think about what I'd see if I looked down: my skin being squished and framed by the rope as he tugs. My breasts were one thing, but my stomach is another. Thoughts of Derek and his commentary, my mom calling me husky, the time one of my bandmates pinched the fat of my hip and said she knew of a great diet I could try fill my mind, and I clench my jaw.

"Presley, darlin'." I take a long inhale at the reminder of where I am. Kade kisses the top of my round shoulder.

"Remember what I told you before. Let your mind be free of those bad thoughts. You're beautiful. Your body is beautiful. Every part of you is worthy and deserves to be loved. Just feel the ropes. Feel my hands worship you. Can you do that?"

I exhale the tight breath constricting my lungs and manage to whisper a "yes" through the years of sadness and anger clogging my throat.

"Brave girl," he murmurs, his gentle features entering my vision. "I'm so proud of you."

Kade's words squeeze like a boa constrictor around my heart. I don't know how someone can repeatedly know exactly what I need to hear at the right time, but he always does.

He gives me a short kiss and breathes with me for another moment before he goes back to tying.

I focus on his broad chest and arms as he continues to weave and tug. I still feel the rope digging into my skin, but I don't let my thoughts from before infiltrate this moment. Instead, I watch as Kade works with his rope as if it's part of him.

It's clear he loves doing this, and for a moment, I wonder why. When he brought up rope before, I thought it was just a thing he wanted to do in the bedroom. But this—what I've felt so far and the care he's put into tying me—goes beyond the sexual nature of it. It's like the rope is a support system to hold and guide me through what I'm feeling, and Kade is the watchful shepherd, the caring, kind, and sensitive man that I've come to know.

Kade ties another part of the rope, and after a minute, he drops the two long ends to the ground then moves to my back. I want to ask what he's doing, but then he brushes the inside of my legs, and I gasp from the unexpected touch. He doesn't stop his movement, reaching his hand through the space and grabbing the ropes. He draws them up as he stands to his full height, sliding them into the creases of my thighs. When he tugs sharply upward, a curse escapes my lips. My body feels as if it's on fire and that just stoked the flame.

"Jesus, Presley," Kade groans, his voice thick with desire. "You're making a mess for me." He drags a finger through the sticky arousal between my thighs to make a point, then he grinds the rough fabric of his jeans against my bare ass. I can feel his hot arousal pressing into me, and I automatically arch back, wanting to feel more of him.

He chuckles and clicks his tongue against the back of his teeth.

"Kade—"

His hand comes down on my ass, and I cry out.

"You're a greedy girl," he tuts. "Be patient. I'm almost done."

Before I can whine like the greedy girl he's claimed I am, I feel him tug again, and in the next minute, he's looped the rope from my shoulders down to my wrists so I'm immobilized with my arms flat at my sides like I'm cocooned. The ropes aren't tight enough that they'll cause any damage or stop me from playing my fiddle tonight.

While I can walk, getting away without the use of my arms would be hard. This kind of situation may scare some, and I think if it were anyone but Kade, I'd be scared, too, but being at his mercy like this with no way out only gets me wetter.

Kade stands in front of me. "How do you feel?" He tests and tugs the ropes in various spots, making my skin burn in a delicious way I've never felt before, not even when he spanked me. When his palm gently squeezes my breast, I groan and lean into his touch. There are so many sensations going on in my body right now that I'm not sure how to feel.

"I—" I exhale a short breath. "I don't know," I tell him honestly.

Kade hums, his palms lightly skimming my tied arms. "Then let's figure it out together." He grasps my biceps and stares into my eyes with soft features. "Close your eyes for a moment."

I do as he says, and then he turns my body so I'm facing the door we came in earlier.

"I'm going to ask you to open your eyes, but first," he says quietly against my ear, "take a few deep inhales for me, and concentrate on my hands, on the feeling of my rope hugging you."

I nod, leaning into his strong body and this experience with him. I let him ground me as I pull in a long breath like I'm drawing from my calming inhaler. My body relaxes, and I focus on the new sensations of his ropes biting into my sensitive flesh and his hands on my arms. I feel the cool air of the room as it brushes against my overheated skin, notice how the small space is quiet except for our breathing. I hear a low whirring as the ceiling fan turns.

"Tell me." Kade's rumbling voice vibrates against my ear. "What does the rope feel like to you?"

My lips part to answer him just as he moves his palms lightly from my arms to my sides, caressing the rolls and slopes of my waist until his hands rest on the flare of my hips. With my breathing even and my focus on the ropes, I don't flinch, I just feel. I rest my back against his muscled chest, and the corners of my lips turn up. "They feel like a hug, almost like a weighted blanket."

Kade gently kisses the side of my head. "Good. And do they hurt?"

"A little, but not in a bad way. I like it."

"Hmm, can you tell me why you like the pain?"

My brain rummages for an answer, but Kade stops my spiraling with a light pinch to my ass. I gasp and say the first thing I can think of. "Because it makes me feel. I become aware of my body in a way that helps me stop thinking so much. It's like I'm just a physical form instead of always soaking in my thoughts, and—" A bit of fear stings in my gut, and I hold back what I was about to say.

"Presley," Kade urges, his hand rubbing the place he'd pinched to soothe it. "Say what you were going to say. Don't be afraid. I'm not judging you."

"I like that you're the one to cause it." I exhale. "Because I know you'll also be the one to take it away. I know I'm safe to just feel and let go—that I can finally be at home in my body."

Kade is silent, and I know he said not to open my eyes, but I turn my head so I can look at him. When my lids open and adjust to the light, his lips are relaxed, and his hazel eyes are soft with an unreadable gleam in them. He grips my biceps and kisses my nose.

"Thank you for sharing that with me." His words echo the night in the loft. "Now look forward."

Curiosity kicks up in my belly, and I turn my head. Kade's hands move to my hips, and my brain takes a second to make sense of what I'm seeing. My nude reflection stares back at me in a floor-length mirror that's hanging on the back of the door. My heart pounds in my ears, and I suck in my stomach as I try to drop my gaze, but Kade steps in front of me, placing his finger under my chin.

"Don't look away, Presley. There's a reason I wanted you in front of this mirror. Lean into whatever you're feeling and feel it, but do not close those beautiful eyes on me. On *you*."

My arms tug against my bindings as I try to calm my racing heart.

"Do you think you can?"

I search Kade's eyes, and they're so full of care and adoration for me. I've never seen that kind of adoration from a person before—not even my own mother.

"Yes," I finally nod, trusting him and the reason he's put me in front of the mirror.

He steps back behind me, his hands moving to my hips again so I can see my full rope-bound form in the mirror.

He rests his chin on my shoulder. "Look at you, Presley. Look at how incredible your body is. How fucking beautiful you are."

I bite the inside of my cheek and focus on his words and his touch, resisting the urge to close my eyes. Kade continues to stroke my skin as I stare at the woman in the mirror, finally letting my stomach relax. For a moment, I don't blink, I don't fidget, I just look. It's like having an out-of-body experience, similar to the night Kade spanked me. I know the woman I'm looking at is me, but at the same time, she isn't.

This woman looks more confident than me. Her perfectly imperfect body is covered in beautiful red-and-tan rope that was woven in careful and practiced detail. Her rolls, stretch marks, and cellulite are all on display. The harsh light from above casts a less-than-flattering glow on her pale skin. But that doesn't matter, because she's beautiful, and her body is strong. It's as if the man behind me has turned me into a work of art.

The back of Kade's hand against my cheek has me sucking in a breath. It's then I realize I'm crying, just like I did that night in the loft. He wipes the tears away while his eyes remain on us in the mirror.

My attention shifts from myself to how our bodies look together. The yin and yang of his broad shoulders and narrow waist behind the soft curves of my body. The sight of his tanned left arm against my pale skin and black and gray tattoos. His shaggy, dusty-colored hair compared to my platinum-and-violet waves.

In many physical ways, Kade and I are opposites. But in many other ways, we're the same. We're both just lost people looking for connection, for kindness, for care, for love. And somehow, despite our differences, we found that in each other.

He tugs on a lock of my hair while continuing to look at our reflection. "I want to play a little game," he breathes against my ear.

I turn my body slightly to look up at him, wanting to see his eyes without looking through a mirror. The movement reminds me that I have rope digging into my skin and the burn it's causing the longer we stand here. But like I told Kade, I enjoy the subtle pain. It's keeping me focused and in my body, not in my head.

"What kind of game?" My voice comes out huskier than normal.

Kade swallows, his stubbled throat working. "You tell me three things you like about your body, and I'll give you whatever you want." He punctuates the T as he gently places a whisper of a kiss on my lips before nudging me back so that we're looking at each other through the mirror once more.

"That's it?"

"That's it." He grins, kissing my neck before resting his chin on my shoulder.

We stare at each other for a long moment while I think, his fingers gripping my hips, and his hard length resting against my backside. The heat of it reminds me of what I'm planning to ask for.

"My eyes," I say, picking one of the easiest things first.

He hums, his hands trailing toward my pussy. "I like your eyes, too. They remind me of sapphires." He cups the space between my legs, applying gentle pressure until he's rubbing my clit with the palm of his hand. "What else do you love?"

I stifle a cry at the delicious feel of him, attempting to thrust my hips up to relieve the ache. He shakes his head and pulls his hand away. "If what you want is for me to make it better, Lemon, you have to tell me two more things."

I can't help the groan that leaves my lips, and he chuckles, his hot breath fluttering over the skin of my neck.

"Two more," he repeats.

I stare at us in the mirror again, Kade's hands now unmoving on my hips. "My breasts. Everyone thinks large boobs are great, but I like being part of the itty-bitty titty committee."

That has him smiling wider until his dimples show. "Your tits are perfect, darlin'." His hands travel upward, leaving fire in their wake as he cups my breasts and squeezes. "They fit perfectly in my hands. And they look exquisite in my ropes, don't you think?"

He flicks my nipples, and I nearly melt into his body. "They do." I exhale, my pussy getting wetter at his teasing.

He removes his hands once more and puts them back on my hips. "Last one."

I could say my hair or my smile. Those are always ones that people like me who are insecure about their appearance say. The ones that people in larger bodies are taught to say.

With a small sigh, I study myself, the newfound beauty of my body in Kade's ropes. In a way, I look like a painting, especially with him standing next to me. He's too handsome to be real sometimes.

Kade moves his thumbs back and forth across my hips, patiently waiting for my answer, and I finally open my lips. "My stomach."

Kade's eyes widen and light up like a Christmas tree, a slow grin a mile wide spreading across his face. Slowly, I watch as his large hands slide from my hips across my waist, the expanse of his palms coming to lie flat against the skin of my midsection. I exhale a breath as he holds my middle, the pressure of his fingers pressing the rope further into my skin.

"And why do you love your stomach, Presley?" he asks, though this time, his voice is tentative like he's afraid his question will make me change my mind.

I look at his hands on the rolls of my stomach, the part of my body I was taught to hate. It's just fat and skin, and if you really think about it, it's ridiculous the world puts so much disdain and condemnation into something so uncomplicated.

My gaze connects with Kade's in our reflection, the corners of my lips tipping up in a small smile because I know my answer. "Because it's part of me."

"It's a beautiful part of you," he replies without hesitation.

My skin flushes from head to toe at his praise, and he kisses my shoulder then trails his soft lips up the side of my neck until he's nuzzling my ear.

"Now tell me, what does my Lemon want as her prize?"

My eyes close as he teases the shell of my ear like he loves to do. I move my butt back against him again, feeling his cock twitch through the fabric of his jeans. He practically hisses as I grind into him, my core fluttering in anticipation. I'm done playing now. I want him. I want all of him.

"Presley," he groans, my name laced with his impatience. "Tell me what you want."

I make him wait a moment longer, sliding my ass along his erection before I finally give in. "I want your cock, Kade. Give me all of you."

CHAPTER 31

Kade

STILL STANDING BEHIND PRESLEY, I grab the ropes woven between her shoulder blades and turn her. She groans as we walk toward the makeshift double bed, my intricate work rubbing her sensitive skin. Each little intake of breath and every sound of her discomfort has my cock straining against my zipper.

I would keep her tied longer if we had more time for aftercare, but I keep reminding myself we're on a timeline. I'm seriously regretting picking tonight of all nights to do this, but at the same time, I knew we couldn't wait any longer.

Stopping Presley at the edge of the bed, I make quick work of untying her. I let my ropes fall to the ground, the soft sounds of Presley's relief sending a shiver down my spine. I gently rub her arms, bringing the blood back to the surface.

"How do you feel? Are your arms good?" I ask. I didn't tie the rope as tightly as I could've. Since this was her first time, I didn't want to take it too far. Besides, she has her big gig tonight, so I didn't want to risk her being sore.

The big smile I've grown to love lights up her face, and she brings her hand to my cheek, brushing her thumb over my stubble. "You're always taking care of me."

"I like taking care of you," I say.

Presley leans in and kisses me, her tongue running along the seam of my lips. I like that she's taking charge of the kiss, that I can feel her passion in every movement she makes. Her hand threads into my hair, gripping the long ends until I moan. My mouth opens, and she strokes her tongue along mine as I bring my palms to her bare ass. My fingers dig into the round flesh, pressing the heat of her pussy into my jeans. I moan again, this time with the need to be touched by her, to be inside her, to claim her.

Presley pulls away, but before I can tug her back into me, she gently pushes me down on the beds. I bounce from the force and then chuckle, my eyes connecting with hers. Instead of joining me like I expect, Presley stays standing, her naked body on display for me and covered in the marks from my ropes. Her eyes rove over my half-clothed body. She's a goddamn beautiful sight, and the pride I feel for her grows even stronger than it was before.

Gone is the quiet and awkward woman who stood with her head down and tried to blend in. Now she's calmer, more confident, and settling into her own skin—and it's all because of her. She's learning to let herself be free, to let herself feel, experience, and be seen. She's amazing and everything I didn't think I deserved in this world.

"Lemon darlin'?" I ask. Her special nickname stops her perusal of my erection pressed behind my zipper. Her gaze connects with mine again, and she grins, her eyes sparkling. "Are you going to just watch me all night, or do you want me to fuck that sweet pussy of yours?"

She bites her lower lip but still doesn't get on the bed. Instead, she puts her hands on the ankles of my jeans. "Unbuckle your belt."

Oh, fuck. Always with the surprises. With our eyes still locked, I do as she says. Once my belt is free, I release the button and pull down the zipper. Presley tugs on my pants, and I lift my hips, letting her free me of the starchy fabric. My hard cock slaps against my lower abdomen, and she stops to look, my Wranglers still in her hands. Just as she had, I didn't deem underwear necessary, and it's clear she wasn't expecting me to have gone commando.

She sucks in a breath as she stares at the steel length that's now dripping pre-cum onto my skin. The energy in the room shifts as we both realize I'm now the one in a vulnerable position. I have to admit it feels odd because sex with me is rough and hard and I'm always the one in control. But this time with Presley is going to be different. I don't need any more than this moment to know that.

My breath turns shallow as her eyes burn a path over every detail of my body, her gaze taking in each line and lean muscle as I wait for her to have her fill. When they stop over the scar on my left arm from surgery, her features soften, and her throat bobs. After a moment, her gaze meets mine again, and a lopsided smile lifts my lips.

"Come here, Presley," I say in an attempt to regain control, wanting and ready to feel her naked body against mine.

She shakes her head then tosses my jeans to the ground. Before I can ask her what she's doing, she grabs my ankles and spreads my legs apart. My insides coil at what I think she's about to do.

Proving my theory right, my beautiful woman gets on her hands and knees and crawls between my legs. With a shy look in her eyes, her palms glide up my legs and stop when they reach my inner thighs. She digs her fingernails into the sensitive skin, and a carnal sound bursts from my lips as I throw my head back into the pillows.

"Presley." I swallow. "You don't have to." I look at her from beneath my lashes to find her smiling coyly. Her hands begin to slide closer to my cock, the head of it red and swollen with my need for her.

"You said I could have whatever I want."

I curse as her fingers brush along the thick vein on the underside of my shaft. My cock strains, and I nearly cry from her touch, from finally having her hands on me after many nights of imagining it. I force myself to breathe and lock eyes with her as she cups my balls and squeezes.

"Fuck, Lemon. Do that again." She does, this time a bit harder before she wraps her hand around me and gives me a swift pump that has my hips bucking off the bed.

"You're so hot," Presley says as she watches her hand jack me through heavy eyes, licking her lips when pre-cum falls on her knuckles. I don't take my eyes off her as she swipes her fingers through the white liquid then uses it to lubricate her motions. Fuck. I can hardly believe this is the same woman who had a hard time looking me in the eye when we first met.

"Presley," I moan. She only smiles to herself and doesn't let up, her hand working my cock faster and harder until it almost becomes pain given how hard I am.

"Darlin', if you keep doing that—" Her wet lips wrap around the tip of my cock, and she sucks, her eyes connecting with mine in a smile. "Oh, fuck. Jesus," I curse, my hips automatically thrusting me into the heat of her warm mouth.

To her credit, Presley doesn't falter with the sudden movement. She relaxes her lips so she can take more of me down while her other hand squeezes my heavy sac. "God." My voice is heady and almost sounds like it's not my own. "That smart mouth of yours feels so fucking good."

My praise has her sucking harder and her mouth moving further down my length. I close my eyes and get lost in the feeling of her, in the way she's completely taken over every part of me, body and soul. When the hand cupping my balls drifts lower, her finger brushing over the sensitive skin between my balls and the crease of my ass, I buck off the bed.

"Fuck." My hand flies to her hair, and I grip the top of her platinum head to stop her movement. She pops off my cock, and the sound it makes sends even more blood south. "You're done playing," I grunt. My heart is pounding in my ears from holding off my orgasm.

She purses her swollen lips playfully. "You didn't like it?" Her question isn't serious; she knows damn well I liked it too much. My Lemon just wants to tease me like I've teased her. I can admire that, but I'm ready to fuck her into the mattress until she's screaming my name for this entire ranch to hear.

I tug on her hair until she gasps at the sensation. "Get up here."

With a coy smile still planted on her face, she crawls from between my legs until she's by my side, her head against the pillows. I pull her into me, my lips sealing over hers as I hitch my leg over her hip so my cock presses into the plush skin of her stomach. I love that there's no flinching at the sensation now. She gasps into my mouth, letting me taste the salt of my pre-cum on her lips as she moves her leg between both of mine until her wet pussy slides against my shaft. We both moan into each other at the feeling, our bodies grinding as our hands explore and touch the new territory of our naked bodies.

My lips detach from hers, and I bite her earlobe, pulling away so I can suck the skin of her neck and then along her collarbone. She chants my name as I shift her underneath me, my mouth seeking her breasts. I wrap my lips around one of her nipples and suck, biting the hard bud and enjoying the way she cries out from the pain and pleasure. Her hands grip my shoulders, and I slide my hand down her body until I reach her sex.

"Jesus, Lemon. Your cunt is weeping for me." I put pressure on her clit, and she cries out. "Such a good fucking girl."

Her hips buck wildly into me as I rub her. "I need you inside me, Kade. Please," she begs. "Please, please, please." Her eyes are shut as she says it, her mouth open in pleasure as I continue to tease her.

"Open your eyes." I smack her pussy the way I did that day in the truck. She gasps, her dilated blue eyes meeting mine. "Tell me you want my cock, Presley."

"I want your cock, please, Kade."

"Tell me how you want it."

I smack her clit again, a little harder this time. "Oh god! Hard, Kade. Please, fuck me hard."

A slow smile creeps onto my lips as I pull back from her body and stand. She looks confused at the sudden loss, and I chuckle, smoothing my hands down her thighs. "Relax, I just need to grab a condom."

Her cheeks turn pink as she watches me take a packet from the nightstand. I open the foil square then make a show of rolling the latex down my length, smiling wider when she groans with impatience. I'm as eager as she is to be inside her, and I love how easily she's expressing how much she wants me—just like I want her.

I crawl back on the mattress, my cock solid against my abs as I position myself over her body. I'm not usually a missionary type of guy, but with Presley, I want to see the look on her face as I enter her. I want to watch her eyes roll back into her head as she comes on my cock and milks me dry.

I capture her lips with mine, kissing her thoroughly as I slide my cock through her arousal. Her wet pussy envelopes me and lubricates my length. Presley's hands grip my shoulders, and she whimpers into my mouth, her hips moving up to seek more friction.

Giving into what she wants, I take my cock in my hand and rub the crown of it over her clit before dipping just the first inch into her tight entrance. I groan at the heat of her, and she sucks in a breath at the intrusion, my name leaving her lips.

I feed my cock in another inch, then another, my forehead pressing to hers as she takes half of me in.

"Fuck, Presley." Her hands move from my shoulders down my sides until they're at my hips. I think she's going to dig her fingernails in, but then she uses me as leverage and thrusts her hips upward so my length is sheathed fully inside her.

"Oh!" She cries out with me, gripping my waist tightly as her body stills. I halt my movement so she can adjust to my size and press my face into her neck. I lick and suck the salty skin over her pulse point as she inhales a shaky breath.

"Relax for me, Lemon darlin'." She nods, and I slowly feel her body ease as a contented sigh leaves her. The sound of it hits me right in the chest, but I don't have time to think about it because her inner walls release, and I completely bottom out. My balls are now resting against the arousal that's dripping out of her.

I lift my head to meet hers and hover my lips over her mouth. "You're amazing," I praise. "You take my cock so well."

Her skin flushes. "And you, Kade Montgomery, have a dirty mouth."

"You like it."

She answers me with a heated kiss, and I take that as a sign she's ready for me to move again. As our tongues explore each other's mouths, I start to punch forward in shallow thrusts. She whimpers at the feeling, and my cock twitches inside her.

Fuck, I'm not going to last long. This is all too much, and Presley is too beautiful, too perfect.

"Kade," she murmurs. "Please go harder."

Unable to deny her request, I pick up the pace and piston my hips in a rhythm that has them slapping against hers. The lewd noise echoes in the small space, and we both cry out. Presley grips my hips harder to ask me for more, so I pull back until my cock is almost all the way out of her, then I plunge back inside as one of my hands finds her clit and rubs.

"Yes, Kade! Just like that."

I thrust again and flick her clit, but it still isn't enough for me. I want to be deeper, so deep she can feel me everywhere.

Keeping my cock inside her, I move backward so I'm kneeling. Presley watches me with interest as I wrap my arms around her thighs and tug her down my length, her head sliding off the pillows. When I punch my hips forward, ass flexing, she yells out my name at the depth of my thrust, and her hands fly out to grip my forearms.

She keens loudly, so I repeat the motion again and again, watching my cock dip in and out of her wet pussy, coated with her arousal. I continue to fuck her harder and faster until my balls draw up and the base of my spine starts to tingle.

"Touch yourself," I command.

Without hesitating, Presley finds her clit while I dig my fingers into the softness of her thighs. Her eyes close, and her mouth falls open as she rubs herself. The sight of her in the throes of pleasure with my cock buried deep inside her pussy almost does me in.

"Look at me," I grunt. "I need you to come. Fucking come with me, Presley."

Her blue eyes lock on mine, and she nods. I thrust harder, hitting that sweet spot inside her that has her crying out and writhing beneath me. Her inner walls grip my cock, and I know she's close.

"That's it," I praise, my balls slapping against the arousal dripping from her cunt. I plunge into her wildly, taking in the way her body moves from the force of me, absorbing every punch of my hips. I love how the marks of my ropes look against her pale skin, and her eyes are full of endless emotion that squeezes my heart. Fuck, I'm a goner for this woman.

"Kade!" She rubs her clit harder, and her body starts to arch off the bed, pushing her breasts forward as she starts to shake.

"Come for me, Lemon. Let me feel your tight pussy come all over my cock."

My filthy words send her crashing over the edge, and our eyes lock as the hand she has on my forearm digs into me so hard I think her nails draw blood. The sharp sting of it mixed with her pussy gripping me has me losing all sense of space and time.

I thrust into her as she comes, prolonging her release as mine explodes from me. White sparks cloud my vision from the intensity of it, and I fill the condom, shooting ropes of cum into the rubber as the best orgasm of my life overtakes me, my shoulders shaking with my own release.

When I have no more energy left to hold me up, I carefully fall forward, my cock still pulsing inside her as her own aftershocks spark against my softening length. I rest against her, our naked and sweaty bodies molding together as we come down from the high we just experienced together, one I'm not sure I'll ever recover from.

When I finally catch my breath, I slide out of her, not caring about the mess I'll make by not getting up to dispose of the rubber. She turns lazily to face me, her blue eyes sated and face flushed from exertion, but the smile on her face has my heart exploding with happiness.

I tuck a strand of damp violet hair behind her ear. I want to say something, but there aren't any words to say other than ones that might scare her. Hell, ones that might scare me.

So instead, I pull her into me and lay a soft kiss on her forehead. That will have to be enough for now.

.

CHAPTER 32

Kade

WE'RE STANDING NEXT TO Presley's car, and both of us are having a hard time leaving each other after what we just shared.

"I'll be there as soon as I can." I kiss her forehead, and she leans into it, causing me to linger. If I had any say, I'd skip dinner with my family, and we'd move her gig to another night so we could lie in bed until sunrise. Okay—we would have done more than just lie there, but that's beside the point.

Tonight is important to Presley, and I've avoided my family long enough. It's time for me to face my demons and speak with them like Presley suggested. And I need to take the olive branch Gavin extended—at least I hope that's what it is.

Presley pulls back and smiles up at me. "The band doesn't go on until seven. Take your time. Your family is important."

I want to tell her she's important, too, more important than I think I've even come to fully realize yet, but I hold it in, saving that information for when we have more time together. When we've both had time to process what we shared tonight.

I brush a lock of wavy hair behind her ear. She looks pretty tonight in light makeup, purple locks styled so they frame her diamond face. Come to think of it, this is the first time I've seen her dressed in clothes like this. She's wearing black loose-fitting trousers, a white tank underneath a sheer black button up, and a pair of horseshoe earrings that she's paired with a long silver necklace.

I decide to tell her what I'm thinking. "You look really pretty."

She looks down at herself and waves a hand over her body. "I didn't have a costume, but I call this my Cher from *Clueless* look."

"I've never seen it."

She scoffs. "You're joking."

"You think I'm watching '90s romcoms?"

Presley shoots me a chiding look. "Are you saying I'm old?"

I roll my eyes and tickle her sides. "You're perfect." Her giggles fill the air, a sound I never thought I'd hear fall from her lips, and I pull her against me. Her soft body fits perfectly into mine, and I'm struck with how right she feels against me. How right everything with her feels.

I hug her tighter to me and breathe in her fresh scent. I used to think the day Dad died had broken me somehow, but in the time since my accident, I've started to see that I've always been broken. I've always had an endless dark pit inside me that could only be managed and numbed with vices on the outside or with anger. But now—

Presley rubs her hand down my back and looks up at me. "You okay?"

I stare into her concerned eyes and nod. "Wondering if I need a costume or not."

She studies me skeptically, but if I talk about my feelings right now, we'll both be really late.

"Cowboy hat, cowboy boots..." She looks me up and down. "You're a cowboy."

I chuckle and kiss that smart mouth of hers. We melt into each other as my lips move against hers, and I absorb the small moan that escapes her when our tongues meet. I swear if gravity didn't exist, I'd be floating in the clouds right now.

The sound of my phone pinging in my pocket startles us. Reluctantly, I release her and pull it out to look at the screen. It's a text from Gavin. Then I see the time—I'm now ten minutes late to dinner.

"Go, Kade." She smiles.

"I'll be there before you go on, I promise. But no matter what, you're going to kill it. And if you get anxious, remember earlier when you saw yourself in the mirror, how you felt in my ropes. How you felt about yourself. You're amazing, Presley. Believe it."

She scrunches her nose up like a bunny, exactly how she did that first day I met her, but this time, I think it's to prevent tears from forming. Then she leans forward and kisses my chin. "Thank you. Now go. Listen to your family, and ask them to do the same for you."

Her words wrap around my heart and squeeze. I know she's right. I do need to listen to them and try not to let my anger get the best of me.

I swallow down the swirl of emotions that threatens to choke me and kiss her one more time. "Drive safe."

With a shine in her eyes, Presley picks up the violin case she set down next to her before placing it in the back of her car. Once she's safely buckled in and the engine has started, I wave her off then make my way to the main house.

I text Gavin that I'll be there soon then stick my phone in my pocket as I whistle "The Kind of Love We Make" by Luke Combs. I smile up at the evening sky, enjoying that the weather is getting cooler as we enter November. Soon, the holidays will roll around, and the image of Presley around the dinner table with my family for Thanksgiving invades my mind.

I think of how she'd look sitting next to me and how it would feel. Of course, my family and I would be speaking to each other, and the dinner would be relaxed and fun. I'd have my hand on her thigh while we ate, and she'd be laughing with Momma, Blake, and Gav at some raunchy joke Gran told. I know Presley hasn't had much time getting to know my family, and part of that is my fault, but I know they'll love her. Just like I—

I stop in my tracks a few feet from my childhood home. *Love.* Do I love Presley? I put my hand over my rapidly beating heart as more images of her flood behind my eyelids. The day we met and how, even before I really knew her, I wanted to kiss her. The way it feels like we've been two magnets drawn together this entire time. How my heart seemed to know she was something special to me before my mind did. And while I'm not a super religious man, I can't deny it seems as if the Divine has been on our side, throwing us together at every turn.

My body warms, and that dark pit in my stomach shrinks a bit more, just like it has been doing over the last month.

Love. I love Presley, the shy and awkward city girl who I've learned isn't as shy and awkward as I once thought. The epiphany has me standing a little taller, and the nervousness I've felt about talking to my family eases a bit. I never thought I could be one for relationships, but I'm starting to think that was never true—I just hadn't found anyone worth having, worth fighting for. But Presley...

I think of her sapphire-blue eyes and what it feels like to hold her in my arms. How I crave to see her laugh, her smile. She's become my anchor, the blood in my veins that keeps my heart beating. Our relationship may be new, but I don't care. It's the first thing I know to be true in a very long time.

"Kade?" The sound of my name in Gavin's concerned tone has me falling back into reality. He's standing on the porch, his eyes pinched in confusion. "Are you going to come in?"

I stare into my brother's green eyes and try to hold on to my newfound realization. A smile pulls at my lips, and I exhale a breath. Gavin looks at me funny, which I can understand; I haven't smiled genuinely around him for a while now.

"Yeah, I'm coming," I say. He looks hesitant but nods, stepping aside so I can make my way up the small set of stairs to the house.

I push open the screen door to the only home I've ever known, feeling like an intruder. I've come by a couple of times since my interaction with Momma and Gran to grab clothes, but I ensured nobody was home when I did. Being inside now, knowing my family is here, eats away at the good feeling I had before I stepped in. But I push the sensation aside, Presley's last words telling me to listen to them echoing in my mind. I can do this. I can have a civil conversation with my family. Then maybe my vision of us sitting together at Thanksgiving could be a reality.

I step further inside, my nostrils assaulted by the smell of a home-cooked meal. The familiar aroma of rosemary and thyme tingles my nose—Momma must've cooked my favorite roast chicken. That dark pit in my stomach grows a little smaller still at the gesture. When was the last time she cooked that? It's been over a year...when Dad was still alive.

For the first time in a long time, hope sprouts inside me even if a sadness comes with the memory. Maybe this dinner is more than about including me in the dude ranch decisions—maybe they want to make amends with me. I know I have a lot to apologize for, but could they finally see how they've hurt me, too? Have they finally listened in the silence of my absence? Maybe the time away from each other was needed.

Soft feminine chatter reaches my ears as I turn the corner to the kitchen, Gavin on my heels. When Momma, Gran, and Blake see me, they stop talking. For a moment, the air is sucked out of the room, and I can hear my blood whooshing loudly in my ears. The hope I felt ebbs as I'm reminded of the night of my accident, when I found them all eating barbecue and laughing. I stand there awkwardly as Gavin walks past me to the open seat at the head of the table, just to the left of Blake.

I stare at the table filled with chicken, cheesy potatoes, and corn. Tall glasses of cold sweet tea are sweating next to the plates. I don't have to look up to know they're all staring at me. I try to grab on to the strength I just felt outside and then start to list things off in my head like Presley taught me. *Horse, books, sloth, flowers.* The last one has me thinking of Presley's tattoos, the violets she told me she got because she found them beautiful and delicate. I know if she were here with me, she'd be holding my hand and urging me to sit. So with a deep breath, I finally look up.

Gran smiles at me. "Sit down, boy, the food is getting cold."

The familiarity of her tone and command has me doing what she says. I remove my hat and place it on a hook on the wall next to Gavin's then run my hands through my still damp hair while seating myself at the end of the table. Blake is on my left, and Momma and Gran sit across from her to my right.

Blake smiles at me as I try to get comfortable, my gut churning from the warmth of it. We haven't spoken much since I called her Blakey girl. I did try to bring it up and truly apologize, but every time she was around, Gavin was with her or I couldn't get the words out. I don't deserve that smile.

"You look good, Kade," she says. Her brown eyes look me over from head to toe. "There's something different about you."

There *is* something different—a woman who's getting ready to play her heart out onstage. A woman I'm dying to get back to even though we just saw each other.

"It's that long hair of his," Gran teases.

I comb my hand through my hair again. "It's not that long," I say, attempting to keep my tone playful. Before Dad died, he and Gran would tease me about my hair, but I like it longer. And judging by how Presley's constantly threading her fingers through it when she gets the chance, she likes it, too. I'll never cut it now.

Blake comes to my defense. "I think it looks good."

I tip my head in thanks, falling into the sort of ease I felt with her before I fucked it up.

"Let's eat, then," Momma says.

After Gran says grace, the food is passed around, and we fall into silence that I wouldn't exactly call comfortable. As I chew my favorite dinner, I find it doesn't hit the spot like it used to. I've got too much bottled up inside me that needs to come out, but I manage to force the food down.

About three-quarters of the way through my meal, I contemplate saying something. The nerves in my stomach are becoming too much. But at the same time, the prideful and stubborn part of me wants my family to speak first. I look across the table at Gavin, who's sitting with his eyes on me as he chews a bite of food. We stare at each other for a moment. It's difficult to get a read on him, because I expected him to look mad. But he looks...nervous?

Normally, he'd rub the back of his neck with his hand, but instead, his jaw ticks, and his eyes look unsure. I bite back a sigh and break eye contact, not wanting to think too much of it. If he wants to say something, I'm sure he'll say it. He always does when it comes to me, even if he tries to hold back.

"Do you want more?" Gran asks, her eyes on my near-empty plate. "You didn't take much."

"I'm fine, thank you."

"Are you sure, baby?" Momma chimes in.

Her motherly tone squeezes like a fist around my heart. Before things went to shit, she liked to tell me I'd always be her baby. The nickname has me reeling as I remember how much I've missed her, and a wave of regret sloshes in my core. I've been selfish and immature, not trying to make amends with her. I know she's in pain, too—she lost her husband, for crying out loud. That pain has to be hard to deal with, especially since he left us in a tough spot and lied to her, too. I can see that more clearly now. And I can't help but wonder: If Presley were given the chance to speak with her mom again, would she?

I swallow down the thickness I feel in my throat and shake my head. "I'm fine, Momma." My words placate her, and we once again fall into a silence filled only by the sounds of forks scraping on plates and chewing.

I sip my sweet tea, letting the cold, sugary liquid ease my flipping stomach as everyone finishes their food. Once the plates are cleared, I dig my fingers into my thighs, unable to wait any longer, pride be damned.

"Should we talk about the land leases, then?"

That awkward tension in the air pulls tight like a cinch around a horse's belly. I scan the table to find the four of them staring at each other as if they know something I don't.

When Gavin's eyes seek mine, I raise a tentative eyebrow at him. "What's going on?" I ask.

There's another pregnant pause before Gavin clears his throat. "We want to talk to you about something, Kade." His tone is serious. It reminds me of the day he came to find me in the fields to tell me Dad had a heart attack and didn't make it. The hair on the back of my neck stands on end.

"You said you wanted to talk to me about the sublease and ideas for the ranch." Gavin glances at Blake, and I see she looks sad, almost regretful. "What's going on, Blake?" I ask, taking a different approach. My tone is a half-octave higher than usual.

"Kade," Gavin interjects. "We *did* invite you here to talk about that, but we need to speak with you about something else first."

My jaw flexes, and images of the papers I found on the table two weeks ago appear behind my eyelids. Those papers were nearly complete and only needed a signature from Gavin—I don't know why I didn't think of that before.

Those decisions were already made. I know he said they wanted to talk about new ideas, but I thought I'd at least get an apology or some say on the contracts I found.

The dark pit in my stomach I thought was shrinking now expands, and the light surrounding it dims with my newfound realization. I was right when I had an inkling this dinner may not be what I thought. I narrow my eyes, the air in my lungs turning to ash and clogging my airway, making my eyes sting.

"What is this dinner really about?" The urge to stand up and walk out is strong, but Blake's clammy hand on my forearm stops me.

"We do want your input on the subleases and new ideas—that wasn't a lie, I promise." She pauses. When her brown eyes bore into mine, I see the sadness that was there the night of my accident. "But as Gavin said, there's something we'd like to talk to you about first."

My Adam's apple bobs as I clench my jaw so hard I think my molars might crack. Presley's soothing voice enters my mind, and I try to list off words again to calm myself, but the anger inside me is too much now.

"About what, then?" I manage to bite out. "Make it quick."

Gavin puffs out a breath of air. "We're concerned, Kade."

My eyes snap to his as more anger bubbles at his words. "So your solution was to lie to me again so you could get me here?"

"Like Blake said, we didn't lie to you." He sighs.

I sit back and throw the napkin from my lap onto the table. "But you omitted part of the truth. You'll never change, will you, Gav?"

He opens his mouth to speak, but Momma beats him to it. "Don't blame your brother. I asked him to get you here, and he said you wouldn't come if we just wanted to talk."

"I would have."

"You know that's not true," Gavin says.

I shake my head. I would have if they'd come to me and told me they were ready to listen and hear me out. That's why I came here tonight, because I thought they would include me. I thought we could try to make things at least a little better.

I exhale a tense breath. "Even if it's not true, that means you knew I wouldn't speak with you on one issue, so you used something you knew meant a lot to me to get me here. You manipulated me."

"You're right, Kade. It was wrong of us," Gran utters, "I see that now. But can't you see we just wanted to talk to you? We were that desperate."

"Yet nobody came and was honest with me. If you were, I would've talked."

"Because you proved you could talk without flying off the handle before?" Gavin says. "We've all tried that."

"No. Like I've said, you talked *at* me, not to me. Don't you get that?"

Gavin rubs the back of his neck, and this time, Blake speaks. "You're right. We should've been honest. But we all love you, and we didn't know what else to do."

I suck a breath of air in through my teeth, willing myself not to do what Gavin thinks I will and fly off the handle. Four sets of eyes peer at me, but I feel like they're looking through me, not really seeing me.

Black creeps at the sides of my vision, and suddenly, I feel like I'm back at Devil's Rock, my feet half over the rock ledge. The canyon below acts like a representation of the dark pit growing inside me at a rapid rate. *Fuck*. I wish more than anything that Presley was here. I need to hold on to her so I don't fall.

"Kade," Gavin says.

I blink away the spots from my vision. "Say it, then," I bite out, resigning myself to hearing what they have to say. I won't run away like Gavin wants. And if this is the last time we ever speak, I might as well know exactly what my family thinks of me. That way, I'll never fall for this bullshit again.

"Kade," Momma starts. "Ever since we talked, I haven't been able to stop thinking about what you said. About your—" She pauses, and her eyes turn glassy. Gavin places a hand on hers, and she continues. "About your depression."

My stomach sours. I regret saying those damn words to her. Even if they are the truth, I should've known they'd come back to bite me. "We're all depressed, Momma. How can you not be, living in Randall?"

She shakes her head. "No, I'm sorry I've ignored the signs for so long with you. I think I saw it before your daddy died, but I didn't pay it any mind. Like you said, it's a way of life around here."

My skin starts to crawl as the urge to drown myself in a bottle of whiskey comes back to me for the first time in weeks. "I'm fine." I grit out the words.

"You're not fine. You've not been fine for a long time," Momma insists.

I clamp my eyes shut and pray for strength. Here they are, talking at me again. "How would you all know? We haven't talked in almost two weeks. Hell, we haven't really talked in a year!"

"Because you've been avoiding us! Drinking all the time, working all the time, being with multiple women!" Momma cries.

Momma grips Gavin's hand as her eyes fill to the brim with tears. My heart cracks, and I dig my nails into my palms, attempting to breathe. I want to scream that I wasn't avoiding them because I was depressed. I was avoiding them to give us all space, to allow them to come to me when they could finally talk to me and include me in their plans.

But relationships are a two-way street. I told Gran and Momma where they could find me if they ever needed me, and they didn't come. They avoided me, too. They all did until Gavin invited me here tonight, to a dinner I thought was an olive branch.

Instead, I feel like I'm on an episode of *Intervention*. Little do they know, I haven't touched alcohol in weeks. They don't know that I enjoy the work I do or that Presley is the only woman I want. They don't know that before I sat down at this dinner, I was feeling better than I have in forever.

But I don't scream any of that. I don't say anything at all, because I know it would fall on deaf ears.

"We want to help you," Gavin says. "We love you."

I turn my attention to my big brother, the man I looked up to when we were kids despite his faults. No man is perfect, but to me, he was always one of the good ones. I see that he cares for me. I *know* that he cares for me. But how can he not understand his methods are wrong?

"I don't need to be saved by you, Gavin." My eyes turn to the rest of them before they land on Blake. "I don't need to be saved by any of you."

"Kade," Blake says softly. "I'll admit this isn't how we should've approached you. It was wrong of us, but we just want to talk. What you think and feel is important to us. It's not about saving you; it's about helping you get better."

"And none of you need help?" I ask. They all stare at me like I have two heads. My eyes bounce from Gavin to Momma and then to Gran. "Do you really think that by fixing me, we fix this family? I'm sorry, but I'm not the only one who's broken." Silence fills the room, and they know damn well I'm right. "Dad dying exposed the cracks is all. But this family was broken long before that."

A soft, painful sound breaks from Momma's lips, cracking my heart open.

"What do you mean by that, Kade?" Gavin asks.

I blink at him, surprised by his question, that he's not yelling at me to apologize to our Momma or telling me it's not true. His green gaze bores into mine, and for once, I feel as if he might be listening.

"Y'all thought you knew him, but you didn't. You didn't see the side I saw. You didn't see his constant drinking to escape his thoughts and ease his tired body. You weren't there when we drank ourselves stupid most nights and he talked about what a burden this place was to keep going."

"We have a good life here," Gran interrupts. "Your daddy loved this place. He didn't think it was a burden." Her tone is that of a mother defending her late son.

I huff. "I'm not saying he didn't love it. He did. But it was a burden. It still is." My gaze finds Gavin's again. "Why do you think he said he'd leave this place to me?"

Gavin crosses his arms over his chest. His eyes are filled with pain. "Why?"

I lick my lips, slightly shocked he's still listening. "Because, Gav, I'm already damaged."

"Kade," Momma argues.

"No, let me say this." I swallow hard. "Dad wanted to leave the land to me because I understand what it takes to maintain it. Blood, sweat, tears, sacrifice, and a lot of heartbreak. He looked at you, Gav, and he knew without you even having to say it that you wanted to leave Randall. Even though you're older than me, your mind wasn't soiled by the harshness of this place. Despite what you may think, you were always happier, more optimistic than I ever was. This place, this land, it hadn't left its mark on you yet. Not like it had on me."

Gavin studies me, processing what I just said. I know it's hard for him to understand or see what Dad's words and my relationship with him did to me, and it's hard for me to explain. I may have always come off as a flirty boy who told jokes and smiled a lot, but ever since I was old enough to be Dad's buddy, that genuine part of me was gone—or should I say, buried. I'm starting to see that, for so many years now, I've played the part of the carefree younger son, and I fooled everyone into believing that was the real me when really, I care too much. I feel too much.

The bridge of my nose stings as I continue to stare into my big brother's eyes. "I hate that he left the place to you, Gav. Not because I'm jealous, but because now it's ruined you. Dad's lies, his truth, the burden of keeping this place running, it's marked you now, too. It's marked all of us."

"Kade," Gavin says, his voice so pained it hurts me deep down into my soul. "You can't really believe that."

The words I've never spoken out loud until now settle deep into my tired bones, and I finally let them free. "You were his oldest son. You were everything to him. I was his buddy, his friend. I loved him, but he primed me to take this land, Gavin, to live here forever. This life wasn't meant for you."

He shakes his head. "I don't think that's true. I can understand why you'd believe that, but while I'll admit I thought of a different life for myself, this land has always been my home. This is my way of life, and if you'd stop and think for a second, you'd understand why I lied about the state Dad left us in. Not only did I want to protect his memory, but I was also trying to protect you from having to deal with the burden of Dad's mistakes."

"It's not the same, though; he didn't want this for you."

"But at some point, he did, because he left the land to me even if he told you he'd buck the tradition. But despite all that—I've told you this many times before, but I'll say it again, so, please, hear me this time—no matter whose name is on the deed, this is our family's property. A piece of paper doesn't mean anything. We all share in the burden of it." He reaches over to Blake, resting his hand on top of hers. "All of us."

"If what you say is true, Gav, then why have you kept me out of everything? I told you multiple times that I wanted to help. Then after the accident, I tried to warm up to the idea of the dude ranch, but you all kept me out of the big decisions. You even left me out of the land sublease conversation, the idea *I* gave you."

Gavin looks down at his hand over Blake's. When he looks back into my eyes, I can see the apology and regret that lies in them. "I take responsibility for that. I could see you were struggling long before you started drinking again. You were withdrawn after the accident and healing, so I didn't want to risk you falling backward and ruining the relationship I thought we were rebuilding." He pauses again, the muscles of his throat flexing as he swallows. "When you got the all clear from your doctor, I thought things would get better for you, that with you back on your feet, we'd be able to include you more. But then you started drinking and sleeping around, and with the way we argued...I got scared."

"Scared of what?"

The small kitchen goes quiet, and I feel like we're all frozen in time. Anxiety tickles the back of my neck, and my jaw ticks.

"Scared of what, Gavin?"

"Of losing you!" The loud boom of his admission seems to bounce off the walls. He's not normally one to yell like that, so it shocks us all. A soft cry escapes from Momma, and I stare in stunned silence at the wide eyes of my brother.

"Goddammit, Kade," he says, quieter this time. "I love you. And I'm so sorry for this mess, for everything, including tonight. I've been trying to do the right thing, and instead, I've done a lot of things wrong. I swear, no matter how misguided I was, everything I did was because I thought I could help you and protect you. But in that process, I feel as if I've lost you." When I don't say anything, he asks, "Have I lost you, Kade?"

Tears burn at the corners of my eyes. Gavin's finally saying the things I've wanted him to say for so long. I know his apology is genuine—I can hear it in his voice and see it in his eyes. While it doesn't make up for everything that's happened, I can't deny I feel a tiny bit of relief from his honesty.

But his question is a hard one to answer, because in many ways, I feel like I've been lost—not only from my family, but also from myself—for a long time now. I don't even know if I've ever truly been found.

"I don't know," I voice. "I'm sorry."

Gavin sits back in his chair and exhales a shuddering breath while Momma weeps and Gran tries to console her. The urge to leave hits me hard again as the pain I'm causing by speaking my truth to my family weighs on me.

"Tell me what I can do to make this better, Kade, and I'll do it," Gavin pleads. "I'll sign the ranch over to you—we'll stop the dude ranch and sell the land if you want—but you mean more than any of it. I mean that, little brother. We don't want to lose you. Please, tell me what we can do."

Everyone at the table stops breathing at his offer, including me. My ears ring, and I swear my heart is beating so loud the room can hear it. My eyes are locked with Gavin's, his hopeful gaze shooting a dagger through my heart. He's just offered me everything I wanted, everything I was asking for. But it all feels wrong.

My shoulders hang heavy as I try to think of the words to say, but none come to me. The dinner in my stomach churns violently as the darkness inside of me threatens to flood through my entire being. I stand up from my spot at the table so fast I see black spots behind my eyelids.

"I think I'm going to go."

Gavin gets up and takes a few steps toward me. "Don't run away from this, Kade. Please. We can talk this through."

I force a small smile on my face. He's right; we *could* talk this through. But there's a reason the offer he gave me felt wrong—it's because I don't think this is what I want anymore. More than that, Gavin and Blake do a fine job of running this place. When I look at them together, I know they're happy. It makes me wonder if the land has ever truly been as much of a burden to Gavin as I thought or if I was blinded by Dad's words and actions.

Presley's caring eyes appear in my mind, and I think of our conversation at Devil's Rock, a conversation I've repeated to myself many times since then. What if she's right? What if this is my opportunity to try to find myself outside of Randall, outside of the Montgomery Family Ranch and the plans my dad had for me?

The idea sparks something in my soul, but at the same time, a nagging voice in my head says it's impossible, that I don't deserve to have more. That all I get is to be a prisoner to this place until the day I get buried alongside Emmett Montgomery.

"Kade?"

I blink and refocus on my brother's stubbled jaw.

"Talk to me, little brother."

My gaze sweeps over my family and Blake sitting at the table. Their concerned faces only add to how badly I feel right now. I turn back to Gavin and lean in to hug him. The action shocks him, but I keep hugging him until his arms slide around my waist. I pat him on the back, ignoring the eyes I can feel watching us. "This is your ranch, Gav. You and Blake have done what Dad couldn't, what I'm not even sure I could do. You saved it."

He pulls away and shakes his head. I know he's confused by my words, and maybe I am, too. But I need him to know what I'm thinking. "You're part of that. You've helped more than you know—"

"It's okay." I stop him. "You don't have to placate me. I'm a big boy." I clap my hands on his arms and step back then look at my family and Blake. "I'm fine. Really." The lie is a bitter pill to swallow, but I can't stay here anymore.

"Kade," Gavin tries again. "Please, stay."

"I'm sorry I've been so horrible—and I mean that." While I meant a lot of the things that I said, I'm seeing things a lot clearer. In a way, my anger with Gavin has stemmed from me not understanding we've been fighting for the same things. We've both wanted to protect each other in our own way. And as far as Momma, Gran, and Blake go, I know they love me and just want to support me. They didn't deserve what I said to them, even if I was in pain.

Everyone at this table has done the best they could, and I think I need to figure out my own shit now. Without them trying to fix or save me.

I look at the clock and see it's close to seven. Presley is probably getting ready to go onstage soon, and I'm itching to get to her. I bet she's off to the side of the stage saying her words to herself and mustering up the bravery I've watched her build.

Thinking of her smile makes a little bit of that darkness cease. Maybe it's time I learned from her. Maybe it's time I faced whatever it is I'm feeling inside head on.

"Kade," Momma says. "Just sit, and we'll talk more. We can talk about something else, catch up. You can tell us what's been going on between you and the city girl."

I smile a little. "Presley. Her name is Presley." My heart skips a beat as I say her name. "I need to go."

"Kade," Gavin tries one more time.

I press my hand into his shoulder and squeeze. "I'm fine, okay? I just need some space to think. And I promised Presley I'd be at Night Hawk tonight."

His pupils dart back and forth as if he's searching for a lie. Eventually, he releases a tense breath and nods. "I love you, little brother."

I bring him into another hug. He holds me tighter this time, and when I pull back, his eyes are watery.

Before I leave, I hug Momma and kiss her on the cheek. I tell her I love her and that I'm sorry before kissing Gran and Blake on the crowns of their heads and saying the same. Then I walk out the door and pull in a long breath of earthy night air.

With the persistent thought of Presley about to go onstage, I haul ass toward the hands' quarters where my truck is parked. When I arrive, I throw open the door and grab my car keys off the kitchen table, tossing them in my hands as I turn to leave. But when I pass the small kitchenette, a flash of familiar silver catches my eye on the counter.

I stop in my tracks, and my palms turn clammy as I turn my body to face Dad's flask. The monogrammed M etched in the silver stares at me, as if it's beckoning me toward it. Against my better judgment, I put my keys in my pocket and walk over to pick it up. I hold the family heirloom in my hands, feeling the coolness of it against my palm. It's funny how such a small, inanimate object can feel like it's alive.

Before I know what I'm doing, I grab the bottle of whiskey I had in the cupboard from weeks ago and move to the small dining table. I sit, opening the flask and filling it with the brown liquid. I put the cap back on then stare at it, my fingers tracing the M.

For a moment, I hear Dad's voice in my head, asking, *What are you doing, Kade?* But I don't answer. I only continue to stare.

CHAPTER 33

Presley

MY HEART POUNDS AS the song "Honky Tonkin's What I Do Best" by Marty Stuart and Travis Tritt flies out of me and the warm vibrations of my fiddle echo through Night Hawk. The people on the dance floor sing along, dance, and clap as I lose myself in playing the last song of the night.

I've felt a lot of things onstage before, but nothing quite like this. I feel...exhilarated. Stronger, confident, and more capable than I ever have before. Part of that has to do with the fact that I'm doing what I love, what I was born for—and my heart is rejoicing, almost bursting from my chest. And the other part has to do with the man I left at the ranch. The man I still haven't seen hide nor hair of.

Sweat drips from my brow as I play the last few notes, looking to the audience where Kade said he'd be one more time—but he's still not there. My good feeling ceases, but then the song ends, and the cheers of the crowd drown out my thoughts for a moment.

"Everyone give a big round of applause for our special guest, Presley James!" Andy, the lead singer, says into the mic. More cheers and hollers erupt, and a flush appears on my cheeks as I bow, soaking in this moment of happiness before I motion for everyone to clap for the rest of the band.

After more clapping and bowing, making my cheeks turn so red I probably look like a red color swatch, the music over the loudspeaker starts up, and I'm walking off the stage feeling several different emotions.

"Presley, that was fucking killer!" Jake shouts, giving me a hug I would normally find awkward but one I find myself leaning into, another thing that's changing about me.

I pull back with a chuckle, my fiddle still in one hand. "Thanks, Jake."

"No, thank you. You were incredible."

With a gentle smile on my face, I search for Kade again—but still, no dice.

"He's not here," Jake says.

I think I become redder than I already am, which should be impossible. Of course Jake knows who I'm looking for.

He glances over the crowd as well. "I was about to text him."

I attempt another smile at Jake. I looked for Kade several times throughout the night, and every time I didn't see him, I tried to tell myself it was a good thing, that dinner went well. But now that the adrenaline of being onstage is wearing off, something doesn't feel right. He promised he'd be here—and Kade doesn't lie.

With Jake's eyes on me, I pull out the phone I had tucked in my back pocket to see if he's texted, but there's nothing there. At least not from him.

There is one text from Derek, which only adds to the growing anxiety I'm feeling. I bite my lip and click it open.

> DEREK: I'm on probation. I hope you're fucking happy.

I delete the message, and with a few quick taps, I do what I should've done when I first moved here: I block him. I didn't have the strength or the bravery to do it before. In a way, Derek was like a cigarette—cancerous and bad for me, something I knew I shouldn't have done but did anyway. But I don't need him, and I don't want him.

As I slide my phone back in my pocket, a weight lifts from my shoulders, and I breathe a sigh of relief. My asshole ex isn't part of my life anymore; he's part of my past. One that I'm learning to let go of so I can focus on my future, a future I hope involves a man who isn't here.

Fear sours my insides. "Do you mind if I take off?" I ask Jake. I glance at the large crowd. "I can stay to help if you need me."

He shakes his head. "Go check on him," he says. The hint of concern in his voice only serves to feed my anxiety, though he quickly covers it. "You've worked hard enough for tonight. But I think this might have to be a regular occurrence."

"Hell yes, it does!" Andy appears at Jake's side. He's got a dusty-colored cowboy hat on over his red hair. A moment later, the guitarist, bassist, and drummer flank him, all grinning widely at me.

"We actually wanted to talk to you about playing with us more," Andy says. "You're extremely talented, and we all had fun tonight."

"What Andy wants to say is that we're going on a little tour around Texas after Christmas," the drummer, Brent, says. "And we'd love to have you join us."

Excitement sparks in my veins at the prospect of it, of being back on the road and playing my fiddle every night, feeling the vibrations of music in my soul once again. Like I did tonight—and with a band that's been nothing but kind and supportive of me since I've met them.

Every part of me wants to say yes, but then I feel my message-less phone burning a hole in my pocket. Kade's smiling face swims before my vision, and my excitement dissipates. *Where is he?*

"It's just some shows in honky-tonks, but we have a couple in Dallas and even one in Nashville down the line if we all jive together outside of gigs," Andy adds. "Which I'm sure we will."

I smile at him and take out my phone, giving it to Andy. "Can you put your number in? I'll think about it."

Andy takes my phone as Jake watches warily. I feel his questioning gaze on me, and I bet he's wondering why I didn't just say yes.

In the past, after feeling so great onstage—plus getting all that appreciation and love—I would have probably said yes and hoped this band was different from my last. And while I think they are, I have two good jobs here in Randall, a nice place to stay, and people in my life now that I care about. One person in particular.

The urge to find Kade gets stronger. When Andy gives me back my phone and I still don't see any messages or calls from Kade, the overwhelming sense that he needs me hits me hard, and I have to hold off a shiver.

I force a smile as I nod at the band. "Thanks, I'll call you later this week."

"Great!" they all chime.

"Well, we see some ladies who want our attention." Andy wiggles his eyebrows. "We'll chat later."

He shakes Jake's hand, and the four men walk off, leaving Jake with me again. "When you find Kade, will you text me?" Jake asks.

"Yes, of course," I say, looking into the dark-brown eyes of Kade's concerned friend. Now I'm very worried. "I'll see you later. And thanks for tonight."

Jake squeezes my bicep. "No, thank you."

I nod at him then step away to head toward the back room and pack up my fiddle. I try to call Kade, but it goes straight to voicemail. My hackles rise as I grab my purse, running to my car.

What if something happened? I think of what Kade told me at Devil's Rock, how Gavin treated him this morning. Now I don't know why I didn't insist on staying with him like I had earlier. I can always play fiddle—there will always be gigs. But did Kade need me tonight, and I wasn't there for him? Guilt roils through me. The first person to really care about me, and I'm already screwing it up.

I put my stuff in my car, and then I'm off, hurtling down the road. By now, I know the way back home like the back of my hand. It doesn't matter that it's dark—I could close my eyes and still know the way back.

The hairs on my arms stand on end when it dawns on me what I just thought. The song playing on the radio fades out, and my heartbeat thumps in my ears so it's all I can hear. "Home," I say out loud. "Home. I'm home."

My already rampant thoughts flip about my head like they're on spin cycle, and then I'm laughing. *Home.*

I reflect on my time in Randall, how I've pushed myself beyond my comfort zone. How I've smiled more than I have my entire life. How I feel like this dense fog that's been suffocating me has lifted and I can finally breathe. Do I have my moments? Yes. I'm only human. But for the first time in a long time, I feel content. At home. Not just in myself, but here, in Randall. With Kade.

I let out a laugh again, one that frees up the weight on my chest that's felt so heavy. Then I smile, Kade's handsome, stubbled face filling my every thought. Every action he's done over the last few weeks only makes me want to be with him more. To fill my time with him and all the things that I love.

Then I'm laughing again. Am I having a mental breakdown? Breakup? That's silly. There's no such thing. But I feel free. Holy crap, I'm happy. I'm in love. Not just with Kade, but with my life.

I step on the gas pedal and go a little faster, the spark in my stomach that's telling me to get to Kade burning brighter. When the driveway to the Montgomery Family Ranch comes into view, I breathe a sigh of relief. I drive past the house and don't see his truck there, so I keep going to the hands' quarters, hoping that's where he'll be.

When I pull up and see his truck, hope lights in my chest. I park next to it and kill the engine before rushing into the house. My stomach drops when he's not there—instead, an open whiskey bottle is sitting on the counter next to his cell phone. Crap. Crap. Crap. I try to think of where he might be, and for a second, I come up empty. But then it clicks.

I turn for the door and sprint to the barn. I see the light through the windows as I approach and suck in a breath. With the muscles I've built up doing ranch work, I pull the sliding door open with almost too much force, and it bangs against the frame. I wince but continue to where I know Kade is.

I run up the stairs, and when I reach the loft, I'm sweating, and my chest is heaving with shortness of breath, but I see him. He's here. His broad back is to me as he stares out into the darkness through the open loft door, but he's here.

There's no way he didn't hear me, but he acts as if he doesn't, his body as motionless as water on a windless day.

"Kade," I say quietly. At the sound of his name, his shoulders tense up, then in the next breath, they slump again. "Kade?" He still doesn't face me, nor does he say anything.

I walk tentatively to him and lean on the wooden railing next to him. My arm gently touches his as I settle in and turn my head to look at him. He is staring off into nothingness while he grips his silver flask in his fingers so hard they're starting to turn white. I attempt to study his face, to get a read on him, but his features are blank.

I bite my lip as I debate what to do or say. But I settle on silence, staring out into the night along with him.

"I'm sorry I wasn't there."

The sudden sound of his voice makes me jump. Then I'm hit with how much pain I hear laced through his words. I gently touch his forearm, feeling the lean muscles bunch underneath my palm, but I don't move my hand.

"I bet you were amazing." His tone is sad, the kind of sad that makes me want to pull him in my arms and hug him, tell him it will be alright. I keep the pressure of my hand on him steady and inhale an easy breath as if any sudden expression will spook him.

"Kade, what happened?"

He clenches his jaw, his eyes moving from the night sky to his flask. "I think I need help, Presley."

His statement stuns me, words I didn't expect to hear sinking through me like a stone to the bottom of the ocean. I swallow and try to maintain my composure. "What do you need help with, baby?"

The endearment slips easily from my lips, and he finally turns to me. His hardened gaze dips to my mouth as if he can't believe I said it, either, then his composure fractures. His features relax slightly, and he starts blinking rapidly as he struggles to stop tears from falling.

"I don't know." His voice cracks, and my heart shatters at the confusion in his words. I want to give in to my desire to pull him into my arms. I want to comb my fingers through his soft hair and tell him that it'll all be okay. But Kade isn't someone who appreciates lies, and the truth is, I *don't* know that.

I trail my hand up his arm instead and rest it on his elbow. "It's okay," I assure him. "We can figure it out together."

His eyes stay glued to mine for a moment. Then as quickly as the softness in his gaze arrived, it leaves. His expression turns hard. "You should go."

He pulls his arm away from me, and I shake my head. "I'm staying."

"Presley." Kade sighs. "Please go."

I don't move, and I'm not planning to. He can say whatever he wants to me, but I'm not going to leave. The Presley that arrived in Randall would've, but not this version of me and not after what we've shared together. Not after how he's stood by me and helped me work through my own hardships.

"Presley," he says again. "I don't want you to see me like this." He whispers the second part, but I hear it all the same.

"Like what?"

His head drops to his chest, and for a moment, I think he won't answer me. But then he barely whispers, "Weak."

If my heart wasn't already shattered, it would be obliterated now, because the man before me is anything but weak. Gently, I grab the wrist of the hand still holding the flask. He looks down at it, and I stroke the soft skin over his pulse.

"Tell me what happened to make you feel that way."

Kade presses his eyes shut then releases a sigh. "They didn't want to talk about the dude ranch. They wanted to talk about my, um…"

I don't say anything as I wait for him to finish, though internally, I'm livid for him. The fact that they lied to him again only makes my blood boil, and I have the urge to run up to the house and give his family a piece of my mind. It's a feeling I haven't ever felt to this extent before, the desire to protect someone with my whole being.

I squeeze Kade's wrist to assure him once more that I'm here. At the touch, his tired eyes meet mine again. "They wanted to talk about my drinking—about my depression." He says the last part with such shame in his chest, which only serves to make me angrier. I hate that he feels the need to be ashamed of it or his coping mechanisms.

While Kade hasn't said he has depression to me outright, I understand he struggles with it and have known since I met him. Our night at Devil's Rock, what he shared with me about his life and his accident only deepened my understanding of it, of him. And while I haven't lost a loved one or been faced with a failing business like he has, I know how it feels to think nothing will ever be okay again, like nobody would care if you were gone. My parents have only ever proved that to me time and time again.

"Kade—"

He pulls his wrist from my touch and starts to pace the loft floor. His steps are heavy as he drags one hand through his messy hair while he grips the flask in the other. Eventually, he stops and holds the flask out to me, his hand trembling.

"I didn't even drink anything. I haven't—God, Presley. I haven't even been drinking at all. I told you at Devil's Rock I was trying, and fuck—" He pulls at the ends of his hair.

Unable to hold myself back any longer, I take a few steps to him and wrap my arms around his waist. His body stiffens, and I think he's going to pull back, but then he sinks into my arms like a deadweight and begins to shake.

The clunk of the metal flask falling to the floor seems to vibrate up through my feet as Kade's arms wrap around me. He grips me so tight against his chest that my breath whooshes from me and I gasp for air, but I don't care. I crush him tighter to me as he hides his face in my neck, his wet tears dropping to my skin.

"Feel whatever you need to feel." I repeat the words he's said to me so many times now. "Let me take care of you."

His shoulders shake in silent sobs, and I rub my hands down the length of his back as his heart releases all the emotions he's been holding in. Regret riddles me when I think back to Devil's Rock, how he expressed to me he wasn't sure what happened the night of his accident. I should've paid more attention to his words, to what he *wasn't* saying. He's been through a lot in such a short amount of time—it's no wonder he's having a hard time, why drinking and women became a crutch for him. I'd want to numb myself, too.

"Kade," I say against his ear. "Listen to me, alright?"

He doesn't respond; he just grips me tighter.

"You're not weak."

He starts to pull back then, but I don't let him.

"You're not." My voice is firmer now. "You're the strongest person I've ever met. Being vulnerable doesn't make you weak. Having depression doesn't make you weak. You asked for help—that's more than a lot of people do, baby."

His watery eyes stare into mine, and I bring one of my hands up to cup his damp cheek. "Tell me how I can help you, and I will. I'll drive you to the hospital, I'll stay with you all night, I'll follow you around twenty-four hours a day—just tell me what you need. I'm here for you, Kade, and I'm not leaving."

"You're too good for me, Presley."

I shake my head. "Then you're too good for me." He tries to pull back again, but I just grip him tighter, making him look into my eyes. "Stop thinking."

He blinks at me, then a hint of a smile curls at the corners of his lips. "You're using my own words against me, Lemon darlin'."

The weight on my chest lightens a bit at his use of my special nickname. "Is it working?"

He turns and kisses the inside of my palm before resting the weight of his head against it. His heavy eyes close, features warming as if he's drawing in my strength.

"Despite what you think of yourself right now, Kade, you're a good man. You'll get through this, and I'll be there to help you, I promise."

His eyes flutter open, and I see a tear clinging to one of his long lashes. "Why?" he asks. "I couldn't even keep my promise to be there for you tonight. I'm a fuckup, Presley. I stared at a flask for I don't know how long instead of being there for you—I'm not any better than your asshole ex."

I shake my head fiercely. "No, you're not, Kade. You're nothing like him."

"You don't know me that well. I'm—"

"But I *do* know you, Kade. You've shown me who you are. You're not what your brother or anyone else thinks of you. I can see through your bullshit, and I'm not buying it. I'm not going to let you push me away. So please. Just stop." I suck in a breath as I try to hold back tears now.

"But I don't deserve you, Presley." He exhales.

I take his face in both my hands now. "Do you think I would allow someone who didn't deserve me to tie me up? That I'd trust them with my body like I trust you? Do you think so little of me?" My words come out angry, but I need him to hear me, to understand.

A sound of protest leaves his mouth. "No, Presley, I fucking love you, I think the world of you, I—" He stops, mouth and eyes wide.

We stare at each other, and my shattered heart begins to mend as his declaration wraps around me like a fierce embrace.

The rough brush of Kade's thumb against my cheek has me blinking, and I realize I'm crying now. "I didn't mean to make you cry, Lemon. I shouldn't have said that—"

"Can you say it again?"

Kade doesn't hesitate. "I love you. *Fuck*, I love you, Presley."

I want to swallow down the sob I feel bubbling out of me, but I can't contain it. It bursts forth like a dam that's broken, and my tears fall in earnest now. Kade crushes me to him, and I lay my head down on his chest so my lips are at his neck.

"Nobody has ever said they loved me and meant it before."

Kade's lips press to the crown of my head, and the next words that leave his mouth are said with conviction. "I mean it, Presley. I mean it more than I've ever meant anything."

A shiver works its way through my body, and I look up into his eyes.

"You don't have to say it back," he adds. I know it's early, but I wanted—no, I *needed*—to say it."

More tears spill from me as a gentle smile plays at my lips. "I love you, too, Kade." My words are as sure and strong as his were so he can hear the truth in them.

The muscles in his throat work as he swallows, fresh tears blurring his awed stare as he tucks a piece of hair behind my ear. I squeeze my arms around his waist.

"You deserve me, Kade. And you deserve to be happy. Whatever it takes, I'm going to make sure you are."

Kade leans his forehead against mine and continues to hold me. I don't know how long we stand there, but we take comfort in each other, and I relish in his steady breaths against my cheek.

While I don't know what the future will bring, I do know one thing: The Montgomery Family Ranch isn't what makes me feel at home—it's Kade.

CHAPTER 34

Kade

"I DIDN'T EXPECT TO see you in here so soon, Kade," Dr. Ellis says, her eyes warm.

I run my hand through my hair, feeling stupid for being at the doctor, but when my eyes find Presley's, I feel anchored again. She gives me that look that tells me to answer, and I smile sheepishly at my doctor while taking a hold of her hand. "Um, well, I trust you, and my girlfriend said I should talk to you."

Presley rolls her eyes at my statement while her cheeks blush at the use of the word "girlfriend." It's been over a week since that night in the loft, the night we both told each other we were in love. And since then, "girlfriend" has become my new favorite nickname. Turns out, I *am* a relationship guy.

Dr. Ellis crosses her arms over her chest and goes into serious doctor mode. "I'm happy to help you in any way I can."

Presley squeezes my hand. "I've been dealing with some depression and, um, alcoholism." The words feel thick on my tongue. Being angry or snide made it easier to admit these things—I could almost pretend they were a joke, even though I was being serious. But now that I'm taking things more seriously and getting help, it feels harder to admit that I'm struggling, that I have a problem.

Dr. Ellis nods. "How long has this been going on?"

I swallow again. I want to say since my dad died, but that isn't exactly the truth. "I had my first drink when I was fourteen." I pause, and Presley grips my hand tighter. "And the depression,

I think I've struggled with that for a long time. It's gotten worse after my accident."

She hums. "I know we talked about this the last time you were in, but depression after a heart attack is three times more common than in the general population. And given that it sounds like you have a possible undiagnosed history, I can understand why you'd be struggling more in the last few months."

I shouldn't feel comforted by that statistic, but I do anyway, like maybe this isn't all my fault. Though I'm sure Presley would say none of it is my fault.

"As far as the alcoholism goes, Kade, you didn't tell me that your drinking had been more than social when we went over your history in the hospital. If you've been consuming alcohol since adolescence, your heart could've been weakened, making a cardiac event more likely. Given that you've had a heart attack, it's even more important that you try to get that under control."

Embarrassment creeps up my neck, and the room gets hot. I look down at my hand where it's laced with Presley's and try to find strength. I owe it to her, to my family, to own my shit, to get help. With another pulse to Presley's hand, I meet Dr. Ellis's understanding eyes.

"I know that it's easier said than done, and I'm sure you've heard this before, but the first step is admitting that you have a problem and that you need help. While I wish you'd been honest with me about this before, I'm glad you've come to me now. The good news is, there are many things that can help you. Antidepressants and therapy are options. There are also free groups like Alcoholics Anonymous—I can recommend one here in the city if you'd like, though I'm sure I could find some online options if that's easier for you."

I bite the inside of my cheek, attempting to ignore what Dad would say about this if he were alive. He'd call me ridiculous and hand me another beer. But he isn't here, and I want to continue to be here if for no other reason than to wake up next to Presley every morning and see her smile.

I nod at the doctor. "What is my next step, then?"

"Do you have a primary care physician?" I shake my head. "No problem. I'll put in a referral for you. You should be able to set up an appointment, and, depending on what you need, they can prescribe you antidepressants or refer you to a psychiatrist. I'll also put the AA group information in your patient portal."

"Thank you."

"In the meantime, do you have a support system to help you?"

The answer seems obvious, but I know she's asking because she has to. When I open my mouth to answer, Presley beats me to it. "Yes, he does."

I lift the back of her hand and kiss it, causing Dr. Ellis to smile wider. "I'm glad, Kade, and I'm proud of you for coming to me. I know it must not have been easy."

"My support system is pushy," I tease.

Dr. Ellis chuckles. "Something tells me you need that."

Presley huffs a laugh in likely agreement. "Thank you, Dr. Ellis."

"It's no trouble. And Kade?"

"Yeah?"

"Maybe try some goat yoga." She winks.

"Goat yoga?" Presley asks awhile later as I park in front of the hands' quarters.

With a bashful smile, I tell her the story of the last time I was in Dr. Ellis's office. I earned a smack and an eye roll when I admitted to flirting with her.

"You're not upset?" I ask.

"Why would I be?" she asks, unbuckling her seatbelt. I unbuckle my own, then we both climb out of the truck. When I meet her on the passenger side, I back her up until she's against the door, my arms caging her in. Her breathing picks up, and I grin down at her.

"I'm not saying you should be. I just wanted to make sure you weren't," I tell her honestly. "I come with a lot of baggage, if you haven't noticed."

Presley blinks up at me, the mid-afternoon sun shining down on top of us. I step a little closer so the brim of my cowboy hat shades her eyes. She lifts her hand to my cheek and rubs the stubble under her thumb. "I do, too, if you haven't figured that out yet."

With a sigh, I lean into her hand. I think of Derek and the trouble he's caused. "That doesn't matter to me. But if you have any other baggage that I don't know about, at least tell me so I'm not surprised," I tease.

Her lips tip up in a sullen smile. "Just a crazy ex and parents who don't care about me."

I kiss her forehead, wanting to convey how much she means to me in the lingering kiss—that she doesn't need idiot people in her life when she has me. By the time I pull back, her expression is warmer. Her thumb trails over my cheekbone again.

"Your baggage doesn't matter, Kade. I like that you're honest with me, that you aren't afraid to own what you've done. Now I'm not saying I won't ever be jealous of women hitting on you, but I trust you."

My chest expands, and I lean in to kiss her. She opens her mouth to mine, and I press her harder against the truck, the softness of her body fitting against mine like it was meant to be there. When our kisses become more heated, she lifts her hips so her jean-covered sex grinds against me. I curse against her lips and let out a low groan.

"Gavin and Blake should be here any minute," I say between her kisses. But instead of stopping, she gets more aggressive. I chuckle against her lips, my cock stirring to life.

"Just kiss me," she murmurs before brushing her violin-calloused fingers down my arm. I shiver then trail my hand up, sliding between her breasts until I'm gripping her throat the way she likes. A moan escapes her lips, and I swallow it with my mouth. The sounds of her pleasure vibrating through me only encourage me to kiss her harder.

"Kade," she says as she breaks the kiss. "I've missed you."

Her hand digs into the flesh of my ass cheek, and the pressure on my cock intensifies. "You see me every day," I tease. I press my thumb harder into her neck and take satisfaction in the way she writhes against me.

"You know what I mean," she pants.

I *do* know what she means. Since that night in the loft, we've taken it easy. We've kissed and touched and held one another, but I understood why she wanted to wait to have sex again. And if I'm being honest, it's been nice to just be surrounded and supported by her, to remind myself that I don't need sex or booze every day to be okay.

My lips seal over hers again, and I surrender to her kisses, to the feel, smell, and taste of her. Everything about Presley is fucking perfect, and I can't believe this woman is all mine.

Just as I grip her leg to hitch it over my hip, a throat clears. Presley detaches her lips, and I release her neck and thigh before she hides her face in my chest.

"I warned you," I chuckle. I kiss the crown of her head then meet the embarrassed eyes of Gavin. Blake just looks amused. I pull Presley in front of me to hide my erection and wrap my hands around her waist. I make sure she feels what she's done to me then give her a little squeeze that says, *You'll pay for this later.* Presley's purple-painted nails dig into my arms, and I smirk at her response before turning my attention to Blake and Gavin.

"Howdy," I say.

Gavin nods in greeting, his features still colored with embarrassment, and Blake smiles back at me. The three of us have talked a couple of times since the ambush of a dinner, and I told them both why Presley and I went to the city today, but there's still tension between us. However, I'm hoping that will fade over time as we work our issues out.

"Howdy, yourself," Blake says. "Do you need us to come back later?" Her tone is playful, and I'll confess it's nice after how serious all our recent interactions have been.

"Yes—"

"No." Presley cuts me off. "Now is good." As she steps away, she makes a point to brush that fine ass of hers against my semi, and I have to grit my teeth. Oh yeah, she's paying for that later.

She looks over her shoulder to wink at me, and my chest fills with happiness. It's been a sight to see her blossom and become more confident. I love that she's getting more comfortable in her skin, especially around people other than me.

"Presley," Blake calls to get her attention. "I've got some paint colors I want you to look at while the boys talk. Are you okay with that?"

Presley checks in with me, silently asking if I'll be okay. I told her I asked Blake and Gavin to meet with us specifically because I need to speak with my brother, but I love that she still wants to make sure I'm okay being left alone with him.

"Go, Lemon," I say. "I'll find you in a bit."

"Great!" Blake says happily, stepping forward to link elbows with Presley.

As she tugs her toward the main stable, I stifle my laughter watching my girlfriend awkwardly walk away with an animated Blake. They don't know each other well yet, but I'd like to think that they could be friends. Blake is a good person, and Presley deserves to have more people in her life that care about her.

Once they disappear into the barn, I turn to face a silent Gavin. He steps toward me, gravel crunching under his boots, and only stops when we're almost toe-to-toe. When he doesn't speak, I study his face under the brim of his worn dark-brown cowboy hat, noticing the dark circles under his eyes from what I'm guessing is lack of sleep. I hadn't really taken time to notice it before, but my brother looks older. He may only be twenty-five, but he's no longer the young and hopeful boy that he once was. But I suppose that's what life does to us all, especially a hard life like ours.

"Do you want to walk or sit?" he asks, his voice gravelly.

I take in a breath of fresh air and look up at the Texas sky. "Let's walk."

We fall into step next to each other, walking along the unpaved road that will loop us around the main part of the ranch. There are a few hands around, including Art, who we greet as we walk by. Eventually, we get away from the stables and the people until the only sounds are our footsteps and birds chirping.

"So," I say, "you're probably wondering how the doctor visit went." I shove my hands into my pockets and turn to look at my brother's profile, one that looks so much like Dad's.

Gavin's steps slow at my words, his eyes meeting mine. "You don't have to tell me unless you want to."

Pleasant surprise and appreciation overtake me at his statement. This is a lot different from his usual demand for information. "I want to."

Gavin's jaw tightens as if my words made him emotional—happy, even. "Then I'd like to know."

I clear my throat and let the information I got today from Dr. Ellis fall from my lips. Gavin listens, his jaw remaining tense as I speak. "Presley already did some research on our drive back, and I think I'm going to see a psychiatrist. She found a couple of online ones who have sliding-scale payment methods, though it'll still be tough to swing since my money is already going to my hospital bills and current heart meds—"

Gavin stops walking, clapping both hands on my shoulders. "Kade, stop."

A flash of anger lights in me, afraid he's mad at me for some reason, but I stop talking at his stern tone and meet his gaze.

"Whatever you need, we'll figure it out. The last thing I want you to worry about is the cost of something that will help you. Let me—let our family—help you."

"But—"

"No, Kade. I don't care if you get pissed at me about this, but you're my brother." His voice breaks, and he stops speaking to compose himself. When he looks back up at me, his green eyes are wet. "You're my brother, and I'm not letting you do this alone. If I have to work more, that's fine. But I've got your back in this. No matter what."

His hands on my shoulders grip me tighter as I try to think of words to say. When I can't, I do the only thing I know to do: I pull him into me and hug him. We stand there for a long moment, the world moving around us as we both process the gravity of his words.

When Gavin pulls back, he wipes his eyes with the back of his hand, trying to remove the evidence of his tears. It's something Dad did, too, and it makes me smile. Gavin sees my grin and matches it.

"What are you thinking about?" he asks.

"How Dad would've told us to get a grip and taken us out to Devil's Rock."

Gavin huffs out a sad laugh. "Yes, he would've."

We start to walk again, and I kick a large rock with my boot. "Do you miss him?"

Gavin is silent for a moment before he answers. "Of course I do." He lets out a long sigh. "I think what I miss the most is the way he made Momma smile."

My gut churns thinking of all the relationships I want to repair. Momma is at the top of the list. We've spoken once since dinner, and we both apologized to each other, but we have a long way to go.

"Yeah, I miss that, too."

We continue to walk in silence for a while until we reach a pasture where Willy, Big John, and some of the other geldings are grazing. I whistle to my horse, and Willy nickers at me, trotting over to us at the fence line. Gavin and I stop to give him some attention.

"Gav," I say after a minute.

He stops petting Willy's neck. "Yeah?"

"Presley got an offer to travel Texas after the new year with that band she played with last week."

He smiles at the news. "That's great."

I run my palm down Willy's long face. "I want to go with her."

Gavin's square features stay neutral, but I can see surprise flash briefly in his eyes.

"I've talked to Presley about it, and the gigs are short. We'd be gone for probably three days at a time tops, and the band can pay me a bit to help with setup and teardown to make up for the money I'm losing when I'm not here. But the ranch would be our home base, and we'll work when we're here." I gesture to the land around us. "This place, it will always be my home. It's everything I thought I wanted. But—"

Laughter reaches our ears, and we look up to see Presley and Blake in the distance. I watch my girl for a moment, my heart beating faster in my chest as I think about traveling with her, waking up next to her and experiencing new things with her.

"But it's not anymore?" Gavin finishes for me.

I meet his green eyes again. "It's complicated."

"Everything always is, little brother. That's life."

I let out a sad chuckle. "Yes, that's life."

Gavin sighs. "I think it's a good idea."

"You do?" I wasn't sure how he'd react, but this is going better than I expected. He nods, though I can see he wants to say something else. "What is it?"

Gavin scratches Willy behind the ear before answering. "When you said at dinner that you didn't want the land, that it was mine and Blake's now, did you already know you wanted to leave?"

I puff out a breath through my lips. "Traveling with Presley wasn't an option yet, but I've been thinking about it for a bit now." I look around once more at the plains and pastures, at the horse I love so much. "But Gav, I think I need the space, some room to grow and breathe. I think you need it, too. But I know it might not seem fair to you because you were always the one who wanted to leave."

Gavin turns his gaze to Blake in the distance, her head tossed back in laughter. The ghost of a smile plays at his lips as he turns back to me. "It's not what I want anymore. At least not in the same way. Blake and I have dreams, but our families and businesses are here. We enjoy what we're building together. Yes, someday we want to travel a bit, but we're happy."

I bow my head, thinking about how much things have changed. I never would've thought he'd say those words. With another glance at Presley, I can't help but wonder where I would be if she hadn't come to Night Hawk, if she hadn't been brave enough to walk away from her situation. I'm so glad she did.

Itching to get back to her, I step away from Willy and start walking again. Gavin falls in step easily beside me.

"It's funny," I say. "We've kind of traded places."

"Yeah, I guess we have."

"But I'm serious, Gavin. I'll find someone to replace me and Presley when we're not here. And when you want to travel, Presley and I can cover you when she's not playing a gig—"

"Kade." Gavin stops my rambling. "I told you—whatever you need, I'm going to support you. We'll figure out ranch coverage, alright? Don't worry about it."

"I just want you to know I'm not leaving you, that you don't have to do this alone, either, big brother."

"I won't be alone—I've got Blake, Gran, and Momma. And like you said, you'll be back. You're too much of a country bumpkin to stay in the city for long."

I chuckle. "Okay, you're probably right about that. Though I guess I'll figure that out for myself."

Gavin puts his hand on the back of my neck like Dad used to do after a talk. The weight of it has a ball forming in my throat.

"Dad would be proud of you. *I'm* proud of you."

"You don't have to lie to me. You know I don't like that."

Gavin stops us again. "I want you to listen to me, Kade." He takes a breath and looks me dead in the eye. "I've been a shit brother to you. I've lied to you, to our family. And while I can't take it back, I can tell you I'm sorry. And I can tell you that I'm not lying to you now. I'm proud of you, of the man you're becoming. You're stronger than me, stronger than Dad ever was. You're getting help, and that's more than most people can say. It's more than I can say."

My mouth goes dry, and I look into my brother's tired eyes. I place my hand over his on my shoulder. "Are you okay, Gav?"

He lets out a shuddering breath, and my chest smarts. "I've been having nightmares. Blake has, too. I thought they would get better the longer we got away from the accident, but—"

"Gav," I say, my brain putting together what he's saying. "You've been having nightmares about my accident?"

He nods. "Like I said, Kade: I can't lose you."

Water fills my eyes, and I hug my brother again. "You won't lose me. You won't. Not if I can help it."

Gavin pulls back and keeps eye contact with me. I can't help but feel guilty that I never realized how hard that night was on him. I've been selfish and an asshole. I see that now.

"I'm holding you to that." His voice is tight as he chokes back tears.

"You can talk to me, Gavin, if you want. I can't promise we won't fight or have our moments, but I'm here for you. And I've got a long list of headshrinkers now, if you need one." I grin in an attempt to lighten the mood.

That does the trick, and he smiles back at me. We're closer to the stables now, and the velvety tone of Presley's laughter washes over me as her purple hair comes into view, causing the hairs on my arms to stand on end. God, I want to hear that sound for the rest of my life—and I want to be the one who makes her laugh, smile, and curse.

"Look who's back," Blake says when she spots us.

Presley's face lights up when she sees me, her eyes silently asking, *How did it go?* I quicken my stride, eating up the ground between us until I'm pulling her into my arms. My lips descend upon hers, and she lets out a gasp into my mouth as I kiss her. I don't care that Gavin and Blake can see us; I needed to feel her lips on mine.

When I pull back, she's flushing bright red, but the smile tugging at her lips tells me that part of her loves how much I want the world to know she's mine and I'm hers.

I gather Presley snugly under my arm, and together, we face my brother and Blake. Gavin mirrors my stance with Blake, holding her close just as I do Presley. When Blake's eyes meet mine, a silent conversation passes between us, one that says despite all the things that remain unresolved, everything is going to be okay. She places her hand over Gavin's heart, and I nod gently at her.

"Gavin, I forgot something at the house—want to come get it with me?" Blake asks, a sly look on her face.

I rub Presley's arm and grin at my brother. Blake didn't forget anything at the house—of that, I'm sure. I waggle my eyebrows at him, and he shakes his head.

"Yeah, baby. Let's go." Before he walks off, he gives me one last glance. "See you both at dinner?" His shoulders appear relaxed, as if a heavy weight has been lifted. It takes away some of the pressure in my chest, and my own body settles.

I gaze down at Presley, and she tips her chin in agreement.

"Yeah, we'll be there," I say. I squeeze her shoulders, and my heart skips a beat, loving that she wants to be part of my life in this way.

Once we say our goodbyes and Blake and Gavin are out of sight, Presley turns in my arms and kisses me softly. "Everything go okay?"

"I think so." I exhale, truly believing the words for once.

"Good, I'm glad." She pecks my lips then tugs me so I'm following her.

I stumble a bit at the unexpected movement but quickly recover, chuckling. "Where are you taking me?"

She keeps her hand in mine but continues to walk backward as she looks up at me through hooded eyes. "I think I left something in my bedroom. Want to help me figure out what it is?"

I bark out a laugh and tug her into me. "I'll always help you, Lemon. You never have to ask." My words wrap around us, the double meaning intentional. She smiles up at me, her sapphire eyes glimmering with love as I pull her tighter against me.

With the sun shining down on us and the future looking brighter, Presley and I walk toward our "for now" home. Together.

Epilogue

PRESLEY

Five Months Later

THE MONTGOMERY FAMILY DUDE Ranch is officially open for business. Okay, well, not *officially*, but tonight is a town barbecue that Blake and Gavin have asked my band to play at.

Mostly, it's for the people of Randall to see all the work that's been done to the place. But as Blake told us, "It's a great time to get pictures for social media and make a marketing push for summer customers."

Just as I turn off my curling iron, I hear the click of the front door closing and the familiar sound of Kade's boots on the floor. My heart rate picks up, and I can't stop myself from smiling. The last five months have been the best five months of my life. Not only have I been traveling with a band I love, but I've also been spending my days with the *man* I love.

Has every day been easy? Of course not. But they've also been exciting, new, and fun. Which isn't surprising, because every day is at least one of those things with Kade, even the bad days.

"Presley?" Kade's baritone voice calls from the living area. "Are you in here?"

I take a moment to look at myself in the mirror, smoothing my hands over the leather on my hips and grabbing my new cowboy hat off the counter, placing it on my head. To celebrate tonight and all the hard work Kade's done—not only with the dude ranch but also on himself—I thought it would be fun to surprise him with a little outfit I found in Dallas yesterday.

Kade had stayed in Randall to help his family get some last-minute things done, and I went to my show. I was gone for less than twenty-four hours, but I missed him. I've gotten so used to him being with me at shows over the last few months that I felt like I was missing a part of me. I know he felt it, too, because I swear the man called or texted at least once an hour to make sure I was good. It was sweet, and my band teased me mercilessly for it.

When I'm satisfied with how I look, I call out, "I'm in the bedroom!"

I walk out of the bathroom and put my hands on my hips. I've never done something like this before, so I'm not exactly sure if I should pose or something. I glance at the queen bed covered in a lemon-patterned comforter—Kade and I replaced the two twin beds a few months ago—and wonder if I should lay on it. But then the door swings open, and I realize it's too late, so I'm sort of standing there awkwardly when Kade's buckskin cowboy hat comes into view.

"What time is the band getting here—" The question dies on Kade's lips as his widened hazel eyes take in my sexy cowgirl outfit complete with leather chaps. His mouth falls open a bit before his gaze drops down my body once. Twice. Then a third time before he makes eye contact with me again.

"Do you like it?" I ask, trailing a finger between the valley of my breasts. They're held by a skimpy tan halter vest that shows off my midriff. The fact that I'm wearing this, especially something that shows my stomach and my butt, is a miracle in itself. But when I'm around Kade, I feel like the most beautiful woman in the world. My confidence only grows every day I'm with him and when I'm onstage, doing what I love most.

"Do I *like* it, Lemon?" His voice comes out husky as he closes and locks the door then takes a dangerous step toward me. "I more than fucking like it." Another step. "I fucking *love* it." He stops just short of me, and when I move to close the gap, he stops me by holding out his hand. "Spin for me, Cowgirl. Let me see that sexy body of yours. I missed it."

My cheeks flush, and I bite my lower lip. Standing in front of him is one thing, but spinning for him?

Kade sees my hesitance and reaches out to take my chin between his fingers. "Don't make me put you over my knee and spank you." His words go straight to my clit, and I involuntarily squeeze my thighs together. He chuckles. "Should've known that wouldn't work." He takes his hand from my face and taps his chin thoughtfully. "How about you spin for me, and I'll let you come on my tongue before you ride my *cock*." He elongates the word *cock* so I feel the K sound in my belly.

"Kade." His name is a breathy moan on my lips, and my knees almost buckle. He knows I love when he talks dirty to me, especially when he's demanding—it makes me feel cared for and cherished, like I'm the only one he wants and ever has or will.

"Do it, Lemon. Or maybe I won't let you come at all," he teases.

With that threat, I do as he asks. I know he'll make good on it, and I need him tonight, even if the memory of the last time he edged me was a good one in the end.

I start to turn, and he interjects. "Slowly. Let me see how nicely you dressed up for me."

My mouth goes dry, and my body feels like it's been lit on fire as I slowly turn. Kade expels a throaty growl as he takes in my form. When my bare butt faces him, he curses.

"A thong *and* assless chaps, Lemon? You're spoiling me."

By the time I face him, my pussy is wet, and my hands are begging to touch him.

"When did you get this outfit?" he asks lustfully.

"At a store in Dallas." I give in to my desire to touch him and brush my hands down his chest, making him shiver beneath my touch. When I reach the hem of his white T-shirt, he doesn't stop me as I pull it out of his Wranglers. He lifts his arms, and I shuck it off his body, throwing it to the floor. I reach for his belt next, unbuckling it with practiced ease before I unzip his fly.

"Eager?" His nose brushes the shell of my ear.

"For you?" I trail my fingers over his growing erection. "Always."

Kade grabs my hands with another growl and pushes me toward the bed. The backs of my knees hit the mattress, and I drop flat on my back, my body jiggling from the force. Once upon a time, that would've made me self-conscious, but not anymore. Kade's hungry gaze devours my body as I push up on the bed, then he removes his hat and frisbees it to the floor before taking mine. With a smirk, he puts my hat on his head.

"What's that saying, darlin'?" he asks playfully. "Oh, yes, wear the hat, ride the cowgirl."

I laugh as he crawls over me, his lips crashing into mine for the first time in over twenty-four hours. He licks into my mouth, stroking my tongue as he takes my wrists, moving my arms above my head so I'm pinned.

He breaks from my lips, tossing my hat to the side with his before trailing wet, open-mouthed kisses down my neck, sucking on the small mark my fiddle leaves there. Kade loves to call it my "violin hickey." I've tried to get him to call it what it is—"fiddler's neck"—but he won't hear it. He said he googled it, and you can call it that, too. I mean, that's true, but I like to tease him about it anyway.

He sucks on the mark again, and I moan, my hips bucking against his. "God, I missed you," he murmurs, kissing my mouth again.

"I missed you, too, baby."

"I'm going with you next time." He moves his lips between my breasts, unbuttoning the vest to expose my chest.

"I'd like that," I rasp before he sucks one of my nipples into his mouth, causing me to gasp. He continues his worship of my breasts for only a moment before he licks a path downward. I prop myself up on my forearms so I can watch the top of his blond head pay attention to each and every faded red and white mark on my stomach.

My heart nearly explodes at the love this man has for me. How he knows and adores every single part of me, even the ones I struggle to find beautiful.

I lay my head back down on the mattress when his face meets my pussy. Without hesitation, I clench my thighs around his head as he sucks my clit through the fabric of my dark-brown thong.

"Always so fucking wet for me." Kade groans. He pries my thighs apart then moves his strong hands to the elastic of the underwear. I start to lift my hips so he can pull them down, but before I can, a ripping noise fills the air.

"Kade!" I gasp, my head flying up. He's grinning at me over the top of my sex as he chucks the now torn underwear to the floor.

"They had to go, darlin'. I need to lick this pussy clean, and they're in my way. Besides, I want you to keep these chaps on." With a devilish smile, he puts his mouth to my now bare clit and sucks. I buck, my hands flying to his hair.

True to his word, he licks and sucks every part of me. His tongue dips into my soaked entrance as he laps me up and hums his enjoyment. Needing to come, I press his face into my pussy, undulating my hips against his mouth.

"That's it, darlin'," he mumbles into me. "Use me."

"Kade!" He seals his mouth over my bundle of nerves again then licks at my folds like he's starved. When he slips two fingers inside me, I grip the digits and arch off the bed. "I'm going to come."

His teeth run over my clit, and I grip my thighs tight around his head again, encasing him. I feel him smile into my pussy—he loves when I do that. With another few flicks of his tongue, I come so violently my body shakes, and I scream his name. He continues to work his fingers in and out of me, letting me ride my release as he eats me clean like he wanted.

After I catch my breath, I drop my thighs open and tug on his hair. His dilated pupils meet mine, and he grins like a dog, his face wet with my arousal.

"I need you inside me."

At my request, he climbs back up my body, the bulge in his jeans dragging across my sensitive clit.

"Oh, fuck," I cry. Kade's mouth crushes mine, and he swallows my vocalization before massaging his tongue against my own. I can taste myself on him, and it only makes me want him more. "Kade," I whine.

He tears his swollen lips from mine and then gets up off the bed, his eyes on me as he removes his jeans and boxers before going to the nightstand to grab a condom. I sit up and beckon him over, taking the foil packet from him. He brushes a lock of now sweaty purple hair from my forehead as I fist his hard length in my hand. When I pump it a few times, he moans for me, then I slide the rubber down his length and kiss the tip of it.

"God, you're perfect," he whispers, voice full of awe.

"You're perfect, too, baby." I tug on his hand until he lays on the bed. When he's settled, I get on top of him this time, kissing his lips and grinding my wet pussy over his cock. He hisses and throws his head back against the pillows, his hands coming to grip my hips.

"I want to try something," I say before leaning down to kiss his chest.

When I sit back up, he has an eyebrow raised at me. I move his hands from my hips, then, with a bit of awkwardness, I reverse myself so my chap-framed ass is facing him.

Kade lets out a loud groan. "I think I've died and gone to heaven. Praise Jesus."

I can't help the giggle that escapes me as I press my ass back, his cock nestled between my pussy lips. He curses from the sensation then brings his hands down to slap both ass cheeks.

"Kade!" He does it again and again as I grind myself back, my clit pulsing from each smack.

"Get on my cock, Lemon," he commands. "Ride me."

Like the dirty gentleman he is, Kade's hands move to the sides of my chaps, and he tugs up on the leather to help lift me. I take his cock, coated in my arousal, and place it at my entrance. Kade curses again as I slowly sink down, my eyes rolling in the back of my head as his cock disappears inside me inch by inch.

"Fuck, baby. You feel so good. I missed your pussy."

"Just my pussy?" I manage to say.

He smacks my ass again then uses the chaps to pull me down until he's fully seated.

"Oh my god!" His cock feels impossibly deep inside me. I feel so full, the heat of him burning me as he thrusts upward over and over. The shallow and rough motion vibrates through my body, and I cry out again.

"Move, darlin'. Ride my cock like the good fucking cowgirl you are."

At his encouragement, I lean forward, my hands gripping his muscular thighs as I work myself up and down his length, a bead of sweat dripping down my forehead.

"That's it. So fucking good."

I move faster at his praise. Kade's strong hands are still gripping my chaps so he can use them for more leverage to go deeper. When his cock hits my G-spot, I swear I see stars, and I scream so loud anyone wandering outside would've heard me.

"God, Presley," Kade murmurs, his pace picking up. The sound of our coupling echoes through the room as he plows into me with reckless abandon. When the bed starts to squeak, I can't help but grin, thinking of the time he made his little comment about testing the guest bed for squeaking. This bed has definitely been tested out—and I like that it squeaks.

Kade swats my ass again and changes his pace so his hips move in a small circle. Then he thrusts upward so hard my breasts shake, and I scream again.

"Fuck, darlin'." Kade groans, the throaty kind that tells me he's on the brink of his release. "I need you to touch yourself. Can you do that for me?"

"Yes!" I sob.

I shift my body and glide my fingers around my oversensitive clit. My inner walls squeeze his cock, and I feel myself teetering on the edge alongside him. Kade fucks me faster, and I grip around him as tightly as I can.

"I'm coming," I keen, my back arching in complete pleasure. Kade's movements turn shallow, and with a final upward thrust, I feel his cock pulse inside me, and my name spills from his lips. Fireworks spark behind my eyes as my release shakes my body, and I fall forward. Kade fucks me through our collective orgasms, and we float together.

When I'm no longer able to hold myself up, I slide off his softening length and fall onto the bed next to him. We both lie together, the melody of our heavy breathing now the soundtrack to the aftermath of our coupling. Eventually, Kade moves, kissing my forehead before he gets up to dispose of the condom.

When he comes back a minute later, he has a lazy smile on his face, and he's holding a wet washcloth. I lay against the pillows as he takes my outfit off and cleans between my legs with the gentle care he always has for me. While he does it, he tells me how much he loves me, how lucky he is to have me in his life, and how hot what I just did for him was. Eventually, I have to tell him to stop or I'll combust from being over-complimented.

He continues to compliment me anyway, but when he's finally satisfied and I'm taken care of, he lays down, tugging me to him. I place my head on his damp chest and listen to his heartbeat. It's crazy to think that, at one time, it wasn't beating. That if Blake hadn't saved him, I wouldn't be here with him right now. We wouldn't have spent the last five months building a life together.

It's an unconventional life but a wonderful one, busy with travel and work. We not only help his family with the dude ranch, but we also tour around the South with my band, a band I've come to love just like a little family. And just like a family should, they appreciate my talent and never put me down. We're even recording an album at the end of this month in the hopes that we can get some interest from record labels—and this time, I know I'd sign on the dotted line without running.

Then there's Night Hawk. We still help Jake from time to time even though he's hired a few new people. My cowboy still likes to teach line dancing, and I usually work those nights with him, but Jake's been keeping an eye out for added support. Kade, however, insists he's fine and that being around alcohol is something he can't avoid, especially since so many of my gigs are in bars. He's doing his to manage it, and I'm so proud of him.

He's done everything he can to support himself in the last five months, including going on antidepressants and attending online therapy once a week as well as regular AA meetings. While he struggled with everything at first, it gets easier every day. Yes, he still has his days—he's human—but he's honest when he needs help, and we deal with it together. He even inspired me to start going to a therapist for my anxiety, and Blake and Gavin started seeing someone for their PTSD and grief.

Kade's heart continues to beat loudly in my ear, and I take comfort in its steady pace. I wind my leg through his and mold my body against his side before placing a kiss over his heart. A moment later, his finger is beneath my chin, and he's lifting my gaze to his.

"Are you okay?" he asks, his brow pinched in concern.

I slide up a bit so I can press a kiss to his lips. "I'm just glad you're here."

He tucks some hair behind my ear then kisses me slow and deep. It's the kind of kiss that's tender yet strong at the same time, one that tells me he knows what I was thinking, that he's glad he's here, too. That he's glad I'm here.

When he pulls back, he kisses my nose and then smiles excitedly. "You want to see something?"

I can't help but match his infectious smile. "What is it?"

He pulls himself away from me to find his jeans on the floor. He picks them up, takes something from his pocket, and then comes back to bed. With a dimpled smile still on his face, he hands the item to me. I stare at the blue chip that says "Five Months Sober" on it.

I grip the chip in my hand and stare up into his soulful hazel eyes. "You're amazing, Kade. I'm so proud of you."

He beams at me. "I never thought a little chip like that could make me feel so good. But it does."

I kiss the chip then hand it back to him. He wraps his hand in mine so the chip is pressed between both of our palms and squeezes. "I couldn't have done it without you."

I shake my head. "You could've, Kade. You're the strongest person I know. You did this—don't forget that. It was all you."

He sighs and grips my hand tighter. "I know we could argue about this again, and maybe my psychiatrist would say this is codependent, but I mean it. I couldn't have done it without you." He leans his forehead against mine. "I wouldn't have wanted to do this without you. You're my rock, Presley. I love you."

I exhale a short breath and smile against his lips as he kisses me softly. "I'll accept that."

He chuckles and tickles my sides. Soon, I'm pinned beneath him, and his cock is hardening between my legs.

I groan. "We can't go again, you sex-crazed man. I need to get ready for tonight, and the band will be here in"—I stretch to see the clock on the wall and gasp—"thirty minutes!" I push at his chest, and Kade huffs, reluctantly rolling off me so I can get up.

I run around the room naked, collecting our clothes and throwing them in the hamper, and Kade watches me from the bed with a smirk.

"Are you going to get ready or come to the show naked?" I ask him.

"That does sound kind of fun." Kade stands, pulling my naked backside against him. "I'd love to see you try to concentrate with my dick in your line of sight."

I bark a laugh and push him off me as I pick up a bra from my suitcase. "I imagine if you put that on the dude ranch's social media, you'd get a lot of customers. I mean, you got me to Randall."

He goes silent as I slip my bra on. A moment later, I feel Kade's hands at my back, and he clasps the hook together so I don't have to. I turn in his arms, and he's staring down at me in wonder and a hint of confusion.

"Why are you looking at me like that?" I ask.

He crosses his arms over his chest. "You came to Randall because you saw me on social media?"

My cheeks heat. "I never told you that?" He shakes his head. "I was doomscrolling, trying to figure out what to do, and I came across Night Hawk's social media post. The picture was of you, shirtless and on a bull, and it made me stop scrolling. Of course, I never imagined that a super-hot young cowboy would ever be into me, but you caught my eye, and I stopped. Then I saw it was a job posting and clicked. And boom! Here I am."

By the time I finish blabbering, Kade is grinning at me. "Super-hot young cowboy, huh?" I shove him and try to walk away, but he pulls me back. "You came to Randall because of me," he states.

I blush red. "Because of the *job*, but I wouldn't have seen the job if I hadn't stopped to look at your chest." I smirk, staring at said chest.

Kade tugs me to him and winds his hands into my hair. He kisses me roughly, his lips demanding my submission as I open my mouth to him.

When we're both breathless and panting, he pulls back, his eyes shining with tears. "I love you, Presley. Fuck, I love you so much it doesn't even seem like the right word. Obsessed, maybe," he teases.

I laugh at his antics and gaze into his eyes, the eyes of the man who has become my family. He's given me a safe place to land and a home. No matter what happens, I know he'll be there with me, and I'll be there for him.

"I'm obsessed with you, too, Kade."

My cowboy tucks me into him, and I burrow my face into his chest, listening to his heartbeat and deciding the world can wait a few more minutes. I'm happy and content right where I am.

Epilogue

KADE

Seven Years Sober

"You're going to be a dad." I clap Gavin on the back. "To a girl."

Gavin chuckles, but I don't miss the warm smile tugging at the corner of his lips as he watches a very pregnant Blake in the distance. She's serving up the pink cake that revealed the gender of their baby to some of the partygoers while chatting with her mom and Jake.

"You'll have to give me some tips," he says, taking a sip of his soda.

A smile of my own graces my lips as I think of my little family. I've been with Presley for just about seven years now. After three years, we got married, then two years ago, we had a new little life grace us with her presence. While it was unexpected, James Hope Presley, who we affectionately call "Jamie," has been the best thing to happen to us.

As if on cue, a blonde head zooms past Gavin, and then little hands are tugging at my jeans. "Daddy, up!"

My smile widens as I bend down to pick up my giggling toddler. The pigtail braids I put in her short blonde hair are falling out from all the running around she's been doing, and her face is covered in what looks like frosting.

"You're a mess, baby girl."

"Auntie Blake give Jamie cake!"

"I can see that." Jamie gives me a toothy grin and lays a wet, sticky raspberry on my cheek before dissolving into giggles. I cringe at the mess now transferred onto my stubble but give my kid a well-deserved raspberry on her tummy in return.

"Daddy, no!" She squirms, her little legs kicking me. I give her another raspberry then tickle her sides. She dissolves into more giggles and squeals, "Uncle Gav, help!"

"I don't know, Jamie. You *did* get frosting on your daddy's pretty face." He laughs.

She giggles louder, her little cheeks turning pink as I tickle her again.

"Don't tickle her too long, Kade—you know what happens," Presley says, arriving out of nowhere with a smirk on her face and a wet wipe in her hand.

"Yeah, Daddy! Don't make me-a-pee," Jamie insists through her hiccups of laughter. "I'm a big girl."

Gavin snickers as I stop my onslaught. "She's definitely your kid."

I beam at that. My kid is cute and hilarious, so I take that as a compliment as Jamie lays another messy raspberry on my cheek.

"Thanks for that, baby girl."

"Welcome," she says. Her tone is so serious that we all laugh. "Down, please."

"Since you asked so nicely," I tease, kissing the crown of her head before setting her on her feet.

Just as she's about to run away, my wife stops her. "Let me wipe your face, Jamie," she says, bending down to clean the mess from her lips and cheeks. The moment she's finished, Jaime takes off running in Blake's direction, probably to try to con her into giving her another slice of cake.

Presley stands and smiles at me, tucking a piece of freshly dyed pink hair behind her ear. She wanted a change from her usual purple, and Jamie got to pick the color. It's taken me a bit to get used to it, but my wife looks hot no matter what color her hair is.

After Presley cleans my cheek off with the wipe, I pull her into my side, stroking her hip. She leans her head against my shoulder.

"You tired, Lemon darlin'?" I ask.

She chuckles. "I'm in my thirties. I'm always tired."

"Ain't that the truth," Gavin adds.

"I wouldn't know," I tease. "I'm still young, unlike all of you folks."

Presley hip-checks me. "Yeah, yeah. You won't be able to rub that in much longer—you're turning thirty soon." She turns to my brother. "And just you wait, Gavin. You think you're tired now? You don't know tired until you're up with a newborn every couple of hours."

Gavin doesn't balk, he just smiles. "Looking forward to it."

"He says that now." I think of the sleepless nights with Jamie when she was born. "Soon, he'll be showing up at our door begging us to babysit."

"Like you didn't do that?" Gavin asks.

I give him a sheepish grin. "Okay, guilty. But to be fair, I only did that when my beautiful wife left me alone with a colicky baby so she could go be a country star."

Presley blushes. "A, it was one night, Kade. For one gig. And B, I'm not a country star."

"Says the woman who just played sold-out shows back-to-back at the Grand Ole Opry," Gavin says.

Presley blushes further at my brother's praise. "I wasn't the star. I was the fiddle player for the country star."

Gavin and I both give her matching looks that say, *Stop being so humble,* but I know she won't. That's just how Presley is. In the last five years, I've watched her go from playing in a small-town band and recording an album to playing gigs on her own—and then, in the last two years, getting asked to play with the biggest names in country music. But no matter who she plays with or what stages she plays on, she acts as if it isn't that big of a deal.

"In all seriousness," Presley continues, "if you or Blake ever need a babysitter, we'll be happy to help. Jamie is excited about her baby cousin and can't wait to take care of her."

I smile at that. Ever since she found out Auntie Blake had a baby in her tummy, it's all she can talk about.

"We appreciate it. Speaking of," Gavin's voice turns more serious. "We can take Jamie tonight if you both want. I know today is a big day for you, Kade."

Presley squeezes me around the middle, and I press a soft kiss to her head. I'm seven years sober today. When Blake realized her baby shower was the same day, she offered to move it, but I told her that was silly. Yes, it's important that I honor my milestones, but it's also important to me that my family celebrates theirs and that life goes on as normal. Because while I still have hard days sometimes, I'm okay. I'm better than okay. And I have a family who loves and supports me when I feel like I may not be.

"That would be nice, actually," Presley says to Gavin before I can answer. "Unless you want to spend time with Jamie?" She looks up knowingly at me.

My heart warms. My wife knows that I'd rather be with both my girls on days like today. It's funny when I think about how much I've changed since the day I met Presley. Now, I'd rather be on the couch watching a movie with my family than go out. But alone time with Presley is always something I want and crave, especially when we don't have to worry about Jamie running into the room while we're trying to have sex. Let's just say my ropes haven't come out to play in quite awhile.

My heart rate picks up at the image of my wife's pliant body bound and at my mercy. I shift on my feet, the crotch of my jeans suddenly feeling too tight and my clothes itchy against my skin.

"I think we should take my big brother up on his offer," I respond, my voice a bit deeper than normal. Presley's blue eyes dart to mine, and then she blushes. My wife knows what I'm thinking. Then I lean my head down to kiss her, and Gavin clears his throat awkwardly just as our lips touch.

"Alright, maybe I should go check on Blake." He rubs the back of his neck.

I chuckle and pull away from my wife's very kissable lips. "Actually, I wanted to talk to you about something quickly. Walk with me?"

Gavin's green eyes turn serious. Ever since the day we walked around the property and talked the week after my breakdown, it's kind of become our thing—when we need to work something out between us, we go for a walk or to Devil's Rock like we did with Dad.

But that's when we have time, which doesn't happen often these days. I work with a sober-living center in the city a few days a week, something I started doing last year to give back. I still travel with Presley, taking care of Jamie when we go on the road. Amidst that, I also help with our family's booming dude ranch operation, which was just featured in a bunch of magazines' "Best Southern Vacation Ideas" for the third straight year in a row. That means we're all about to get even busier, especially with Gavin and Blake's baby on the way.

"Yeah, of course," Gavin answers.

I turn to Presley. "We'll be back in a bit."

"Take your time. I have to go stop Jamie from getting Blake to give in to her. That girl does not need another slice of cake—she'll be up past her bedtime."

"I don't know. If Gavin's taking care of her, he can deal with the sugar high and the inevitable sugar-crash meltdown." I smirk, and Presley taps her chin.

"Good point. Blake!" she yells over to her. Blake looks up from our daughter with an amused smile. "Jamie can have another slice."

Gavin groans as Presley and I laugh.

"You said you'd take her," I remind him.

"Just remember," Gavin shoots back. "Payback is a bitch."

This time, Presley and I are groaning. Something tells me my brother's kid is going to be stubborn as hell. But I smile at the image of our kids playing together, a new generation of Montgomerys—but girls this time. It's going to be wonderful and frightening all at once, but I can't wait for it. I know Gran and Momma are excited, too. They love having Jamie around because it "keeps them young," and they can't wait for a second granddaughter.

After Presley leaves to join Blake and Jamie, Gavin and I take off down the path around the property. We're having an off week for the dude ranch, so there are no guests around, but some of the workers are milling about.

Once we're out of earshot, Gavin clears his throat. "What did you want to talk to me about?"

I hear the nervousness in his tone, so I clap him on the back. "It's nothing bad, Gav. Take it easy."

Gavin releases a breath then cracks a small smile. "Okay. It was just the last time we went on a walk, you told me you wanted to move to Texas again full-time and build a house on the property, so..."

This time, I punch him in the shoulder. "Jackass."

He chuckles. "Sorry, I couldn't resist. You know I love having you here with us."

I nod. I *do* know that. After Presley amicably left the band she met through Jake at Night Hawk, we moved to Nashville for a while since she'd been working there so much. But when she got pregnant, we both decided we wanted to be closer to family so Jamie could grow up like I did. That was important to Presley, especially since she didn't have parents or extended family who cared about her growing up.

So as soon as it made sense, I asked Gavin if we could build a place on our land. He was shocked to say the least, but it didn't take a genius to see how happy he was. He also reminded me it was my land, too—a fact that he solidified even more when he added my name to the deed after Jamie was born.

Seven years ago, I didn't want it, didn't think I needed it anymore. But I understood why Gavin included me—not only because he knew Dad would've wanted it, but also because my child, and now his child, deserve to share in the legacy we all built.

"So what is it?" Gavin asks, breaking me from my thoughts. "Do you want to build a bigger house because Presley is pregnant again?"

I think my eyes turn into saucers. "No, no, nothing like that. I mean, not that I don't want another Jamie, but not right now. I think my wife is in the same boat. And the house is plenty big as it is."

Gavin smirks. "Then what is it?"

I look out over our land, the land we've all worked so hard to save and build into something truly amazing over the years. "Blake and I talked this morning."

"About what?"

I stick my hands in my pockets and stop to face my brother. He pauses, staring at me with a curious gaze.

"She mentioned you said something about wanting to name your baby after Dad but you were nervous to ask me about it."

Gavin's lips press together. "I'm sorry, Kade. She shouldn't have said anything."

I clap my brother on the shoulder and give him a reassuring squeeze. "No, I'm glad she did. I think it's a great idea."

He stares at me cautiously, as if he thinks I'm lying. "Really?"

"I mean, I don't think I've ever heard of a girl named Emmett before, but I *did* name my kid James for Presley's last name, so…"

That has Gavin barking out a laugh. "We'd name her Emmy."

I grin so wide my cheeks hurt. Blake had already told me, but I couldn't pass up the chance to tease my brother. "That's a way better idea."

He shakes his head, and we fall in step next to each other again.

"I didn't know how you'd feel about it," he says a moment later.

"Truthfully, I was shocked when Blake told me. But I'm not upset. I could've named Jamie after him, but I liked the idea of carrying on Presley's name with her. And you have to admit, my kid looks like a Jamie," I say proudly.

"Her name suits her." We walk a bit more before Gavin asks, "Why were you shocked?"

I kick a rock with my boot. "Because I know your relationship with Dad was complicated. And given how he left things when he died, it didn't even occur to me you'd want to name your baby after him."

"Both of our relationships with him were complicated," he volleys.

"I can't disagree with you there. But why do you want to?"

Gavin hesitates, then he stops walking again and faces me. "Despite my differences with him and everything he did, I realize that he did what he thought he had to do. Was it always right? No. But he was trying to protect his family."

Before I was sober, Gavin's words would've made me angry, and I would've wanted to reach for a drink. But now that I'm a dad and have had therapy where I talked until I was blue in the face about my relationship with my father, I get what Gavin is saying. I know Dad only ever did the best he could to raise us with what he knew, with the tools he had at his disposal. I forgave him for everything he said and did years ago now.

"Is there any other reason?" I ask. I have a gut feeling it's more than that for him.

"He was a good man with a strong work ethic. And despite his mistakes, he loved us. He loved us more than I think we even knew. He made sure we always had each other, Kade. And while his death almost ripped us apart, it brought us back together. This is my way of not only honoring him but also honoring you, honoring our relationship. If my daughter is half the person that you are, that he was—" Gavin clears the emotion in his throat then pauses to gather himself. "There's one more thing."

I just nod, unable to trust myself to speak right now. Gavin's emotion—his words—are affecting me more than I expected but not in a bad way.

"Her middle name is going to be Kade."

Kade. "Emmy Kade Montgomery."

Gavin nods.

I tug my brother to me in a long and fierce hug—a hug that you can only share with a brother, a person who's been by your side as you went to hell and back.

When I pull away, his eyes are teary like they were all those years ago when I first told him I was getting help and that I needed space. This conversation is emotional, too, but for an entirely different reason.

"I'm proud of you, Kade, of the man you've become. You make me want to be better every day."

I squeeze his biceps. "You're a good man, Gav, the best man. Thank you for even thinking to do that. I—I don't know what else to say except that I'm honored."

His next words are almost a whisper. "I can't wait to meet her."

"You're going to be a great dad."

"You think?"

"I know."

Before I can say another word, a streak of blonde hair zips between us then starts circling our legs.

"Look! I'm a pony!" Jamie giggles. She makes a nickering noise that has Gavin and I chuckling, then she circles us again and again. Soon, Presley walks over to us with Blake on her tail.

"I'm so sorry. She ran over here so fast." Presley laughs. "Maybe you'll get lucky, and she'll pass out after a bath."

"If not, we'll watch a movie," Blake says as she sidles up to Gavin. She rests her head on his shoulder, and he places his hand on the swell of her belly. My heart warms at the picture they make, and I stare in awe at her stomach. *Emmy Kade*. A niece named after me and Dad.

Presley tucks into my side, and I snap out of my little trance. When she sees my still-glassy eyes and slightly shocked expression, she frowns a bit.

"You okay, baby?" Her voice is hushed so a still-galloping Jamie doesn't hear.

I give my attention to Gavin then to Blake. The latter is giving me a look that says she knows what Gavin told me. Her warm brown eyes smile at me, and she places her hand over the one my brother has on her stomach.

With a smile of my own, I gaze down at my wife, the person who means more to me than anything in this world.

"I'm great." I know she doesn't completely buy it, but I'll tell her everything when we're alone. I tug on a lock of pink hair. "You ready to get out of here, wife?"

She bites her lower lip and stares at my mouth. "If you are."

"I am." My body starts to heat as I picture what that smart mouth I love so much can do to me. "Jamie, Mommy and Daddy are going to go now. You're having a sleepover with Uncle Gavin and Auntie Blake."

Jamie neighs her agreement, and I shake my head. What a weirdo my beautiful wife and I created.

After Presley and I say our goodbyes to Jamie and the rest of the family scattered around the food area—and Momma reminds us it's chili night tomorrow while warning us not to be late, I pull my wife into my side, and we walk down the path to the little house we built. It's just past the barn that has our favorite loft.

When we approach it, I eye the sliding door and grin slyly. "What do you say we make a pit stop?"

She follows my gaze then smirks cheekily. "I've actually been a *very* bad girl."

My cock jumps. "Oh, yeah? What did you do?"

She leans forward, taking my lip between her teeth then biting down. "I haven't had sex with my husband today."

I hiss from the sting then chuckle. "You're right. That is *very* bad. I think you need to be spanked. Don't you agree?"

"Yes, Kade," she hums.

I growl and smack her butt through her jeans. "Then let me teach you a lesson, Lemon darlin'."

Presley expels a breathy laugh. Before I can blink, she takes off toward the barn, and I follow—hot on her heels.

Want More Kade & Presley?
Get Their Bonus Chapter at www.patreon.com/kaylagrosse

Read More Books by Kayla Grosse

SILVER FOXED
a dad's best friend, spicy age gap novella with a plus-size female
lead and her sexy silver fox.

TRICK SHOT (BROTHER PUCKERS BOOK #1)
a spicy MMF novella with a plus-size female lead and male
lead...and their hot hockey player

PUCK SHY (BROTHER PUCKERS BOOK #2)
a spicy novella with a plus-size female lead and her golden
retriever hockey player

REIN ME IN (THE COWBOYS OF NIGHT HAWK #1)
a late brother's best friend, small town, cowboy romance with a
plus-size cowgirl

I LIKE YOU LIKE THAT
a second chance, rock star romance with a plus-size female lead

AXES AND O'S
Available November 4th, 2024
a super spicy MMF snowed-in lumbersnack romance

FALLING FOR THE MANNY
a single mom, contemporary romance by author duo
Kayla Nicole

For Exclusive Bonus Stories, Artwork, and More Visit:
www.patreon.com/kaylagrosse

Find Kayla:

Website: www.kaylagrosse.com
Instagram: @kaylawriteslife
Facebook: Kaylaholics Facebook Group
TikTok: @kaylagrossewriter
Twitter: @kaylagrosse

Acknowledgments

THANK YOU SO VERY much for reading Kade and Presley's story—and for completing the Montgomery boys' journey with me...what an emotional ride it has been.

When I wrote *Rein Me In*, I never planned for it to be a series, but Kade spoke to me, yelling at me that he must be redeemed. I'm so happy that I could give him his wish, and that both his and Presley's story could be told and shared with the world.

This story was a lot different than any other I've written. Not only did it deal with grief and healing, but it also dealt with addiction, mental health, and body image. If you've read my previous books, you know that my plus-size characters tend to be confident in themselves and happy in their bodies. As you now know, that was not the case with Presley. However, I felt that her story was an important one to tell. A story that is similar to mine and so many other people in this world. I hope that you felt healed through her journey as much as I did. And that you walk away from this story knowing that it always gets better. That you are loved, just the way you are.

Now to the thank-yous!

First, I always have to thank YOU, my dear reader, for supporting me on this author journey. Thank you for reading, sharing, and loving my stories. Without you, I would not be able to continue to share important books like this one. You have no idea how much it means that you've picked up *Rope Me In*. So thank you!

To my alpha, beta, and sensitivity readers, Taylor, Allie, Elliot, Nic, Dallas, Melissa, and Jackie, thank you so much for helping make Kade and Presley's story shine. I couldn't have made it through this writing process without you. Thank you for giving me valuable feedback and always cheering me on.

Thank you to my author friends, Bailey Hannah and Nicole Reeves, and to my Melissas for listening to my incessant rants and voice notes about this book, and to Melissa Frey for editing this beast of a book.

Thank you to my Smut Obsessed and Smut VIP Patrons, Kasandra R, Lindsey M, Jenn M, Kaitlyn J, Jackie B, Jessica M, MGN, Kaitlen, Sasha, Jee, Sarah S, Carlee R, and Micheala L, for all your love. Your constant support means the world to me. Thank you!

Lastly, thank you to my family and friends who have supported me through my own grief and mental health journey. Without you, I would not be here. You know who you are.

Till next time...

Xoxo,
Kayla

P.S. If you or someone you know is struggling with depression or need help, please contact the 988 Suicide & Crisis Lifeline by calling or texting 988. You can also visit http://www.988lifeline.org/ for help.

Love you.

Printed in Great Britain
by Amazon